This book is sold subject to the condition it shall not, by way of trade or otherwise, be lent, re-sold, duplicated, hired out,
or otherwise circulated.
without the publisher's prior written consent in any form of binding or cover other than that in which it is published and without a similar condition
including this condition being
imposed on the subsequent
purchaser.

This book is a work of fiction. Any references to historical events, actual
people, or real places are used for fictitious purposes. Other names,
characters, places, and events are products of the author's imagination.

…well, some of it is anyway.

Copyright ©2024 Bryan Wayne Dull

TABLE OF CONTENTS

VOICES CARRY - 6 -

IT ALWAYS FEELS LIKE - 29 -

A LITTLE RESPECT - 35 -

VALERIE - 47 -

TENDERNESS - 52 -

SAVE IT FOR LATER - 60 -

THIS IS THE DAY - 69 -

MONEY FOR NOTHING - 79 -

I WANT CANDY - 85 -

THE SAFETY DANCE - 97 -

PSYCHO KILLER - 111 -

THIS CHARMING MAN - 130 -

UNDER PRESSURE - 143 -

ALIVE AND KICKING - 163 -

YOU MIGHT THINK - 173 -

HEAD OVER HEELS - 189 -

EVERYWHERE - 201 -

SOMETHING ABOUT YOU - 214 -

WEST END GIRLS - 223 -

NEW SENSATION - 235 -

INBETWEEN DAYS - 246 -

DON'T STAND SO CLOSE TO ME - 253 -

BLUE MONDAY - 260 -

OWNER OF A LONELY HEART - 268 -

MIRROR IN THE BATHROOM - 274 -
ONE THING LEADS TO ANOTHER - 283 -
THIS MUST BE THE PLACE - 287 -
MANIAC - 300 -
SWEET DREAMS - 309 -
THE KILLING MOON - 314 -
SEND ME AN ANGEL - 334 -
PICTURES OF YOU - 360 -

FOR MORE SONGS, CHECK OUT
THE WOLVES OF NOWHERE, OHIO
PLAYLIST ON SPOTIFY

THIS BOOK IS DEDICATED TO THE ONLY PLACE I EVER CALLED HOME DURING AN ERA GONE BUT NOT FORGOTTEN.

THE HARVEST MOON

THE COLD OPEN

VOICES CARRY

Keep it down.

Anna Blake's hand trembled as she attempted to apply the bold blue eyeshadow with a shaky brush. She wasn't used to wearing makeup, preferring a more natural look with just concealer and mascara. But today was different. Today was her first official date with Jessie Cohen, the boy who made her heart race and cheeks flush every time she thought of him.

For Anna, this date marked a milestone in her high school years as she had been too nervous to start dating until now. Her father had finally given her permission to wear makeup, and since then, she had noticed a shift in how she was perceived at Wadsworth High School. Boys were suddenly taking notice of her, and it only increased her excitement for this date with Jessie.

As she finished applying her makeup, Anna couldn't help but think back to her teenage years. Her bedroom wall used to be adorned with posters of Corey Feldman and Corey Haim, but now it was decorated with a poster from her favorite vampire movie, *The Lost Boys*. She longed for her own fairytale romance like the ones depicted in those movies, but it had seemed out of reach until now.

With Halloween just around the corner, everyone appeared to have plans for Saturday night. Even Anna's parents were getting ready for a costume party hosted by her father's workplace. They were running late, which meant Jessie wouldn't have to meet them just yet.

In the quiet of her room, Anna could hear the sounds of kids roaming the streets for trick-or-treating and parties. She stood before the mirror, wondering if she had chosen the right shade of makeup for tonight. As the door closed behind her with a hollow sound, Anna couldn't help but remember an argument she once had with her father, where he punched through their front door in anger as if he had punched through their illusion of safety. But tonight, she pushed those thoughts away and focused on the excitement of her first real high school date.

Anna twirled in her pink dress, the tulle skirt brushing against her legs and the puff sleeves framing her face. She smiled as she remembered Molly Ringwald's iconic moment in *Sixteen Candles*, feeling like a modern-day princess herself. The delicate sweetheart neckline and royalty like pink hue only added to her irresistible appearance. Her vibrant red hair was pulled up into a messy bun, with a few stray strands falling around her face. She had to secure a few clips to tame the length of her hair, but it completed the look perfectly.

As she stood by the window of her bedroom, Anna heard an unexpected yell from the street behind her house. It was followed by an abrupt silence that piqued her curiosity. Stepping closer, she strained to see outside and figure out what was going on. The flickering light poles cast erratic shadows across her backyard, making it difficult to see clearly. But there was nothing amiss in her view—no one walking along the sidewalk or street behind her house. However, at the corner of the chain link fence surrounding her home, something caught her eye. It wobbled back and forth in the wind, its torn and shredded appearance resembling a tattered bag caught in a storm.

The evenings had been getting darker earlier, thanks to daylight saving time ending. Anna could barely make out details through the dim lighting outside, but she could feel the wind blowing fiercely against her skin. Colored leaves danced across the grass and road beneath the radiant light of the full moon—the first of the month. The serene scene brought a sense of calm over Anna, as if all was right in the world for just a moment.

With a dramatic sweep of his arm, Phillip threw open Anna's bedroom door. The booming echo of his voice filled the room

"Alright! We're about to leave." Anna let out a shrill shriek, springing to her feet in surprise. Her heart pounded fiercely against her ribcage, her hand pressed tight against it in response, as people often do when caught off guard, trying to steady her racing heartbeat and catch her breath.

He is always doing this! This is pissing me off, she thought.

"Dad!" she groaned, irritation pricking at her nerves. Worried about the time, Phillip glanced up from his wrist, his daughter's irritated gaze drawing him away from the ticking hands of his watch. "Do you mind?"

A dull guilt flickered across Phillip's face as Anna's words struggled to sink in. He shrugged his shoulders, not fully comprehending why Anna was so upset. "The door, dad! Knock on it!" Anna's frustration was palpable as she scolded him. "I'm bad about that, aren't I?" Phillip stammered, scrunching up his forehead and waving a distracted hand in the air. Her nod was stiff, her gaze unyielding as she caught her breath. "Yes, all the time, Dad."

"I'm sorry. I forget sometimes, is all," Phillip explained, struggling to come to terms with his daughter's accelerated transition into womanhood. "It's just that it all happens so quickly, and suddenly you're all grown up, looking lovely in your dress."

Anna pressed her lips together, uncertain about how to respond to her father without sounding disrespectful. "Yes, Daddy—that's how time works," she smiled, her words falling somewhat short. Sighing, Phillip shook his head, choosing to sidestep the sarcasm lacing her words.

Lately, Anna had been displaying a more assertive demeanor, a response he deemed reasonable given the circumstances. "Are you prepared for your date, then?" he inquired, a touch of anxiety threading his words.

With her arms gracefully raised, Anna twirled, her new dress flaring out around her. She shot her father an innocent grin, fully aware he'd see through her 'costume' excuse.

"You look like that girl in those movies you like. Um, Ally, something or another," he commented playfully.

"Molly Ringwald," Anna replied, her eyes rolling in slight frustration at his recurring inability to recall actors' names.

"The dark-haired one?" he ventured.

"No. She's the other one with the red hair, like me."

"I see," he nodded, though he might not entirely grasp the comparison. "I intended to come up here and provide you with the contact number for where we'll be," Phillip said as he reached into his pocket and handed Anna a piece of paper, neatly folded and perfect for tucking inside a purse.

"If you find yourself needing anything, feeling uncomfortable, or needing a ride home, you know what to do," he said, his voice gentle but serious.

Anna took the paper, her fingers lingering over the smooth edges. "I understand, Daddy," she said, her grin a mix of embarrassment and appreciation, her cheeks flushing slightly.

Phillip hesitated, then added, "Just... just be careful, okay? Don't do anything you might regret later, anything that could make you or us feel ashamed."

Anna's eyes widened; her shock evident. "No, Daddy," she replied, her voice firm, though her fingers began to fiddle with the objects on her desk, betraying her sense of insult.

Phillip nodded, as if reassuring himself. "When are you leaving?" he asked, trying to change the subject.

Anna glanced out the window, hoping to see Jessie. "Shouldn't take too long. His place is just down the road, and the party isn't far either. We figured we'd walk."

Phillip relaxed slightly. "Ah, I see. So you probably won't need a ride, then."

"Guess not," Anna said, a hint of disappointment in her voice.

Sensing the shift in her mood, Phillip decided to wrap up the conversation. "Before you head out tonight, make sure to lock the door. It's a bit tricky, so you might need to lift it a bit to get it to close properly. It'll feel like it's locked, but it might not be."

Given the neighborhood's safety, leaving the house was generally worry-free. Anna, known for misplacing her key, only carried the one for the doorknob. "Got it. Make sure the door's secure," she quipped, giving her father a mock-serious look.

Phillip rolled his eyes and headed out, saying, "Remember, curfew is midnight. Don't make me regret extending it."

Anna sighed and asked her father to close the door behind him. Phillip's hand gripped the knob, the door swinging shut slowly. He watched as his daughter's more mature face disappeared behind the narrowing gap. For a moment, he let his hand rest on her bedroom door, a wave of nostalgia washing over him. He sighed, reminiscing about a younger Anna and the simpler times. Shaking off the sentiment, he descended the staircase to face his wife, Maria, who looked rather annoyed. Her irritation deepened as Phillip shot her a sarcastic grin.

Bounding down the stairs, Phillip caught a glimpse of Maria's displeased expression. "You know we were supposed to leave ten minutes ago, Phillip!" she scolded.

He smiled reassuringly. "It's alright. The place isn't far, and what's the harm in being fashionably late?"

Maria giggled. "That would be fine if you were still fashionable. How long have you had this suit?" She adjusted his tie, her fingers deftly straightening it.

Phillip shrugged. "Not that long. Maybe late seventies?" He stretched the truth.

"Phillip Blake, you lie like a rug!" Maria exclaimed, laughing. "You've had that suit since Anna was a toddler."

Phillip didn't argue; he knew better than to contest her memory. Without Maria, he might be lost in the chaos of their household. Suddenly, a concern interrupted his thoughts. He needed to ask Maria a crucial question, one that embarrassed him to even consider. "Have you talked to her? You know, about the way things are with adults and boys and all that?"

Maria's smile was understanding. "Years ago, dear," she assured him.

"Years? Really?"

They exited the house and headed toward the detached garage. Phillip, preoccupied, left the front door slightly ajar, vulnerable to a strong gust of wind. Anna Blake's parents climbed into her father's blue '87 Chevy Cavalier, off to a party, while Anna herself waited for her date, anticipating the sound of the doorbell.

Outside Anna's bedroom door, Miss Boots-Boots Bittenbacher, the family cat, pawed at the wood. Anna, waiting for her hair curler to heat up, aimed to add an extra bounce to her red curls. She heard her kitty's whining and rolled her eyes, contemplating whether to let Boots in. Her pink and purple Caboodle, filled with crimpers and scrunchies, teetered precariously on her vanity table as she stood up.

"Come on, you little gremlin," Anna sighed playfully, pretending to be annoyed. She looked down at her feline companion with its big, endearing eyes. The cat's friskiness was apparent. "Who's a little chubby furball?" she cooed as Boots clung to her arm with its back legs.

A sudden draft sent a chill through Anna's room, making her shiver. The door slammed shut with a loud bang, driven by the wind blowing through the ajar front door. Both Anna and Boots jumped. This wasn't just the usual chill; it felt unsettling. *This is weird.*

Her date, Jessie Cohen, was now over thirty minutes late. Anxiety gnawed at her. Had she been stood up? The thought was devastating. This was her first real date, and it meant the world to her.

Anna quickly reopened the door and closed the window, peering outside with growing concern. Boots, sensing the tension, leaped onto Anna's bed and began batting at a pen, her energy frantic as she arched her back.

Something caught Anna's eye—a strange object wedged in the corner of the chain-link fence surrounding her yard. She wondered, Is it a bag? A piece of cardboard? What could be stuck there? The fence, with its jagged interlaced wires, was typical for the neighborhood. As she thought about it, she couldn't recall any house on her block having a nice wooden fence.

Her anticipation swelled, a taut wire of tension humming beneath her skin. "He'll be coming up the street any moment now," she murmured to herself, fingers jittering against the fabric of her dress. The thrill of his imminent arrival sent a shiver through her, mingling with the unease gnawing at her gut.

A soft trill broke through her thoughts, drawing her attention to the floor where Boots, her feline companion, gazed up at her with wide, pleading eyes. Anna couldn't resist the call. Miss Boots-Boots had a way of demanding affection that was impossible to ignore, her adorable antics melting Anna's resolve with every chirp and purr.

Annoyance simmered beneath the surface as Anna cradled the cat in her arms, the warmth of the fur a stark contrast to the chill of

Undaunted, Anna lunged forward, her muscles coiled with determination. As the wolf leaped towards her, she swung the curling iron with all her might, the metal connecting with a searing impact against the creature's flesh. A pained yelp echoed through the room as the beast recoiled, its once threatening demeanor faltering in the face of agony.

The collision sent shockwaves through the room; the force of the impact akin to a battering ram against crumbling walls. Despite the chaos, Anna held fast to her weapon, her movements fluid and purposeful. With a graceful twist, she evaded the falling beast, its claws scraping against the hardwood floor in a desperate bid for stability.

Seizing her chance, Anna bolted from the room, the echo of her footsteps mingling with the creature's anguished cries. With a final glance over her shoulder, she slammed the door shut behind her, the barrier a feeble defense against the unknown horrors lurking within. Racing down the stairs, each step a frantic dance with danger, she prayed for escape, her heart racing with fear and adrenaline.

No. That's not how it will get me, she thought with determination.

As Anna descended the staircase, the kitchen beckoned from her right, a beacon of both familiarity and trepidation. Her footsteps quickened down the narrow hallway, her eyes darting to the cramped space beneath the stairs—a tempting refuge, but one that offered only temporary solace. With a grim resolve, she pushed past the urge to hide, knowing her salvation lay in the hands of her neighbors, their distant voices her only lifeline in the encroaching darkness.

A fleeting thought crossed her mind as she passed the shadowy doorway beneath the stairs—a whispered promise of safety in silence. But the echo of her own footsteps, hollow against the empty walls, urged her forward, a reserved request for aid.

The kitchen loomed ahead, a once familial sanctuary. With a sense of urgency, Anna darted towards the countertop, her fingers closing around the familiar wooden block housing an arsenal of steel. Knives of every shape and size gleamed in the dim light, but she wasted no time in deliberation. In her trembling hand, the chef's knife glinted with deadly promise, its edge a razor sharp reminder of the perils that lurked beyond the safety of her home.

With a steadying breath, Anna gripped the knife tightly, her reflection shimmering in its polished surface—a portrait of determination etched with the pallor of fear.

Good enough, she told herself

Anna approached the sliding glass door, her pulse thundering in her ears, each beat a frantic rhythm matching the savage assault echoing from her bedroom above. The flimsy barrier of her bedroom door stood little chance against the relentless onslaught of the beast, its ferocity splintering the wood with each bone rattling impact, the sound of claws tearing through timber a discordant symphony of dread.

With trembling hands, Anna grasped the handle of the glass door, her movements frantic with desperation. But the door remained obstinately still, a silent hindrance barring her escape, adding fuel to the fire of her rising panic.

Outside, the creature snarled and snapped, its primal hunger driving it to tear through the barricade separating it from its prey. Anna's heart clenched with terror as she fought to free herself from the confines of her prison, tears mingling with sweat as she wrestled with the stubborn obstacle blocking her path.

Her fingers brushed against the familiar shape of the security stick; a symbol of safety now transformed into an impediment to her survival. With a sob of frustration, Anna removed the makeshift barrier, each second ticking away like a countdown to her demise.

Above, the beast's growls grew more frenzied, its hunger driving it to new heights of savagery. With a final surge of adrenaline, Anna flung open the glass door, her escape fraught with peril as she fled into the night, the creature's bloodcurdling cries echoing in her wake, a haunting reminder of the dangers lurking on the floor above.

It's almost out, she thought.

Anna slammed the door with all her might, the hollow thud echoing through the still night. With a sinking realization, she knew there was no way to secure it from the outside, leaving her vulnerable to whatever horrors lurked beyond. Heart pounding in her chest, she bolted from the screened porch, her bare feet pounding against the cool grass, the knife clenched tightly in her trembling hand.

A quick glance over her shoulder revealed nothing but darkness behind her. The kitchen remained shrouded in shadow, its secrets hidden behind the glass doors and the window above the sink. Anna's breath hitched in her throat as she realized the absence of any sign of pursuit offered little comfort in the face of the unknown.

Barefoot and chilled to the bone, Anna pushed herself onward, each step a desperate bid for survival. The back corner of the fence loomed ahead, another beacon of hope. With a sob of relief, she quickened her pace, the thought of tearing her dress a small price to pay for the promise of safety beyond.

As she approached the fence, Anna's thoughts were consumed by the fabric caught on its rusted edges, a nagging reminder of the obstacles that lay ahead. Yet, even as fear threatened to consume her, the idea of calling out for help remained a distant echo in the recesses of her mind. For now, her sole focus was on surmounting the barrier between her and the relentless predator hot on her heels.

This could be good. I can jump the fence using the cloth from scrapping me, Anna planned.

She reached out, her hand navigating the jagged edges of the fence as she attempted to scale its barrier. Midway over, her progress halted abruptly as her foot caught on the gap between the fences twisted steel ends, sending her crashing to her knees. With a sickening twist, her ankle buckled beneath her, pain shooting through her as she collided with the ground. Her pink dress snagged on the fence, trapping her in a web of fabric and metal, a predicament she fought desperately to escape.

Tears mingled with frustration as Anna struggled to disentangle herself, the sharp edges of the fence tearing at the delicate fabric with each tug. The wind whispered against her back, its mournful sighs carrying a grim revelation. Beside her, a discarded sheet fluttered in the breeze, its white surface marred by crimson stains and ragged holes where eyes should have been.

Anna finally freed herself from the grasp of the fence using her now frigid hands, her gaze drawn inexorably to the gruesome tableau before her. Through the holes in the sheet, lifeless brown eyes stared back at her, their empty gaze haunting her soul.

As she recoiled from the sight, Anna's fingers brushed against something cold and wet, the sensation jolting her back to reality. Horror washed over her as she realized her hand was immersed in human innards, her skin coated in a slick layer of congealed blood and torn meat.

Confusion and revulsion warred within her as she stared at the grisly evidence of the creature's savagery. Trembling, she lifted the gore-streaked hand to her face, the grotesque reality of her situation sinking in with nauseating clarity.

With a heavy heart, Anna's gaze drifted to the scattered petals strewn across the ground, a poignant reminder of shattered dreams and lost innocence. Despite the dread coiling in her chest, she knew she had to face the truth, no matter how devastating it might be.

Gingerly, she reached out, her trembling hand brushing against the fabric of the ghost costume draped over the lifeless form before her. As she peeled back the cloth, her worst fears were realized in the ghastly visage of her date, Jessie Cohen, his once vibrant spirit silenced by the ravenous hunger of the beast.

The horror before Anna unfolded like a macabre tableau, a symphony of horror conducted by the creature's savage brutality. Jessie's lifeless body lay broken and mutilated from the merciless onslaught he had endured. Tears mingled with the blood soaked earth beneath Anna's feet as she gazed upon the shattered remnants of a life snuffed out too soon.

Her knees trembled, the sensation of dread seeping into her bones as she knelt beside Jessie's corpse. With a shuddering breath, she covered her face, unable to bear the sight of his mangled form any longer. The truth was undeniable—Jessie's body would never move again, leaving Anna with no choice but to seek help.

Using the cold concrete for support, Anna struggled to her feet, her muscles screaming in protest. Before she could fully rise, a presence on the sidewalk caught her attention. Dread coiled in the pit of her stomach as she met the creature's gaze, its eyes burning with a malevolent intensity.

Anna knew she had to act fast, but fear held her in its grip, rendering her paralyzed. With a steely resolve, she retrieved the knife from the ground, steeling herself for the task ahead. Making eye contact with the wolf, she held its gaze, refusing to back down in the face of danger.

As the creature crept closer, Anna studied its monstrous form, her mind racing to comprehend the entity before her. Though it bore the semblance of a wolf, its size and demeanor were unlike any animal she had ever seen. With each labored breath, its emaciated frame was laid bare, revealing the grotesque truth lurking beneath its mangy exterior.

This isn't right. It looks sick, she thought.

The creature's front paws bore a disturbing resemblance to fingers, their elongated form twisted and disjointed. Below the torso, the transition from fur to flesh was jarring, the skin exposed as the hair receded, giving way to an unsettling semblance of humanity.

This one's a boy, she noticed.

Shaking, Anna reached for the first item she could find, a stone, the weight of fear pressing down on her as her knees threatened to buckle beneath her. With a swift motion, she flung the stone across the street, hoping to divert the attention of the massive wolf, if only for a fleeting moment—it worked. Now was her chance to escape, and she wasted no time in putting distance between herself and the looming threat.

With every ounce of strength she could muster, Anna propelled herself over the fence, her heart pounding in her chest as she landed in the bushes below. The rustling of foliage caught the creature's attention, its menacing gaze fixed upon her with predatory intent.

The wolf grunted and growled as it watched Anna dashing across her backyard. *Leave her alone! Damn you! You don't have to. We're not even hungry anymore*, a low, exhausted voice said to the beast.

You have no say! This is what you do. This is what we do now. Now go!

As Anna dashed alongside the fence, the wolf's relentless barks echoed in her ears, driving her forward with a surge of adrenaline. Glancing to her right, she saw the creature effortlessly leap over the chain-link barrier, closing the distance between them with terrifying speed. Now faced with a life-or-death struggle, Anna's instincts kicked in, propelling her towards the glass door with newfound urgency.

The sound of grass and dry leaves crunching beneath the wolf's paws filled the air as it closed in on her. With trembling hands, Anna grasped the door handle and pulled the glass, the metal groaning in protest as she partially opened the door. It was a narrow escape, but it was all she needed. With a final burst of effort, she squeezed her slender frame through the gap, her dress snagging on the doorframe as she fought to make her way inside.

Just as Anna thought she was safe, agony seared through her right calf as the wolf's fangs sank deep into her muscle. With a cry of pain, her upper body collided with the cold linoleum of the kitchen floor, while her lower half remained trapped on the porch. The relentless beast tugged at her leg, its growls reverberating through the air like the snarls of a rabid animal.

Realizing escape was futile, Anna knew she had to fight back. With a desperate lunge, she seized the sharp kitchen knife, her shivering hand finding purchase on its handle. Rolling onto her back, she turned to face the wolf, the blade gleaming in the dim light of the kitchen. With every ounce of strength she could muster, she swung the knife wildly, hoping to strike a blow that would free her from the jaws of death.

You're going to rip her apart. There is no need for this!
Within the monstrous form, a voice whispered with empathy, a stark contrast to the avatar of rage and hunger it embodied. Confident and arrogant, the creature toyed with its prey, assured of its inevitable triumph. But Anna refused to yield without a fight.

As the wolf abruptly released her leg, its demeanor shifted. The ferocity in its eyes softened, the furrowed brow relaxing as its jaws loosened their grip on her lower limb. For a fleeting moment, the beast looked remorseful, a brief flicker of regret crossing its features. Though the pain in her leg remained unbearable, Anna scarcely noticed the creature's sudden change of heart as she wielded the knife with determined precision.

With a swift motion, she slashed at the mongrel's snout, drawing blood and eliciting a pained yelp from the creature. Seizing the opportunity, Anna delivered a forceful kick to its face, sending it staggering backward. In a whirl of motion, she smeared her blood across the linoleum floor, then pushed the glass door closed and locked it with her now cold, numb fingers.

Summoning every ounce of strength, Anna forced herself to rise, her uninjured leg trembling beneath her. With gritted teeth, she limped towards the kitchen entrance, her back pressed against the wall for support. In her haste, the knife slipped from her grasp, clattering onto the blood-drenched floor with a metallic clang.

As she sank to the ground from the pain, her gaze fell upon the lifeless form of her friend across her backyard, a wave of shock and grief washing over her. With fearful hands, she wiped away the mix of blood, sweat, and tears from her face, her eyes drawn to the open front door. Bloody paw prints stained the threshold, leading inside and up the stairs, a grim reminder of the horrors lurking within. In the eerie calm that followed, the only sound was the howling wind, whispering tales of darkness and despair.

I have to close the door, she knew.

A fleeting glance at the kitchen revealed the yellow rotary phone hanging next to the entryway. The living room lay beyond, filled with untouched furniture and pristine carpeting. Though instinct urged her to call for help, Anna knew securing the door was paramount.

I can't risk it seeing me. Just the thought of it lurking back there is terrifying enough, she thought as she limped towards the front foyer, each step accompanied by a grunt of pain.

Suddenly, a sharp *donk* reverberated through the house, causing Anna to freeze in her tracks. She turned towards the kitchen, half expecting to see the creature hurling itself against the glass doors.

Donk. Again, the sound echoed, yet there was no sign of the beast outside, no frantic pounding against the windows.

As the noise grew louder, Anna's heart hammered in her chest, her breaths coming in ragged gasps.

The creature's relentless assault echoed through the house, its exact location eluding Anna's grasp. As she stepped back into the kitchen, a deafening crash shattered the silence, the window above the sink exploding into a shower of glass fragments. With a primal roar, the massive beast burst through the broken window, its desperation evident in every lunge.

Yelping in pain, the creature collided with the olive-colored refrigerator, its bruised form indication to the ferocity of its entry. Anna's cries mingled with a defeated moan, uncertainty clouding her chances of survival. With bated breath, she turned towards the closet under the stairs, a small refuge in the face of overwhelming dread.

Huddling in the cramped space, Anna drew her knees close to her chest, her sobs muffled by the leather of an old baseball glove. Once a cherished memento of simpler times spent playing catch with her father, it now offered little solace in the grip of possible death.

If there is a glove here, the has to be a—knowing what she was looking for.

The wolf rose to its feet, saliva dripping from its jaws as it prepared to resume its hunt for Anna. Through the slats of the closet door, she watched its every move, her heart pounding in her chest. The creature growled menacingly, its brow furrowed in determination, while foam frothed around its mouth, an indication of its exhaustion.

Anna fought to control her breathing, but despite her best efforts, the sound escaped her lips, drawing the wolf's attention like a beacon in the night. With a sinking feeling, she reached for the old softball bat resting against the closet wall, clutching it tightly to her sweat soaked face.

As the werewolf prowled, Anna held her breath, praying it wouldn't detect her presence. She winced as it shook its body, scattering blood and foam across the hallway floor. With cautious steps, it made its way towards the front door, leaving a trail of destruction in its wake. Anna waited in tense silence, the hours stretching endlessly as she remained trapped in the tiny closet, her fear mounting with each passing moment.

Phillip Blake pulled into his driveway; his senses dulled by the alcohol coursing through his veins. Though he knew it was irresponsible to drive under the influence, he brushed it off as a mere suggestion rather than a hard and fast rule. Beside him, his wife Maria slumbered fitfully due to the effects of the tequila shots and the warmth of the car lulling her into a deep sleep. Each time her head bumped against the car window, Phillip couldn't suppress a chuckle.

As he brought the car to a stop, Phillip's gaze drifted to the house looming before him. Something felt off. With a furrowed brow, he noticed the front door standing ajar, a glaring contradiction of the instructions he asked Anna to follow. *That girl. I swear to God. If a robber doesn't kill her, I will,* he thought.

"Stay in the car," he instructed his wife, who complied sluggishly due to intoxication. With a mix of concern and inebriation, Maria ventured, "Is everything okay?"

"It's probably fine. I just want to check the house first. I think Anna may have left the front door open again, despite my reminders," Phillip murmured, his words tinged with the faint scent of champagne from Maria's breath. She added a whispered critique, "Your fault for not fixing it, tight ass." It wasn't an entirely baseless accusation—Phillip's frugality was notorious, down to the most mundane of household items—if he could successfully pull the two-ply toilet paper apart to create another roll, he would.

As Phillip approached the house, a sense of unease settled over him like a heavy shroud. He could have taken the shortcut through the side entrance near the laundry room, but his instincts urged him towards the front. The door stood wide open, a stark invitation. His steps faltered as he noticed the crimson streaks marbling the once pristine steps, the sight jolting him into sobriety.

Pushing the door further ajar, Phillip stepped cautiously into the foyer, taking in the sight of bloodied paw prints and the chaos that had engulfed his home. "Anna?" he called out, his voice trembling with dread, hoping his daughter would answer.

A rustling sound emanated from the stairwell, unnerving Phillip. His daughter emerged from the darkness of the closet, her hair matted with blood and her dress stained with grass and filth, clutching a baseball bat with shaking hands. "Daddy!" she cried out, her voice laced with desperation.

Concern etched deep lines on Phillip's face as he took in Anna's makeshift bandage and the fear in her eyes. Her words tumbled out in a frantic stream, recounting a harrowing encounter with a monstrous intruder. Phillip's attempts to reassure her faltered as he considered the gravity of her words. "Can you walk? Do we need to get you to the hospital?" he asked, his voice tinged with urgency.

Anna nodded, touching her makeshift tourniquet, pleading, "Yeah, but we need to go now, please!"

"Did a dog do that?"

"It wasn't a dog! It was a huge—giant—a wolf!"

"Well, it seems like it's probably gone now."

"Just look out there, Daddy. Please! I'm telling you; his body is out there! I tried to escape but found him—dead!" Anna's voice rose in frustration, her yells desperate for acknowledgment.

"Okay, okay. Just stay by the door and keep watch. I'll check the rest of the house. Close the door and lock it," Phillip directed, his tone edged with concern. Anna nodded, clutching the bat tightly to her chest as she pushed the door, leaving it slightly ajar.

Phillip navigated the hallway, his footsteps heavy with trepidation. Each sight of destruction elicited a mixture of disbelief and expletives. "Jesus Christ," he muttered, his breath hitching as he entered the kitchen. The shattered window and dented refrigerator bore witness to the unfolded chaos. "What the hell? How big was this thing?"

"It was huge! I...I told you!" Anna's response was strained, her words punctuated with frustration. "I already told you! Why don't you believe me?"

"Well, I doubt it's still here," Phillip huffed, his eyes scanning the wreckage in the kitchen, his foot nudging the scattered glass fragments. He stood with his hands on his waist, surveying the mess. "Your mother is going to have a coronary when she sees this."

But Anna's anxiety was fixated elsewhere. Her gaze darted around the room and up the stairs, her paranoia mounting. "Daddy, can you please check upstairs? I don't think it's gone—you know?"

Phillip hesitated with evident skepticism. "I'm sure it's fine," he retorted, his stance unwavering in the hallway and kitchen entrance.

Anna begged, "Please!"

"Anna," he sighed, meeting her anxious eyes, "animals don't tend to linger in one place for too long. They move on, looking for food or other trouble. I'm telling you—"

A dark shadow loomed behind Phillip, casting an ominous silhouette over him. Wrinkled lids gave way to piercing yellow eyes, and foul smelling teeth, flecked with bits of meat, were bared as the wolf parted its jaws. Strings of saliva dripped from the bottom of its menacing muzzle, splattering onto Phillip's bald spot. He felt a warm, viscous substance land on his head, prompting an involuntary shudder. Trying to wipe it away, he patted his scalp, only to realize the wetness between his fingers was far thicker than water. He brought his hand to his face, his heart racing as he recognized the heavy, translucent substance tinged with red. It was blood.

Anna's horrified scream sliced through the air as the wolf rose onto its hind legs, looming menacingly over her father. Its jaws unhinged, accommodating the top half of Phillip's head, confirming the dreadful truth of her warnings.

The wolf's long canines descended onto Anna's father, piercing his eyes. Anna watched as the monster picked her father from the ground and began hurling his body back and forth, like a chew toy. Phillip ignored the pain of his legs crashing into the walls, punching the beast as hard as possible, hoping it would force the wolf to let go of him. Like his legs crashing repeatedly into the walls, Phillip could feel the monster breaking his neck with every fling of its head. Crimson fluid oozed from Phillip's face—a mix of blood and white eye fluid surrounded the sharp edges of the wolf's incisors as it flung him about with every head tug.

Anna screamed at the wolf to let her daddy go, but it didn't. It never had any intention to do so, ignoring her screams. Her retaliation made it personal, and with the practical human sound of its mind now muted, the pure animal rage had taken over. It knew what it was doing. The werewolf knew Anna was in the closet. Instead of quickly depriving her of her life, it waited. It would murder her father now in front of Anna, wanting her to watch. It was bigger than a man with murderous intentions—cold, calculated, and patient. They say there are only two innocent things in the world: children and animals. This creature was neither.

Phillip's shrieking ceased as the wolf snapped his neck.

Anna's voice wavered as she mumbled, "D—Dad. Daddy!" The wolf fixed its large, pale eyes on her, a twisted pride in its gaze, as if taunting her:

See what you made me do. I can do this all day.

Anna's cry pierced the air as she charged towards the monstrous wolf, wielding her baseball bat with determination. The creature growled, dropping back onto all fours, bracing for her assault. With a fierce swing, Anna brought the bat crashing down on the wolf's forehead, eliciting a howl of agony. It clutched its head with long, dark hands, but quickly regained its composure, dark pupils eclipsing the golden irises, preparing for one final strike.

Anna pivoted to flee through the front door, but stumbled over her father's lifeless form, crashing to the ground. Blood streamed from her nose as she crawled towards the exit, crying for help, her focus fractured by the growling predator stalking behind her. The sound of claws scraping against hardwood filled the air, drowning out her sobs. With a sinking dread, Anna realized she had no hope of escape. As she reached the door, her vision clearing, she saw the wolf extend its clawed hand towards her, piercing her right leg and pinning it to the cold floor.

In her agony, Anna longed for her father's comfort, her screams echoing through the house. Each movement tore her leg further, the once pristine floor now stained with the blood of the Blakes. Anna's gaze flickered to the living room, where she spotted her cat, Boots Boots Bittenbacher, cowering behind the couch, a wordless witness to torture her owner endured.

She's safe at least, she thought, attempting to find the good of a horrific situation.

With tears welling in her eyes, Boots watched her beloved human's final moments with growing distress. As the menacing creature loomed over Anna, a silent question echoed in her mind: Who will care for my kitty once I'm gone, her inner voice softening. With a weak meow, Boots expressed her concern, her feline instincts sensing the imminent danger. Anna, lying on the floor, turned her gaze towards her faithful companion, her heart heavy with sorrow. She knew their time together was slipping away. "I'm so…sorry," Anna managed to force out, her voice strained with anguish, apologizing for leaving Boots behind. Tilting her head in response, Boots meowed softly, her concern evident as the wolf drew nearer.

The wolf's claws pierced Anna's back, dragging her across the floor towards the kitchen, her father's lifeless form a grim reminder of the horror. The shards of glass sliced into her stomach, but Anna braced herself for the inevitable agony yet to come. As the wolf prepared to devour her, Anna's gaze fell upon her father's twisted neck and vacant stare.

Daddy!" she tried to cry out, her voice raspy from screaming. But as she stared into her father's lifeless eyes, a chilling realization washed over her. The trauma inflicted upon her body had stolen her voice, leaving her to face her nightmare in silence, never to have the high school romance she yearned for.

This is it.

"Please let me know—" Maria's voice trailed off in the car, accompanied by the upbeat rhythm of Huey Lewis's music resonating from the speakers. She basked in the warmth of the heater, unaware of the chaos unfolding within her own home. Maria's earlier indulgence in alcohol had taken its toll, leaving her unconscious in the passenger seat with her head resting against the chilly window.

As the music played on, Maria's senses stirred, her bleary eyes struggling to focus. A glance at the dashboard clock revealed her husband had been inside for nearly ten minutes. Impatience prickled at her consciousness.

A dark silhouette near the front door caught Maria's attention, drawing her gaze through the fog of her inebriation. Leaning closer to the window, she squinted, attempting to discern the intruder's identity.

"The hell is that? An animal?" she muttered to herself, puzzled by its presence. "Why would there be a dog in our house?"

Maria stepped out of the car, peering over its roof for a better view. Initially attempting to scare the creature away, her efforts ceased when she noticed it carrying something in its mouth. As it turned towards her and its yellow eyes locked onto hers, Maria's unease grew.

Retreating to the safety of her car, Maria locked all the doors, her heart pounding in her chest. As the animal approached, its gruesome offering became clear: a torn lower limb, the fabric clinging to shredded flesh and dried blood. With horror, Maria recognized her daughter's leg, the birthmark confirming her worst fears.

Screaming in fear, Maria pounded on the horn, desperately praying for salvation. The deafening noise startled the wolf, causing it to retreat as alarmed neighbors began to stir.

Meanwhile, Boots observed from a safe distance, understanding home was no longer safe. With a final glance, she disappeared into the nearby woods, leaving behind the shattered remnants of a once loving household.

After this, there would be no more love in their home. It was taken away by a creature many would never see—something many would never accept as truth, now or ever.

A werewolf.

NOWHERE, OHIO

A Novel by
Bryan Wayne Dull

CHAPTER ONE

IT ALWAYS FEELS LIKE

Someone's watching.

Ryan Hatcher lay awake, a certainty gnawing at the edges of his consciousness like a rat. It had been a week since he first glimpsed the shadowy figure lurking outside his bedroom window, its presence casting a gloom over his nights, infecting his sleep with a creeping unease that refused to dissipate. His room had become a battleground, every corner fraught with unseen horrors lurking just beyond the veil of darkness.

Desperate for reprieve, he sought refuge in unlikely places, dragging his pillow and faded blue blanket into the bathroom, seeking solace within the porcelain confines of the bathtub. But the respite was fleeting, the cold enamel offering little comfort against the chill of fear that gripped him.

It was only after hours of restless tossing and turning that he stumbled upon the sanctuary of the living room couch, its worn cushions embracing him like an old friend. Clutching his fuzzy grey slippers with raccoon faces smiling up at him, he curled into the familiar embrace of the plush fabric, seeking solace in its warmth.

Yet even in this makeshift haven, Ryan found no respite from the shadows haunting his dreams. Night after night, he awoke in the small hours, his heart pounding in his chest as he dared to open his eyes, nearly expecting to find himself face-to-face with the specter frequenting his waking nightmares.

His fingers throbbed with phantom pain from the tension gripping him even in slumber. Each morning brought a new ritual of stretching and flexing, a futile attempt to ease the ache that lingered long after the darkness had fled.

But it was not just his body that bore the scars of his nightly battles. The weight of his fears pressed down upon him; a burden too heavy for him to bear. School, family, friends—their concerns loomed large in his mind, overshadowed by the ever-present specter of dread that hung over him like a shroud.

As he lay there in the dim light of the early morning, Ryan's gaze wandered down the long, shadowy hallway stretching out before him. The closet door at its end stood silent and foreboding, its once golden knob now conspicuously absent, a quiet indication the intruder had breached the sanctity of his home.

The curtains fluttered delicately in the breeze, casting shifting patterns of light and shadow across the room. Behind him, the windows stood guard, their panes offering a tantalizing glimpse of the world beyond. But even as he strained to peer through the darkness, Ryan knew some horrors could not be banished with the light of day.

The silhouette of a man loomed before the closet door, casting a long shadow down the dim hallway. Ryan's heart raced as he tried to discern if it was the same ominous figure he had spotted lurking near his home. He couldn't bear the thought of another entity encroaching upon his sanctuary. Ryan once believed the darkness didn't have eyes, but now realized it was staring at him. Why is it doing that, he wondered, as the darkness stood silently as it kept its secret watch.

Memories flooded back to the night he first encountered the mysterious figure outside his window. Startled from his sleep, he had peered out into the night, expecting to see nothing but the stillness of his suburban neighborhood. Yet, amidst the mundane landscape, a shadowy presence had materialized, its form fixed upon his home with an intensity that sent shivers down Ryan's spine.

His unease deepened as he recalled the break-in that had plagued his family upon their return from visiting his grandparents. The invasion of their home had left an indelible mark on Ryan's psyche, a lingering fear that gnawed at him even now. He thought about the broken glass and full toilets they defecated in using the nice towels to cover their mess. Though the culprits had been apprehended, their malicious intent still haunted him, casting a shadow of paranoia over his every waking moment.

And then there was Ryan himself, a constant ball of nerves and anxiety amidst the relative calm of his family. His siblings embodied freedom and attitude, leaving him to grapple with the weight of responsibility that seemed to weigh heavier with each passing day. Despite his mother's assurances he was simply the "middle child," Ryan couldn't shake the feeling he was somehow destined for disaster.

Try as he might to find solace in his fantasies and distractions, Ryan remained tethered to his fears, unable to escape the relentless grip of his own pessimism. It was little wonder that sleep eluded him, his mind consumed by the endless parade of worst case scenarios that played out in his restless dreams.

The shadow remained fixed on the house, its quiet watch unbroken. Ryan hesitantly extended his hand toward the window, a tentative wave meant to acknowledge the eerie presence looming outside. In response, the darkness shifted, revealing two pinpricks of white that pierced through the gloom. Startled, Ryan recoiled, retreating beneath the safety of his covers.

His mother's words echoed in his mind, a feeble attempt to quell his rising panic. "Ghosts just want to be seen or heard," she had said, "they don't mean to harm anyone." But as he lay there, trembling in the darkness, Ryan couldn't shake the feeling of unease that clung to him like a second skin. If the apparition truly sought visibility, why did it loom so menacingly outside his window?

For days, the specter had lingered in the same spot, a silent being keeping watch over the house from its perch beneath the gnarled branches of the old spruce tree. Its presence had been an unwelcome intrusion, a constant source of unease for Ryan as he struggled to make sense of its intentions.

But tonight, something had changed. As Ryan peered out from beneath his blankets, he saw the shadow shift, its form twisting and contorting in the darkness. For the first time since its arrival, the specter moved, its movements fluid and purposeful as it turned its gaze toward the house.

Anxiety ran down Ryan's body as he realized the apparitions attention was no longer fixed solely on him. Whatever malevolent force had brought it to his doorstep had been unleashed, and Ryan knew with a sinking heart that he was no longer safe within the confines of his own home.

It slithered through the dim recesses of the house, a spectral presence gliding unseen. Ryan's senses faltered in its wake, unsure if what loomed before him was a figment of his imagination or a tangible nightmare. Its form, diminutive and stooped, lingered in the shadows, its head perhaps devoid of hair, though the darkness cloaked any certainty.

No mere trick of the mind, this apparition defied dismissal as a simple coat rack mistaken for a person. At the end of the hallway, where only a door stood, the abyss writhed, a manifestation of malevolence.

With deliberate patience, the shade crept nearer, each movement a calculated advance. Ryan clutched his blanket close, seeking solace in its frail barrier, reminiscent of a child hiding from unseen frights.

Halting before his sister's bedroom, the darkness pulsed with an enigmatic energy. Was it lost, Ryan wondered, daring to peek at the indistinct outline, searching for any semblance of humanity in its form? Once the target of its spectral pursuit, now he questioned if another was its quarry. A lament of defeat echoed through the halls as the entity lingered, its presence an unmistakable weight before descending the stairs, vanishing into the night.

Ryan scrambled to his knees on the couch cushions that bore the marks of past indiscretions hidden beneath layers of spilled paint. He watched in awe as the ghostly figure's legs, previously unseen, carried it towards the gnarled blue spruce, its purpose shrouded in mystery. What desires drove this ethereal wanderer? Ryan pondered until the being dissolved into the ether, leaving behind only questions and the whisper of its fleeting presence.

A thud reverberated down the hallway, its source concealed in the murky depths. Ryan's gaze darted towards the sound, but there was nothing to see, no spectral figure lurking in the shadows. As a door squealed open, Ryan instinctively sought refuge, flattening himself against the floor, his heart pounding in dread. "It's coming for me!" he gasped, his voice barely a whisper.

The floorboards groaned under the weight of the unseen intruder; its intentions shrouded in uncertainty. Another door creaked open, but fear paralyzed Ryan, keeping him hidden beneath his makeshift shelter. "Where is he?" a voice called out, tinged with frustration and concern.

Thump... thump... thump-thump-thump-thump.

The sound of approaching footsteps grew louder and more frantic, each beat a terrifying countdown to confrontation. Squinting through the fabric, Ryan braced himself for the inevitable moment when the sheets would be ripped away, his fingers clutching desperately at the fabric, a feeble barrier against the unknown assailant.

With each tug, the unseen presence outside struggled to breach Ryan's defenses, accompanied by frustrated huffs and moans. "Ryan! Why are you on the couch?" his mother's voice suddenly pierced the darkness, her irritation unmistakable.

Reluctantly, Ryan emerged from his hiding place, meeting his mother's gaze mixed with apprehension and defiance. "I can't sleep in my room. Can't I just stay out here?" he asked, his voice tinged with desperation.

"No," his mother replied firmly, her frustration evident. "We bought a house so you can have a room and not live like a bridge and tunnel hobo hanging outside a train station."

Rolling his eyes, Ryan swung his legs over the edge of the couch, his irritation simmering beneath the surface. "What's the matter with you?" he retorted, his frustration mirroring hers.

Rebecca Hatcher, Ryan's mother, paused, a flicker of realization crossing her features as she recalled his earlier tales of the spectral figure outside his window. Suppressing a shiver, she forced herself to confront the unsettling possibility. Perhaps her sensitivity to the unknown had been passed down to her son, a legacy she had hoped to spare him.

As Ryan watched his mother, a pang of concern tugged at his heart. He had noticed the subtle changes in her appearance, the streak of white hair that had appeared seemingly overnight. "Is your stomach acting up again?" he inquired, his tone gentle.

Rebecca sighed, her facade crumbling under his scrutiny. "No better, no worse. It is what it is," she admitted, her voice tinged with resignation.

"It's getting worse, isn't it?" Ryan pressed, refusing to be placated by half-truths.

Rebecca hesitated, grappling with her fears and uncertainties. "Nothing you should worry about right now, love," she deflected, her words tinged with regret.

Guiding Ryan towards his room, Rebecca felt the weight of her secret bearing down on her. How could she tell her son the truth? How could she burden him with the knowledge of her mortality?

As they reached his door, Ryan collapsed onto his bed, his exhaustion evident. "Will you tell me when I should?" he murmured, his voice tinged with vulnerability.

"Should what?"

"Worry about you."

Rebecca hesitated, her heart aching at the thought of what lay ahead. "Of course," she promised, though the lie weighed heavily on her conscience.

With a gentle caress, Rebecca bid her son goodnight, slipping quietly from the room. As she crossed the hall, a sudden chill danced down her spine, a reminder of the unseen forces lurking.

Entering her own bedroom, Rebecca settled into the empty bed, the absence of her husband a stark reminder of the loneliness which now consumed her. As she drifted into sleep, the weight of her being pressed down on her, a burden too heavy to bear alone.

CHAPTER TWO

A LITTLE RESPECT

Rebecca stood in her cluttered kitchen, the morning sun casting a soft glow through the curtains. Her gaze lingered on the array of breakfast options laid out on the counter, each one a testament to her recent culinary inclinations. Lately, she found herself inexplicably drawn to breakfast foods, the kind brimming with sugary sweetness and childhood nostalgia.

The memories flooded back as she recalled the days when her children were younger, their tiny faces scrunched in defiance at the sight of anything remotely green or nutritious. Sugary pancakes and bowls of colorful cereals had been her saving grace, the surefire way to coax them into consuming something, anything, to fill their tiny bellies. She hadn't enjoyed resorting to such tactics, but the relentless demands of motherhood often left her with little choice.

Yet, this morning felt different. As she poured herself a cup of Sanka coffee, the familiar bitterness mingling with the scent of her kitchen, she couldn't shake the sense of unease that crept into her thoughts. The first sip left her feeling bloated, the warmth of the liquid settling uncomfortably in her stomach. With a grimace, she set the cup aside, opting instead for a tall glass of water, the coolness soothing against her parched throat. *I'm feeling off again today. It's getting worse*, she feared.

Ryan woke up to the sight of his framed Corvette poster, spanning from 1953 to 1986. He couldn't remember when or why he had it. The wallpaper, decorated with vintage cars from the '30s and '40s, puzzled him. *Why cars? Is it my father's subtle attempt to make me more manly?* If so, it failed—he remained a nerd.

The room felt cold, typical of their old house. Ryan slipped on his raccoon slippers, carefully placed beside his bed to avoid the chilly hardwood floor. The scent of coffee, which he never drank, greeted him on this Sunday morning—the day his mother brewed the good stuff. Unlike the usual mundane breakfast foods, Sundays were dull for Ryan. He had to entertain himself within the house or the neighborhood. But this Sunday held promise because the newest issue of Eastman and Laird's Teenage Mutant Ninja Turtles, "issue seventeen", was out. He was determined to get it.

As Ryan wandered down the hall, his brother Devin burst out of his room, darting ahead of him. Devin lifted his leg and unleashed a fart, directing an invisible cloud towards Ryan's face. "Morning, dorkus!" he teased. Fanning away the smell, Ryan snapped back, "God! You are so obnoxious!"

An assertive "Oy!" came from the kitchen, where their mother scolded them without bothering to find the culprit. Ryan no longer took offense; he just hadn't figured out how to use it to his advantage. Devin would soon regret tormenting his younger brother—*oh, yes. One day.*

"It's too early for your nonsense," Rebecca scolded. Devin, usually quick with an eye roll or a fake apology, responded earnestly, "Okay, mom." Ryan, surprised by his brother's sincerity, sensed things were different now.

The kitchen table was a sugary paradise, offering chocolate-chip pancakes and Strawberry Shortcake cereal—both breakfast options guaranteed to spike blood sugar levels. Ryan and Devin chose the pancakes, drowning them in maple syrup. The pink cereal, with its cute, colorful appeal, was more for their younger sister, Layla.

Layla woke up surrounded by pastel flowers on off-white wallpaper, which gave her an energetic boost. Unlike her brothers, she lingered in her room, savoring the prettiness and greeting her stuffed animals and dolls. Lucy, her beloved Cabbage Patch Kid, held a special place in her heart. Layla sometimes felt guilty leaving her toys alone, but Teddy Ruxpin's storytelling reassured her they would be entertained in her absence.

With a cheerful bounce in her step, Layla emerged from her room. Ryan often imagined a jaunty tune playing in her head as she moved about. Her happiness was infectious, though her brothers teased her about it. Today, she appeared especially bright.

"Ello, mummy!" she greeted with a thick accent.

Devin rolled his eyes at her exuberance, and Ryan snickered. Layla only used the accent at home, dropping it when their parents were around. Ryan understood; he mimicked accents too, a subconscious attempt to fit in. In Norton, Ohio, such opportunities were rare—each year, the town seemed to shrink further from memory.

"Hello, love. Your cereal is on the table. Grab a bowl," Rebecca said.

"Mmmm. Strawberry Shortcake. How delightful," Layla exclaimed, shimmying with excitement.

Devin's ears perked up at a noise from Layla's room near the kitchen. "Did you leave your possessed bear on again?"

Layla paused, then understood. "Teddy is not possessed! He tells stories!" she protested.

"Are you sure he's not teaching them Satan's will?" Devin teased.

"Mother! Devin's saying my toy is the devil again!"

"Devin! What did we say about talking about Satan at the kitchen table?" Rebecca admonished.

Devin sipped his milk, ignoring them. "Don't worry, luv. If anything is possessed, it's your brutha."

Ryan and Layla laughed, while Devin couldn't muster a smile. He was great at dishing out insults but terrible at taking them. Normally, he'd have a retort ready, but this time, he chose to let it go.

Rebecca leaned against the counter, her gaze drifting out the window as she observed her kids eating. Despite feeling weak today, she was resolute in providing them with a decent meal. Ryan, always the first to finish, set down his plate and made his way towards the kitchen entryway. His eyes fixated on the linoleum floor, its pattern resembling bricks, as he prepared for what could potentially be his most daring slide to the sink yet. Devin and Layla, sensing the impending spectacle, paused in their meal, their attention fully captured by the greatest feat about to unfold.

As Ryan dashed forward, a surge of determination fueled his movements. With each step, he calculated his momentum, ensuring he positioned his legs just right for the ultimate slide. His confidence soared; this time, he was sure he would succeed. Unbeknownst to him, his siblings silently rooted for him, their hopes riding on his success.

In a split second, he felt the exhilarating rush as he glided across the linoleum floor. For a moment, victory was within his grasp. But then, just as he neared the sink, disaster struck. His right foot lost traction, sending him teetering on the edge of a fall.

Despite the mishap, laughter erupted from his siblings, their amusement echoing in the kitchen. Ryan himself couldn't help but laugh quietly at his near miss, even as he realized he had slid farther than ever before.

As he picked himself up, a determined gleam shone in his eyes. One day, he silently vowed, he would conquer that slide and reach the sink. And when he did, it would be a momentous achievement, celebrated by all who witnessed it.

"Where are you in such a hurry to get to?" Rebecca asked.

Ryan shrugged. "Going to get Scott and walk to Loyal Oak to get the latest Teenage Mutant Ninja Turtles comic."

Rebecca, not fully understanding, replied, "Oh! That sounds nice!"

Devin scoffed. "What's the deal with these turtles? Isn't there a cartoon on now?"

Ryan seized the moment to explain. "The cartoon is for kids, but the comics are much grittier, with more violence and adult language. In the comics, they all have red bandanas, not different colors. You can tell who is who by their weapons. Master Splinter gave them names after Italian Renaissance artists: Leonardo, Donatello, Raphael, and Michelangelo."

Devin stared at him, baffled by his enthusiasm. "Thank God you explained. I thought it was going to be something stupid."

Their mother shot Devin a disapproving look. "Sounds pretty cool, Ryan. Just have fun today before school tomorrow."

Ryan nodded and went to get dressed. Rebecca sighed and asked, "Are you going with the Donovans for trick-or-treating tomorrow?"

Devin replied nonchalantly, "Probably. It's what we always do, isn't it?"

Rebecca nodded. "Do we have to? There are other people," Devin suggested.

"I think it's nice. They're good friends, even if your father and theirs haven't seen eye to eye since your dad changed jobs."

"I'm going to feel out of place. Valerie will have Eric, Ryan will have his girlfriend, Christina, and Scott. Then there's this little suck-up," he said, pointing at Layla.

Layla giggled. "I like Christina. She's nice to me."

Rebecca's neutral expression turned into a frown. She didn't care much for Christina, finding her overly needy when it came to Ryan, though she had no issue with Eric, the delinquent—but in small town, friends were hard to come by. There was something about the way Christina looked at her son that Rebecca didn't like. Mothers rarely relish another woman capturing their son's attention.

Devin ran his hand through his dark hair, a mirror image of his father's. He exhaled loudly, his lips flapping in a sign of dissatisfaction. Steering away from the conversation, he moved to his mother. "You feeling alright today? Need anything?" he asked.

Rebecca smiled, resting her frail hand on his shoulder. "Just a bit tuckered. I'll take a nap after you all head out. LayLoo takes care of herself most of the time. I'll be alright." She winked at her son, hoping to ease his worry, if only for today.

As the afternoon sun cast long shadows over the Hatchers' gravel driveway, a vibrant red '86 Mazda 626 eased its way down the winding path. The crunch of gravel beneath its tires echoed through the quiet neighborhood, drawing the attention of Melvin Craggs, who was busy unloading materials from his weathered mustard-colored '79 Ford Courier.

As the car came to a halt, Melvin's brow furrowed in recognition, and a sense of disapproval crept over him. He squinted, the lines of irritation deepening on his weathered face as he observed the driver emerging from the vehicle. The sight did little to improve his mood.

Calvin Hatcher, dark-haired, thick-bearded, and overweight, hadn't lived with his family for months. Today, the alcoholic father decided to visit. Melvin, tired and worn far too young for his mid-thirties, didn't need to know more. Their animosity was rooted in an old disagreement about erecting a fence to shield Melvin's neglected pool—the sole pool in the Holiday Heights subdivision that had remained untouched for years, much to the disappointment of summer swimmers. Unpleasant words had been exchanged, creating a lingering tension between them. Melvin chose to ignore him, while Calvin acted obnoxiously, often greeting his neighbor with a sarcastic "how do you do" if he was outside. Today was no different.

"Hey there, Melvin!" Calvin shouted, exiting his car with a Cheshire cat grin. Melvin's upper lip curled, and his eye squinted. Raising his old arthritic hand, he flipped Calvin the middle finger. Cal laughed and pointed. "I wouldn't expect anything less from you, Melvin."

Melvin watched as Calvin approached the front door, fumbling with his keys. Muttering obscenities under his breath— "shit, dammit, son of a bitch"—each time he chose the wrong key, he finally found the right one. The house key was marked with an H to make it easier to find, but Calvin's frazzled mind had forgotten even that.

"Is anyone here?" Cal called out, stumbling over the threshold. His voice echoed through the hall, and each family member reacted. Rebecca, his wife, felt a surge of annoyance. Devin's anger flared at his father's sudden appearance. Ryan remained indifferent, while Layla's face lit up with excitement.

Layla jumped up from the table and dashed down the stairs. "Daddy!" she exclaimed, throwing herself into his open arms. Calvin hugged her tightly, a smile breaking across his face. "Are you coming with us for Trick or Treat, Daddy?" she asked, hope shining in her eyes.

"Of course. I mean, I won't be getting candy because I'm an old man," Calvin chuckled. Rebecca appeared at the top of the stairs, her eyes narrowing. "Go finish your breakfast, LayLoo," she ordered, her tone sharp with frustration at the sight of her estranged husband.

"Hey, Dad!" Ryan called from the kitchen.

"Hey, bud!"

Ryan stayed put, knowing the routine. Dad would come in; Mom would argue with him out of earshot. Only then would he get to spend time with his father. Still, he felt a small surge of happiness seeing his dad more at ease around the kids. Rebecca stomped down the stairs, her frustration evident. "You can't just come into the house. We've talked about this. You don't live here anymore."

Calvin shrugged, his confidence unshaken. "Seeing as how I'm paying the mortgage and my kids live here, I'm going to trump that statement."

"Ya want to play that card, do ye?"

Cal raised his hands in a gesture of peace. "There are some things in my office. Let me just get them, and I'll be out of your hair until tomorrow when the kids go out for Halloween." Rebecca inhaled deeply, conceding defeat. She gestured towards the second set of stairs leading to the family room. "Go ahead." Cal descended with a smirk, his attitude a mix of sarcasm and arrogance. Rebecca rolled her eyes, secretly finding it endearing.

Adjacent to the closet, a doorway led to the laundry room, its entrance adorned with a decorative curtain swaying gently with the faint breeze filtering in through the open window. Inside, the rhythmic whir of the washing machine and the gentle swish of clothes in the dryer provided a soothing background accompaniment to the room's functionality.

Across from the laundry room, nestled in the corner, was Cal's office—a cozy sanctuary tucked away from the hustle and bustle of daily life. The room was small but efficiently organized, with every item meticulously placed to maximize space. A filing cabinet stood against one wall, its drawers neatly labeled and arranged in alphabetical order.

In the center of the room sat a sturdy desk, its surface adorned with a vintage word processor, its keys worn from years of use. A soft lamp bathed the desk in warm light, casting comforting shadows across the room. A worn leather chair awaited its occupant, inviting them to sit and immerse themselves in whatever task lay ahead.

In one corner of the office stood a glass display case, its polished wood frame gleaming in the ambient light. Inside, rows of red velvet cradled Cal's prized possession—the carefully curated collection of firearms he held dear. Each weapon meticulously maintained and lovingly displayed.

Rebecca despised having guns in the house; her family never had one in Manchester, England, where she grew up. After Devin was born, they moved to Norton, attracted by the affordable price of the house on half an acre, perfect for Cal's salary at Seiberling Tire &

Rubber Co. The plant's closure in 1980 strained their finances, but the house, with its acres of woods stretching to neighboring areas, remained irresistible.

Calvin insisted on owning guns to protect the family from potential threats lurking in the woods. Rebecca reluctantly agreed, though she suspected he was more interested in the collection itself. One weapon turned into several until she put her foot down, leading him to start collecting knives instead.

"Do you still have the key for this if you need it?" Calvin asked, noticing Rebecca quietly standing in the doorway.

"Yeah. It's in the shoebox on the top shelf of our closet, along with the other five pieces of firepower you have hiding. You have enough now your sons could dual wield them," she replied.

Calvin snickered and made his way back to the family room, carefully navigating around the metal pole in the laundry area. He paused, taking in the view.

As one stepped into the Hatcher family room, they were greeted by a cozy yet unassuming space that exuded warmth and familiarity. The scent of aged wood mingled with hints of vanilla scented candles, creating an inviting feel that enveloped visitors like a comforting embrace.

In the center of the room sat a well-loved couch, its cushions adorned with handmade quilts and mismatched throw pillows which added a touch of charm to the space. A solitary armchair stood nearby, its weathered upholstery bearing the marks of countless evenings spent curled up with a good book or engaged in lively conversation.

Against one wall, a vintage television set and Hi-Fi system rested on a sturdy wooden stand, their outdated appearance due to the family's fondness for nostalgia. Despite their age, both still served their purpose admirably, providing endless entertainment and serving as a focal point for family gatherings.

The walls were adorned with wood paneling, their rich, earthy tones lending the room a rustic charm reminiscent of a cozy log cabin retreat. While the décor was simple and unassuming, it held a certain rustic elegance that spoke to the family's down-to-earth nature and appreciation for life's simple pleasures.

Every Christmas, a towering evergreen stood proudly in the corner near the stairs, its branches adorned with twinkling lights and homemade ornaments lovingly crafted by little hands. The sight of the tree never failed to elicit a mix of joy and exasperation from Cal as he grumbled about the inevitable mess of fallen needles and tangled lights.

Along the staircase, a flat railing provided the perfect vantage point for adventurous children to slide down, their laughter echoing through the room as they indulged in the simple leisure of childhood play. Whether engrossed in a game of Atari 2600 or gathered around the television for a family movie night, the family room was a sanctuary where cherished memories were made.

Rebecca's words sliced through the air, halting Calvin's thoughts. "Ya can't keep doing this, Cal," she said, her voice tinged with concern. "It's like you're stringing them along, makin' 'em believe you'll come back."

"I will come back, though," Calvin insisted, his gaze steady. Rebecca understood his intentions but urged him to change the subject. "How are you holding up?"

A heavy sigh escaped Rebecca's lips. "Eatin's become impossible. I manage to sip water now and then, but even that's a struggle. My stomach feels like it's being torn apart, but I guess that's just par for the course."

Calvin winced, imagining his wife's suffering. "Are you absolutely sure there's nothing—"

"Yes, Cal. Stage IIIC gastric cancer—maybe IV," Rebecca cut in sharply. "I doubt there's a miracle cure hidin' somewhere, unless you've got insider info the doctors don't." Calvin clenched his jaw, suppressing the urge to lash out at her dismissal of his concerns. Instead, he drew strength from the files clutched in his hands, mustering the courage to broach a difficult topic. "I think I should move back in."

"Are you out of your mind?" Rebecca scoffed; her tone laced with incredulity.

"No, Rebecca. I've been sober for a month now. I'm trying to get my life together, and I believe being with you again could help," Calvin stated firmly.

"Absolutely not."

"Fine. Just hear me out," Calvin urged, taking a deep breath. "Think about it. The doctors have given you only a few weeks. Do you want our kids to find you... like that? Do you want them to be the ones to call for help, or worse, find you gone?"

Rebecca folded her arms, her expression softening as she allowed him to continue. "If... when... they need to know, it's better coming from me."

Shaking her head, Rebecca fought the urge to argue. "You know I'm right, Rebecca," Calvin persisted, his voice asserting. "It would devastate them to discover you like that. What if Layla found you?"

"Okay, fine!" Rebecca relented. "But there's no guarantee they won't be the ones to find me or call for help."

Calvin threw his hands up in exasperation. "Maybe, but at least I have some time off. Let me spend these last weeks with you."

Rebecca folded her arms, considering his proposal, but she knew she needed more time to decide. "I'll think about it. But what you did... that night... it's not something I can easily forgive, even with the time I have left."

As Calvin climbed the stairs, Rebecca watched him go, torn between her anger and the longing to have him by her side, if only for a little while longer. Marriage was never easy, especially when faced with the harsh realities of life and the painful choices it demanded.

Devin donned his headphones, engulfing himself in the thunderous sounds of *Appetite for Destruction* until his curiosity prodded him. "Wait! What are you doing?" he asked, his voice rising slightly. Ryan, who had nearly shut the door, smirked and leaned back in. "Always so predictable. The moment she enters the picture, you perk up," Ryan thought to himself.

"I'm heading to Scott's, we're going to grab my comic and some Garbage Pail cards," Devin said, his gaze drifting as he concocted a plan to catch a glimpse of Valerie, Scott's older sister.

"Let me give you a ride in the Turbo," Devin insisted, his tone sounding more like a demand.

"Why do you keep doing this to yourself? You know she's dating that jerk, Eric, who—by the way—is part of your crew in the neighborhood," Ryan pointed out.

"Is it wrong to stop by? Our parents were good friends with their parents," Devin justified.

"Yeah, were. Past tense," Ryan rebutted, swiftly dismantling Devin's excuse.

"Just let me take you!"

"Five bucks."

"What? No! I'm doing you the favor here!" Devin insisted.

"Uh-uh. Not this time," Ryan declared, relishing his newfound leverage. "I'm the one doing you the favor here, lover boy." Devin reluctantly fished out a crumpled five-dollar bill. "Here," he muttered, tossing it at Ryan. "See you downstairs," Ryan chimed as he shut his brother's door.

Feeling triumphant with the extra cash, Ryan headed down the hall to inform their mother of their departure and bid his father farewell. After enduring a brief interrogation, Rebecca reluctantly agreed to let them use her car, The Turbo—a brown Dodge Daytona with yellow and orange stripes, brown leather and adorned with 'Turbo' on the back doors. Ryan snagged the keys from the homemade holder near the kitchen entrance, a memento crafted by Devin in shop class two years prior and descended the stairs.

Directly across from the staircase was Layla's room. Rebecca always harbored a fear Layla might wander out in the middle of the night and suffer an accident. Fortunately, it had never come to pass in their six years on Greengate Drive.

As Ryan passed by Layla's room, he caught sight of her playing with her Cabbage Patch Kid. But something was off. There, beside Layla, sat a young girl in a tattered pink dress, her legs mangled and covered in blood. Ryan's heart raced as he froze, unsure of what to do. The sight of the decaying figure shook him, and he hesitated before bursting into Layla's room, ready to protect her from the spectral entity he might have glimpsed the previous night.

Layla, unperturbed by Ryan's sudden intrusion, looked up calmly. "What's wrong?" she asked, her gaze steady. Ryan stumbled over his words, fabricating a feeble excuse to mask his alarm. "Uh, thought I heard something. Sorry," he muttered, retreating back into the hallway, his mind reeling with confusion and unease.

Once Ryan had retreated downstairs, Layla turned her attention back to the spectral presence beside her. "It's okay," she reassured the ghost gently. "He means well." With a serene smile, Layla approached her tea set on the dresser and addressed her ethereal companion, "Was there something you wanted to talk about?"

CHAPTER THREE

VALERIE

Time was slipping away as they neared the Donovan house. Ryan would have spoken earlier if he hadn't been preoccupied with comparing his attire to his brother's. Devin wore a blue and grey flannel, unbuttoned, over a plain black shirt, while Ryan sported a red Lacoste polo with the iconic alligator logo on the chest. Their mother would *have a go at them* later for leaving without coats or hoodies. The autumn leaves painted the neighborhood in vibrant hues, but there was little time to appreciate the changing scenery; they needed to talk.

"You should start talking to Dad again. He seemed disappointed you brushed him off earlier," Ryan ventured. Devin shook his head gently, disappointment etched on his face. "No. I can't," Devin replied firmly. Ryan focused on the road ahead, with Scott's house in his view. "He's going to come back eventually, you know. It's only a matter of time until Mom—" "I know! Damn it!" Devin cut in, frustration bubbling up. "There are things you don't understand. Things you don't need to know."

"Then tell me. Help me understand why Dad is so distant," Ryan pressed. With a clenched jaw, Devin thumped the steering wheel in frustration, torn between wanting to confide in his brother and knowing it wasn't the right time. "He's not the same. Something changed him, and I don't know if we'll ever get him back," Devin confessed.

Ryan couldn't argue. Their father had become a different person over the past few years, and while Devin knew part of the story, Ryan and Layla remained oblivious—*well, at least Layla probably didn't notice*. To her, their father was still the infallible hero. It must be comforting to be so innocent. Calvin had become consumed by work and alcohol, losing sight of what truly mattered—their family and their future.

Anxiety crept in as they approached the Donovan's ranch-style home. Rick Donovan, the patriarch, was a formidable figure—large, often mean, and usually drunk by noon. Due to their fathers' past working relationship, Rick harbored resentment toward Calvin, perhaps fueled by jealousy.

Norton, Ohio, served as a bedroom community for those commuting to Akron, mainly plant workers. Akron was a vital cog in the Midwestern Rust Belt machine, where Calvin and Rick had served as supervisors in the B.F. Goodrich plant. Their friendship blossomed as they bonded over work and family, often sharing meals and spending time together. However, when a recession hit Akron, their lives took a turn for the worse.

Calvin transitioned to a district manager role for Musicland in 1987, leaving behind his blue-collar roots for a white-collar position. Rick understood the decision but remained at the plant until it ceased production, leaving him jobless and struggling to make ends meet. Over time, Rick spiraled into depression, battling anxiety, hatred, weight gain, and alcoholism. While Calvin continued to work, he too found solace in alcohol, a habit that would eventually tear their friendship—and their families—apart. Two men, once inseparable friends, now found themselves on parallel paths of emotional turmoil, unaware of the shared struggles.

The Turbo eased into the driveway, bringing Scott to his feet in anticipation of Ryan's arrival for their trip to the store. As the brothers stepped out of the car, Scott quipped, "I thought we were walking." Ryan, casual as ever, nodded towards Devin, implying that driving had been his brother's idea. "We are. My brother just wanted to tag along and admire your sister," he remarked with a smirk.

Devin's jaw dropped, stunned by his younger brother's newfound audacity. Quickly swatting the back of Ryan's head, Devin admonished, "Shut up, you little brat!" Despite the sting, Ryan wore a satisfied grin; enduring a smack was a small price for a good jab.

Intrigued, Devin inquired about Scott's sister. "Is she around?" Scott, casting a knowing glance at Ryan, decided to tease. "Why the sudden interest?"

"To talk about tomorrow."

"What's the real reason—really?" Scott whispered the last part, aiming to provoke.

"That's *really* a big 'ol case of none of your business," Devin shot back, attempting to assert himself. Unfazed, Scott met Devin's towering presence with boldness, while Ryan's relaxed demeanor balanced out Scott's assertiveness.

Scott shrugged on his Ohio State hoodie, locking eyes with Devin. "You won't do anything. You know why? Because if you touch me, my sister will never give you the time of day—like you had a chance anyway," he taunted. Sneering, Devin headed towards the front door to see Scott's sister.

Leaning against the car, Scott and Ryan braced themselves for the inevitable spectacle of Devin trying to engage in conversation with a girl. While Devin wasn't lacking in looks, his awkwardness and demeanor around girls gave off an eccentric vibe.

Devin's hand trembled as he pressed the doorbell, eliciting a worn chime, a melody of years past. This encounter could go either way—perhaps a successful conversation or, worst-case scenario, an awkward encounter with Scott's dad in his underwear. Devin prayed fervently for the former.

The door creaked open slowly, revealing Valerie Donovan, a five-foot-six blonde beauty. She stood with her hand in her hair, adjusting the scrunchie holding it to the side. Valerie wore purple leggings, a black leotard paired with pink leg warmers, and a cropped white sweatshirt adorned with a faded Miami Vice logo. Even in casual attire, whether exercising or relaxing at home, she exuded an aura akin to Venus herself. Devin couldn't help but think of the Bananarama song; there was something about her that stirred a desire for romance, yet it also brought forth a surge of anxiety, momentarily robbing him of coherent speech.

"Hey! What's up?" she greeted with a smile, but Devin found himself at a loss for words. The topics he had planned to discuss mere minutes ago evaporated from his mind. The ensuing conversation resembled the antics of the mentally challenged buzzard from the Looney Tunes cartoons.

"Uh, I, uh, tomorrow. The thing. Trick or treating! Are we still, um, you know... like... going to meet up at a certain time?" he stammered.

Observing from the driveway, Ryan and Scott marveled at Devin's inability to converse with a girl. "Dude," Scott remarked, elbowing Ryan in the arm, "This is making my coochie dry up, and I'm not even a chick." Ryan nodded, witnessing the train wreck unfold before him.

"Oh yeah! I think we are going to meet at your house at six or seven. I think," Valerie replied, giggling at the end of her sentence. Devin cherished her laughter. If she were a glass of champagne, her laugh would be the bubbles floating to the top, tickling your mouth.

"Who's at the door?" a booming voice resonated from inside the house. Valerie rolled her eyes, bracing herself for her father's potential embarrassment. "Just Devin and Ryan, dad," she sighed. Rick's heavy steps approached the front door, a massive figure holding a Coors emerged, grinning. "The Hatcher brothers. What brought you here today, forgetting Ryan's practically part of the furniture?" Mouth hanging open, uncertain how to respond, Devin replied, "Finalizing plans for tomorrow, sir. Are you joining us?"

Rick groaned, "I guess. The whole street is on watch duty to prevent any trouble." He paused, pointing to Valerie with his thumb. "This one is dating the troublemaker. Not sure about the rest."

"Ugh! Dad, come on! He's not that bad!" Valerie interjected. Rick ignored his daughter's remark and focused on grilling Devin.

"Your dad still running the music stores?" Rick asked.

"Yes, sir."

"Yeah, well—I guess he was smart to leave. Here I am, waiting for something big to come my way."

"Something will turn up," Devin said, trying to appease the father. Rick sneered, eyeing Devin and then Ryan. "I bet you guys are doing alright with all those fat checks your dad is raking in," Rick insinuated, his tone growing aggressive. The rude insinuation irked Devin, bringing out his smart-ass personality. "I wouldn't know.

He's not living with us right now, and even if he was, I'm not his accountant."

Valerie stifled a laugh, amused by Devin's response. Devin glanced at her and grinned, pleased to have made her laugh at her father's expense. Rick sucked his teeth, debating whether to engage further, but to Valerie's surprise, he backed down. "I hope your mom is doing okay," he said before retreating to the television showing the Cleveland Browns-Cincinnati Bengals game.

"I'll see you at school tomorrow and then for trick-or-treating," Valerie smiled, warming Devin's heart. "Oh! Eric will be joining us. That's cool, right? I mean, you two are friends and hang out and stuff." Devin's warm feeling began to fade as reality set in; Eric, his friend, was dating the girl of his dreams.

"Yeah, sure. That's cool," Devin replied with a long sigh, releasing the tension in his chest.

"Okay. See ya," Valerie waved as she closed the door. Devin waved back, walking away from the front door towards the car.

"Hey, Devin," Scott began to mock, "I, uh, was like, you know, wondering—about the thing tomorrow, if, like, you could be, ya know, be—a bigger dweeb?" Ryan laughed at Scott's impression of his brother until Devin intervened, gently grabbing their foreheads and playfully knocking them together. "Shut up, trout-sniffers!"

Devin drove home, leaving Ryan and Scott to walk to the store. As they watched him drive away, Ryan realized he would have to walk back home alone, as Scott lived near the main road. "Worth it," he smiled, seeking confirmation from Scott, his best friend. "Yeah, it was!" Scott agreed with a nod.

They performed their handshake, a simple slide of their hands against each other. It wasn't original, but it worked for them. They walked along the roadside, chatting about anything and everything coming to mind.

CHAPTER FOUR

TENDERNESS

The Loyal Oak Market loomed like a foreboding relic, an ancient barn renovated into a drive-thru convenience store, its long shadows stretching across the desolate road. Years ago, Ryan had dismissed it as just an old barn until his mother made a fateful stop for supplies. When Garbage Pail Kid cards became popular, the market transformed into Ryan's shortcut for acquiring a pack effortlessly. The barn's interior, with its rustic beams and creaky floors, harbored more than convenience; it concealed a plethora of beer, a secret haven for adults. Fortunately, the local churches retained their congregations, sparing Ryan and Scott from the prying eyes of adults.

"Here." Ryan yanked on Scott's hood, drawing his attention. He handed over a five-dollar bill. "What's this for?"

Ryan grinned, divulging, "Convinced my brother to chauffeur me to your place so he could catch a glimpse of your sister." Scott stared at Ryan's unchanged expression. Concern crept into Ryan. "Did I upset you?"

"That is the most selfish thing, taking money from your vulnerable, desperate brother. I have never been—prouder of you than I am right now!" Laughter echoed as they entered the shadowy barn store for their collectibles and snacks.

Years earlier, Jennifer Brayer, the neighborhood's go-to babysitter, stood behind the Oak's register, watching two familiar figures stroll in. "Hey Jennifer!" they chorused. A smile graced Jennifer's face. "Hey Ryan!... Scott."

Scott had been a challenge for Jennifer during his younger days, a source of self-consciousness. With adorable curls framing her face, Jennifer couldn't escape Scott's early flirtations, which began in fifth grade when she was a Norton High senior. "Hey Jennifer," Scott purred, raising his eyebrows suggestively. Jennifer's subtle smile fueled Scott's belief she harbored interest.

"Did the new TMNT come in?" Ryan inquired. Jennifer shook her head regretfully. "No. Sorry, bud. It got delayed a couple of weeks. Sorry about that." Ryan's disappointment was obvious, but his spirits lifted at the sight of series fourteen Garbage Pail Kid card packages on the counter. Calculating his purchase, he figured he could snag three packs and a Tootsie Roll Pop and still have enough.

As Ryan finalized his transaction, Jennifer fought to keep her curly black hair from obscuring her eyes. "How's your brother and sister?" she inquired. Unwrapping his sucker, Ryan replied, "Devin's still a pain, and Layla remains the sweet one until my parents stop looking; then, she's not sometimes." A shared laugh accompanied Jennifer's offer of a bag, which Ryan declined, anticipating potential trades with Scott.

Scott, meanwhile, approached the counter, placing two packs of cards and a sucker. Jennifer squinted at him. Scott's attempt at seduction was evident as he placed the sucker in his mouth and attempted what he considered 'sexy eyes.' He asked, "You like Tootsie Pops?" Jennifer released a shallow breath, uncertain of his intentions but ready to knock him down a peg or two. The transition to high school hadn't softened her resolve.

"I can get to the middle fast with just a few licks. Know what I mean?" Scott's crude remark hung in the air, leaving an awkward silence. Jennifer, fully aware of his insinuation, couldn't help but grimace. Offended, Scott scoffed at the idea she found him repulsive.

"Please. It would be a privilege, and you would love it," Scott insisted, prompting Jennifer to burst into laughter at the audacity of the eighth grader making advances. Unfazed, Scott mumbled, "Oh, blow me," as he began to walk away, visibly embarrassed.

Jennifer, not one to let such comments slide, snapped her fingers to get Scott's attention. As he turned back, expecting a different reaction, Jennifer pointed to the front of her toothy smile. "You see this gap in between my teeth?" she teased. Ryan, curious about the commotion, walked over to join them. "If I were to blow you, there would still be room left over," she quipped.

Shocked, Scott stood with his mouth open while Ryan erupted into loud laughter, nearly falling to the ground, his sides hurting. "Whatever," Scott scoffed as he walked from the entrance, and Ryan continued laughing all the way to Wadsworth Road, the supposedly "busy" street they had to cross to return to their housing development.

"What a bitch! She didn't have to be that mean. I'm still a kid," Scott complained. Ryan, whose laughter began to slow, replied, "Talk like an adult, get treated like one." Scott shook his head as he opened his first pack of GPK cards. "Shut up, Ryan!"

Feeling a bit guilty about his prolonged laughter, Ryan began to open a pack of cards, carefully chewing on the hard stick of gum, hoping it wouldn't break his teeth. The conversation shifted as they discussed more mature topics influenced by Scott's dad, Rick, who had become more vocal about adult matters due to job loss.

"Can I ask you a question?" Ryan asked hesitantly. Scott, intrigued, raised his eyebrows, removing the sucker from his mouth. It was a departure from their usual conversations, and Ryan, navigating unfamiliar territory, sought answers about Scott's surprisingly advanced knowledge of grown-up stuff.

"My dad has these videos. He watches them when everyone is asleep but lets them play when he's passed out on the couch. I just sit at the top of the stairs and watch them through the bars from the rail," Scott explained. As they walked, Ryan looked down at his feet, contemplating Scott's home.

"Did he always do that?" Ryan asked. Scott sifted through his cards, searching for the Zipped Kip card with a boy featuring a zipper for a mouth and eyes, or its alternate, Jack Tracks. "Don't think so. Just when he lost his job."

"What about your mom?" Ryan asked.

"What about her?" Scott winced.

"I mean, like, you know, she's around for stuff like that."

"Gross. Have you seen my mother lately?" Scott replied, shivering at the thought, offended Ryan would mention her in that context. "He drinks and gets angry a lot." Ryan nodded and had to ask one final question because he was Scott's friend. "He doesn't hit you or anyone, does he?"

"Nah. He yells a lot. Makes us out like we're the losers, that we're the dumb ones, and he's right all the time. My dad is harsh on my sister more than anyone. My mom stays quiet and doesn't talk much anymore. Not to anyone." Scott stopped talking, realizing how distressing it was to have a family as they are now. "Just don't tell anyone because it's kind of embarrassing."

Ryan nodded and reassured, "I won't tell anyone. I swear." Scott faked a smile and shook his head, knowing his best friend since third grade wouldn't spill his family's dirty laundry. Scott didn't think he was the only kid with a shaky home life. Many in the three communities had households with little money and depressed adults from manufacturing jobs ending. The decline began in the 1960s and worsened over time. The residents would endure Rubber City's financial hardships for many years. However, Ryan would never truly understand the difficulties of others until he became older. He was content where he was, even with death looming over him, a truth he would face even when no one else wanted to.

"You want to hang out in the woods and trade cards?" Scott wondered. As enticing as it was, Ryan felt guilty for not being at home with his mom. "No. I think I'm going to go home now," he replied. Understanding the situation, Scott didn't whine or nag Ryan to hang out longer. Instead, Scott nodded and told him to take it easy as they parted ways at his driveway.

Ryan observed as Scott made his way through his garage to the side door, letting out a sigh. He knew he would have to journey home with nothing but his thoughts. Glancing at Scott's home, he noticed Valerie peering out her bedroom window. Their eyes met, and Ryan couldn't help but sense loneliness emanating from her.

Valerie offered a smile and waved at Ryan. Caught off guard by the unexpected acknowledgment, he pondered how to respond. Should he give an enthusiastic wave back? Or perhaps a more subdued one? Eventually, Ryan decided on a slow wave, infused with a hint of empathy, wanting her to feel reassured now that he understood the dynamics of life in the Donovan household. Valerie's smile deepened, her eyes lingering on Ryan as if wordlessly wishing for someone to rescue her.

Ryan held onto a glimmer of hope someone would. *She deserves better.*

The temperature had dropped substantially since Ryan left his house. Dark clouds took over the sky, and Ryan felt like he was the last person on Earth. Houses appeared empty, with no light emerging from the windows, and no children played outside as they usually did on weekends. Over the years, the neighborhood roads he had known became more vacant as people left for better jobs. It was a lonely, desolate feeling walking through Holiday Heights, which had become lost in its unkemptness.

Ryan saw his home in the distance. His family lived in the last house on a dead-end street, so he wasn't surprised when a car pulled into his driveway. He still became excited about the prospect of having a visitor, but as usual, the car used the driveway to turn around. Ryan looked ahead at the car reversing itself and gazed through its windows at the spruce tree in his yard. The strange occurrences of the last week replayed in his mind, particularly the shadow appearing in the hallway and traveled to his front yard, stopping at the tree.

As the car drove off, it revealed a man standing in front of the spruce—*it's him*. It was no longer a shadow. Ryan recognized the figure by its stature: short with hunched shoulders and a balding head. Remnants of dark mist outlined its body, but it was unmistakably a man. The man's eyes were large, and his chest heaved, growing angrier with every passing second. His black polyester tracksuit remained still as the wind blew harder.

They stared at one another for what felt like minutes to Ryan. The phantom began to gasp for air, and his body started to tear apart from the bottom of his chin down to his chest, with four lines of blood pouring down. Ryan put his hands up to his chin, ready to hide his face. He didn't want to look away, but the terror he witnessed from afar was too much. The dark spirit quickly put its arms out, pushing away whatever was attacking him, causing Ryan to fall backward. It was so far away but felt so close.

The man opened his mouth, yelling for help, but no sound came out. Blackness surrounded him, flowing upward as pieces of dark mist separated and dissipated in the air. The man's head bent backward as five holes appeared on his neck before an unseen force pulled out his throat. Ryan couldn't comprehend what was happening—*is this how you died?* A wad of human innards with parts of the larynx and vocal cord floated before it fell onto the grass. The short, balding man in the black tracksuit clutched his throat as blood spewed through his fingers. Ryan finally covered his eyes, waiting for the vision to disappear, never wanting to see the man again. When Ryan gently pulled his hands away from his eyes, the body in front of the spruce tree had vanished, leaving only the overcast sky, the wind, and his house ahead. He breathed out slowly, his heart racing. He hoped this would be the last time, but he knew deep down it wouldn't be.

Shaken from the entity appearing more vividly than before, Ryan walked through the front door to the sound of painful moans and retching. He had become all too familiar with these sounds lately. Glancing up the stairs, he saw Layla standing near her bedroom door, her face filled with worry. Ryan motioned for her to stay put before running up the stairs and into the hallway bathroom. There, he found his mother with her head in the toilet, and his brother holding her hair back.

"We've been here for a while now," Devin said, his voice carrying a rare tone of camaraderie. Rebecca tapped on the side of the toilet, trying to speak but only managing to vomit again. After spitting out excess saliva, she croaked, "It won't be long now. I had to eat something. Forced meh self to swallow some food."

Ryan looked over at Devin, the unspoken question clear in his eyes. Devin shrugged, his expression mirroring Ryan's helplessness. Rebecca, tired and full of fear, sat up and tried to lighten the mood. "It's a good day today, innit?" she joked weakly. Her boys smiled, appreciating her attempt at humor, but neither could muster a laugh.

"Yeah, mom. It's a lovely day," Ryan replied. Rebecca stretched her arms out, inviting her sons to help her up. "Help your old mum to the bedroom then?" Ryan and Devin gently lifted her to her feet.

As they turned toward the bathroom door, Layla's worried face came into view. Tears welled in her eyes as she asked, "Is mum going to be okay?" Rebecca mustered enough energy to shuffle over to her, allowing Layla to hug her legs. Rebecca leaned down, placing her hands on Layla's back. "Don't you worry about me, dearie. Everyone has their good and not-so-good days. Today wasn't so good, is all, but it doesn't mean tomorrow won't be better."

Layla clung to her mother's comforting voice, even if the words felt hollow. She knew her mother wasn't well despite the reassurances. All she could do was rely on her brothers and hope her father would return home soon. "Go and hang out in your room, Layla, please," Ryan gently urged his sister.

"But I've been in there all day with—," Layla began to protest.

"Just do it, Layla! Pretty please with sugar on top! Go play in your room while we help mom!" Devin interjected. Layla stomped her foot in defiance and marched back to her room, mumbling complaints.

The boys guided their mother to the main bedroom across from Ryan's. Rebecca collapsed onto the bed, pulling her legs up with effort. "I need a big spoon and a little spoon," she murmured. Ryan and Devin understood and climbed onto the bed, Ryan snuggling close to his mother with his back to her, while Devin followed suit. They rested together, emotionally exhausted.

"That's mah good lads. You're mah good boys. I don't care what anyone says about ya," Rebecca murmured. It was meant to be a joke, but neither laughed. The warmth of their bodies brought a momentary solace as they began to drift off.

Meanwhile, Layla continued to grumble about being treated like a child. Her room was dark, lit only by the glow of her Lite Brite. She sat cross-legged on the floor, working on a picture with her multicolored pegs. "It's not fair, ya know? I understand what's going on. They don't have to pretend with me," she muttered. Layla knew her mother had cancer but didn't grasp the full extent of the illness. She was more confused than angry.

As she sighed, her mood shifted. She focused on her art, her fingers hovering over the pegs. "What color should I do next?" she wondered aloud.

A bloodied hand appeared beside her, blue with torn, loose skin, pointing at the pegs. Layla watched its pointer finger wave around, searching with a bent nail. That must feel bloody awful, Layla thought, mimicking her mother's accent. She sensed something terrible had happened to the person behind her.

Layla didn't look back. She wasn't scared—she simply didn't want to stare at the torn body. It would be terribly rude. She remembered her mother explaining why it wasn't polite to stare when she had fixated on a girl with a physical deformity at the mall— *"It's because they are self-conscious about it. It reminds them they're different and don't want to be. But it's our differences that make us not like the rest, innit?"* Her mother always had a way of explaining things to her, and right now, the advice was good to remember.

The mutilated hand quickly made a fist, startling Layla. The sound of crunching, popping bones and joints made her shudder. Maybe her hands hurt, she thought, trying to make the best of what was happening. The hand pointed again, finally choosing a clear peg.

"The clear one? Okay. We've used a lot of clear pegs and some blue. Where do you want this one to go?" The hand hovered beside her. As she shifted forward, more decayed bones cracked, frightening her.

The hand indicated another clear peg, forming a large oval on the lit board. Two blue rectangles attached to the bottom and two orange triangles on top created the outline of a cat. Layla recognized the image before it was complete but wanted her new friend to enjoy the process.

"It's a very pretty kitty," Layla smiled, looking at the lit pegs resembling a cat. Below the image, pink pegs spelled out the word— SEE?

CHAPTER FIVE

SAVE IT FOR LATER

Rolling Acres Mall lay quiet about an hour before security sealed its doors for the night. The rain dampened consumer traffic, dissuading people from various corners of Akron. With summer a distant memory and the holidays not yet in full swing, the mall held an air of quiet anticipation. However, the work at hand remained, and Jerry Lawter, employed at Musicland, had a choice to make. The boxes of merchandise awaited unpacking, processing, and placement on the store floor, but Jerry, in his characteristic manner, decided it could all wait until the next morning.

Jerry leaned against the counter, staring at the unopened boxes. Procrastination was the teenage norm for many part-time employees, and Jerry was no exception. Convinced the boxes contained nothing more than copies of U2's "Rattle and Hum" and Jane's Addiction's "Nothing Shocking", he deemed it unnecessary to open and shelve them immediately, remembering he didn't get paid enough to care. "I'll leave a note for the morning opener," he muttered to himself, grabbing a scrap of paper and scribbling a quick message.

Managing the merchandising racks and showcasing new releases was a straightforward task due to the existing space. The records and neglected cheap headphones on the wall had gathered a thin layer of dust. In the world of Musicland, the mantra was clear – "We Got What's Hot."

Jerry performed the bare minimum duties, counting down the registers and recording the day's sales in the company logbook. He glanced at the clock. There's no way I'm staying late, he thought, his mind already at the gathering at a friend's house near Norton High. Vacuuming the floor or tidying up the records seemed unnecessary to Jerry. As a part-time retail manager, or, as he liked to think of himself, a 'warm body', he was only scheduled when no one else could work or when full-time management took time off and needed someone to close – a shift nobody preferred.

Jerry's shift happened to overlap with the presence of a cute girl he had noticed working at Merry-Go-Round, often modeling the trendy looks they advertised. He didn't know her name, but he wanted to assuming she was still in high school since she didn't usually work. Jerry, a freshman at the University of Akron, contemplated the age difference—she might not be eighteen, he thought. The race against time began as he hurriedly set the alarm, opened the gate, and saw a group leaving Merry-Go-Round heading towards the parking lot. He fumbled with the key, the lock resisting his efforts.

"Come on, not now," he hissed, yanking and cursing at the stubborn lock instead of remembering the need to lift the gate to facilitate the key's turn. The race was on – could he lock the gate before they exited the building?

Jerry's hopes sank as the group exited the mall through the doors next to Gadzooks, making their way to the parking lot near the theater – the designated parking area for employees on the south side. There went my chance, he thought. The missed opportunity disappointed him, but Jerry had a party to attend, and a change of clothes awaited in the back seat of his yellow Aries K to facilitate a quick transformation. The rain starting the night before Halloween continued, and as he walked, dodging puddles of collected water, Jerry noticed a few parking light lamps flickering, signaling the need for maintenance or a bulb change. The sudden illumination then darkness made him uneasy as he slowly walked to his vehicle.

Passing under the yellow Rolling Acres Theater entrance sign adorned with bold red lettering, Jerry glanced at the backlit frames showcasing new movie posters. The Ghostbusters logo, featuring the iconic ghost holding two fingers, caught his eye through the glass, accompanied by a tagline reading, *Guess Who's Coming to Save the World Again?* Excitement surged through him at the prospect of a sequel to one of his favorite films. Eager to get a closer look, Jerry approached the box office, only to realize it had already shut down for the night, with the doors securely locked.

The parking lot held only a few cars at this late hour. Some belonged to mall employees, while others were likely owned by those watching the latest releases at the theater—perhaps the fourth *Halloween* film, bringing back Michael Myers. The night held the anticipation of cinema, whether it was *Night of the Demons*, *Alien Nation*, or *Mystic Pizza*.

As Jerry walked by, the trees and bushes beside the theater wobbled, casting eerie shadows in the dim light. Slowing his brisk pace, Jerry turned his head towards the plants, their leaves now tinged with autumn red, and the pine tree to his right. A sudden rustle, high-pitched and frenetic, echoed from the foliage. A squirrel darted out, its erratic movements causing Jerry to step back and take a deep breath, embarrassed at being startled by a woodland creature.

As Jerry stood amidst the whispering trees, a flicker of movement drew his gaze, prompting him to lean forward and peer into the shadowy depths beyond. His eyes narrowed, straining to discern the source of the disturbance amidst the tangled underbrush.

There, nestled among the gnarled branches and dappled moonlight, lay a figure cloaked in darkness, its form barely discernible against the backdrop of rustling leaves and pine needles. A shiver coursed through Jerry's frame as a sense of unease washed over him, prickling at his senses like unseen tendrils of mist.

With bated breath, he watched as the figure stirred, its movements slow and deliberate, as if weighed down by some invisible burden. As the moonlight danced across its ashen skin, Jerry caught a glimpse of scars marring its fragile frame, proof to the trials it had endured.

A surge of concern welled within Jerry as he realized the extent of the creature's plight. Without hesitation, he began to extend his arm, fingers outstretched in a gesture of compassion and aid. Despite the uncertainty gnawing at his insides, he remained steadfast in his resolve to help, determined to ease the suffering of this enigmatic being, even if only for a fleeting moment.

"You don't have to be afraid of me. I'm not goin' to—" Jerry started, but his words trailed off as the branches shifted, unveiling large, piercing golden eyes. A shiver coursed through him. It was a wolf, but not like any wolf Jerry had ever seen.

"Jesus!" he yelled involuntarily.

Amidst the dusky shadows of the forest, the wolf stood, its form illuminated by the pale glow of the moon above. Its hackles raised in a menacing display, it bared its teeth in a primal snarl and the glint of moonlight reflecting off its razor-sharp fangs. A low, guttural growl rumbled from deep within its throat, reverberating through the stillness of the night.

As saliva dripped from its snout, glistening like molten silver in the moon's ethereal light, Jerry felt a sudden surge of fear coursing through his veins. His heart pounded in his chest, a steady drumbeat of distress echoing in his ears, as he stood frozen in place, his right arm still outstretched in a futile attempt to defend himself against the formidable predator before him.

It turned its massive body towards Jerry, and without hesitation, it opened its mouth wide, clamping down around Jerry's arm near his shoulder. A short shriek escaped Jerry's lips before the wolf, in one swift jerk of its unwieldy head, tore his arm off. Blood poured onto the sidewalk from Jerry's mangled shoulder, the gaping wound—a horrifying tribute to the unexpected brutality unfolding.

Jerry stumbled to his feet, panic setting in as the wolf emerged from the shadows and bushes, now fully visible in the dimly lit parking lot. Desperation fueled his thoughts—there has to be a way to escape. There must be more doors, more exits. Using his remaining hand to cover the bloody stump of his missing arm, Jerry shuffled around the bushes, moving hastily up the sidewalk leading to the theater's side. The wolf, gnawing on the remnants of Jerry's dismembered digits, ominously stalked its newfound prey.

As Jerry reached the corner, he spotted an exit door meant for the late-night movie audience to access the parking lot. With his bloody left hand, he repeatedly pulled on the handle, the slippery grip causing increased fear and frustration. Gasping for breath, he pressed his face against the cold window, realizing the only way to unlock it was to use the push bar on the opposite side. In desperation, Jerry slammed his bloody hand against the glass, hoping to attract the attention of anyone nearby.

"Please! Somebody help me!" Jerry's desperate pleas echoed through the glass door as he continued to pull on the handle with no one on the other side to assist. Wiping the mucus from his nose onto his black Members Only jacket, he choked back frightened gasps. "Please," he weakly begged for any patrons or employees within earshot, defeated, slowly collapsing to his knees. His blood stained hand left a smeared handprint down the glass door as he put his head between his knees, holding his hand against the torn wound, blood spewing onto the grass and concrete. Jerry was losing blood rapidly, the wolf trailing behind him ensuring a gruesome end unless help arrived soon.

Jerry's fading consciousness struggled against the encroaching darkness; his senses dulled by the overwhelming pain throbbing through his battered body. With half-opened eyes, he forced himself to focus, his gaze drawn to the looming figure that approached from the shadows.

The werewolf emerged from the dense undergrowth; its massive form silhouetted against the moonlit clearing. Every movement was deliberate, calculated, as if the creature reveled in the anticipation of the kill. It stayed within Jerry's line of sight, a silent tormentor, relishing the fear radiating from its prey.

As it drew closer, Jerry could see the patches of missing fur marring its disfigured form, revealing the scars and wounds that adorned its twisted frame. From its snarling muzzle to its human-like paws and back feet, the creature bore the marks of countless battles.

Despite the agony that wracked his body, Jerry summoned the last vestiges of his strength, his voice slurred but defiant with false bravado. "Come on," he spat, his words tinged with bitterness and desperation. "Finish me off, you ugly piece of shit. Get it over with!"

The mongrel lowered its head, bringing its muzzle terrifyingly close to Jerry's face, their foreheads almost touching. Jerry, avoiding direct eye contact with the looming threat, felt the creature's hot breath against his ear, each exhale carrying a repugnant odor—a nauseating blend of warmth and the foul remnants of decaying tissue trapped between the beast's teeth. The scent made his stomach churn, adding another layer to his horror.

The wolf inhaled deeply, savoring the scent of Jerry's blood and sweat, its nostrils flaring with each intake. Jerry could hear the deep, guttural rumble of the creature's growl vibrating through its chest, a sound which reverberated through the very ground beneath him. The tension in the air was palpable, each moment stretching into an eternity as the beast relished the anticipation of its meal.

Suddenly, the wolf opened its mouth wide, revealing rows of jagged, yellowed teeth before clamping down with brutal force. The creature bit through the crotch of Jerry's jeans, the fabric tearing with a sickening rip. Pain exploded through Jerry's body as the wolf's powerful jaws crushed and shredded Jerry's body. His upper torso was violently tossed from side to side, like a rag doll in the grip of a monstrous predator. Blood sprayed from the wound, splattering the sidewalk and staining the nearby bushes dark crimson.

Jerry's vision blurred, the edges of his vision dimming as the pain and blood loss. He could feel the warmth of his own blood pooling beneath him, mixing with the dirt and grime of the pavement. The last sounds he heard were the crunch of bones and the wet, gruesome chewing of the wolf as it feasted on him, each bite sending waves of agony through his fading consciousness.

With brutal force, the wolf clamped its powerful jaws around Jerry's head, and with a swift, savage motion, it slammed his skull onto the unforgiving pavement. The sickening crunch echoed in the night, the back of Jerry's skull shattering like fragile glass beneath the monstrous pressure. Blood pooled and spread across the ground, a dark, spreading stain against the grey concrete.

The beast's hunger wasn't sated. It shifted its grip, teeth sinking deeper into flesh with a precision born of primal instinct. With a feral snarl, it tore through more of the fabric of Jerry's jeans, ripping away his genitals in a spray of blood and torn tissue. The remnants dangled grotesquely from the fresh, gaping wound, adding to the macabre tableau.

Slowly, almost with a twisted sense of satisfaction, the wolf opened its bloodied maw. Jerry's lifeless body, now a ragged and broken shell, slid from the creature's jaws and crumpled onto the ground. The corpse lay sprawled on the sidewalk, a testament to the horror that had just unfolded. Blood trickled into the cracks of the pavement, pooling around the body and seeping into the surrounding bushes, marking the scene with a permanent, gruesome reminder of the beast's savagery.

"Why do we kill when we aren't even hungry? Isn't it a waste?" His voice trembled, the echo of humanity still lingering in his words. His chest heaved as he fought for control, his fingers curling into claws. Under the full moon, the transformation raged within him. His eyes flickered between the man he used to be and the beast he had become. Every breath was a struggle as the battle for dominance between the primal creature and the remnants of his weary soul.

You take mankind and their resourcefulness for granted, which is why our body is scarred," the monster began:

You tear off an arm; they have another.

You slice one side of the face. Tear away the other. As long as they move, they can kill.

You must finish.

You are animal now.

I just don't want it anymore.

You do not get to make that decision. The animal inside and out is more powerful than your human will to fight it. Why do so?

You will let go and allow me to take over or be driven mad. You are nothing without me, small and fearful with an aging body, tired by the mere thought of leaving your home.

You know I'm right.

You think, and I listen. All the days I have not taken over your body and mind, you think of your worthlessness.

You will allow me to take over both parts of you.

The human voice began to talk low and slow, claiming defeat after fighting against his heightened animal instincts. *I can't do it anymore. It's too hard. I had nothing, but at least I feel better when I'm not hunting with you.*

It will not matter. You will let me take over when I can. You will make peace with us, existing. We will live the way you always wanted to, and in exchange, I will hunt.

It's like dealing with the devil.

No. You have to agree to the devil's terms. You did not have a choice. Your gift was given to you without consent. The devil wishes they could do what I do, what others like us do.

The man's voice intertwined with the beast's guttural growl, creating a chilling harmony. Reason and consciousness struggled against primal, untamed instinct. The beast, a dark shadow of dormant savagery, stirred within him, sometimes breaking free. This curse, or twisted gift, cloaked his humanity in a veil of anonymity, allowing compassion to evaporate in the chaos it caused.

Around a quarter past eleven, the final showing of the Halloween IV ended—the one where Michael Myers returns. Theatergoers conversed casually, their laughter and conversation filling the lobby, unaware of marring the glass door with dark streaks. As the first couple neared the exit, ready to push the bar, they found the door stuck. A burly man named Jake, who had come with his girlfriend, leaned his weight into it, grunting with effort. The door suddenly gave way, causing Jake to stumble forward and crash onto the sidewalk.

He landed on something soft and wet. Jake's eyes widened in horror when he realized he was lying on a mutilated body. With blood smeared on his hands and face; the remains of Jerry Lawter were grotesquely splayed beneath him. The theater erupted in screams, but Jake's desperate cries rose above them all. He scrambled away, frantically wiping his blood-streaked face, the macabre scene forever etched itself into his mind.

CHAPTER SIX

THIS IS THE DAY

The eerie news of animal mauling seeped through the airwaves, a haunting melody that lingered long after the dawn of Halloween morning. Radios crackled with updates, while television screens flashed with grim headlines, casting a shadow over the day's festivities. Media outlets, hungry for sensationalism, drew chilling comparisons between the recent deaths and the grim tally of previous months. Local authorities, notorious for their reluctance to divulge details, provided little more than speculation, leaving the community on edge, reminiscent of the tense atmosphere gripping Akron and Canton in the late '80s.

In the quaint homes scattered across the three pillow towns—Norton, Barberton, and Wadsworth—families halted their morning routines; their conversations punctuated by murmurs of concern. Homemakers, usually immersed in the humdrum of domesticity, now paused to ponder the safety of their children as they prepared for the night's festivities. Worry etched lines on their faces as they dialed their husbands' workplaces, seeking reassurance in the face of uncertainty. Among them, Rebecca Hatcher, typically pragmatic, brushed off concerns until concrete details emerged. I have more pressing matters at hand right now, she thought, steeling herself against the rising tide of panic, while residents inundated local radio stations with impassioned petitions and opinions on the fate of Halloween night.

Heated debates echoed across the airwaves, the voices of the community rising and falling like waves crashing against the shore. Some drew parallels to cinematic tragedies, evoking the ill-fated decisions of fictional mayors in *Jaws*, while others clung to statistics and probabilities, hoping to calm the rising tide of fear. Yet, amidst the cacophony of opinions, the final decision lay in the hands of the townsfolk, each voice a thread in the intricate tapestry of communal discourse.

In the bustling household with three rambunctious children, the morning routine was a delicate dance of chaos and camaraderie. Ryan, the quiet observer among his siblings, preferred the solitude of night showers, his thoughts drifting to his mother as he lingered beneath the warm spray. His concern for her weighed heavy on his mind, a constant companion in the midst of his adolescent musings.

Meanwhile, Devin, ever the image-conscious teenager, devoted precious hours to grooming himself, his reflection a canvas for his meticulous attention. His dark hair, a stark contrast to Ryan's unruly locks, fell in carefully tousled waves. Layla, the spirited youngest sibling, flitted about the house with boundless energy, her laughter a symphony of joy amidst the morning bustle.

"Devin, for the love of all that is holy, get out of the bathroom and let your sister have a turn!" Rebecca's voice cut through the chaos, a fusion of exasperation and amusement as she brandished a spatula in frustration. Devin, unfazed by his mother's gripe, grumbled in protest, his hands fumbling with the stubborn cowlick at the nape of his neck. "I'm almost done, Ma! This hair is giving me a headache," he retorted, his frustration mounting with each failed attempt to tame his unruly locks.

"You're fine. You're as handsome as your father, a regular heartthrob. Now, move it or lose it!" Rebecca's tone carried a hint of sarcasm as she ushered Devin out of the bathroom, his protests fading into the background as he retreated to his room.

Meanwhile, Ryan, ever the observer, lingered in the doorway, his thoughts drifting to his mother as she navigated the delicate balance of motherhood and illness. *What if she needed help? What if something happened while he was away?* His heart ached with a sense of guilt, a nagging feeling gnawing at him with each passing moment.

As breakfast preparations continued in the bustling kitchen, the weight of unspoken worries hung heavy in the air, a reminder of the fragility of family and the bonds holding them together.

Confused, Ryan furrowed his brow. "But you're the one who wanted him gone for a bit, right?"

Their mother's response was swift, her tone guarded. "It's complicated, okay? Just hurry and eat your eggs. If you're quick about it, you might get a ride to the bus stop."

Ryan's mind raced as he pushed his eggs around his plate. Missing out on the opportunity to talk to Christina White, his other best friend, weighed heavily on him. Christy, as she was affectionately known, lived down the street and tended to be clingy. Though he enjoyed her company, there were moments when her exuberance felt overwhelming. In his mind, he likened their dynamic to characters from Peanuts, with himself as Linus and Christy as Sally, prone to gushing whenever he was around.

"I don't want to do that!" Layla interjected with concern. "If we do, we won't talk to Christina as much."

Rebecca's smile was knowing as she anticipated Ryan's next words. "Oh...yeah. That would be a real bummer," he retorted, the edge of sarcasm creeping into his tone as he feigned indifference towards Christina. Yet, beneath his jest, a pang of guilt nagged at him. He didn't want Layla to feel sad because of his momentary lapse in empathy.

Despite Layla's protests, Ryan felt a sense of duty towards her. Though she was perfectly capable of walking to the bus stop alone, they rode the same bus, and he couldn't shake the feeling of responsibility towards his younger sister. However, as he contemplated his upcoming transition to high school, he knew he had to temper his overprotectiveness.

As they gathered their belongings and prepared to leave for school, Rebecca lingered at the kitchen table, her solitude plain in the empty house. Sorting through the pile of mail, her eyes lingered on a shiny envelope bearing the word "Mastercard," a flicker of curiosity sparking within her.

Outside, Ryan and Layla stepped onto the street, while Devin climbed into Eric Flanagan's '83 Pontiac Fiero. Ryan quickened his pace, eager to catch his brother before he left. "Got a sec?" he called out, hoping for a moment of his brother's attention amidst the morning bustle.

Eric glanced at him dismissively, his focus already shifting back to Devin. "You wantin' a ride?" Devin's voice was casual, his attention diverted elsewhere as he prepared to depart.

Eric Flanagan's reputation preceded him like a storm cloud, a living embodiment of mischief in the neighborhood. He was infamous for his nocturnal escapades, leaving a trail of toilet paper strewn across lawns, eggs splattered against windows, and mailboxes battered. But his exploits didn't stop at the borders of the subdivision; he ventured further, leaving behind a legacy of vandalism. One notorious incident involved a classmate's car, coated in a concoction of maple syrup and aluminum foil, a sticky metallic mess that peeled away paint like a scene from a disaster movie.

With his flaming red hair, sprinkled freckles, and a glint of mischief in his eye, Eric epitomized juvenile delinquency. Ryan couldn't shake the notion that Eric could be the embodiment of chaos itself, a mischievous imp with an exaggerated overbite, capable of biting through an apple even if it were chained to a fence.

"Well, see, I would," Eric drawled, his grin dripping with smugness, "but it turns out I don't want to. See, I don't tote around dorky little trout sniffers in my ride."

Ryan absorbed the insults stoically, already foreseeing the verbal sparring match about to unfold. Eric's barrage of insults continued unabated, while Ryan's older brother simply observed, resigned to the routine.

Devin yearned for a connection with Eric but struggled to reconcile his friend's abusive behavior with the admiration Valerie, the girl he adored, seemed to hold for him.

Summoning an unexpected surge of courage, Ryan retaliated against Eric. "Calm down there, slick. You have a hoopty-ass Fiero, not a new Acura, which you couldn't even afford anyway. But suppose one day you manage to save enough money from whatever convenience stores you decide to knock off like the dime store hood you are. You might want to think about some dental work because that mouth, I mean, damn! Whenever you talk, I think of donkey sounds coming from it, being that you are an ass and all."

Anticipating Eric's reaction, Devin braced himself for the fallout. "You're dead…you little queer," Eric snarled, his rage intense. He revved his engine, a juvenile tactic meant to assert dominance over a thirteen-year-old. Ryan scoffed as Eric glanced at him. Devin shook his head at his brother, silently conveying that he had screwed up.

As Eric's car sputtered away, Ryan's bravado ebbed, replaced by a creeping sense of apprehension. He couldn't shake the feeling of unease, but now wasn't the time for reflection as he and Layla made their way to the bus stop. Glancing back, Ryan noticed Layla staring intently at the spruce tree in their front yard, her hands outstretched in a familiar gesture.

"LayLoo, what are you doing?" he called out, jolting her back to reality. Confused, Layla looked at her brother and gestured towards the tree. She began to speak, then hesitated, realizing there was nothing there anymore. "Nothing," she replied, puzzled, as she rejoined Ryan.

"Did you see something?" he inquired, sensing a familiarity with her experience. Unaware of Ryan's own encounter the day before, Layla fibbed. "It was nothing. I thought I saw something in the woods." They continued their journey, an awkward tension lingering between them until they met up with Christy at the corner of Greengate Drive and Jean Lane.

Christina's anticipation simmered as she awaited the arrival of her potential beau and his younger sibling. He'll warm up to me being his girlfriend someday soon, she assured herself, observing their approach. Her attire spoke volumes: a chic grey coat complemented her platinum locks, accentuated by a white scarf. Black jeans and a red-grey plaid vest, all from Contempo Casuals, completed her ensemble, topped off with a wide-brimmed, felt bowler hat reminiscent of Debbie Gibson's iconic style.

"Hi, Ryan!" she greeted warmly as Ryan strolled towards her, hands nestled in his jean jacket pockets. Ryan returned the smile, replying, "Hey, Christie." Layla, ever observant, caught her brother's unease and giggled. "Hush, you," he teased, earning a unspoken vow of secrecy from Layla, expressed through playful gestures.

"Hey, Christina?" Layla piped up, skipping ahead to take her hand. "Have you seen a cat around here lately?" Christina glanced back at Ryan, sharing a knowing smile before addressing Layla's query. "I've spotted a few felines around, occasionally emerging from the woods. What does this one look like?"

"It's a girl, and my friend said she's white. That's all I know," Layla explained. Ryan interjected, slightly exasperated, "What friend? You barely talk to anyone in your class." "I do too have friends!" Layla retorted. "Just because you don't see them doesn't mean they don't exist!"

Ryan raised his hands in mock surrender to Layla's ten-year-old indignation, earning a playful scolding from Christina's amused gaze. Once the commotion settled, Christina inquired, "Is there anything specific to look out for?" Layla paused, then exclaimed, "Oh! She might have colored patches on her legs, like she's wearing boots." Christina nodded in understanding, promising to notify them if she stumbled upon a lost kitty.

"Okay, but make sure you tell Ryan, not Devin. He's been a bit of a troublemaker lately," Layla cautioned. Ryan and Christina exchanged surprised glances at Layla's unexpected candor. It was a side of her they hadn't seen before.

"LayLoo!" Ryan laugh inwardly.

"What? It's what mom says all the time. It's not news or anything. Besides, you know you feel the same way." Ryan refrained from disagreement, opting for maturity. "Yeah, well, just because you can say something doesn't mean you should sometimes." Layla nodded, her reaction ambiguous—whether to silence him or to ponder his words. *Maybe I should throw her a bone*— "To be fair, though, he hasn't been himself for a while now, huh?" Layla hesitated to agree, reluctance evident. Children resist change; her family dynamic had shifted irreversibly.

Christina regarded Ryan with admiration, uncertain how to console his sister amidst their home turmoil. "He'll be back to his old self, and maybe even better," he comforted Layla, wrapping his arm around her. Layla nodded, skipping ahead, humming a tune unfamiliar to Ryan.

"She's a sweet kid," Christina murmured to Ryan, her breath tickling his ear, sending shivers down his spine.

"Yeah, well, just wait a few years, and let's see how we feel about her then," he teased, acknowledging imminent puberty.

They approached their bus stop in silence, Christina attuned to Ryan's myriad expressions—contentment, joy, sadness, irritation. Ryan's current demeanor intrigued her.

"Hey," Christina nudged Ryan, hands tucked in her pockets, "What's on your mind?" Ryan averted his gaze, a common evasion tactic. She nudged him again, smiling. Meeting her eyes briefly, Ryan glanced at the ground, then back at Christina. Amidst autumn's hues, she blended into the scenery with her hat and attire.

"Nothing. It's just...," Ryan gestured in frustration, struggling to articulate his feelings. "What?" Christina prodded, intertwining her arm with his.

"What? What is it?"

Ryan exhaled heavily, pondering how to express himself. "Have you, you know, noticed anything strange lately?"

"Like what?"

He shook his head, fearing ridicule or gossip. Christina tugged his arm, urging him to confide. "We've been through a lot together," she reminded him, attempting to ease his reluctance. "You've been there since I moved in with my grandparents. You played Barbies with me when my parents didn't show up some weekends, not that I wanted them to," she reminisced, offering comfort.

Ryan refrained from probing into Christina's living situation, wary of stirring up discomfort. Conflict avoidance was his forte; he aimed to shield Christina from any potential embarrassment or frustration stemming from her home circumstances. "You don't have to worry about me. I promise," she reassured him.

He gazed at Christina, steeling himself to divulge his unsettling experiences. "I've been noticing shadows lately—figures of people," he began. "About a week ago, I spotted something in the street, peering towards my house and bedroom window. It looked like a man, but then it vanished. A few nights back, a shadow emerged at the end of the hallway, then crept towards LayLoo's room upstairs, lingering momentarily before descending the stairs and vanishing outside by the spruce tree in our front yard. Yesterday, the shadow...

it seemed more defined, like a man. Maybe someone who met their end with their throat slashed? I'm not sure."

Unbeknownst to him, Layla eavesdropped from a distance, her curiosity piqued by her brother's conversation.

"To add to the oddity, I thought I glimpsed someone in her bedroom," Ryan continued, gesturing subtly towards Layla. "It might have been nothing, just a trick of my peripheral vision." Layla breathed a sigh of relief, knowing her brother had seen her spectral friend who frequented her room.

A heavy silence enveloped them as they neared the bus stop. Layla pondered whether to speak up, while Christina struggled to find the right words. Meanwhile, Ryan felt a twinge of embarrassment for broaching the topic.

"I think you're carrying a heavy load," Christina offered, empathy coloring her words. "It's a lot for anyone to handle—having two siblings, an absent father, and a sick mother. No one should feel obligated to bear such a weight alone."

Ryan mulled over Christina's words, wondering if they stemmed from her own familial struggles. He considered delving deeper but held back as the bus pulled up, interrupting their conversation.

Glancing around, Ryan inquired, "Where's Scott?" His friend, typically present halfway to the bus stop, was conspicuously absent.

Eric and Devin pulled up at the Donovan's house to collect Valerie for school. Typically, she awaited them in the driveway, but today broke from routine; she was nowhere in sight. It wasn't the first time Eric had been kept waiting, nor would it likely be the last. Usually, a revving engine would prompt her appearance, but today she wasn't in a hurry.

"I'll go check the door," volunteered Devin, eager to assist. Valerie cracked open the door, revealing only a portion of her face. "You coming with us today?" Devin inquired. She shook her head, revealing a bruise near her eye. Devin instinctively placed his hand on the doorframe.

"No one's feeling well. We're staying home today," she whispered. Devin gently pushed the door ajar, needing confirmation of what he suspected. "I'll be better tomorrow," she insisted, attempting to close the door, but Devin resisted. "Devin! Let go of the door!" Eventually, it opened enough to reveal the bruises and swollen side of her face. Valerie lowered her gaze, embarrassed. Devin clenched his fists, suppressing his anger. He knew Rick, her father, was responsible.

"Please, don't tell anyone," she stated. "He's never done this before. He's just not himself since he got laid off from the tire factory." Devin pressed his hands to his temples, nodding to reassure her.

He wanted to mention the widespread job losses in the area, but refrained, thinking, it's tough all over. That's not an excuse to hit your kids! "Please," she pleaded again. Devin averted his gaze, murmuring, "Okay," before departing. It was the first time Devin left Valerie's house feeling anger—not directed at her, but at the tumult of emotions within. The thought of informing someone tugged at him, but he feared Valerie might sever ties if he did. Yet, justice demanded action. He resolved to respect Valerie's desire and maintain silence, at least for now. However, a simmering rage urged him to burst in and confront her father, to mete out justice by beating the shit out of him with his own hands.

Devin eased back into the passenger seat of the Fiero, his expression weighed down with concern. Eric glanced at him, awaiting an explanation. "She's not feeling great today," Devin disclosed. "Said she'll be okay by tomorrow."

Eric nodded, though doubt lingered in his mind like a shadow. "You sure Val's alright?" he pressed, searching for reassurance.

"Absolutely," Devin assured, the lie slipping from his lips without hesitation. "You should check in on her later."

Eric couldn't shake his unease, having caught sight of the half-opened door and Devin's tense demeanor moments earlier. He recognized the telltale signs—the subtle shifts in behavior spoke volumes of hidden turmoil. He knew them intimately, having endured them himself. The echoes of past trauma reverberated in his bones, a constant reminder of the darkness lurking beneath the surface of man.

"Whatever you say, man," Eric conceded with a heavy sigh, maneuvering the car out of the driveway. But inwardly, he grappled with a torrent of conflicting emotions. It might be a one-off occurrence, he mused, but it rarely ends there—I can't stand by and watch someone suffer. Brushing a lock of red hair from his eyes, Eric rolled down the windows, blasting Def Leppard to drown out the tumult of thoughts racing through his mind as he sped towards school, his anger simmering just beneath the surface.

Two boys on the cusp of manhood, products of vastly different backgrounds yet united by their affection for the same girl. Both gripped by a seething fury at the injustice of her suffering, yet acutely aware of the consequences of intervening. But what Valerie truly needed wasn't a hero; it was understanding—something in short supply from those around her.

CHAPTER SEVEN

MONEY FOR NOTHING

Rebecca stepped out of her house, clutching an envelope, relishing the freedom of barefootedness as she traversed the yard. But the early morning chill quickly bit at her feet, reminding her that spring hadn't quite thawed the grass enough for comfort. Still, a spark of joy ignited within her—a rare sensation in recent months. She knew the contents of the envelope held the promise of a better future for her and her children, though its true power remained locked within, for now.

Melvin Craggs, who was in the middle of outfitting fishing rods with fresh line, spotted Rebecca's fragile figure making its way to the mailbox. While Melvin usually kept to himself, Rebecca held a special place in his heart among the neighbors. Despite his gruff exterior, she treated him with kindness, unlike others who shied away from his perceived crabby demeanor, a reputation he had cultivated over the years.

Melvin's gaze lingered on Rebecca, observing the stark transformation from a full-bodied woman to a frail figure, her clothes, now hanging off her frame, betraying the toll of unseen struggles.

A silent exchange passed between them as Rebecca waved in acknowledgment before heading back towards her home. Melvin reciprocated the gesture, an unspoken invitation for her to linger, a rare gesture from the reclusive man. He retreated into the shelter of his garage, stealing a glance around to ensure privacy.

"He's not around yet," Rebecca reassured, referring to her husband. Melvin offered a quick grin before retreating further into his sanctuary. "What are you up to?" Rebecca inquired with genuine curiosity.

Hailing from Maine, Melvin's thick New England accent melded his words together in a way that felt familiar to Rebecca, hailing from the United Kingdom.

"What are you up to then?" Melvin replied, gesturing towards the walls adorned with tools and various implements. His orange Syracuse football hat tipped slightly as he wiped his hands on his overalls. "And what's under there?" Rebecca pointed to the shrouded object, her interest piqued.

Melvin nodded in permission. "It's a motorcycle!" he declared proudly, unveiling the sleek black AJS beneath the tarp. Rebecca's eyes widened in awe as she circled the vintage bike, her fingers trailing over the gold emblem adorning its side.

"It's an AJS?" she marveled, already knowing the answer.

"Yep, '53 Model 20 500," Melvin confirmed, his voice tinged with nostalgia.

"How did you manage to get a British bike here?" Rebecca inquired; her curiosity piqued.

"Had a buddy who lived over there before he moved here. Fought in Japan together. Lost him to cancer in the end," Melvin explained, his voice heavy with reminiscence.

"There seems to be a lot of that going around," Rebecca sighed, her thoughts drifting to her own battles.

"Is there anything wrong with it?" she asked, steering the conversation away from somber thoughts.

"Nah, just keep it in shape out of habit. Lost the itch to ride, I guess," Melvin admitted, a hint of melancholy in his tone.

"Would you consider selling it?" Rebecca inquired.

Melvin met her gaze with a hint of surprise, pondering her request. "Not yet. Guess I'm not ready to part ways just yet," he decided, his tone final.

Rebecca's lips formed a disappointed pout, but she quickly shifted gears. "How does it ride?" she asked, eager to steer the conversation towards brighter horizons.

"Well, it's got 20 horsepower at 6800 RPMs," Melvin explained, his passion for the machine evident.

Rebecca nodded, though the technical jargon sailed over her head. "Right... Well, just so you know, I have no idea what ya just said," she admitted with a sheepish grin.

Melvin laughed and provided a better frame of reference, "It gets up to eighty-five miles per hour, so you won't be doing any real high speeds like bikes deese days." Rebecca nodded again, admiring the bike, taking her back to a place she called home, England.

After an awkward silence, Melvin leaned into his workbench and asked, "How ya been feelin'?" Rebecca was surprised he had taken an interest in her health and answered, "It's hard to eat and drink because me throat is swollen. Even if I could, don't have an appetite anyway."

He felt awkward asking, but Melvin knew Calvin hadn't lived in their house for weeks. As much as he despised Cal, he knew it was probably time for him to come home soon and thought Rebecca felt the same way whether she wanted to admit it or not.

"Husband goin' to come home?" he asked. Rebecca turned her back to look at all the tools on his garage wall near the bike and sighed. "Probably. Kids need their dad around now. It's probably about time."

"What the word you Brits like to use? Wanker? Twat?... He's a bit of a wanker?" Melvin insinuated. Unsurprised by his comment, Rebecca turned, smiled, and replied, "He is sometimes, yeah. But he's my wanker, ain't he? But he's the only wanker I got, so."

When Rebecca kicked her husband out of her home, it wasn't because of infidelity, looks, or arguments over money. He had become a different person, refusing to lay off the alcohol. Something happened—something she never thought Calvin would, or could, ever do. Rebecca could only hope he had learned from his mistake to be the father he needed to be for their children.

"How's da kids den?" he asked, changing the subject.

"The girl is adorable. The girliest girl I have ever seen. The middle one is beginning to grow a backbone I don't care for, not one bit. Still, good for 'em. He's still very considerate and sweet, probably to a fault, I think. The oldest lad, well, he's like me."

Melvin grabbed a wrench from the bench and tapped it on his palm. "He can't be that bad. Otha' than hanging 'round the hooligan, he seems like he's okay."

"He's moody, stubborn, like his 'ol ma, always thinkin' he has something to prove. S'pose he's like his father in dat way. Always talkin' 'bout doin' things, just never does 'em. It's no wonder he doesn't like his dad," Rebecca said aloud, voicing thoughts keeping her up at night with no one in her bed to speak with about them.

Sucking his teeth, Melvin thought about the options he could offer to help his neighbor. "Boy sounds bored. Can't blame 'em. He lives in this little place with little to do 'round here. When young boys figure it out, usually gets 'em in trouble because nuthin else is excitin'," he explained, remembering his childhood. "Idle hands and whatnot." Feeling fatigued, Rebecca nodded and began to walk away back to her house.

"Tell da boy to come here den when he ain't got nothin' to do. Got things needed doing in the house and in da back. Maybe help clean the pool before I cover it for the season, get that husband of yours off my back. Ain't dat funny? We yelled at each other 'bout dat inconvenience filled with chlorine back der, and I get his son to do it instead!" Melvin mused with a deep, throaty laugh.

Rebecca laughed, not so much at what he said but that Melvin Craggs, the cranky neighbor, had a sense of humor. "That's terrible!" she laughed, choking on her words, gasping for air. "He'll do it. I'll call when he's goin' to come by."

"A'ight then," he agreed.

The lovely giggle left her feeling a bit vulnerable—something that hadn't occurred in a while, she mused as she stepped back into the chilly air to make her way home. Just before leaving Melvin's driveway, she pivoted towards him and inquired, "What compensation are you planning to offer him? Devin will certainly be curious."

Lighting a Marlboro, Melvin yelled, "He helps me get things done before Thanksgiving, and he will get what's coming to him. Dat and my pleasant company." Unsure of what his intentions were, Rebecca questioned his motives. "Why Thanksgiving?"

"Boy needs a deadline. Don't want my place looking like white trash lives here anymore anyway," he answered. Rebecca knew not to step in Melvin's bullshit as she walked away, ensuring she had lifted the red flag on the side of her mailbox.

Rebecca walked through the cold grass again and entered the front door of her house when something hard hit the side of her body. She fell onto the ground, her ankle twisted, biting her lip to keep from drawing attention to herself. Rebecca touched the ground, confused and hurt, feeling for anything that may have hit her. Maybe a stone, rock, pinecone, or even a stick. There was nothing. Rebecca looked at the trunk of the spruce and then at its fullness, thinking about the presence Ryan spoke of.

Convinced it was kids playing a prank using blackberries growing in the woods, Rebecca looked past the spruce and into the woods. She would occasionally use them in pies she baked. The trail behind the Hatcher's home reached past the cornfield and the pond where people would fish. People would park outside the house on the dead-end street, which annoyed Rebecca, but it was a small price to pay for the land providing so many memories for her kids.

But kids should be in school now, she thought.

She wasn't succumbing to insanity—*absolutely not!* Rebecca was resolute about it. An unseen force propelled her to the ground, directing her towards the front door. There was no other plausible explanation in her mind. Hobbling back inside the house, ascending the stairs, and making her way to the kitchen, Rebecca retrieved a glass from the light-colored wood cabinet and filled it with tap water. Her mouth had become parched, and she sought relief for her swollen throat. After five gulps, Rebecca choked on her pills, struggling to swallow her water. Reluctantly, she admitted to herself she was encountering difficulties with eating and would soon need to transition to a liquid diet. It's approaching. My body is no longer functioning as it should, she knew. Rebecca acknowledged that her inevitable fate was drawing nearer. She had grown weary from traversing the yard, ascending the stairs—and merely rousing herself to feign strength for her kids this morning.

Rebecca gazed through the kitchen window over the sink, observing shadowy figures in her backyard. They stood at a distance; their outlines outlined against the backdrop of the woods where the property line blurred. With arms outstretched, they remained concealed within the shadows of the trees, their gaze fixed on the sky. The eerie spectacle unsettled her; it was shrouded in an enigma she couldn't unravel. Yet, deep down, she understood—she always did. It was a knowing passed down, her son inheriting the same intuition. The boy gets it honest, she shuddered at the thought.

Not again, she thought, closing her eyelids, an uneasy feeling settling in. She wished for them to disappear, their presence casting a somber atmosphere. Since childhood, she sensed they and others like them needed to move on, yet she remained clueless about how to convey this message. Rebecca reluctantly opened her eyes, finding the dark figures had vanished. However, an ominous intuition lingered, telling her it wouldn't be the last time. "They'll come for me when this bloody disease eventually takes me," she whispered as a cold dread filled her veins.

As she turned away from the window, a sense of dread crept over her, wrapping her in its cold embrace. She couldn't shake the feeling the shadowy figures had left behind something more than just their absence—a warning, perhaps, of what was to come. And as she shuffled back to her bedroom, the weight of impending doom settled heavily upon her shoulders, casting a dark cloud over her once hopeful spirit.

CHAPTER EIGHT

I WANT CANDY

The challenge of being at the last stop on a bus route was the limited seating available. Fortunately, Ryan could always count on Colin Hill to have a spot reserved for him as he strolled down the aisle. A quick point at the vacant space, a nod from Colin, and Ryan would happily settle in beside him for the brief journey to school.

Colin wasn't the most approachable person when it came to making friends, not due to unkindness but because of a few idiosyncrasies making socializing challenging. One unmistakable trait was the lingering aroma of cooked cabbage and a hint of meatloaf that clung to him. Additionally, his voice emitted a peculiar croaking sound, a result of his narrow windpipes, accompanied by a lisp which sometimes made it difficult for others to comprehend him. Uninterested in typical childhood activities like collecting cards or climbing trees, Colin kept to himself during recess, finding solace in his shared love for television and movies—a common interest with Ryan.

Ryan never pondered Colin's ethnicity; it never occurred to him. Colin, his bus mate, diverged from the typical white kids in Norton, his darker complexion shrouding his background in mystery. With a shade darker than Ryan's, Colin remained an enigma. It took time for Ryan to summon the courage to breach the subject, revealing Colin's Hispanic heritage, though the specifics eluded him. In Ryan's childhood perspective, racial distinctions held little sway.

"Want a Crunch bar? My mom gave me a bag for the kids in my classes," Ryan offered, extending the bag to Colin. The gesture ignited a spark in Colin's eyes, momentarily lifting him from his usual lethargy. "Oh, yeah! Sweet!" he exclaimed, diving into the bag. "I've never had one of these before." Ryan was taken aback. "Really?"

"My mom doesn't usually let us have much candy," Colin explained, cramming the entire party-sized chocolate bar into his mouth. Ryan nodded and slumped in his seat, knees resting on the pleather in front, sifting through his Garbage Pail Kid doubles, even triples. His collection was formidable, as thick as a Swenson's Drive-In double cheeseburger. Colin watched in awe, thumbing through the cards, arranging them in numerical order. He felt a pang of envy, a touch of jealousy. Yet, amidst these emotions, a sense of camaraderie blossomed, a shared appreciation for their mutual passion for collecting. Despite their disparities, they found unity in the joy of exchanging cards, transcending the boundaries of race and upbringing.

An eerie sensation washed over Ryan, a prickling at the back of his neck hinting at an unseen presence. Amidst the chatter of other kids, a sharp, high-pitched noise pierced through—a familiar sound, the gossiping giggles of girls. Ryan turned to see Christina and her friend Michelle sharing laughter. Christina noticed Ryan's gaze and waved nervously. Ryan's mind raced with doubt. *Was she telling our secret, that massive revelation I trusted her with? But then again, she's never told on me before. It's probably nothing. Yeah, nothing.* With an effort, he pushed aside his unease and forced a smile, waving back.

"What did you have for breakfast?" Colin's voice cut through Ryan's thoughts.

Turning to Colin, Ryan asked, "What did you say?"

"What did you have to eat this morning?" Colin repeated.

"Why?" Ryan wondered, piqued by curiosity.

"Just curious," Colin replied.

"Eggs," Ryan answered. Colin nodded, then hesitated before asking, "Fried or scrambled?"

"Scrambled."

"So, when your mom makes them, does she just crack the egg in the pan and push it around as it cooks?"

Ryan realized Colin's curiosity was insatiable. He was always probing into others' lives, stringing together questions to keep the conversation flowing. But he never overstepped boundaries; his inquiries were always general.

"She cracks the eggs into a bowl, adds a bit of milk, maybe some salt and pepper, then stirs it and pours it into the pan," Ryan explained, introducing Colin to a new breakfast technique. "What's the point of the milk?" Colin wondered. Ryan chuckled. "I think it makes the eggs fluffier." Colin scribbled down Ryan's insights in a small spiral-bound pad he produced from his bookbag.

"Cool. Thanks!" Colin concluded his round of questioning. "Did you watch Perfect Strangers last Friday? Wasn't it great when Balki—"

"Hey, Colin! Interested in snagging the doubles?" Ryan interjected, changing the subject. Sometimes, he just had to derail that train; put a quarter in him, and Colin would make you listen to the whole thing.

Colin's eyes widened in disbelief, his voice carrying a tinge of astonishment. "Whoa! Seriously?" The incredulity in his tone echoed through the bus, his mind struggling to grasp the idea of receiving something without strings attached. Ryan's response was casual, almost indifferent, as he shrugged off the significance of his gesture. "No problem. They'll probably just sit in the stack and fade if you don't use them."

For once, Colin fell silent, his jaw slack as he examined the grotesque images and cleverly named characters adorning his newfound cards. With each breath, a small wheeze escaped Colin's lips, gradually escalating in intensity. Concern etched across Ryan's face as he turned towards his friend, noting the irregularity in his breathing. "Do you have asthma or something?" he inquired; his voice tinged with worry.

Slowly tearing his gaze away from the captivating cards, Colin shrugged uncertainly. "I don't know," he admitted with some embarrassment. "Sounds like you're not breathing right," Ryan observed, his concern deepening. Colin glanced back at the cards, a sense of unease settling over him. "Maybe. We don't get to go to the doctor much, and I don't want to ask. It's just how I've always breathed."

Ryan leaned back in his seat, a sense of trust lingering in his mind as he hoped Colin would find a solution soon. The worn vinyl seat beneath him bore the scars of countless bored kids, the evidence of their mischief etched into its surface by pencils and pens. Recalling the faint echoes of girl giggles from moments ago, Ryan's gaze drifted towards Christina, her animated conversation with others captivating him from afar. With a sigh, he closed his eyes, waiting for the bus to arrive at school, bracing himself for the candy-fueled chaos awaiting in the bustling halls and classrooms.

As Ryan traversed the bustling corridors of the school, the remnants of Halloween celebrations lay strewn across the floor, in the form of discarded candy wrappers, mostly Tootsie Rolls. Despite the festive ambiance, subdued whispers among teachers and counselors warned against the donning of rubber masks, emphasizing the importance of visibility and identification within the school premises.

For Ryan, the allure of Halloween had waned with each passing year, its once exciting festivities now overshadowed by the vibrant hues of autumn. He found solace in the crisp air outside, tinged with the scent of fallen leaves, far more appealing than the confined spaces of the school halls.

Lunchtime approached, a dreaded interlude for Ryan, particularly in the absence of his usual companions. The bustling lunchroom, usually abuzz with chatter and laughter was daunting, fraught with the uncertainty of finding a suitable place to sit. Yet, amidst the sea of faces, Ryan couldn't shake the looming presence of Stephanie Melker, a persistent figure from his grade school days.

Stephanie's unwavering infatuation had transformed into a relentless pursuit, her advances bordering on obsession. With her disarming charm, tousled brown curls, freckled cheeks, and sharp wit, Stephanie was a force to be reckoned with. Ryan vividly recalled one unsettling encounter when she had cornered him against the cold brick exterior of the school building, her relentless pursuit interrupted only by the shrill call of the departing school bus.

As Ryan found himself seated alone in the lunchroom, he couldn't help but feel a sense of unease as Stephanie's gaze bore into him from across the room. Unbeknownst to him, his mere presence sparked resentment in Christina, her eyes narrowed in disapproval.

"Scoot," Stephanie's voice, tinged with longing, broke through the tension as she approached his table. Ryan obediently shifted over on the worn picnic-style bench, making room for her. Christina's disdainful gaze bore into Ryan, her silent disapproval unmistakable as she watched their interaction unfold.

"Do you eat a lot of meat?" Stephanie's question, though innocuous, cut through the strained air as she slurped the last remnants of her chocolate milk. Ryan's gaze fell to his hamburger, but what he saw made his blood run cold. The meat, once ordinary, now pulsed and writhed, a grotesque display turning his stomach.

As Stephanie's voice droned on in the background, Ryan's mind spiraled into a nightmarish reverie, images of the man with the mutilated throat flooding his thoughts. The raw meat on his plate came alive, a grotesque mockery of sustenance, its throbbing movements mirroring the unsettling rhythm of his own unease.

In the dimly lit cafeteria, a sinister whisper slithered through the air like a chilling breeze, weaving its way into Ryan's consciousness with an eerie intensity. "*Stop it. End it. We know the path. Don't go out tonight*", it gargled, the words dripping with desperation as they clawed at Ryan's mind, urging him to heed their warning. With a nervous hand, he glanced towards the source of the voice, his heart hammering in his chest as he beheld the ghastly sight before him.

There, beneath the table, lurked the head of a man in a dark tracksuit, his features contorted in a grotesque grimace as he locked eyes with Ryan. Blood gushed from a gaping wound in his throat, staining the floor with a sickening crimson hue as he struggled to form coherent words. His gaze bore into Ryan's soul, a mute plea for salvation amidst the torment of his own demise.

With a shudder, Ryan tore his gaze away, his stomach churning with sickening fear and revulsion. The taste of bile rose in his throat, and with a violent lurch, he turned away, retching as he expelled the remnants of his meal into a crumpled napkin. He dared not look back; the memory of the man's haunting visage etched into his mind like a nightmare he could not escape.

"He's gone now. It's over," Ryan whispered to himself, his voice shaky with a blend of relief and dread. But deep down, he knew the horror he had witnessed would linger long after the cafeteria emptied, and the echoes of Stephanie's voice returned from the darkness.

Stephanie leaned in, her voice dripping with a mix of condescension and concern. "Do you know what kind of chemicals you could be ingesting by eating that?" she asked, her gaze fixed on Ryan's lunch tray.

With a furrowed brow, Ryan glanced down at the burger, his stomach churning with unease as he inspected it to assure himself it cooked. "This is school food," he replied, his voice tinged with skepticism. "I don't think this is probably real beef."

Stephanie's laughter cut through the tense mood, echoing off the cafeteria walls. Ryan couldn't fathom what she found so amusing, but in an attempt to diffuse the tension, he forced a nervous giggle, mirroring her laughter.

Beyond her attraction to Ryan, Stephanie reveled in her role as a self-proclaimed expert on societal issues, never missing an opportunity to share her opinions, whether they were welcome or not. One of her favorite topics? Dietary habits.

As the conversation veered towards the dubious origins of school cafeteria fare, Stephanie's tone took on a lecturing quality. "You ever notice the boobs coming in on the sixth graders are a little too, um, big for their age? You know why?" she remarked, her voice laced with a mix of curiosity and authority.

Ryan's eyes darted around the cafeteria, searching for the elusive evidence Stephanie spoke of. But all he found was the unappetizing sight of his lunch tray, devoid of anything but the questionable meal before him.

"It's because of the chicken," Stephanie declared, her voice tinged with certainty.

Perplexed, Ryan attempted to follow Stephanie's train of thought, his mind still reeling from the unsettling vision that had plagued him moments before. "Wait. What? What do you mean?" he asked, struggling to keep up.

Stephanie leaned back, her posture exuding confidence as she launched into an impromptu lecture on the perils of consuming meat. "Steroids," she stated simply, before launching into a detailed explanation. "Farmers are now pumping chickens full of steroids, so they grow faster. However, the steroids remain in the meat, causing both men and women to develop faster when they are young."

Ryan nodded, attempting to process the information as Christina slid into the seat beside him, effectively interrupting Stephanie's monologue. With a grateful glance at Christina, Ryan thanked her for the timely intervention, grateful to be spared from any further lectures on the dangers of cafeteria cuisine.

"Oh my God, Stephanie! Your pearls! They look so good on you," Christina exclaimed, her tone dripping with faux admiration. "I wish I had the confidence to put on old people's jewelry, but you can definitely pull it off!"

Stephanie's smile faltered for a moment, her grip on her pearls tightening imperceptibly. She wore them every day, a subtle display of her family's social standing, though it often came off as pretentious. With an eighth grader's bravado, she sometimes adopted a more mature attire, complete with plaid skirts and blazers boasting oversized shoulder pads. Her parents' membership at the Fairlawn Country Club, infamous for its history of discrimination, only added to her air of superiority.

Despite her best efforts, Ryan couldn't fathom why Stephanie was interested in him. He lacked the pedigree or connections that typically appealed to girls like her. *Maybe*, he mused, *she enjoys the thrill of rebellion, bringing home a boy she knew her parents wouldn't like?*

Stephanie plastered on a tight smile, fully aware of Christina's thinly veiled insults. "Thank you," she replied through gritted teeth. "I saw you with that cute hat this morning! I love it! It's like you're taking someone else's style and making it your own. It's so cute!" Her words dripped with sarcasm, the tension between them apparent.

The girls shared a laugh, their words laden with barbed intent. Ryan watched with amusement, finding their exchange oddly entertaining. He suppressed a grin, marveling at their verbal sparring like a spectator at a high-stakes duel. In a strange way, their animosity towards each other only served to make him feel more desired. *This*, he thought with a chuckle, *was every guy's dream.*

Ryan never considered himself anyone special. He wasn't popular, didn't excel at anything, and didn't have a penchant for sports. Content with being in the background most of the time, he believed as long as he was friendly and earned good grades, it was all that mattered—at least, according to his mother. Perhaps, though, that's what drew the attention of both Christina and Stephanie.

"So, what were you two talking about?" Christina pretended to care.

"Well, I was just telling Ryan here about the dangers of eating meat," Stephanie informed, her bottom lip quivering dramatically, "and all the additives they put in animals and how it affects our bodies." She placed her hand on her chest, emphasizing the presumed role of hormones in chicken.

"Really?" Christina asked with indifference.

"Yes. I mean, when you think about it, how can you eat such beautiful creatures?" Stephanie mused. Christina sucked in her lips and nodded, seemingly agreeing, but Ryan knew better. He began to smile, sensing insincerity.

Here it comes.

"So, are you being rhetorical, or do you want some recipes?" The condescension from Christina was unmistakable. Ryan's eyes widened, unable to believe the comeback and burn shooting from his friend's mouth.

Stephanie, unamused, placed her tongue against the back of her bottom front teeth, searching for a comeback to rival Christina's highbrow insult. She rose from her seat, put her hand on Ryan's shoulder, leaned down, and kissed him on the cheek. With a contemptuous smile aimed at Christina, Steph whispered, "Bye. I'll definitely see you later, Ryan." Christina squinted and smirked at Steph with rage in her eyes as she walked away. Ryan looked at his friend differently than he had before. After several years of friendship, something about Christina felt natural, not in a familiar friendship kind of way.

Christina turned her face to Ryan's and, with a raised eyebrow, stated, "Whadda bitch." Ryan choked on his food at the rude but amusing statement. "You, me, and Scott tonight, right?" she asked regarding trick-or-treating that evening. Nodding his head, "Yeah, well, LayLoo will hang around. I'm not sure what Devin and Valerie are doing, but Eric will probably be there, and I want to stay away from him."

"Why?" she wondered.

"Well, I kind of said some things that may have pissed him off a little bit."

Surprised, Christina scooted closer to him, teasing, "My, my. The quiet, passive boy in school, Ryan Hatcher, finally grew a pair. What happened? I'm sure it's not that bad."

"I insulted his car and may have implied he needed dental work," he quickly countered. She took a fry from Ryan's tray, shoved it in her mouth, and mumbled, "You're right. You're dead where you stand." He shrugged his shoulder and nodded, thinking, tell me something I don't know. A senior began to play a local radio station with a boombox he toted around, with *Obsession* by Animotion echoing through the cafeteria

"I'll see you tonight, champ. Grandma is taking me to get my costume on layaway. So, I won't be on the bus." The good news continued as Ryan would have to walk home with his little sister with no other witnesses if Eric decided to beat the piss out of him. "You're welcome, by the way, for interfering with Miss Nose in the Air." Ryan mouthed thank you as she began to walk away, but something told her to stop and say something to her friend. Christina opened her mouth to Ryan's right ear and whispered, insinuating, "You can do better than her, Ryan. Don't settle. Be brave and go for what you want."

Ryan's dark green eyes looked into Christina's blue. They stared at each other face-to-face. He began to blush, and she pictured kissing him on the mouth. It would be the first for both, but neither would move closer. Instead, they looked away, embarrassed, thinking one wouldn't want the other to kiss them—but they both wanted to.

For years, Christina harbored unspoken feelings for Ryan, deeply appreciating his unwavering friendship. No matter how insecure or needy she felt, Ryan remained a steadfast presence, even forging connections with her grandparents, affectionately referring to them as grandma and grandpa.

Ryan, on the other hand, had never entertained romantic notions about Christina until recently. When his mother battled cancer, Christina provided a comforting ear, allowing him to express his fears and emotions without interruption. Witnessing Ryan's vulnerability, shedding tears for the first time as a young adult, stirred something within Christina. She realized Ryan's significance in her life had deepened, yet the prospect of jeopardizing their friendship by confessing her newfound feelings left her hesitant and anxious.

"See you tonight," Christina reiterated before retreating, a faint blush coloring her cheeks. Ryan nodded in response, observing her attempt to adopt a more outgoing demeanor as she navigated toward another table, concealing her inner turmoil.

As the school day sluggishly dragged on, Ryan's sole desire was to board any bus and return home to his mother. The passing minutes felt interminable, each tick of the oversized classroom clocks seemingly taunting him with their exaggerated movements. Ryan mused over the necessity of such ostentatious timepieces, pondering whether they synchronized with the school bell's chime.

Finally, the clock struck 2:30 PM, signaling the end of the school day. Amidst the chaotic dispersal of students, Ryan made his way to the bus area, his fingers trailing along the familiar brick wall. The smooth wood handle of the staircase beckoned him as he descended, each step a fleeting moment etched in the annals of his memory. Had Scott and Christina been by his side, Ryan would have savored these mundane details, unaware of their eventual significance in his recollections—cherished moments he would reflect on later in life.

Stepping onto the bus, Ryan's eyes darted around, searching for Christina. His heart sank when he spotted her sitting next to Michelle, their laughter filling the air. Instinct whispered for him to join them, but the cloud of Malibu Musk surrounding Michelle like a suffocating fog made him hesitate. While he enjoyed Michelle's company, the overwhelming scent was stifling.

Instead, Ryan found solace beside his younger friend, Colin. "Mind if I sit here?" he asked, sliding into the seat next to him. Colin shook his head, his gaze fixed on the grimy window, cobwebs clinging to the edges like forgotten memories. Ryan settled in, pondering their conversation.

"Are you going out tonight?" Colin turned towards him, breaking the silence hanging between them. "Yeah, just roaming around the neighborhood, you know, keeping it low-key," Ryan replied.

"Do your parents go with you?" Ryan probed, curious about Colin's family dynamics.

Colin's shoulders drooped slightly. "Nah, Mom's got her hands full with the little ones at home. She doesn't want us straying too far," he explained.

"I get it," Ryan nodded, shifting the topic. "So, what's your costume?"

"Just a ghost. Found some old sheets lying around," Colin shrugged, his excitement dimming as he spoke. Ryan sensed a tinge of melancholy in his friend's voice, realizing Halloween held little significance for him.

Suddenly, Colin's face lit up. "Hey, my birthday's coming up in two weeks. Want to come?" he asked eagerly.

Ryan hesitated, thoughts swirling in his mind. He couldn't shake the image of his own home—would it meet Colin's expectations? "Sure," he replied, handing Colin a pad of paper. "Write down the details, and I'll check with my mom."

As Colin scribbled down his information, Ryan wrestled with guilt. *Does his house smell like him?* It was one thing to endure a barrage of questions on a twenty-minute bus ride, but to go in and have to listen for multiple hours—*I just don't know.* He didn't want to use his mother's illness as an excuse, yet he also craved privacy in his time of need. "What are you planning for your party?" he asked, trying to divert his thoughts.

Colin's enthusiasm bubbled over. "Just pizza and a movie, nothing fancy," he grinned. Ryan nodded, relieved his decision wasn't solely his burden to bear. Their conversation drifted to pizza toppings, and Colin's relentless questioning brought a smile to Ryan's lips, despite his internal turmoil.

As the bus rolled to a stop in front of Colin's house, a flurry of activity erupted as several kids streamed off the bus alongside him. They dashed eagerly toward a weather-beaten, cerulean house that sag under the weight of its own history. Its peeling paint and crooked shutters whispered tales of neglect and abandonment, a stark contrast to the lively energy of the children converging upon it.

Ryan watched the scene unfold with curiosity and admiration. Their coordinated movement spoke volumes about their camaraderie and shared experiences. He couldn't help but feel a pang of envy mingled with relief; while he valued his solitude, there was something comforting about the idea of belonging to such a tight-knit group.

As he observed the kids disappear into the worn threshold of Colin's house, Ryan couldn't shake the feeling of anticipation building within him. He imagined the laughter echoing through the halls, the warmth of companionship enveloping him in its embrace. It reassured him to know that even if he didn't attend Colin's party in a few weeks, he had these faces, these connections, to turn to.

With a newfound sense of determination, Ryan made a vow to himself. He would embrace this opportunity to step outside his comfort zone, to immerse himself in the unknown depths of social interaction. Little did he know, this decision would mark the beginning of a journey that would shape his life in ways he could never have imagined.

CHAPTER NINE

THE SAFETY DANCE

The news of multiple animal attacks had given the locals an excuse to carry their registered weapons in holsters attached to their belts. Residents and their quasi-neighborhood watch program consisted of meeting once a year as an excuse to drink and grill out. They gathered on the street next to the Hatcher's home, in front of the woods, for Halloween night.

Silvia Donovan was the least vocal of the four, standing around, waiting for their kids to come out in their costumes. She looked and dressed older than her age, sporting large glasses with the neck cord attached to the arms for convenience and long skirts with long-sleeved button-up blouses. The dresses in her wardrobe were mainly denim, flowered, or khaki-colored. Rick joked, her khaki skirts made her look like a Mormon.

Adults roaming the neighborhood with holstered weapons weren't a new concept. For the last few years, someone, or maybe individuals, had begun vandalizing houses and cars with toilet paper and eggs, occasionally with a side of graffiti. They all knew who the culprit was.

A crisp breeze rustled the leaves as residents milled about, their hands resting casually on their holstered weapons. Shadows from the trees danced across the ground, adding an eerie touch to the already tense environment. The scent of grilled meat wafted through the air, mingling with the aroma of cheap beer.

Calvin Hatcher and Rick Donovan stood a few feet apart, an unspoken truce between them. Calvin's face was etched with lines of weariness, his eyes darting around as if searching for something—or someone. Rick took a swig of his Pabst Blue Ribbon, finding the cold can a familiar comfort in his hand.

"Did you know the kid?" Rick's voice was low, almost swallowed by the night.

Calvin buried his hands deeper into his Notre Dame hoodie, his fingers curling into fists. Since he was the district manager for Musicland, it was an obvious question he knew he would be asked.

"I met him once. He didn't work at the store long. He seemed like a good kid, ya know?" His voice was flat, the words rehearsed.

A murmur of agreement passed through the small group, their faces illuminated by the soft glow of the streetlights. Silvia Donovan, her large glasses catching the light, shifted uncomfortably. "Is what they're sayin' on the news and radio pretty close to the truth?" she asked, her voice barely above a whisper.

Calvin exhaled slowly, his breath visible in the cool air. "I didn't see the body, but going by the people who saw it, yeah, he was pretty torn up." He glanced at his empty hands, wishing for the familiar weight of a drink.

Silvia's eyes flickered to her husband, then back to Calvin. She looked older than her years, her clothes practical and worn. She tugged at the cord of her glasses, a nervous habit.

The group fell silent, their thoughts drifting to the recent vandalism. Toilet paper and eggs had become a common sight, the work of a known troublemaker. As if on cue, Eric Flanagan sauntered up the street, flanked by Valerie and Scott. The trio's laughter cut through the stillness, drawing the attention of the watchful adults.

The night air seemed to thicken with tension. Calvin's eyes narrowed as he watched the trio, a flicker of unease crossing his face. Rick's grip tightened on his beer can, the aluminum crinkling slightly under the pressure. Silvia nervously reached for the cord of her glasses again.

"Looks like they're at it again," Rick muttered, his voice a mix of frustration and resignation.

Calvin nodded slowly, his gaze fixed on Eric. "We need to keep an eye on them. Last thing we need is more trouble tonight."

Silvia glanced at her husband, then back at Calvin. "Do you really think they're the ones causing all the problems?" Her voice wavered, a hint of doubt creeping in.

Rick sighed, shaking his head. "Who else would it be? They've been a thorn in our side for years."

The trio continued their approach, oblivious to the scrutiny they were under. Eric's laugh was loud and carefree, a stark contrast to the somber mood of the gathered adults. Valerie and Scott followed suit, their own laughter echoing in the night.

As they passed by, Eric gave a mock salute to the adults. "Evening, folks," he drawled, with a smirk playing on his lips.

Calvin's jaw tightened, but he said nothing. Rick merely grunted in response, his eyes never leaving the trio.

Silvia exhaled softly, the tension in her shoulders easing just a fraction. "I hope tonight stays quiet," she murmured, more to herself than anyone else.

Rick's grip tightened on his beer can, his eyes squinted. "Here we go," he muttered under his breath, the words lost in the autumn wind.

He glared at Eric from a hundred feet away, his eyes narrowing in disdain as he watched his daughter with the thug. It was ironic, considering his own tendency to knock around his family when he had too much to drink. Valerie's outfit didn't help his mood—a white leotard and leggings with pointed pink ears and makeup to make her look like a sexy cat, the default hot girl costume. The sight of her made his blood boil.

Eric stood next to her, flaunting a white lab coat with torn-off sleeves, a fake tattoo of a heart impaled by an arrow, black Z. Cavaricci pants, a white tee shirt, and a blue Fisher-Price stethoscope from a child's pretend medical kit. Scott's costume was more casual, but the adults couldn't help but notice Eric's black bookbag. Rick's scowl deepened as he eyed the bag straps on Eric's shoulders. "What the hell are you supposed to be?" he scoffed.

Eric glanced down at his outfit, a smirk playing on his lips. "Oh! Yeah. I'm the love doctor." His tone dripped with sarcasm, music to a father's ears.

Rebecca rolled her eyes, shivering from the cool nighttime breeze. "Do you want my coat, dear?" Cal offered; his voice softer. Rebecca stubbornly shook her head, but Cal ignored her protest and took off his coat, shoving it toward her. She snatched it from him with a huff, grudgingly putting it on.

"I'll see what's taking the kids so long," Calvin muttered, heading towards the garage. His steps were heavy, each one echoing his frustration.

Inside, Calvin turned left, opening the closet and grabbing a coat off the hanger to replace the one he had given Rebecca. "C'mon, you all! Time to get this party started!" he yelled from the bottom of the stairs. His voice carried a forced cheerfulness, a mask he wore for Layla more than anyone else. He felt the weight of his family's disdain, but he was there to prove he could be better. *I am better,* he told himself, trying to believe it.

Ryan was the first to emerge from the middle landing with a leopard vest over a white tee shirt and grey slacks. "Who are you supposed to be?" his father asked. Putting his thumbs under his vest, pushing the print forward, "Bueller…Ferris Bueller."

Devin stomped down the stairs, annoyed that he was even going out. "Aren't I a little old to be trick or treating now?" Calvin shrugged, suggesting, "You don't have to, but I think Valerie thought you were hanging out with them tonight." Devin hated his dad knew how to play him. It was even more embarrassing he harbored deep affection for Valerie, yet chose to keep it concealed, as though it were a shameful secret known to all. Although with Devin's teenage temperament, he would become angry if someone brought it up.

Indifferently, Devin threw the string connected to a cereal box filled with plastic knives stuck inside it around his neck with attitude as he scoffed. With a box marked "Cereal Killer" in red ink laying over his red flannel shirt, Devin put his hands in the air, palms up, and asked, "Well?"

"Clever," his dad answered, thinking he could have just said Judd Nelson from The Breakfast Club with his outfit. It would have been easier than the time it took to make the "outfit" he had on. "Make sure you get candy for me," Cal playfully demanded, attempting to be friendly towards his eldest. Devin bumped shoulders with his father and muttered, "Whatever," as he made his way to the garage.

Layla Hatcher, dressed to the nines in a pink dress with silver sequins and a lovely plastic crown, graced her subjects with her divine presence. She slowly descended the staircase, letting the boys soak in her splendor.

"Are you ready for the annual Trick or Treat celebration?" Calvin asked, bowing theatrically to Layla.

Layla curtsied, mimicking her mother's accent with exaggerated elegance, "Yes, daddy. Tonight will be splendid, the best year yet."

Ryan rolled his eyes, cutting a glance towards his father. The drama was over the top, but he had to give Layla credit for staying in character. Calvin, on the other hand, wondered if Layla had been watching too many animated Disney films, losing touch with reality.

As they headed toward the door, Calvin paused and looked at Ryan. "Wear a jacket, it's too cold out," he instructed.

Ryan grinned and reached into the closet, pulling out his dad's grey leather coat, the one that looked just like the one Matthew Broderick wore in the film.

Ryan walked up his driveway to find Scott standing there in khaki pants and a Red Wings jersey, dressed as Cameron Fry from the eighties classic Ferris Bueller's Day Off. "I can't believe you went with it!" Ryan exclaimed; his excitement evident.

Scott smiled, pleased to see the surprise on his friend's face. "A bet is a bet," he shrugged, his hands stuffed in his pockets for warmth. Scott was always the one kid who never needed a coat, no matter how freezing it was outside.

"I couldn't find any proof of where they were in that scene," Scott admitted, referring to the pool scene in Ferris Bueller's Day Off. The bet revolved around whose house the trio was at after visiting the city. Ryan insisted it couldn't be Cameron's house because the siding didn't match and there was no pool in the exterior shot. Scott countered that Cameron's house was in the woods, with leaves in the water, and the only way to be sure was to see the house when Ferris called him outside at the beginning of the film. But there was no clear shot of the house, so it was decided Ryan won the bet.

The parents gathered the kids and delivered their annual safety talk. Ryan stood nearby, catching Eric's eye as he mouthed, "I'm going to get you." The urban legend of razor blades hidden in candy bars had parents on high alert during and after trick-or-treating. The lecture wasn't really for the older kids; it was aimed at Layla, the youngest, who had a habit of munching on chocolate before getting home.

Devin, Eric, and Valerie headed off towards the other end of Holiday Heights, near Wadsworth Road. Meanwhile, the younger ones started their candy hunt near the Hatcher's house, where Rebecca handed out the first batch of treats. Ryan's group needed to meet Christina at her grandmother's house before beginning their route.

"Oh my gosh! Don't you all look great!" Christina's grandmother, Josephine—or Jo—gushed, admiring Layla's princess costume. When she looked up at Ryan and Scott, her confused expression revealed she had no idea who they were supposed to be. "Christy's coming down in a sec. She's just finishing the final details on her outfit," Jo explained. Leaning in, she whispered, "I don't care for it myself, but I can't make her change it now."

Ryan's curiosity piqued, wondering what Christina would emerge as from the staircase.

Scott meandered around the front porch, eventually drifting onto the lawn, unable to keep still. Ryan often wondered if his best friend had an anxiety or attention disorder, as he never was able to stay in one place long enough for a meaningful conversation. Yet, Ryan enjoyed walking with him; at least during those moments, they could talk.

Suddenly, an angel emerged from the front door—a fallen angel with blonde hair. Christina scanned the group, seeking someone to praise her outfit, especially Ryan. Her appearance was hard to ignore: the low-cut sweater, the torn bottom exposing her midriff, black boots, thigh-high fishnet stockings, and black wings strapped to her back. Bright red lipstick completed her look.

"What do you think?" she asked, waving her hands in front of her, clearly wanting Ryan's opinion.

"I think you look evil," Layla responded playfully, smiling with a wrinkled nose and making claws with her hands. Christina laughed, playfully sparring with her. Scott looked her up and down, grinning, and quipped, "I think you need to let Jesus into your heart. Do you have a moment to talk about our lord and savior?" Christina punched Scott in the arm as she walked past him, with Layla trailing behind, hanging onto her every word.

"Well?" she asked Ryan, the opinion she cared about most.

Ryan's face reddened as he looked her up and down again, those strange feelings for her stirring up. "I think you look like a badass," he said. It wasn't exactly the response she was hoping for, but it was good enough coming from a guy who rarely voiced his thoughts. She smiled and gestured for everyone to follow her.

It was time to get the candy.

The first house they approached exuded an eerie aura, sending a traveling shudder through his body. Mr. Gleeson, the resident, upheld his peculiar Halloween tradition with unwavering dedication. Positioned outside his door was a weathered rocking chair, its creaking hinges echoing through the night. Mr. Gleeson himself sat there, cloaked in a scarecrow guise, his face obscured by a mask reminiscent of a jack-o'-lantern. A bowl of candy rested on his lap, accompanied by a sign imploring visitors to take only one piece.

Despite its familiarity, the sight never failed to unsettle passersby. The mystery of whether someone inhabited the scarecrow ensemble lingered, inviting speculation year after year. And without fail, there were always those brave (or foolish) souls who dared to test the illusion, prodding at the figure in hopes of uncovering its secrets. Yet, nestled within the fabric and straw was merely an elderly man, finding amusement in the fright he induced.

But not all were ensnared by his antics. A solitary child might be met with a subtle movement, a playful attempt to startle. Only in the presence of a group would the scarecrow come to life, its guardian relishing in the collective gasps and giggles of the children.

This year, however, a subtle alteration marked Mr. Gleeson's facade—a jack-o'-lantern now adorned his head, its features obscured by thin black material. A small but significant change, hinting at unseen intentions beneath the familiar costume. Maybe he's not in costume this year, they wondered.

With hesitant steps, Ryan approached the enigmatic figure, his heartbeat quickening with each footfall. He plucked a piece of candy from the bucket, his fingers nervously pointing at each possible selection. Joining his friends, he attempted to downplay his unease. "Not so bad," he declared, though the tension in his voice betrayed his true feelings.

Scott snickered, teasing Ryan's facade of bravery. *He's not wrong.* Unwilling to verbally admit his apprehension, Ryan countered with a challenge, daring Scott to test his nerves. Christy observed their banter with a shake of her head, her own curiosity piqued.

"I'll go," she announced, her determination evident as she approached the porch. A sudden gust of wind set the rocking chair in motion, causing her to pause. Doubts flickered in her mind, the possibility of an empty husk beneath the costume offering a fleeting reassurance.

As Christy reached out, her hand hovering over the candy bowl, uncertainty mingled with anticipation. *Maybe there's nothing there,* she thought with suspicion.

The group observed as Christy hesitated, contemplating her approach to the candy bowl. "I bet she doesn't do it," remarked Scott, already seeking a wager. Layla shot him a disapproving look, disappointed by Scott's lack of confidence. "You're wrong! Christina is a warrior who never goes back on a challenge, you ignoramus," she retorted, surprising Scott with her fervor. Ryan couldn't help but laugh at his sister's unexpected boldness, acknowledging her with a low five.

Scott turned to Ryan, incredulous at Layla's outburst. "Better watch out, you little trout sniffer, your turn is coming," Scott taunted Layla, who responded with a playful tongue-out gesture, choosing not to stoop to his level. It was her subtle way of asserting the high ground.

Meanwhile, Christy approached the scarecrow with the pumpkin head, her movements deliberate. With a sense of mischief dancing in her eyes, she reached into the bowl, savoring the anticipation. Her fingers traced the edges of the black triangle eyes, a knowing smile playing on her lips. Eventually, she unearthed her favorite treat, a Three Musketeers fun size, and carefully tucked it into her bag.

Turning to face Scott, Christy issued a challenge with a pointed finger. "Your turn, slick. Let's see if you can do it there, big shot," she goaded him. Scott rolled his shoulders in mock preparation, as if gearing up for a marathon or a brawl. "It's getting candy from a bowl, stop being dramatic about it and go down there!" Ryan teased, noticing Scott's exaggerated bravado. Scott shot him a quizzical look. "I don't think I like this more vocal thing you've got going on lately," he remarked, raising an eyebrow.

"Stop stalling," Ryan replied, mockingly jutting out his front teeth and shaking his head. With a resigned shrug, Scott made his way down the driveway. As he reached for a small packet of Smarties, a hand clad in an old gardening glove suddenly clasped his own. Startled, Scott recoiled, sending the candy scattering. The scarecrow lurched to life; its wobbling head too cumbersome to remain upright.

"Sweet fucking Christ!" Scott's expletive pierced the night air, reverberating through the darkness and drawing attention to their group. Mr. Gleeson, hidden behind his pumpkin mask, chuckled at the outburst, settling back into his chair to await the next unsuspecting visitors. Ryan, Christina, and Layla joined in laughter at Scott's expense, their amusement evident. Scott, his pride wounded, refused to meet their gaze. "This is lame. Let's go," he grumbled, striding ahead as Ryan and Christina exchanged mocking glances, unable to resist teasing him.

However, their departure was halted by an oversight—they had forgotten to allow Layla her turn at the candy bowl. As they began to walk away, Christina intervened, gesturing towards Layla, who approached the chair with trepidation. Drawing closer, she nervously bit her lip, desiring reassurance evident in her demeanor. Finally, summoning her courage, she halted a few feet from Mr. Gleeson and, in her squeaky voice, made a polite request. "Could you please not scare this year, mister? Can you be nice to me?" Moved by her innocence, Mr. Gleeson straightened up, nodding in agreement and offering her the bowl. Layla tentatively reached in, retrieving a pouch of chewy sweets with a grateful smile. Thanking him, she dashed back to her brother.

Expressing their appreciation to Mr. Gleeson, the group savored the unexpected kindness amidst the night's tricks. Though Scott initially sulked, his spirits lifted when they encountered the Hutchinsons, who generously distributed whole candy bars—a rare delight. Credit was duly given to Mr. Gleeson; his unwavering commitment to the scarecrow charade, even with his head encased in a pungent, hollowed-out pumpkin, earned their admiration.

As they continued their rounds, Ryan couldn't help but notice Layla's peculiar habit of consuming her candy immediately after receiving it. Sensing her discomfort during each stop, he decided to intervene when she settled on the curb to devour a small packet of gummy worms.

"Layloo? What are you doing?" Ryan questioned, crouching down to her level. Layla hesitated before explaining, "I'm eating candy in front of the people's houses." Perplexed, Ryan pressed for clarification. "Yeah, I get that, but why?" he inquired. "Because you have to show the people you appreciate the food," Layla replied earnestly, puzzled by her brother's lack of understanding. Chuckling quietly, Ryan corrected her misconception. "I think you've mixed that up with restaurants somehow. Like if you eat a steak without A1, that's a compliment to the chef, or if you burp after eating. Something like that." Uncertain but trusting her brother's explanation, Layla rose awkwardly and followed him down the sidewalk.

They were halfway through the neighborhood, and it was time for Ryan to visit his favorite house. Much like Mr. Gleeson's annual scarecrow costume, the next home they approached was occupied by an older gentleman dressed identically. Ryan never learned much about them, as they tended to keep to themselves. However, the husband always greeted them at the door, towering in an authentic-looking Darth Vader ensemble, devoid of the heavy asthmatic breathing and blinking lights. Ryan and Scott harbored a secret hope to hear the man speak, anticipating a voice reminiscent of James Earl Jones, but their wish remained unfulfilled. This year, however, they held onto hope. They just knew it.

"Trick or Treat!" they chorused as the imposing figure with the shiny black helmet loomed over them, awaiting their request for candy and, perhaps, a glimpse of his voice. Delving into a glass bowl, the giant man generously filled Scott's bag first. As the night wore on, the dwindling number of trick-or-treaters meant the neighbors were more liberal with their treats. If their bags weren't overflowing with goodies already, they soon would be.

"How long have you had your costume?" Scott prodded, hoping to coax a response from the tall figure. In response, the man offered an imitation of Vader's iconic asthmatic breathing, eliciting a more animated reaction from the group than they had ever received before. Pumping their fists and hopping with excitement, they celebrated silently, drawing curious glances from passersby who wondered if they were somehow mentally unhinged. Layla, unfamiliar with the source of their excitement, watched on in confusion, having never seen the movie from a galaxy far, far away.

When Layla approached for her turn, she gazed up at the towering figure and complimented, "I like your cape." The man nodded beneath the helmet, patting her head in gratitude without uttering a word. Ryan offered a smile and waved goodbye, cheerfully declaring, "See you next year!" momentarily forgetting the uncertainty of their future encounters. Tonight would linger as a bittersweet memory, as Ryan and his friends faced the reality of entering high school the following year. They would celebrate Halloween differently, no longer embracing the innocence of childhood in the same way.

Meanwhile, the older kids, Devin Hatcher, Valerie Donovan, and Eric Flanagan, had different plans from trick-or-treating. Devin stood vigilant, his eyes darting around to keep lookout, while Eric, driven by a mischievous itch, held a roll of toilet paper, itching to wreak havoc on private property. Valerie, her white cat costume brushing against fallen leaves, sighed dramatically, her boredom evident in every move.

In front of Holiday Heights, a massive oak tree stood solitary, its branches swaying slightly, an inviting target. But the frequent patrols of the neighborhood watch and the constant traffic on Wadsworth Road made any vandalism a risky endeavor.

"Eric, can we just go? Walk somewhere else? This is boring as hell," Valerie complained, flicking a leaf from her costume. Eric, clearly frustrated, clutched his backpack tighter. "Just wait! Okay! Anytime now!" he snapped. Devin, ever watchful, spotted an older woman strolling down the street. Valerie's restlessness grew; she paced, popping a piece of Wrigley's gum, and shot a questioning look at Devin. He responded with a subtle eye roll and a shrug, siding with her.

"Maybe we should go into the woods and do stuff," Devin proposed. Eric turned, confused. "We could at least roll the trees in the woods behind my house. It's better than nothing."

"Won't your folks be there since your house is in front of it?" Eric asked.

"Yeah, but they're probably loaded on beer and snacks, gossiping about whatever. They might not even notice." Valerie leaned into Eric, her head resting on his shoulder, a gesture that made Devin stiffen. "I think that's a good idea. The adults are in full force tonight. No one will be in the woods to watch us," she coaxed, batting her eyelashes.

Eric conceded and started to zip up his bag just as the old woman on the road called out, "Aren't you a little too old to be out trick-or-treating?" Eric, never one for respecting his elders, retorted, "Aren't you a little too old to be living?" The woman gasped, her hand flying to her chest in shock. "Well, I never!"

"Well, ma'am, maybe that's just your problem then," Devin quipped, slapping a high-five with Eric as they all took off running. They darted through the neighbors' lawns, laughing, their footsteps crunching through the fallen leaves as they made their way to Devin's house, ready to cause some trouble in the woods.

The drinking had commenced at the Hatcher's house, and Rebecca bustled about, trying to play hostess despite Calvin's insistence she didn't need to. Rick Donovan, inconsiderate as ever when drinking, repeatedly asked Rebecca, a woman battling stomach cancer, for another Coors. Each request was met with a forced smile, her lips tight as she turned away, scowling once her back was turned.

Calvin's job and the grisly murder from the night before dominated the conversation, despite efforts to avoid it. The discovery of a body behind Rolling Acres Mall brought back haunting memories of the two college girls found raped and murdered in the nearby woods over two years ago. Though the perpetrators were caught, the small towns remained uneasy.

Rick, loud and brash, couldn't resist prodding his old friend. "I bet you make about ten more than you did when we worked together," he teased. Calvin took a measured sip of his beer. "Man, I wish. Then it would be worth it." Silvia, fed up, snapped at her husband, "Would you just leave him alone about it? What difference does it make now? You're not working. You got a decent exit salary. What do you care?"

"I don't, woman. Jesus! I'm just trying to figure out if I should go white collar like Cal here." Silvia, emboldened by a few too many drinks, retorted, "White Collar? Right. That will be the day." Rick's face flushed with anger, a look Silvia knew too well, one that promised retribution later.

"You wouldn't want it anyway, Rick," Calvin interjected. "Your old job was about making sure people met quotas. Now, I have to oversee multiple stores across Ohio and Pennsylvania, catering to an entitled public and dealing with complaints. It's not just one store—it's several. Then I have to investigate and sometimes fire people, taking away their livelihood. In factories, union rules make firing harder, but not in retail." Calvin leaned back in his chair, the weight of his words heavy in the air. "Lady commerce is a fickle bitch. She counts every failure and barely acknowledges success. So, if you don't mind, get off my back and stop being pissed about something that doesn't matter."

Rick's bravado faltered, the reality of Calvin's words sinking in. He had been so obsessed with the money that he never considered the stress. The Rust Belt had already crumbled, and people like Rick were left wondering if it could ever recover. Akron, once a tire manufacturing hub, now felt like a flat tire on a decaying car.

Even Rebecca, watching from the sidelines, didn't know the full extent of Calvin's burden. He had never told her. She wondered if things could have been different if he had. Calvin took the job, believing it was the right thing for his family, but never considered the personal toll. As the night wore on, Rebecca reflected on their life together, thinking maybe he should have spoken up.

The night sky cleared, the full moon casting an eerie glow over Norton, Ohio, and the woods connecting the townships. The wind had died down, but a foreboding still hung in the air. Four mutilated bodies found over the last two days cast a shadow over the celebrations, leaving everyone uneasy and on edge.

CHAPTER TEN

PSYCHO KILLER

"Let's hang out in the woods!" Scott said with enthusiasm, his eyes gleaming with excitement at the spontaneous idea.

Ryan, Scott, Christina, and Layla were trudging back to the Hatcher house. The porch light flickered in the distance, a beacon of adult oblivion. Inside, the adults would soon be immersed in their drinks, blissfully unaware of potential child endangerment or mischief. It was nearing nine o'clock. Ryan's parents had granted the kids a bedtime extension until eleven, as long as morning wouldn't be a struggle. Devin, however, planned to retreat to his room and lose himself in his cassette player.

"Or just hear me out—we don't," Christina quipped, her tone dripping with sarcasm. Layla looked up at her and nodded in agreement, clutching Christina's arm.

"Oh, come on! What's Halloween if there isn't a little creepiness involved?" Scott's eyes sparkled mischievously.

"I don't know, man. Sounds iffy," Ryan said, his voice tinged with uncertainty.

"There's a shocker. Agree with the girlfriend," Scott teased, rolling his eyes. "What's the worst thing that could happen?"

"That is literally the thing someone says before they get murdered, cursed, or whatever. Have you not seen a horror movie before?" Ryan's hands flailed dramatically, causing Layla to giggle and Christina to dodge.

Ryan sighed, knowing he was about to cave in. *Time to man up*, he thought wryly. "Fine," he said, the word feeling heavy on his tongue. Scott pumped his fist in victory, his grin widening.

Layla tugged on Ryan's arm, her voice a worried whisper, "You're not going in the woods, are you?" Her wide eyes pleaded with him.

Ryan knelt down, trying to sound reassuring. "Just for a little bit, okay? You go back inside quietly so no one sees you. We won't be long."

"You promise you'll be fine?" Layla's concerned eyes searched his face. Ryan hesitated, the weight of her trust pressing down on him. He forced a smile, but inside, a small voice warned him not to make promises he couldn't keep. *Layla would be so disappointed if something happened.*

"Don't diddle-dottle, Ryan. Tell your sister it will be fine," Christy said with raised eyebrows. Ryan squinted at her, recognizing the teasing, and replied in a deadpan voice, "It'll be okay. I promise." Layla, reassured but still uncertain, walked to her house's front door while the adults inside chatted and drank.

Ryan watched her disappear inside before turning to Christy with a pained look. "Please don't make me do something like that again," he said quietly.

"Why? Are you mad at me?" Christy asked, a hint of concern in her voice.

Scott started down a well-trodden path, and Ryan followed, leaving Christy to trail behind. "No, I'm not mad," Ryan muttered as he passed her. "But I made a promise like that to her when my mom went for tests. Turned out it wasn't okay. Understand?" Christina felt a stitch of guilt but knew Ryan would be fine after a few minutes of silent treatment.

As they reached an area where the parents could see them if they looked, Ryan murmured, "Scott, get down and be quiet." Scott mimed a salute and crouched low.

Navigating the forest floor was an art form, mastered by those who routinely snuck through without their parents' knowledge. Dancing around twigs and dead leaves, they had perfected their technique during the day, but night posed new challenges. *Which leaves are fresh and which were brittle? Was that a branch or a shadow?*

Snap, crackle.

"Shit! Get down!" Scott whispered urgently, having stepped on a branch near Ryan's yard. They dropped to their stomachs, hearts pounding as they prayed not to be caught. Scott's feet were now in front of Ryan's face, an irresistible target. Ryan slapped them. "Ow! What the hell is your problem?"

"Good going, numb nuts. We're going to get spotted!" Ryan hissed, throwing dirt at Scott.

"We will if you keep talking! Shut up!"

"You shut up!"

Christy shook her head, annoyed by their whispered bickering. a light swept the area as Calvin, having heard the noise, shone a flashlight their way. They lay still, holding their breath. Ryan's mind raced with the fear his dad, armed and paranoid, might mistake them for intruders.

Oh, shit! One of us might die out here tonight!

Calvin peered into the woods, looking for the source of the sound. Finding nothing, he turned off the flashlight and returned to the adult conversation. The trio began crawling slowly, making their way past the berry bushes until they reached the end of the property line.

In the growing darkness, time slipped away. Ryan maneuvered through the undergrowth; confident his parents wouldn't spot him. A brisk wind sent a cold tingle across his skin, and the moon, now veiled by clouds, cast an eerie glow. Leaves of red, orange, and yellow swirled in the wind, dancing across the forest floor.

As Ryan stood, his pinky brushed against something unexpected, a sharp edge cutting into his skin. An eerie sensation gripped him as he looked down, his breath catching in his throat. A bloodied, black wingtip shoe lay partially buried in the leaves, its polished leather marred by streaks of dark, congealed blood. His heart pounded against his ribcage, the sound echoing in his ears like a drum.

He squeezed his eyes shut, willing the gruesome sight to disappear. It's not real, he told himself. Just a trick of the light, a figment of his overactive imagination. But when he forced his eyes open again, the shoe was still there, and now a pale, flesh-torn leg extended from it, the fabric of a pant leg shredded and stained.

Panic surged through him, a cold sweat breaking out on his forehead. His breathing grew rapid and shallow, and his hands shivered as he tried to make sense of the macabre scene. The whispers began then, soft at first, like the rustle of leaves, then growing louder, more insistent. They filled his head, echoing with cries and screams which seemed to come from everywhere and nowhere all at once.

He dropped to his knees, pressing his nose into the dirt, inhaling the scent of damp earth. Covering his ears, he shut his eyes tight, trying to block out the horrific vision and the haunting voices. His fingers dug into the ground, nails scraping against rocks and roots as he rocked back and forth, a desperate mantra spilling from his lips.

I don't want to see you—please go away—I just want to get up—please go away—I have nothing for you—please go away. The words came out in a frantic whisper, barely audible over the noise in his head. Each plea was more desperate than the last, a raw, fervent cry for release from the nightmarish encounter. His voice broke, the syllables merging into a desperate, incoherent babble.

He could feel the weight of the leg, the presence of the apparition looming over him, but he refused to open his eyes. Tears leaked from the corners of his eyes, mingling with the dirt on his face. His body trembled with fear, every muscle taut, ready to spring away if he could only muster the courage to move.

The world around him faded, leaving only the overwhelming dread and the relentless whispers. The leaves rustled faintly, a stark contrast to the violence of the scene before him. He clung to that sound, hoping it would anchor him to reality, even as the horror threatened to consume him entirely.

A force yanked Ryan off the ground by his jacket, which was caught in a firm grip. His heart raced, fear gripping him as he imagined the ghost from his nightmare materializing. Flailing wildly, he saw Scott's familiar face above him. "What the hell, man!" Scott exclaimed, dodging Ryan's panicked punches. Relieved, Ryan scrambled to his feet, brushing dirt off his clothes. "Sorry, I wasn't sure what was grabbing me."

"Who else could it have been? It's just us," Scott asked, seeking an explanation from his friend. Ryan, avoiding the question, suggested that they continue. Scott's expression shifted from concern to delight, like a dog discovering a new toy. He sprinted ahead, carefree and oblivious to any danger.

Christina hummed, "I think we're alone now," observing the deserted surroundings. "There doesn't seem to be anyone around," the guys echoed, sharing a moment of levity. Christina eagerly linked her arm through Ryan's, slipping her hands into his jacket pocket. As he glanced at her, he couldn't help but think if their costumes were more coordinated, Christy could have dressed as Sloane Peterson, completing their group theme. Alas, hindsight is always twenty-twenty.

"Do you ever think about me?" Christina asked, her big blue eyes searching his face. Ryan blushed, feeling the weight of her gaze. "You're like my best friend. Of course, I think about you," he replied, sensing the deeper meaning behind her words.

"I mean, I think about you in more than a friend way," she confessed.

"Oh!" Ryan exclaimed, surprised but not shocked. *Seriously? That's your response, you moron? Why not just say, "Aw, shucks," while you're at it?*

Christina stopped, swinging Ryan toward her, their eyes locking. Amidst his distracted thoughts about ghosts, he felt her hand gently press against his cheek, guiding his face toward hers. "Ryan Hatcher! I would make a great girlfriend, and you know it!" Sighing, Ryan took her hand from his cheek, kissed her knuckles, and nodded. "I know you would."

"Then what is it?" she asked, confusion and hope mingling in her eyes. Ryan closed his eyes, knowing the truth could change everything. "I'm just scared."

Scott's voice echoed from a distance, breaking the moment. "Looks like someone got their wish granted," he called. Ryan and Christina exchanged a glance and continued deeper into the woods. The trees blocked the natural light, and above them, white toilet paper draped over the branches swayed in the wind. Scott showcased the handiwork with a triumphant gesture.

Toilet paper blew off the trees onto the ground. Ryan stopped to inspect the yolk-covered bark and broken eggshells at their feet. "Who did this?" Christina asked.

"I'll give ya three guesses, but you'll only need one," Scott answered. Ryan began to walk under the trees, looking up at the toilet paper rolls, finding the scene oddly calming. Walking backward, facing Scott and Christina, Ryan yelled, "Who else could it be? Eric, right? The neighborhood dime store hood. I wonder what it's like being a cliché."

A shadow moved behind a massive oak tree, and suddenly, a knife pressed against Ryan's throat. A sinister voice whispered mockingly into his left ear, stripping away any bravado. Ryan's hands shot up in surrender as the foul stench of his captor filled his nostrils. The sniveling giggle confirmed his fear – Eric Flanagan, wielding a switchblade, had him in a deadly grip.

Devin emerged from another hiding spot, nervously snickering, revealing his complicity. Valerie, arms crossed, stood nearby, embarrassed by her boyfriend's threatening behavior.

"Hey there, buddy. Not so suave with your words now, are ya?" Eric sneered, the knife gliding over Ryan's Adam's apple, lifting him slightly off the ground. "Who else could it have been? It's just us," Scott reiterated, his voice filled with worry. Valerie argued for Ryan's release, but Eric silenced her with a threatening glance.

Devin, usually supportive of Eric's antics, grew uneasy, sensing the danger. "Come on, man! You scared him enough!" he urged. Eric violently shook his head, insisting Ryan must face consequences for his boldness.

The tension peaked as Christina's desperate cries for help further incensed Eric. "You just made a big mistake orphan. You'll get yours later and I'll make your boyfriend here watch!"

Tensions surged as Christina's voice cut through the air, "Shut up!" Her defiance sparked a sinister giggle from Eric, whose eyes gleamed with sadistic pleasure. Ryan's fists clenched, anger boiling over as Christy's tears mirrored those from her childhood tantrums. The memory fueled his resolve, and with a swift kick to Eric's crotch, Ryan managed to break free. Scott's nervous giggles only escalated the tension.

Eric doubled over, spewing chilling threats about Ryan's mother, his voice dripping with malice. "You're going to get it you little queerbate—Better yet, maybe I'll take it out on your limey mom and just get it over with since she's good as dead anyways!" Devin, momentarily paralyzed by the revelation of Eric's cruelty, felt a surge of rage. With a powerful punch, he connected with Eric's face, shattering the bully's arrogant facade. The kids formed a tense circle, their eyes locked on Eric, the air thick with anticipation.

The sudden arrival of parents added urgency to the scene having heard the commotion only moments ago. Eric, clutching pepper spray, hissed more threats. Devin, wrestling with guilt, extended a hand to Eric, an undeserved gesture considering his actions. Eric's eyes blazed with madness as he pointed the pepper spray at Devin, escalating the danger.

The wind howled through the trees, amplifying the ominous sky. Eric's lips curled into a sinister smile as he unleashed the spray, aiming at Valerie, Devin, Scott, and Christina. Ryan, quick on his feet, dodged the spray. Horror filled him as he saw his friends wiping their faces and eyes to reduce the mist's sting, most of which didn't reach them.

Eric's voice rose above the chaos, "I'll kill all of you!" His threats echoed through the woods as the parents arrived, their faces masks of shock and fear. Valerie's eyes widened, seeing something behind Eric. She tried to scream, her voice caught in her throat, paralyzed by fear. A dark presence loomed behind Eric, shadowed and menacing.

Eric, oblivious to the panic he was invoking, continued, "I have everything in this bag to make you all miserable. Do not fuck with—"

A dark shape lunged from the shadows; its eyes gleaming with predatory intent. The massive wolf, its fur bristling and teeth glinting, clamped its jaws around Eric Flanagan's sides. His scream pierced the night as the beast's fangs sank into his love handles, crunching through ribs like dry twigs. Blood spurted from the wounds, painting the ground and autumn leaves in a gruesome spray.

Eric's body convulsed as the wolf shook him violently, trying to incapacitate him. His screams echoed through the trees, mingling with the sound of bones snapping. Blood sprayed across Valerie's face and soaked her white cat costume, the stark contrast making the scene even more macabre. She wiped the blood from her mouth, staring in horror at her crimson-stained hands. Tears streamed down her face as she watched the wolf fling Eric's body around like a ragdoll.

Eric's fingers clawed at the dirt, his shrieks growing weaker as he tried to drag himself away. The beast's jaws clamped down again, lifting him off the ground with a sickening crunch. Devin, Scott, and Christina, still blinded by the pepper spray, struggled to clear their eyes, their confusion slowly morphing into horror as the scene came into focus.

The Hatchers and Donovans stood frozen, having witnessed the grisly spectacle. The enormous wolf, its fur matted with blood, held Eric in its jaws, shaking him with brutal force. Blood dripped from the leaves above and pooled at the roots of the trees, the forest transformed into a nightmarish tableau. The air was thick with the metallic scent of blood and the echoes of Eric's diminishing screams.

You will leave.

You allowed the meat sacks to see too much.

You will carry this one and pick at its bones.

You will take advantage of this last night until I come again.

The wolf snarled menacingly at the two families, freezing them with fear. Its upper mouth curled, revealing long whiskers pointing toward the ground. Calvin Hatcher positioned himself before the parents, blocking any attempts to move forward with his outstretched arm. The creature momentarily paused, allowing Eric to reach out to Valerie, gasping for air and struggling to scream for help.

No one knew how to react.

It planted its bare, creatural hands and feet into the dirt, preparing for movement. Cold air shot out of its mouth and nose as its blond eyes, with dilated pupils, scanned the potential threat. Eric lay limp in its mouth, gasping for breath. Rebecca Hatcher reached out to Devin, hoping to get his attention as she stepped toward Ryan and

Calvin. Devin remained oblivious, helplessly watching Eric's gruesome fate, while Ryan fixated on the wolf's eyes. Despite its intimidating appearance, Ryan sensed a hint of sadness in those eyes during a brief moment of relaxation—

This isn't an ordinary wolf. There's something vulnerable, something human about it.

Fascination replaced fear for Ryan as he locked eyes with the wolf, an understood exchange passing between them, laden with secrets the creature wished to keep hidden from human comprehension. With a menacing growl, it swiftly vanished into the wilderness, Eric Flanagan clenched within its jaws.

Shocked and terrified, the onlookers remained frozen in place, the image of the wolf etched into their minds as if burned into their retinas. The affected children rubbed their eyes, attempting to banish the lingering stinging sensation.

"What the hell do we do now?" Rick Donovan's voice pierced the tense silence, breaking the spell of disbelief. Traumatized by the horrific scene, Valerie clawed at her skin, trying to rid herself of the imaginary grasp of drying blood, her cries for Eric lost in the darkness as she sprinted after them, driven by desperation.

Devin's vision cleared, his gaze following Valerie's fleeing form, a sense of helplessness washing over him. "No! Valerie!" he shouted, his voice echoing into the night.

Realizing he was armed, Calvin retrieved his gun from its concealed place, his resolve firm. "We need to help him," he declared, his words echoing with determination. But Rebecca, with panic clawing at her heart, urged caution, her voice stuttering with fear. "You…you saw what just happened, Cal! There's no wa…way that boy is still breathing."

"I have to go after it, Becs! Or more will get hurt!" Calvin's resolve was unwavering, his determination driving him forward into the darkness.

Rick Donovan, his own gun drawn, took charge, instructing Silvia to take the children back to safety. Eager to assist, he chased after Calvin, his bulky frame moving with surprising agility.

Meanwhile, Ryan hesitated, torn between following his family into the unknown and staying behind. His gaze lingered on his mother; her apology conveyed with a single glance. "Mom?" he called out, but without a word, Rebecca dashed into the night, leaving Ryan with no choice but to follow, unwilling to let her face the danger alone.

As Devin and the group made their way back, he realized his little brother was missing, a surge of worry coursing through him. Despite his responsibility to the younger children, the urge to assist his parents and Valerie was overpowering.

Layla watched from her bedroom window as her brother returned without the rest of the family, a knot of anxiety tightening in her chest. Locking eyes with Devin, she found solace in his quiet reassurance.

Unable to bear the thought of his family facing danger alone, Devin knew he had to seek help. With a heavy heart, he turned away from the woods, his mind set on finding someone nearby who could assist them.

Rebecca's voice sliced through the night, her urgent cries for caution reverberating in the darkness. Ryan hastened toward the turmoil, his steps faltering as he navigated the shadowed terrain. The dense canopy of trees swallowed every trace of light, plunging Ryan into disorienting darkness. His only guide was the faint echo of past journeys through the woods.

As the voices faded into silence, Ryan slowed, straining his ears for the slightest hint of movement. A rustle to his right, off his intended path, caught his attention. "Tell me where are you, mom?" he called out. Ryan's plea echoed into the night, lost amidst the eerie stillness.

A sharp bark pierced the air, followed by menacing growls, emanating from the direction where leaves had rustled moments before. In the distance, Ryan heard his father's voice, a distant cry near the edge of the cornfields.

Multiple voices mingled in a symphony of taunts and screams, blending together in a chorus of fear and desperation. Ryan, his heart pounding, edged closer to the woods, straining through the tangled branches to glimpse the chaotic scene unfolding before him.

His parents, Rick, and Valerie confronted a towering creature, looming over them on its hind legs. Ryan's breath caught in his throat as he watched the grotesque figure, no longer holding Eric in its jaws but standing over him as he lay motionless on the ground, blood pooling around him.

The abandoned cornfield provided a desolate backdrop, the withered stalks crunching underfoot, their dying whispers a stark contrast to the violence unfolding nearby. In this moment, anonymity held no significance, not when a life hung in the balance.

The werewolf lashed out at Calvin and Rick with long, jagged claws, their guns pointed in disbelief at the unearthly creature before them. Squinting from the edge of the woods, Ryan observed the creature's strange appearance: its furless body was unnaturally thin, as though it had been starved for weeks.

Advancing toward Valerie, the werewolf struck again, sending her sprawling to the ground. Rick's voice cut through the chaos, demanding the creature's attention and urging it to spare his daughter. Ryan strained to see if Valerie was injured, her fate uncertain amidst the chaos. A single gunshot shattered the night, a defiant act of retaliation from her father, ensuring the creature's temporary restraint.

As the werewolf yelped in pain, Ryan watched, mesmerized by its grotesque transformation. Though resembling a wolf, its movements showed a human grace, stumbling on two legs rather than four.

You fool! You stopped! You have no respect for our life! You never did.

You will die tonight.

You will never know how much better it is.

......*So be it,* the exhausted man within the mongrel exhaled. *That's what I have wanted all along.*

"Clear a path, boy!" demanded a voice, cutting through the chaos as a figure stormed past Ryan at the edge of the woods, forcefully pushing through the dense foliage into the open field. It was their neighbor, Melvin Craggs, his arms cradling a shotgun, his expression hardened with determination. Two more gunshots rang out, one from Calvin and the other from Rick, as they continued their desperate struggle against the formidable opponent that was the werewolf. Each bullet pierced its body, but still, the creature proved tough to kill, its dying howls diminishing with each shot, until it began to whine like a wounded animal, asking for mercy. Yet, beneath the animalistic cries, it was the man trapped within who begged for forgiveness.

With the beast cornered, they cautiously approached, studying its form in the dim moonlight. Its sparse hair receded into its body, revealing the vulnerable figure beneath the monstrous exterior. Melvin walked alongside Calvin, his hand resting on his shoulder, gesturing for him to stop. Positioning the shotgun against the creature's forehead, Melvin guided its gaze upward, towards the moon, as it let out one final yowl, a somber acknowledgment of its inevitable fate.

As Melvin prepared to deliver the fatal blow, an eerie transformation unfolded before their eyes. The creature's face contorted, shifting into a semblance of a man's, its canine mouth whispering a heartfelt "Thank you." Melvin hesitated, unsettled by the human aspect of the creature before him, knowing instinctively everything about it was unnatural. Yet, as the body convulsed in reaction to the metal within, the man's eyes reflected a resigned acceptance of his fate, an understanding that death was preferable to a cursed existence.

Naked and vulnerable, the man lay sprawled on the ground, his shivering form a stark contrast to the looming figure of Melvin standing above him. His gaze, once fierce and wild, now held a haunting sadness, as if every line etched into his weathered face told a story of suffering and regret. In the dim moonlight, his eyes shimmered with unshed tears, reflecting the weight of a lifetime of anguish.

As Melvin hesitated, the silence of the night enveloped them, broken only by the ragged breaths of the fallen creature. Each exhale carried with it a lifetime of pain and sorrow, a testimony to the human soul trapped within the monstrous shell. With a heavy heart,

Melvin understood the mercy that lay in the final act, the release from a cursed existence that had brought nothing but torment and despair.

Melvin's hands trembled as he raised the shotgun, the cold metal glinting in the moonlight as it hovered over the man's forehead. For a fleeting moment, their eyes locked in a silent exchange, a wordless desire for understanding and forgiveness passing between them. In that moment, Melvin glimpsed the depths of the man's sorrow, the weight of his burden too heavy to bear.

And then, with a steady hand and a heavy heart, Melvin pulled the trigger. The deafening roar of the shotgun blast shattered the stillness of the night, sending shockwaves rippling through the air. The echoes reverberated through the darkness, carrying with them the weight of the man's sorrow and the burden of his pain. As the last echoes faded into silence, the night held its breath, as if mourning the passing of a tortured soul.

In the aftermath, as the crows scattered into the night, Melvin's soul felt alone, his heart heavy with the weight of what he had done. And though the man's suffering had come to an end, his sadness lingered in the air.

Meanwhile, Calvin draped his coat around Rebecca's shoulders for the second time that night, its warmth a small comfort against the cold night air. She leaned against him, her face contorted in pain as she cradled her abdomen, the aftermath of her reckless bravery weighing heavily on her. Rebecca had acted on instinct, driven by a desperate need to protect, but in her haste, she had underestimated the danger she faced.

A rustling sound behind her snapped her back to the present. She turned to see their youngest son approaching, his eyes wide with concern as he took in the scene. Ryan's gaze lingered on the scratches marring his father's arm, worry etched into his young face. The weight of the night's events settled heavily upon them all.

As they stood there, the tragic reality of the situation began to sink in. The man, now freed from his monstrous form, lay lifeless on the ground as his final moments had been a solemn plea for forgiveness, a desperate yearning for release from the torment that had consumed him. In his eyes, they had seen the heartbreaking story of a life cursed, each day a struggle against the beast within.

Calvin tightened his hold on Rebecca, drawing her closer as they both gazed at the fallen figure. The man's human eyes had spoken volumes, revealing a depth of suffering and sorrow that cut through the horror of his actions. His transformation back into a man had stripped away the fright, leaving behind only the raw, painful truth of his existence.

Rebecca's breath hitched as she rested her head against Calvin's shoulder, the pain in her abdomen a dull throb compared to the ache in her heart. She had thought she could be a hero, perhaps as a way to defy the cancer slowly claiming her body, but now she realized the futility of such thoughts. The real heroism lay in understanding and compassion, in seeing beyond the surface to the tortured soul beneath.

Did that thing do that to my dad? It doesn't look too deep, but he should go to the hospital just in case. Maybe the wolf had, like, rabies or something. "Mom? Dad?"

The lifeless body of the wolf came into Ryan's sight. Naked and twitching, its mouth and nose obliterated by Craggs' shotgun blast. It wasn't a wolf or a large dog; it was a dead, pale man lying in the middle of the cornfield. Sparse, dark hair covered his head, reminding Ryan of alopecia *something or another—I know there's another word there*, a condition a boy at school had.

The group circled around Eric Flanagan's twitching form, his shredded clothes barely clinging to his nearly naked body. Tears streamed down his face, eyes filled with a mix of fear and remorse as he gazed up at those he had threatened moments ago. Ryan stood at a distance, convinced Eric was on the brink of death.

"No, no, my love! You shouldn't see this!" Rebecca cried, placing her arm on Ryan's back and turning him away from the gruesome scene. Confusion and fear laced his voice as he demanded answers. "What the hell was that?" he questioned. "Nothing you need to bother yourself with," his mother replied sternly, her voice fearful. Calvin noticed his son's agitation and turned toward him, his own arm marked with three bleeding scratches, but Ryan's focus remained on the lifeless man on the ground.

"You went after a wolf. I saw it! That wasn't an animal!" Ryan insisted.

Rebecca urgently put a finger to her lips, trying to silence his questioning. "Listen to me, boy! Best you forget about this tonight as best you can. I'm going to."

"But!" Ryan interjected.

"No! Shut your mouth!" she snapped, her tone brooking no argument.

Ryan's posture deflated, and he gave up trying to get answers, realizing he wouldn't prevail against his mother's stern insistence. "We need to take care of this. Take Valerie and go back to the house, and don't say anything about what you saw. Don't need the town thinkin' I'm raisin' a loon." Ryan lowered his brow, understanding the gravity of his mother's warning.

"No one will believe this. We have to make sure no questions are asked. Do you understand?" Ryan nodded and walked away, confused and disappointed in the woman who should stand for truth. But this—*this was different.*

He understood the burden his parents now carried, yet he resented that it fell upon them. The day would come when he'd seek answers, but not tonight. Ryan never fully grasped the term "ignorance is bliss." After tonight, he would have given anything to rewind time and refrain from pursuing the creature into the field.

Valerie, quivering in the frigid night winds, smeared Eric's blood over her costume as she attempted to wipe it away. She walked alongside Ryan on their way back to his house, where Devin and the others anxiously waited. The journey felt long and arduous, the silence between them thick with the weight of the night's surreal events. How could they ever convey the tale of Halloween night in 1988 to anyone? Ryan glanced at Valerie, noticing a slight bleed on her leg from the cuts on her leggings.

When she saw Devin lingering outside the house, tears welled up in her eyes. Valerie rushed over to him, embracing him tightly and sobbing into his shoulder. This moment had occupied Devin's thoughts for years—what her embrace would be like—but reality differed from his dream-like scenario. Ryan observed Valerie

THE HUNTERS MOON

CHAPTER ELEVEN

THIS CHARMING MAN

Everything has changed, but everyone looks the same. Like nothing happened.

The tone had shifted.

As the holidays approached, Layla took it upon herself to replace the cardboard Halloween decorations with Thanksgiving-themed ones she made at school. The Hatcher family had a yearly tradition of taping these school-made decorations onto the windows. It was the usual set – Devin and Ryan had crafted the same ones in the past: a crayon-colored cornucopia, a brown turkey with cardboard feathers attached by a clip, and pilgrim hats. The Jack-o-lantern was removed from the doorstep, and the moveable skeleton hanging on the front door was taken down.

Two weeks had passed since the Halloween monster attack. Everyone appeared to have moved on, never discussing the unsettling event. Ryan couldn't comprehend why no one wanted to talk about it. His closest circle—Devin, Scott, and Christina—were oblivious to what he witnessed that night. He repeatedly contemplated if silence was the best solution.

Devin reveled in the aftermath, soaking in the attention Valerie gave him. Unfortunately, the focus was on Eric and his condition at Akron General and the night of the incident. Ryan wasn't sure if Valerie had disclosed the whole truth to his brother or if she omitted certain parts to avoid sounding mad. Regardless, Ryan figured Devin wouldn't mind as he enjoyed the attention and friendly affection. Christina's attitude towards Ryan, however, remained wishy-washy.

On some days, she clung to Ryan's side at every opportunity, much to his annoyance. On others, she was distant. Ryan often pondered how their conversation might have unfolded if it weren't for the fear interrupting them. *Would we have become a couple? Would I have just wanted to be friends?* All Ryan knew was the days when Christina avoided him were more challenging than when she annoyed him.

His best friend, Scott, appeared unaffected by the attack. Scott wasn't oblivious; he understood what happened with the wolf a couple of weeks ago wasn't natural. However, he chose silence, treating it like a delusion rather than reality. Scott sensed something was troubling both his friend and his sister. He knew Ryan was keeping something from him.

And he was.

Ryan was aware that Scott might not believe him, so he avoided him when he thought questioning might happen.

Even more peculiar were the interactions among the sets of parents who witnessed the incident firsthand. They now engaged in more frequent conversations, like when Calvin and Rick collaborated. Even Ryan's parents were getting along again, although Calvin still rented a small apartment in Akron, somewhat far from his family. Ryan no longer cared if his father ever returned home because the clock was ticking for his mother now—his primary concern. He had become numb to everything else around him, consumed by thoughts of Halloween night.

Who was that man? What happened to the body? Was there even a man? I can't be the only one who saw the wolf's size. Why is no one talking about this? Ryan remained quiet, keeping a hidden secret in his eyes he didn't want anyone to know.

Layla was a different story.

She had always been slightly different from other kids her age, which often left her feeling isolated. It never troubled her much since it meant more time to focus on her grades. Layla found solace in her stuffed animals, playing the roles of both mother and doctor to them as if they were alive. Since the end of October, she had shifted her attention from dolls to an obsession with her Lite-Brite set. She requested more blank pages from the store, creating brightly lit artworks while speaking softly to invisible companions.

Calvin and Rebecca weren't too concerned about this change in their daughter's behavior, attributing it to Layla's unique personality.

While they took no issue with the idea of their daughter talking to the air, Ryan remained on edge.

Ryan had seen the shadow at the end of the hall, terrifying him night after night. He witnessed an apparition reenacting its death, without any context about who or what caused it. He saw it reaching for a bloodied dress shoe attached to a leg in the woods. Normally timid, Ryan was confident he was on the verge of a nervous breakdown. He stayed awake at night in bed, refusing to leave. Some nights, he held his urine when he needed to relieve himself, eventually soiling his underwear and pajamas—*a small price for safety.*

It was Friday, November 17th, marking two weeks since the wolf attacks. Yet, there were no news reports, radio broadcasts, or missing person bulletins regarding the man who perished in the cornfield. No murmurs circulated among homemakers sharing gossip with their husbands about the mysterious events of Halloween night. The silence was too coordinated, too calculated. For Ryan, the absence of any evidence only pointed to one conclusion—the adults disposed of the body and moved on without a second glance.

"When your mom bakes a cake, how does she know it's done? What kind of cake do you enjoy? And how about the frosting?" Colin settled beside Ryan on the bus, his eyes wide with curiosity. The two had been assigned to hang banners for Norton's Fall Festival after talking during class, and now there were no empty seats left.

"She uses a toothpick to check if the insides are cooked through. I like lemon-flavored cake with white icing. Why?" Ryan replied, intrigued by the line of questioning.

"I'm trying to decide what kind of cake I want to make for my birthday party tomorrow."

Oh, shit! That's tomorrow! I totally forgot.

"Why do you have to make the cake? I thought someone else does it for the person's birthday."

Colin shrugged, his crooked smile full of determination. "I just want to do it myself. I want to practice in case I need to make something one day."

Ryan nodded. "Cool." He admired Colin's drive but dreaded attending the party. *What if no one else shows up? It'll be so awkward.*

The bus halted in front of Colin's house. "See you tomorrow, Ryan. The thing starts at eleven o'clock," Colin called out, walking down the aisle.

"In the morning?" Ryan teased, though his heart sank at the early hour. Colin laughed, stepping off the bus.

Dammit! That means I'll have to get up earlier. Ryan had become a night owl, relishing the late mornings on weekends.

Christina slid into the seat beside him. "That's the last time, Miss White," the driver warned.

"Sure thing!" Christina grinned, flipping the bird behind the bus driver's back.

Ryan chuckled, surprised by Christina's boldness. *That's the first time I've seen her do that*, he thought.

"So...you're mad at me," Christina said, her tone direct.

"What? No, I'm not."

Christina sighed in relief. "Will you tell me what's up then?"

Ryan slid down in his seat, shaking his head. Christina leaned closer. "You know I'm just going to keep bugging you until you let me in a little."

"Maybe when we get off the bus. But we have to be quiet. I don't want Layla to know or get scared," Ryan whispered.

The bus stopped at their usual spot. Ryan placed a protective hand on Layla's shoulder, guiding her safely across the road. Layla, oblivious to the darker reality, skipped ahead in her corduroy pants and red cardigan.

"What's bothering you?" Scott asked, joining them on the walk home.

"I've been asking the same thing," Christina chimed in. "Moody McGee over here is being stubborn."

"He's been in a wee bit of a snit," Layla added, her ponytail bouncing.

"Shut it, dingleberry!" Ryan shouted, stifling a laugh. Scott turned right towards his house, leaving Ryan, Christina, and Layla to go left. "Hang out this weekend?" Scott called.

"Probably. I have a thing tomorrow," Ryan replied.

"Just call when you're ready," Scott said, waving goodbye. Christina slipped her hand into Ryan's jean jacket pocket, their fingers intertwining.

The day was brisk but sunny, and Ryan savored the light as winter's shorter days approached. "Do you think we could hang out more this winter than we usually do?" he asked.

Christina's eyes lit up. "Yeah! I mean, sure. That sounds cool."

As Layla ran ahead, Ryan saw his chance. "I want to tell you. I do. It's just—I'm not even sure what the problem is. Even if I did, I'm not sure you'd understand," Ryan said, avoiding her gaze.

"You don't know that!" she insisted. Christina knew she had to be patient with Ryan. "I'll be around next week until Wednesday. We're leaving for South Carolina."

"What's in South Carolina?" Ryan asked.

"An uncle of my mom's side. My cousin Allen is there. He's pretty cool. Obnoxious sometimes, but cool."

Ryan was glad she was getting away for a while. "That's good. You should see your family more." Christina smiled, relieved by his positive tone. She slid her hand out of his pocket, but he didn't let go. Instead, he pulled her closer, wrapping his arm around her. It wasn't the first time they hugged, but it was the first time he initiated it. Ryan's arms circled her waist, and she breathed in, holding her breath as he rested his head on her shoulder. She blew out frigid air, loving every second.

Ryan inhaled the scent of her hair—lavender with a hint of vanilla. "Is this okay?" he asked, his voice cracking.

"Yeah. It's good—new. What's gotten into you?" Christy asked. Ryan sighed.

"You did. You got into my head—in the best way. I'm not good at explaining."

Christina smiled, her heart full. "Well," she trembled, "I think that is just the best." She shuddered, love-drunk and stumbling over her words.

They pulled from one another, a mix of happiness and nerves evident in their expressions. The wind playfully tossed Christina's blonde hair across her face, partially obscuring her bright smile. Ryan's own smile was crooked, a blend of embarrassment and relief he had finally shared something genuine with her, even if it was a bit cheesy. They awkwardly said their goodbyes, each feeling lighter, and walked away with a noticeable skip in their steps. Christina glanced back to see if Ryan was watching her, but he wasn't. If she had waited a moment longer, she would have caught him looking back.

Ryan walked down the driveway, noting his father's car was in the garage instead of its usual spot on the road. *That's strange. He doesn't see us until tomorrow morning.* His concern grew—had something happened to his mother? He was about to rush inside when he heard a giggle from the other side of the yard.

A large flock of blackbirds circled above, their numbers darkening the sky as they occasionally landed to peck at the grass. Ryan moved towards the sound of laughter, finding Layla running around, tapping the air and giggling uncontrollably. Watching her, he realized she was playing some sort of game, stopping periodically to tap the air and then running off again. "Goose!" she finally yelled, dashing towards the patio stairs and then veering sharply towards the large tree with the swing their father had put up.

Layla stopped, looking around with a pout. "That's not fair!... Okay, fine. You can be it now, I guess."

Ryan's gaze returned to the birds; more had joined the flock, appearing unsettled. He ran across the yard, shouting for Layla to come inside. The birds cawed louder, circling lower. Layla, still laughing at her invisible playmates, didn't understand Ryan's urgency. He grabbed her, pulling her back to the driveway near the garage. "No!" he yelled. "Can't you see the birds?"

Layla stilled, watching the flock land on the grass. Ryan dragged her to the patio stairs, both of them stepping backwards, eyes fixed on the shifting sea of blackbirds. From their vantage point, they saw five bare spots where the birds wouldn't go.

"They just want to be seen," Layla explained dimly.

Ryan's gaze fixated on the flurry of feathers outside the window, his unease evident in the tense set of his jaw and the furrow of his brow. He observed the birds' erratic movements, their fluttering wings casting shadows against the invisible forces guiding them. With each twirl and dive, they formed a perfect, untouched circle on the lawn, a indication to the unseen at play.

Beside him, Layla's breath hitched, her eyes wide with fear and fascination. The siblings exchanged a glance, acknowledging the ominous spectacle unfolding before them. As they retreated up the stairs, the ancient wood groaned beneath their weight, a foreboding soundtrack to their retreat.

The circle of grass, untouched by the swirling mass of crows, loomed closer—a void amidst the chaos of feathers and caws.. Ryan felt his heart race, each beat reverberating in his ears like a warning drumroll heralding imminent danger. Beyond the barrier of the sliding glass door, the safety of the kitchen appeared a distant sanctuary, tauntingly out of reach.

In a desperate bid to escape the encroaching menace, Ryan's hand sought Layla's, trembling fingers finding solace in the familiarity of their grip. With a surge of urgency, he pulled her towards the glass door, their footsteps echoing in the tense silence of the room. But as his palm met the icy surface, a wave of dread washed over him—a chilling realization that their means of escape was barred, condemning them to face the looming threat trapped within their own home. "Damn it!" Ryan's curse echoed in the air, frustration and fear intertwining in his voice like tendrils of despair.

Inside, their mother Rebecca was talking to someone, probably Devin. Ryan knocked frantically on the glass, trying to get her attention. She glanced over, motioning for them to wait. *What the hell is she doing?*

The footsteps on the stairs grew louder, each creak of the wooden boards sent a tremor up Ryan's back. His knuckles whitened as he pounded on the window, the glass vibrating with his frantic efforts, a futile attempt to ward off the encroaching dread. Panic clawed at his chest as the sounds drew nearer, a relentless march of impending horror.

A quick glance over his shoulder revealed nothing but darkness, yet the oppressive presence in the air was suffocating, tangible in its malevolence. Layla pressed against his side, her voice a trembling whisper in the suffocating silence. "They don't look right, Ryan. They look bad again."

A hush fell over the world, a chilling stillness choking the very air from their lungs. The large murder of crows outside ceased their ominous cawing, their dark forms frozen in mid-flight, a quiet omen of impending doom. Were they gone? Ryan's fingers tapped lightly on the glass, a request echoing in the emptiness of his mind, praying for salvation from the unseen horror lurking just beyond.

With a hesitant breath, he opened his eyes, relief flooding his senses as the patio appeared normal once more. But the illusion shattered with a sickening scrape of metal against wood, the grill pushed aside by an unseen force. In the reflection of the glass, grotesque figures emerged from the darkness, their decaying forms a grotesque mockery of life.

Rotting corpses surrounded them, their bodies putrid and decayed, a nightmarish tableau of horror. A jaw hung loosely from one face, while another picked at decaying flesh with skeletal fingers. A well-dressed man struggled to keep his crumbling head from toppling off his neck, while blood gushed from the gaping wound of a boy's groin. Each figure bore the scars of their demise, a grotesque display of suffering frozen in time.

Ryan's grip tightened on Layla's hand, a suppressed scream building in his throat as he fought against the overwhelming urge to flee. A rush of warm air heralded their mother's arrival, her silhouette framed in the doorway as she finally opened it to reveal sanctuary within. With a desperate cry, Ryan dragged Layla inside, both collapsing onto the kitchen floor.

"Close the door!" he shouted, his voice, a blend of relief and lingering fear.

Rebecca knelt, her arms reaching out to help her children to their feet. "Was it so damn hard to open the door when we knocked? We were standing right there!" Ryan's voice erupted, the strain of frustration evident in his tone, a rare display since his mother's diagnosis. "Watch yo' tongue with me, boy!" Rebecca shot back, her scowl proving her authority.

"Watch your mouth!" another voice interjected, stern and commanding. Ryan turned, surprised to find his father, Calvin, leaning against the counter, his presence unexpected in this tense moment. *The hell is he doing here?* His father appeared different, freshly shaved and trimmer than usual, a subtle change maybe, but still unsettled Ryan.

Ryan's mind raced with questions. *How could nobody else be curious about this sudden change in dad?* This immediate shift in appearance and attitude didn't just happen overnight. Ryan might have been young, but he knew enough to be suspicious.

Calvin took Rebecca's hand, looking at his kids with a mixture of excitement and apprehension. "So we have a little announcement." Rebecca smiled at him warmly. "Do you want to tell them, Becs?" Rebecca giggled, her cheeks flushing. "That's okay. You can, love."

"You can! I know you want to," Calvin replied, their playful banter making Ryan and Devin cringe. *What's with all the lovey-dovey crap?*

"Sweet Jesus! Can you two get on with it then?" an irritated Devin shouted.

"A'ight then! Get your underwear outta ya bum," Rebecca hissed in a thick accent, clearly annoyed by Devin's attempt to spoil the moment. She took a deep breath and smiled at her children. "So after some discussion, your father and I thought it would be best if he moved back in."

Layla's eyes lit up. "Yay!" she clapped, hopping out from her seat and hugging her daddy. Her excitement bubbled over, joyful at the prospect of them all being a family again. "This is such good news!" she squealed. The high-pitched noise made Devin wrinkle his nose, his face contorting in mock agony. With his eyes closed tight, he joked, "Layla, please don't do that. I think only dogs could hear you," hoping to lighten the moment without hurting her feelings. Rebecca laughed, removing her fingers from her ears, the ringing still faintly there.

"Why?" Ryan asked candidly. "I mean, like, why now?" Calvin and Rebecca exchanged a glance, a mute agreement passing between them about who should speak first.. Rebecca nodded, signaling Calvin to go ahead.

"Well," Calvin began, "The short answer is that we think it's time for us to be together as a family. With your mother going through what she is and how it may be affecting you kids… well… I think some things need mending. We haven't dealt with the news about your mom so well. I love your good ol' mom, and I don't want her to be alone. I want to be around her and all of you. I made a mistake by making it about me and how I couldn't deal with it, but I'm trying to now. After months of thinking, I realized I'd rather have more bad days with all of you than one day of just existing without you."

A slow clap echoed from the end of the dinner table. Calvin looked up to find Devin clapping sarcastically, his expression filled with disdain. "Bravo. Seriously, if I had an Oscar, I'd give it to you for that powerful performance. I'm sure plenty of people would buy it."

Rebecca's eyes flashed with anger, her hand twitching as if she wanted to reach across the table and smack Devin for his disrespect. "That's enough out of you, cheeky little shit!" Devin never bought into the saying one should respect their elders. To him, respect worked both ways, and watching his parents fight a few months back had eroded all respect he had for his dad.

"I swear to Christ, Devin," his mother hissed. Devin threw his arms in the air, frustration etched across his face. "What? Please tell me, what is going to make everything better?" Rebecca put her hands on her forehead, visibly exhausted from talking to her stubborn son.

"It's fine," Calvin assured his wife. "It's a valid question even if there was another way of going about it." Devin and Ryan sat in silence, waiting for their father to gather his thoughts. Calvin, unsure of how his boys would react, hesitated. They were protective of their mother, and he knew Ryan would likely be the more understanding of the two.

"So, I'm on vacation until the beginning of January. I had some time saved up and thought of all the times to be home, now would be it. I haven't had any alcohol since around Halloween. I've been working out more, trying to watch what I eat. Since October, I've had this jolt of energy during the day giving me a drive in a way I have never known before. I know this doesn't make sense because of the suddenness, but I hope you can help me along the way."

Both Ryan and Devin looked away, lost in their thoughts. Devin, ever the pessimist, found it hard to believe people his father's age could undergo such a complete change. Calvin had always treated Devin differently, often berating him about his grades, his friends, and his interests. Devin began shaking his head, clenching his jaw to keep the peace. "Doesn't really matter. I have no say in this. I just hope you're right in thinking everything will be hunky-dory one day, Mom," he finally spoke after minutes of contemplation.

Ryan, deep in his thoughts, was skeptical of the changes his father claimed. It wasn't that he didn't believe his dad could improve, but the sudden transformation in his physical appearance was irksome. *No one changes so drastically in just a few weeks. Do they?*

Ryan's eyes traced his father's figure, taking in the rolled-up sleeves of his white thermal shirt. The hair on Calvin's arms was as black as on his head, and the scratches that had once marred his skin were now gone. It had been a couple of weeks, so the healing wasn't surprising, but something still nagged at Ryan. "The scratches you had on your arm, what caused them?"

Calvin glanced down, recognizing the concern in his son's eyes. "Nothin' big. I just tripped and landed in a thorn bush. That's all."

They stared at each other until Ryan nodded and forced a smile. "Just wonderin'." The conversation about their restored living arrangement had ended, and everyone began to devour their pizza. Devin, Layla, and their father shoveled melted cheese and processed meat into their mouths. Even their mother had a decent appetite, taking more substantial bites than usual, though at a slower pace.

Ryan sat back, observing his family as they ate like wild animals. The noise around him faded, replaced by the sounds of chewing, swallowing, and slurping echoing in his head. He fixated on their mouths, noticing the saliva escaping as they chewed with their mouths open. Strings of saliva stretched between their lips when they opened wide, revealing food stuck between their teeth, and their loud swallowing sounds became too much for Ryan to handle.

Visions of the wolf from days ago flashed before his eyes. His family's mouth noises reminded him of the beast's fangs tearing into Eric Flanagan's skin as it carried him away.

Something was wrong. Ryan didn't know what—*that's a lie*. He did but admitting it to himself would drive him more insane than he already thought he was.

CHAPTER TWELVE

UNDER PRESSURE

On a Saturday morning, Ryan, once again, struggled with sleep. The potential invasion of poltergeists lingering about the house wasn't what kept him up. He wasn't even sure if they were real or if they would cause any physical harm to him or his family. No, it was something else now. It was the idea of something even more terrifying to Ryan if what he witnessed on Halloween was true—the existence of werewolves in Norton, Ohio.

He stumbled into the kitchen with half-shut eyes, sat in his usual place at the table, and placed his forehead on the surface. "Well, you seem to be full bricks in ya feet this mornin'," Rebecca said to her son with a fizzy laugh, the kind where air sputters. *Her accent is thick this morning*, Ryan thought. He moaned, displeased he was up at all. "That moan has a hint of whine to it," she pointed out. "Doughnuts are on the counter courtesy of your dad."

"Is anyone else up?" Ryan yawned as he shuffled his raccoon slippers over the linoleum. The options of fried dough were plenty. It was the first time Ryan had ever gotten first dibs on the doughnuts, and wouldn't you know it; there was a crème-filled long john from Jubilee Doughnuts waiting just for him. He never complained about the lack of options when someone brought home doughnuts. Every Wednesday, his mom took Layla and him to Jubilee, across the street from their schools. They liked to sit in the fifties styled shop at the counter with the round stool they twirled on.

"Layla, but she hasn't been out of her room yet. Your brutha is sleeping in as usual. Your dad is down in the garage coming up with a new project to do now that he's home," Rebecca listed as Ryan shoved the long john in his face. "And you have that get together around eleven this mornin'."

Ryan's body deflated, remembering he had to go to Colin's party. "How did you know about that?"

"The mother, I think, called to make sure," Rebecca informed. Ryan waited to see if his mother would add to the thought, but she went back to tearing off pieces of her glazed doughnut, not enjoying it like she used to. "And?"

"And what?"

"What did you tell her?" Ryan said slowly with raised eyebrows.

"Oh! That you'll be there before noon," she said with a devilish grin.

"Aw, mom!" Ryan slumped in his seat. "Why'd you tell 'em that?" Rebecca shrugged her bony shoulders, not understanding the issue. "I don't think I want to go," Ryan admitted.

Rebecca breathed in heavily, keeping herself from yelling at her son, "You are most certainly going!" Annoyed, Ryan curled his lip at his mom, scoffing at the thought she had some say about where he went. *As if she could make me.*

"It's going to suck. I know it will! I won't have a good time. I'll just be miserable!" Rebecca shook her head in disgust at the thought he would be unhappy at a party. He doesn't know what being miserable is, she thought.

"But it ain't all about you then, now is it?" Rebecca argued, her voice rising as she loomed over Ryan. They stood face-to-face, his confusion plain. "What if you being there is what the boy is looking forward to the most? Maybe he thinks you're great, and that's why he invited you. What if no one else shows up? He'd be stood up by a friend who decided he wasn't worth the time."

Rebecca leaned against the counter, her gaze drifting to the yard. She was lost in a memory of a birthday back home when no one showed up, the heartbreak still fresh to her. "If taking a few hours of your time brings one person a great memory, one they won't forget, ain't it worth it? For the boy to look back on today and remember you being there. We owe it to people, and ourselves, to try and make memories because that's all this life is, Ryan—a series of moments. Might as well make the best ones because there will be bad, even sad ones sometimes, I can assure you."

Her words hung in the air, heavy with unspoken meaning. Ryan wondered if she was talking about herself and her own passing. He decided he'd go to Colin's house, if only to make his mom happy. "Besides, if you don't go, I'm going to send you with your father to Builder's Square to buy lumber and all that." The threat of a hardware store visit, especially for a nerd like him, sealed the deal. Ryan immediately agreed to see Colin because *going to the hardware store is a special level of torture.*

Rebecca watched her son eat another long john before he headed off to shower and get dressed for the get-together. "Are you taking me?" Ryan yelled from down the hall.

"No. Just take your bike or walk," she yelled back. Ryan hadn't ridden his bike in months, having outgrown it. He didn't want a new one, figuring a car was in his near future. *My parents buying a car for me would be badass.*

Ryan entered the bathroom, preparing to leave for the afternoon, as Devin emerged from his room, which he fondly called the dungeon, to discover a lack of doughnut options in the kitchen. "Who the hell ate all the long johns?"

"Your brutha beat ya to it 'dis mornin'," Rebecca cheerfully informed him, grinning behind a coffee mug. Devin, with all his fabricated angst, snatched the pink-frosted strawberry doughnut from the box. "Wait a bit!" she yelled before Devin could walk down the hallway. "You're going next door and helping Mr. Craggs with housework and whatever else he needs for the next couple of weeks."

Devin curled his lips and wrinkled his nose, placing the doughnut back in his hand. "My ass I am. Why?"

Rebecca put her mug on the kitchen table, bracing herself for the upcoming conversation, knowing it might exhaust her. "Watch your tongue with me, boy! You need something else to do besides mope in that dark room of yers. There is something in it for ya when you complete it at the end of the two weeks."

"Like what?" Devin asked with folded arms, indicating skepticism.

"Does it matta? Ya doin' it one way or another," she demanded, laying the accent on thick. Devin petulantly hopped in his seat. "Your other choice is to help your dad with rebuilding the shed. I know how much it may interest you, and you can start by going to the hardware store with him."

The shed in the Hatcher's backyard was a tetanus infection ready to happen. The rickety structure leaned to the right, and remnants of its white paint clung to the rotting wood. It housed mice most of the year; once, Calvin scared a mouse so bad it released its litter suddenly—true story. Weathered wood and wasp nests made the shed a danger zone. It desperately needed rebuilding.

Devin glanced at his options, disliking both. One had a possible reward, the other meant spending time with his father, which he wanted to avoid. "Are we ever going to discuss what happened?" a fed-up Devin asked, not beating around the bush.

"Ain't nothing to discuss. Things happen. It don't make 'em right, but we move on as best we can. Maybe you should too." Devin didn't want to argue with his ill mother, but so much anger festered within him he didn't know how to convey it. "Your father will be the only parent ya got sooner or later. Start figuring ya shit out! Yeah?"

Devin's breathing grew heavy, his lips tight, his face a storm of hate with nowhere to unleash it. "It should have been him."

"What did ya say?" Rebecca's eyes flashed with shock and fury.

"I said it should be his miserable ass on a deathbed soon, not you!" Devin spat out, his words dripping with venom.

Despite the pain coursing through her body, an enraged Rebecca stormed over and slapped Devin's face, the jelly-filled pastry dropping from his mouth. The sting in her palm burned, and she clutched it with her other hand, her lips quivering. She never imagined she would strike her child, the emotional pain far worse than the physical ache in her brittle fingers. "Don't you ever say that again!" she commanded, her mouth quivered as she fought back tears. "Your father isn't a perfect man, but you ain't either. So get off your holier-than-thou pedestal and be a son."

Devin rubbed his cheek, a red mark forming where her hand had struck. Rebecca's voice softened, filled with regret. "I'm sorry. We all go a little crazy sometimes and let the animal out. I know that now," she whispered, recalling the moment weeks ago when she had told her husband to leave.

Devin replaced his harsh words with a vigorous nod. Rising from the table, he picked up the fallen doughnut, now misshapen, and muttered, "I'll be next door," before heading out to assist Mr. Craggs with household chores.

On his way to his room, Devin peeked in on Layla, who was engrossed in her Lite Brite set, inserting colorful pegs into tiny holes. "Hey, Layloo," he greeted, still shaken from the altercation.

Layla's Teddy Ruxpin bear on the dresser shifted its eyes slowly at Devin, the cogs inside whirring. A strange, almost spiritual force appeared to possess the toy, craving acknowledgment from him. Layla turned her hand towards it and remarked, "It's fine."

Devin, oblivious to the subtle movement of the mostly inanimate bear, looked around. "What is?"

Layla paused her creative work, locking eyes with her brother. "Nothing."

"Better grab a doughnut before they disappear, Layloo," Devin suggested.

She nodded, seemingly uninterested in eating. Focused on her mission to craft pictures, she had already amassed a stack of thick black sheets of paper with punched holes. "Okay," she replied, returning to her Lite Brite, subtly signaling her brother to leave.

Devin complied, but had he lingered, he might have seen Layla constructing a hallway on the lightboard, one resembling their house with a white figure standing in it. The figure would have been black, but transparent pegs in that color weren't available, as they wouldn't contrast against the background.

***

Devin Hatcher and Melvin Craggs had never conversed before. Despite living side by side, their interactions were limited to disingenuous waves from Devin's childhood when he was outside with his mom. Devin knew Melvin didn't care for his dad; a sentiment Devin currently shared.

Typically, the Hatchers found Melvin tinkering in his garage during the day, but this time was different. Devin stepped into Melvin's garage, noticing it was more organized than he remembered. Not much caught his eye except for a machine under a black tarp on the left side. A shelf filled with magazines in a water-stained cardboard box piqued Devin's interest. Glancing around to ensure no one was watching, he started thumbing through the different publications, discovering old issues of *Guns and Ammo*, *Playboy*, *Penthouse*, and oddly enough, *Vogue*. "Craggs, you dirty old man. Guns and hot women. Whatever fills your rub tub, I suppose," he muttered to himself.

"What you doin', boy?" Melvin's voice echoed from behind a screen door. "See somethin' you like?"

Startled by Melvin's smoky voice, Devin's heart skipped a beat. "I wasn't! I just…You got a lot of magazines."

"You ain't seen nothin'," Melvin replied. "Why you in my garage?"

Regaining composure, Devin cleared his throat. "My mom said I should come over and help you with your house. Whatever that means."

Melvin scrutinized Devin and nodded. "A'ight."

When Melvin opened the screen door, the stench of cigars and perspiration from inside his home overwhelmed the garage. The smell, a blend of onions on a Skyline chili dog mixed with clothes left in the washer for too long, unsettled Devin, who was used to the cleanliness of his own home.

"Your mama tells me that ya bored. Need somethin' to keep ya busy," Melvin continued.

"If I had more magazines, I wouldn't be," Devin joked, realizing too late the implication of his words. Expecting Melvin to kick him out, he was surprised when the old man raised an eyebrow and looked him up and down.

"Sense of humor. You goin' to need dat," Melvin cracked a smile, walking back into his house. "Come on then. Best you see what you're working wit now. Pull off da Band-Aid, as dey say."

As Devin followed Craggs into what he assumed was the living room, he thought, *how does someone live like this?* Old newspapers and magazines covered most of the hardwood floors, creating a cluttered environment Devin hesitated to tread on for fear of crushing something.

Melvin navigated through the maze of magazines with ease, finding his recliner and settling into it. Devin, curious, examined the spines of the magazines to discern his neighbor's reading preferences. Each stack represented a different type of publication—*Rolling Stone* along one wall, Time Magazine on the opposite side, Newsweek in the middle of the floor near the television, *National Geographic* overflowing from bookshelves, and oddly, Better Homes and Gardens—*Better Homes and Gardens?* Alongside neatly piled Playboys in the corners.

As Melvin settled into his recliner, the room echoed with the sounds of old man groans, exhales, and a small curdle of snot. Devin, standing by the adult magazines, inquired, "Why do you have so many of these magazines?" referring to all of them, not just the adult ones.

"For the articles, genius—whaddya think they're for?" Melvin sarcastically replied. "Why? You want to borrow one?" Devin considered the offer but quickly decided against it for sanitary reasons. "No, thanks. I mean, why keep all of these?"

Lighting a cigar, Melvin sighed, pondering Devin's question. "Don't know for sure. I guess I was tired of living in an empty house." Devin felt a surprising twinge of sympathy for Melvin. There was a profound silence between them until Devin broke it. "So. What do ya want me to do?"

Returning from his thoughts, Melvin pointed to the stacks of magazines. "All 'dem are goin' to be recycled. Maybe make me some money."

Devin glanced around the room at the vast collection and laughed. "No way."

Melvin held Devin's gaze until he understood. "Wait. Like, really? All of these?"

"Yeah. Start putting 'em in the back of the truck. Go to the garage and get the hand cart. It'll make it easier," Melvin suggested. The prospect of parting with the things keeping him connected to the world made Melvin melancholy. Unbeknownst to others, he had learned about music, politics, news, and even decorating from those papers. However, as time went on, the world became stranger to him, and he lost interest. For Melvin Craggs, the world grew more significant with its advancements, and he found himself a lonely stranger, wandering aimlessly. Unsure of what was happening, he waited for nature to take its course.

***

Attempting to gather speed on a bike too small for his size, Ryan pedaled uphill along the bustling street toward Colin's house. Norton wasn't particularly bike-friendly, lacking sidewalks along the roads. The cold air made Ryan's nose run, and he had to pause every few blocks to wipe it on his gloves.

As Ryan approached Colin's place, his anticipation of a warm and lively party filled him with excitement. However, as he neared the house, his enthusiasm waned. The scene before him spoke volumes, painting a picture of neglect and desolation.

The dirt driveway, once probably neat and tidy, now resembled more of a rugged path, its surface marred by patches of dried mud and overgrown weeds. Ryan's gaze swept across the yard, which appeared as though forgotten by time. Toys lay scattered haphazardly: their vibrant colors dulled by a layer of dirt and grime, a small wasteland of their abandonment.

The screened-in porch, a once inviting space, now stood as a dilapidated structure on the verge of collapse. Its blue paint, once vibrant and fresh, now cracked and chipped, peeling away in places, revealing the weathered wood beneath. The chimney, missing several bricks, stood vigilant, weathered by the elements.

The only vehicle parked in the vicinity was a rusted beige van, its once shiny exterior now dulled by rust and neglect. Its presence, incongruous amidst the desolation. *I expected more cars for a party.*

As Ryan took in the scene before him, a sense of unease crept over him. This was not the bustling party mood he had anticipated. Instead, it felt like a forgotten corner of the world, frozen in time, with only whispers of past celebrations lingering in the air.

A gentle knock on the front door prompted a young voice, presumably Carlton, to shout, "Someone's here!" Multiple children's babble overlapped in response. Those must be the other guests, Ryan thought.

The creaking wooden door revealed an overweight woman, appearing to be in her fifties. She had a worn-out but friendly demeanor, asking, "You must be Ryan!"

"Yes, ma'am," Ryan politely replied.

"Well then! A boy with manners? Those tend to be rare, especially with this bunch. Call me Mary. Come on in!" She gestured toward the inside of her house, and Ryan entered slowly. Taking in the air, he realized why Colin often smelled of various foods. The whole place had a distinct odor, a blend of meals lingering over time, as if the home hadn't been ventilated in months. While Ryan couldn't pinpoint any specific smells, it was undeniably pungent.

Navigating through the foyer, Ryan nearly tripped over multiple pairs of shoes on his way to the living room. Kids of various ages and ethnicities were scattered across numerous couches and chairs, engrossed in watching *The Never Ending Story*. Atreyu was about to pass the giant sphinxes with wings, and the boys giggled over the statues' exaggerated features. The same thing had happened in Ryan's class a few months ago when they watched it.

Ryan's eyes darted around, taking in the cluttered room, the piles of mismatched shoes by the door, and the faded wallpaper peeling at the edges. The stridency of children's voices mixed with the movie's soundtrack, creating a chaotic yet oddly inviting surrounding. As he settled into an empty seat, he felt a mix of awkwardness and curiosity, wondering how the day would unfold in this unexpectedly lively setting.

Colin's buddy, Ryan, entered with a jovial announcement. "This is Colin's buddy, Ryan. Say hello, everyone!" Mary yelled. Instantly, all heads turned, youthful anticipation lighting up their faces as they welcomed a new addition to their gathering.

Mary took charge of introductions, her voice resonating through the room, even reaching the two slumbering infants tucked away down the hall. "Pizza's on its way, about thirty minutes out. We snagged a couple of videos from the store on Market Street. Colin's in the kitchen, whipping up his cake. You can catch him in there."

"Making his own cake?" Ryan's curiosity piqued, momentarily forgetting his earlier conversation with the birthday boy.

"It's just a quirky thing he likes to try. There's a store-bought one if that homemade masterpiece is devoured—and trust me, it will be. We'll need it with this many mouths." Mary grinned knowingly, a shared understanding passing between them.

Ryan's brow furrowed slightly, a puzzled smile gracing his lips as he wondered why Colin had taken on the task of baking his own cake. As he stepped onto the faded, yellow linoleum, its once bright hue now dulled with age, Ryan found Colin patiently waiting for the cake to cool.

"Hey, man!" Ryan greeted with a sense of relief, grateful for the respite from the bustling living room that triggered his social anxiety. Colin's smile lit up the room, his raspy voice breaking the silence. "Cool! You made it on time! Just waiting for it to cool down."

Recalling Colin's earlier interrogation about cake making, Ryan attempted to steer the conversation toward a new topic. "Do you enjoy cooking?" he inquired, already anticipating the response.

"I hear it's a way to a person's heart. Well…wait. The way to a man's heart is through his stomach. Yeah. That's it. I heard that on TV, but I'm sure it's the same for a girl too," Colin croaked out with his characteristic froggy voice, surprising Ryan with his unexpected reply.

Ryan nodded in agreement, "I can see that," before stealing a glance into the living room, observing the eclectic group of kids. Some were familiar faces from the bus, like Alicia, the blonde-haired girl closest to Colin, likely due to their similar ages. Occasionally, she would flirt with Ryan, but he never reciprocated. *She's in sixth grade*, Ryan thought, quickly dismissing the notion. *Nope. That's too weird.*

Alicia entered the room, her light brown hair neatly braided in a single French braid—a style Ryan never particularly favored, yet somehow it suited her. As his gaze briefly met hers, she caught him staring. Flustered, Ryan hastily retreated into the kitchen, silently hoping she would remain in place.

However, luck was not on his side. The springs of the couch echoed as Alicia sprang to her feet. "Hey, Ryan!" she exclaimed, her eyebrows raising playfully, indicating her flirtatious mood. "Hi, Alicia," Ryan responded with a sigh.

"I noticed you were looking, so I wanted you to know I noticed. I think you're pretty."

Ryan couldn't help but liken the situation to a real-life Lucy and Schroeder moment, feeling a twinge of amusement at the comparison in his mind. *Why do I think of Peanuts so much in my head?*

"I'll be around if you want to be alone," Alicia added, awkwardly twirling a Blow Pop against her cheek in an attempt at seduction as she sauntered away. Rolling his eyes, Ryan shook his head and redirected his attention to Colin, who was laughing. "You sure do have it easy, don't ya? I mean, girls seem to really like you."

"It's not all fun and games when they're younger than you and say weird things. It's kinda gross," Ryan confessed, pondering whether other guys faced similar situations and if it was specific to him or his surname. Reflecting on his modest approach to life, Ryan acknowledged he didn't strive for popularity or to project toughness; he simply aimed to be pleasant and intelligent, which attracted attention naturally. Yet, amidst the attention, there was only one who truly held his interest.

"Before I forget, I got these two packs of GPK cards. I know you liked the ones I gave you, so here are fresh packs," Ryan presented Colin with his gift, a purchase made with Scott a couple of weeks prior. Forgetting he had them until now, he thought it would be a thoughtful gesture for his younger friend.

"Sweet! These have gum in them?" Colin inquired eagerly.

"Yep," Ryan confirmed.

"Is it good?"

"Assuming you don't break your jaw biting into it—it's still not good. It tastes like cardboard after a minute of chewing—kind of like the Fruit Stripe gum."

A hearty knock echoed from the front door, signaling the arrival of Domino's pizza. The kids sprang from their seats to answer the door, eager for the feast. Mary headed towards the door, accompanied by another woman, presumably a relative. Some returned carrying bags of soda pop with the company's mascot, The Noid, printed on them. The older kids returned bearing trays laden with pizzas, each one marked with the type of topping—two cheese, two sausage, four pepperoni, and two deluxe.

As all the kids gathered around the long dining room table, Ryan counted eighteen people, excluding the infants being cared for by the other woman. Colin has way more friends than I realized, Ryan thought, surprised. Everyone grabbed a paper plate and dug in. Not wanting to appear greedy, Ryan waited until the others had gotten their share.

"Hey! We have a guest! What do we do when that happens?" Mary shouted over the television. The children all moaned, "Be courteous." Mary nodded, waiting for Ryan to grab a slice. A little boy offered his slice of pizza with a bite mark. Ryan shook his head and politely told him, "You have it. I'm trying to cut back on other people's saliva." Not understanding Ryan's remark, he giggled and turned back toward the television set. Having had pizza the night before, the thought of eating it again wasn't appetizing to Ryan.

"Well, Ryan. Did you think you'd ever see a house with this many kids?" Mary asked as the table awaited a response. "No, I don't think I ever have."

"Yeah. We're all like family. They all think of themselves as brothers and sisters even if technically they're not. Except for Julie and John over there, they're actual siblings," Mary explained as she balanced holding one of the crying infants.

Confused, Ryan looked around the table, realizing the nature of this household. *I am so stupid for not putting it together sooner with all these kids.* Colin didn't have this many friends, sort to speak—this was his foster family. Colin was an orphan living in a foster home, waiting to be adopted by a real family. It never occurred to Ryan that other kids he went to school with had a more challenging life than he did. When you meet someone and become friends, people assume they have a life like your own, maybe better. Ryan never fathomed what it was like for Colin; he was just a guy he talked to on the bus.

I feel awful. I don't know why. I just do.

The children fired questions at Ryan about his hobbies, family, and various topics around the table, taking turns almost in order. Each answer from Ryan sparked another question immediately. He now comprehended the source of Colin's curiosity; every kid in the house was like a sponge, eagerly soaking in knowledge about a world they were unfamiliar with.

"Ryan gave me a couple of packs of cards for my birthday!" Colin proudly announced to the table.

"Are they those gross ones that are popular?" Mary asked with disdain.

"He seemed to like the ones I gave him, so I figured it was fine to do," Ryan interjected cautiously, worried he might have inadvertently gotten Colin into trouble.

"I don't care for 'em, but at least he has some kind of hobby, finally," she responded. Colin gazed away, contemplating the abundance of cards released before the current series. "Can you still get the older cards? I think those are better tha…."

Colin's mouth and face abruptly stopped moving, his eyes widened, and his mouth hung open. Ryan waited for him to finish his thought, tilting his head forward in confusion. Glancing around the table, he realized it wasn't just Colin; four other kids had frozen in place. The rest of the table slowed to a crawl as they ate and spoke. Low, sluggish voices turned into background noise as a high-frequency pitch rang in Ryan's ears, compelling him to put a pointer finger in his right ear canal.

Isaiah, a young black boy, froze with the pointed end of a fresh slice of pizza inches from his face. Alicia paused as she picked off a pepperoni. A Latino boy, Luis, one of the older kids, halted mid-laugh. A little ginger-haired boy in kindergarten, Alex, remained still while patiently waiting for another serving. And then there was Colin, mouth agape mid-sentence, staring at Ryan.

Ryan's pulse quickened. He shut his eyes, trying to block out the unsettling sounds until the pops and cracks reclaimed his attention—like static on a television channel after midnight. Hesitating, he cautiously opened his eyelids. The five children, frozen in time, now stared at him with chewed food tumbling from their gaping mouths, dropping onto the table and floor. Unearthly voices, whispers of sadness, began to emanate from them, their eyes shifting upward into their lids. Ryan, desperate to maintain his sanity, placed his other finger into the opposite ear and began chanting, "It's not real. The voices are from exhaustion."

"*Look what it did to me!*" a female voice materialized from Colin. Startled, Ryan withdrew his fingers, discovering blood on his fingertips. "*It hurts so bad,*" a young man's voice echoed through Alicia's open mouth. The five's heads began to shake back and forth. *They're cold*, Ryan realized.

"*What can we do but tell you?*" an older man's voice with a Brooklyn accent came from Isaiah. "*No one whole here to tell. So we cling to you. So cold, but don't want to burn,*" the red-headed boy, Alex, spouted using another man's voice. "*Listen to the little one! The girl!*"

"*Where's my cat?*"

"*I just wanted to have some fun with the redhead.*"

"*Just went for a run.*"

"*All I wanted was some food. A warm place to sleep.*"

"*Had to go to a party.*"

"*Help us. Help you. Tell you, help us. You'll be torn apart like me, from your balls to your stomach, if you don't listen,*" a final voice began, emanating from Luis, "*Help us. Help you. You die if we don't try. You die, we fry! Can you help us? Help them! Save you! Save them! Save us!*" The voices escalated into a haunting crescendo, intensifying the horror gripping the room.

Ryan's friends' bodies began to convulse, their limbs jerking erratically, while the rest of the table moved in eerie slow motion, oblivious to the grotesque phenomenon unfolding. Why would they notice? It was only happening to Ryan, thanks to his cursed sight. He alone witnessed the horrors consuming Colin and the four other foster children, their bodies manipulated in macabre ways. Distorted sounds echoed from each spirit, imitating the moments of their deaths. Yells, gasps, and choking noises polluted the air until Colin shrieked, "*Daddy!*"—the haunting girl's voice again, likely the same as the one he had encountered in Layla's room.

Slapping his hands over his ears this time, Ryan shut his eyes, desperately whispering to himself it wasn't real and malevolent entities weren't tormenting his friends. Ryan's mind flashed back to when darkness in the hall had approached him as he tried sleeping on the couch. Hiding under the blanket had worked then, so he envisioned it now—a massive blue blanket enveloping him, warding off the malevolence. *But this isn't my imagination. This is real somehow.*

The loudness abruptly ceased, and Ryan cautiously shifted his eyes, peering through the cracks between his fingers, grappling with the humiliation of a person his age cowering like a frightened child. Then, with a deep breath, Ryan slid his hands over his face to his chin, bracing himself for the unimaginable sights awaiting him.

The five bodies—Colin, Alicia, Luis, Isaiah, and Alex—reclined in their chairs as the specters of the deceased, possessing them, loomed behind. The dead gazed down at the dismemberments they had endured, now grotesquely projected onto the children. The hijacked bodies, serving as unwitting avatars, slumped over in their chairs, their flesh tearing on various areas of their limbs and torsos.

A red-headed girl in a tattered pink dress peered down at Colin and his shredded torso, a leg missing. An older man stood behind Isaiah, observing him from the left side. The man didn't want to look at the angle; he couldn't help but do so. His head dangled from what remained of his neck. A man wearing a bloody varsity jacket, a ghost Ryan hadn't noticed until now, lingered behind a slumped-over Alicia. He scratched his devoured stomach, spreading blood over his hands and body, perplexed as the mess cascaded over Alicia's hair.

Dressed in black running attire, a man whom Ryan had seen in front of the blue spruce pushed Alex's chair, violently shaking his corpse until it tumbled onto the floor, jolting Ryan. Finally, a teenager clad in regular street clothes stood behind Luis, picking at his groin, attempting to find something no longer there—his genitals. He examined his hands and saw blood and lumpy remains of testicles, screaming without any sound emerging from his mouth.

The tone thickened with horror as the macabre scene unfolded, each detail intensifying the dreadful reality before Ryan's eyes. They were all dead.

Kill it! Help yourself. They are not what they seem. End our suffering. Help us! Save them! The voices intensified, growing louder. Drained, Ryan slumped in his seat, his head landing at the edge of the dining room table, and he tumbled onto the gray, dull carpet floor.

"Ryan? Ryan!" came an urgent call from his friend Colin. Whispers and murmurs surrounded Ryan as he slowly opened his eyes. Beside him, Mary, the foster mother, inquired, "What happened? You all right?" Widening his eyes and attempting to shake off the haze, he observed the kids staring at him, curious about the sudden turn of events. Once his focus sharpened, Ryan realized all five of his new friends were perfectly fine. Everything he had witnessed was merely a hallucination.

But it felt so real. It had to be true. It has to mean something. It has to.

To mask the embarrassment of passing out at the dinner table, Ryan forced a laugh. He needed an excuse to save face. "I guess I'm not used to so many people in one place," he tittered, trying to assure them he would be fine. The girl assisting with the house and the younger kids offered comfort, admitting, "Probably just a bout of anxiety. I get that." Ryan nodded, appreciating the gesture. *Anxiety. If only.*

Alicia suggested Ryan relax on the couch, clearly wanting to sit next to him during the subsequent movie, *Labyrinth*. While it wasn't Ryan's preferred choice, he obliged, watching as the younger kids reveled in the puppetry courtesy of Jim Henson and his team. Musical fantasies never quite appealed to him, although David Bowie seemed to be doing something for the older girls in the house. They shifted in their seats and whispered when the infamous bulge appeared on screen. Meanwhile, the younger ones giggled, much like the boys had earlier when genitalia made an appearance. Ryan pursed his lips, pondering why some movie studio executive hadn't advised Bowie and the director to tone down on the weiner lump, considering it was a kids' film.

It was time for cake, and Colin gleefully took charge of serving the dessert. With a hop in his step, he danced into the kitchen, grabbing paper plates and plastic forks. The air was filled with the sweet aroma of vanilla and frosting. His fingers trembled slightly with excitement as he carefully cut the cake into perfect slices.

Colin's face beamed with pride as he handed everyone a small piece, his smile wide and eyes sparkling with joy. He watched eagerly, anticipating the moment his family would taste his creation. As the first bites were taken, a noticeable shift swept through the room. Eyes widened in surprise, jaws slowed to a cautious chew, and some struggled to swallow, their discomfort masked by strained smiles.

Alicia's face contorted as she fought the urge to spit it out. Unable to hold back, she discreetly turned her head and let the morsel fall into her napkin. One by one, others followed suit, their initial enthusiasm replaced by polite distress. The room was filled with awkward coughs and forced chuckles.

Colin's expression faltered, the pride in his eyes dimming. He glanced around, desperately searching for a sign of approval, but finding none. His cheeks flushed, and his eyes welled up with tears. His mouth quivered as he tried to stay composed. The sting of rejection was sharp and unexpected, cutting deep into his heart. Unable to bear it any longer, he turned abruptly and stormed into the kitchen, the door swinging behind him with a thud.

Ryan, sensing the depth of Colin's hurt, slowly stood from his seat on the couch. Concern etched into his features, he followed Colin into the kitchen, the sounds of hushed apologies and uncomfortable shuffling fading behind him. The kitchen was dimly lit, a stark contrast to the bright cheerfulness filling it moments before. Colin stood by the counter, his shoulders shaking with hampered sobs. Ryan approached him cautiously, reaching out to place a comforting hand on his shoulder, hoping to offer solace amidst the storm of emotions.

Mary watched as Colin frantically read over the box instructions he had retrieved from the trash. His eyes darted over the text, but it was clear he wasn't truly seeing the words. His frustration carved deep lines into his young face, a canvas of mounting despair. As his breath quickened, he turned to Mary, tears streaming down his cheeks, leaving glistening trails.

"No one is ever going to want me! I can't do anything!" he cried, the raw emotion in his voice slicing through the air. He clutched Mary tightly, his small body shaking with the force of his sobs. "I thought someone would want me to come home with them if I cooked well. People like to eat. That's what I heard. I heard it was a way to their hearts!" His voice cracked, each word a plea, a desperate attempt to make sense of his world.

Mary felt her heart shatter as Colin's sobs muffled into her clothes, now soaked with his tears. She wrapped her arms around him, holding him close, trying to offer a refuge from his storm of emotions. She could feel the warmth of his tears seeping through her shirt.

Ryan, standing nearby, heard every word. A lump formed in his throat as he pieced together the puzzle of Colin's behavior. The constant questions about food, the determination to master baking—it all clicked into place. Colin wasn't just trying to learn a skill; he was trying to forge a connection, to make himself wanted, to find a family through the love of food. Ryan's chest tightened with a mix of empathy and helplessness, the weight of Colin's unspoken hopes pressing down on him.

Feeling overwhelmed and unsure of how to intervene, Ryan tiptoed away from the poignant scene. Each step was heavy, his heart aching for the boy who just wanted to be loved. The kitchen, usually a place of comfort and warmth, now filled with an unbearable sadness, the echoes of Colin's cries lingering in the air.

The film concluded, signaling it was time for Ryan to head home. Expressing gratitude and bidding farewell to everyone, he joined Colin outside. The night air was cool, and they carefully navigated the muddy patches in the driveway. Colin glanced at Ryan and suggested, "You should come by more."

Surprised at his own openness, Ryan replied, "You too. I'll give you my address." He realized he had almost avoided inviting Colin to his house just hours earlier; a change in perspective can be incredible.

"That's going to be hard. It's a long walk," Colin explained, kicking at a loose pebble.

Puzzled, Ryan looked around, his brow furrowing in confusion. "Where's your bike?"

Colin's cheeks reddened, a flush creeping up from his neck to his ears. He stared at his worn shoes, scuffed and stained, avoiding

Ryan's eyes. "Don't have one," he admitted, his voice barely audible over the evening breeze.

Ryan felt a wave of guilt wash over him, his chest tightening. He had momentarily forgotten Colin didn't have the same privileges he did. The realization hit him hard, like a punch to the gut. He glanced at his own blue bike, then back at Colin, who was still looking down, embarrassed.

"Can I use your phone?" Ryan asked, his voice gentle.

Colin nodded, his face still flushed, and led Ryan back inside. As they entered, the warmth of the house contrasted with the cold, muddy driveway outside. During their conversation, Ryan learned about the Norton Fall Festival on Wednesday, the 29th. Colin's eyes lit up as he talked about the rides and the food, his excitement bubbling over despite his earlier embarrassment. Ryan, intrigued, motioned for Colin to keep it down with a wry smile, needing to hear his parents' response.

Calling his mom for a ride home, Ryan felt a deep connection with Colin and his foster siblings. The room buzzed with quiet activity, children playing and chatting softly. "Just wanting to create one of those moments," Ryan explained to her, watching Colin and the rest of the foster family. His smile was genuine, reaching his eyes and filling the room with warmth.

Outside, the air was crisp as they walked and discussed the possibility of Ryan joining them at the festival. The thought of a night filled with junk food and rides under the cool autumn sky was enticing. Ryan promised to think about it, making no guarantees but hoping he could make it work. Moments later, Rebecca's car pulled up, the headlights cutting through the dusk. The boys were still chatting, standing close together as if reluctant to part.

Ryan approached the car, leaving his bike behind. Colin's eyes widened in confusion. "Wait! What about your bike?"

With a crooked grin, Ryan turned to him. "It's not my bike anymore. It's yours."

Colin's face twisted in confusion. "What do you mean?"

"I'm too big for it. It's more your size. Happy Birthday!" Ryan said, his voice full of sincerity.

Colin's eyes shimmered with unspoken emotion. He gave Ryan a high five, his lip quivering and his voice raspy as he tried to express his gratitude. "Thanks," he managed, his voice breaking.

As Rebecca reversed down the driveway, Ryan watched Colin sprint into the house, his face lit with joy. He could hear the excited talk as Colin shared the news of his "sorta new bike" with his foster siblings, their faces lighting up with excitement.

Rebecca glanced at Ryan, a soft smile on her face. "That was a nice thing to do."

Ryan nodded but remained silent about the nature of the house being a foster home. He pondered the complexities of the adoption process, why it was such a secret, and why finding families for foster children seemed so challenging. Despite his lack of understanding, one conviction remained steadfast in his heart:

"Every kid should have a bike."

CHAPTER THIRTEEN

ALIVE & KICKING

Surviving Halloween night was nothing short of a miracle for Eric Flanagan. The Lycan's teeth had left grotesque, mutated marks on the sides of his torso, resulting in considerable blood loss. The canines alone, piercing through his lungs, should have spelled his demise.

Remarkably, Eric spent only a week in the hospital, defying doctors' expectations. Professionals advised him to take a week off school for recovery, warning of permanent scars. Eric, however, remained focused on his room, avoiding his abusive father and completing missed school assignments. Valerie's daily delivery of his work became a lifeline fostering an unexpected shift in Eric's perspective on education. Facing death kindled a desire for self-improvement, a longing to escape the purgatory of living with an abusive parent.

Word spread about Eric's animal attack in the Akron area, thanks to his father's opportunistic ad and interviews with the local news station. Conor Flanagan, seeking money for his son's hospital bills he had no intention of paying, resorted to scams to avoid working. Thousands of dollars poured in, mostly squandered on alcohol, as Eric suspected.

As Monday, November 20th approached, the week of Thanksgiving, Eric experienced several nights of uninterrupted sleep. Absent were the belligerent encounters with his father and haunting nightmares. Opening his eyes, he felt refreshed and glanced around his room. Posters of bikini-clad models and bands adorned the wood-paneled walls, reminders of his father's freebies from the local ABC store.

Eric's bedroom floor, cluttered with repeatedly worn clothes and discarded food wrappers, had not seen the light in weeks. A layer of dust coated the ceiling fan blades, prompting a newfound concern for cleanliness. Eric wrinkled his nose at the unpleasant odor his room emitted, a blend of dirty clothes and food remnants. As he checked his own body, relief washed over him as he realized the unpleasant scent didn't emanate from him. Daily showers, a new routine post-attack, ensured personal hygiene.

Wearing only blue and white striped boxers, Eric turned to the mirror on his dresser. Amidst the mess on the floor, he inspected the scarring from the creature's attack. Initially blurry-eyed, he couldn't discern any red marks or protrusions. After wiping his eyes, Eric realized his body was not disfigured; in fact, it appeared better than before. His chest and arms were more toned, with a hint of developing abs on his stomach's top part. Puzzled, Eric wondered if the change was due to his diminished appetite since the attack.

I feel like I should eat, but I have no desire to, he mused, staring at his reflection in disbelief.

Attempting not to fixate on his altered body, Eric resolved to get ready for school. It was his first day back, and for the first time in a long while, he was genuinely looking forward to it. Eager to reunite with his friends, particularly Valerie, he started pulling at his drawers. The old dresser, a hand-me-down from a neighbor when his mother passed away, gave him a hard time as the drawers resisted sliding smoothly on their track.

Frustration mounting, Eric gritted his teeth. He felt a surge of strength, an unfamiliar power coursing through his muscles. With an involuntary yank, the drawer shot out of the dresser, flying across the room and slamming into the wall with a loud crash. The impact left a dent in the wall and splintered the wood of the drawer. Perplexed, Eric stared at his hand, flexing his fingers as if to confirm they were still his. He glanced at the wall, then at the damaged drawer, with a mix of awe and confusion on his face.

Carefully, he collected the fallen clothes, his movements now more cautious. He selected a plain long-sleeved white shirt, leaving the rest for later, and gently slid the drawer back into place. Spotting a pair of jeans on the floor, he picked them up and gave them a sniff.

His newly heightened sense of smell made him more discerning, and these jeans, fortunately, passed the test.

Eric looked into the mirror, his reflection showing a young man with long red hair framing his face. He pushed back his hair from both sides, pulling it back into a low ponytail. While he appreciated his unique long ginger locks, he was tired of hiding his face. It was time for something different.

As he dressed, he couldn't help but feel a mix of excitement and trepidation. His newfound strength was both a gift and a mystery. But for now, he focused on the anticipation of seeing his friends again, ready to face whatever the day might bring.

You are feeling excellent now.

Eric heard it, a sound echoing in the room, *or is it in my head?* There was no one present. He shook his head, contemplating whether he was speaking aloud to himself. His gaze scanned the corners of his room, a growing concern gnawing at him—had the animal attack and near-death experience left an indelible mark on his sanity? With his hair pulled back and dressed in a simple outfit, Eric nervously backed out of his room, a creeping paranoia suggesting he was being stalked. Shaking off the eerie sensation, he shrugged his shoulders, redirecting his focus to brushing his teeth, and eventually tiptoeing around his father.

Conor would typically be passed out on the recliner at this hour, allowing Eric to navigate the house in silence, avoiding the verbal onslaught that could potentially ruin his day. As he glanced around the Flanagan residence, disgust welled up at the state of his home. His dad had allowed it to deteriorate, and now there was an inexplicable urge to clean everything in sight. The pervasive scent inside the house triggered an obsessive-compulsive tick, leaving Eric bewildered and frightened by the changes in his own body.

As Eric reached the front door just as Conor snored himself awake, he knew there was no escaping the impending verbal lashing. He would endure the familiar routine, roll his eyes in defiance, and then leave. It was the same old song and dance he knew too well.

"Where you goin'?" Conor rasped, hacking a wad of phlegm and spitting it into a beer can beside him, accompanied by a full ashtray.

"School. The same place I usually go when you wake up in the chair as I'm leaving," Eric replied, anticipating the confrontation. Conor sat up, ready to stand, his chest puffing outward.

"You bein' smart with me, boyo?" Conor was accustomed to his son staggering backward when he lunged, but this time, it didn't happen.

"You think you're hot shit, don't ya?" Eric remained silent, unwilling to entertain his father's nonsense. Conor, still too intoxicated to bother lifting a foot off his recliner, let alone stand, locked eyes with Eric. They faced each other like gunslingers, poised for a showdown at high noon.

"Get your ass to school! Get a job to pay back the hospital bill you accrued for being a dumb ass in the first place, or I'll take it out of your ass," Conor threatened, reclining in his seat, ready to drift into unconsciousness. Eric had a plethora of potential responses, a myriad of insults he could have hurled, but chose to hold his tongue.

You can't bring attention to yourself now.

"Heh?"

Surveying his surroundings, Eric strained to identify the mysterious voice he had heard. His eyes flicked back to his father, who had closed his drunken eyes and shook his head in disappointment. Eric couldn't help but wonder about the turmoil within a man who had given up, consumed by rage. As he closed the door behind him, a nearby scuttling sound caught his attention. He paused, ears perking up. The noise was faint but persistent, like a whisper in the wind.

Eric's gaze fixated on the front door of his house. Once painted sky blue, it had deteriorated into dark, rotting wood with large clusters of faded paint chipped away over time. Leaning closer, he brought his right ear near the door, listening intently. The sound grew louder, a deafening cacophony of termites gnawing within. Before he could place his ear fully against it, the noise intensified, reverberating through his skull. Startled, Eric pulled back, covering his ears, struggling to comprehend what he had just heard. How and why could he hear it so clearly?

Shaking off the unsettling sensation, Eric made his way to his car. He turned the ignition, relieved when the engine roared to life. Driving to school for the first time in two weeks, he pondered what to expect on his return, sensing things would be different.

Inside the high school, adorned with banners and flyers for the Norton Fall Festival, efforts were underway to attract attendees for the week after Thanksgiving, from Monday, November 27th to Wednesday, the 29th. The idea of a fall festival amidst potential snow seemed odd to some, but the school board sought donations to support all four schools: Norton Primary, Intermediate, Middle, and High School.

Valerie Donovan approached Devin, who stood at his rust-colored locker gathering materials for Science Lab. Her sudden appearance startled him as he closed the locker door, revealing her gorgeous face. "Sorry," she said with a smile which rendered Devin unable to stay upset. Look at those eyes, he thought. He secretly hoped she would gently end things with Eric after his outburst before the accident. Neither Devin nor Valerie had seen Eric since he came home from the hospital, and they were uncertain if he would return yet.

"Have you seen him yet?" Valerie inquired, raising an eyebrow as she referred to Eric. Devin rose onto his toes, scanning the hall as if expecting Eric to appear out of nowhere, as if she posed a trick question. "No. Not yet."

"I've heard things, like he looks so different. I hope he isn't too badly scarred, but that could be kind of hot, right?" Valerie gossiped. Devin deflated, realizing she had no intention of ending things with Eric. Confused and angered, he began, "Why would you want to be with—." The answer to his question appeared, strolling around the corner at the other end of the hall.

Eric emerged, strutting down the hall during the final moments between the second and third periods. As Valerie and Devin spotted him, a mix of guilt and anxiety washed over them. They had both felt terrible for not going after Eric when the animal dragged him away, and Devin worried Eric might hold a grudge, remembering the awful things said on Halloween night.

Valerie's eyes widened as her boyfriend, Eric Flanagan, approached them, casually opening a soda. His shirt clung more tightly to his toned frame, and his walk now had a newfound swagger. His hair, now pulled back, gave him a fresher, more polished look. Even Devin couldn't help but notice how good Eric looked for someone who had been nearly torn in half. He wondered, albeit briefly, how such a transformation was possible.

"Hey guys," Eric greeted, his voice carrying a slight edge of nervousness. Valerie giggled, clearly smitten by Eric's new demeanor. "Hey. You look butt—better," she stammered, her cheeks flushing. "A couple of weeks away seemed to do you good—I mean, did you some good—did some good for you, yeah" Embarrassed by her fumbling, she laughed awkwardly.

Eric laughed under his breath and thanked her, while Devin ground his teeth, annoyed. "Devin!" Eric pointed; his tone suddenly serious. "I need to talk to you at lunch, cool?" Devin forced a half-hearted smile and replied, "Sounds good."

"I'll see you all later. At lunch, I guess," Eric confirmed, turning to walk away. Valerie leaned in for a kiss, but he was already moving, seemingly indifferent to public displays of affection. Disappointed, she watched him walk away, then shrugged and told Devin she would see them in an hour or so.

Devin stood in the hall, his eyes following Valerie's confident stride. As much as he enjoyed looking at her, he couldn't shake his bewilderment at Eric's transformation. How could someone look like the same person but come across so differently, so confidently, in just two weeks, Devin asked himself. All he could do was chalk it up to a possible reevaluation of life, hopefully for Eric's sake.

Lunchtime arrived, and Devin settled into the round table tucked away at the back of the cafeteria, the designated spot for those seeking solitude. He chose the orange chair this time, noting the cafeteria's vibrant assortment of chairs in yellow, orange, blue, and puke green. Sitting solo wasn't his preference, but most of his friends had a different lunch period.

Valerie, meanwhile, occupied a seat with her fashionable clique of girlfriends. As Eric entered through the east entrance, he scanned the room and quickly spotted Devin at their usual spot. A mutual nod acknowledged each other's presence. "Can only stay a minute," Eric mentioned as he approached. Devin kicked out the nearby blue chair, inviting Eric to join. "What's up?" Devin asked, casually adding a straw to his chocolate milk. Eric hesitated, nervously twisting his fist inside the palm of his other hand—a rare display of vulnerability.

"I just wanted to say that I'm sorry," Eric confessed, his voice wavering slightly. Devin furrowed his brow, taken aback by the unexpected apology. It wasn't typical for Eric to express regret. "I said some things, called your mother something I'd never hear myself say, and for if I hurt your brother that night." The memories of Halloween night rushed back to Devin, and he recalled the chaos, the hurtful name he had uttered, and Eric's retaliation.

"Sorry I hit you," Devin mumbled, his gaze dropping to the table. Simultaneously, they nodded and exchanged a casual "cool," followed by a shared laugh. Eric excused himself, mentioning the need to catch up on some work. Devin reassured him, "Go do what you need to do." Watching Eric leave, Devin was left contemplating the recent exchange, feeling a lingering uncertainty about whether Eric would remain the same person and friend. *Maybe he will move on from me as well.*

You cannot fight it. It's in you, no matter how you mask it.

The school day ended, and Eric Flanagan walked to his car in the student parking lot, acutely aware of the curious gazes from his peers. They wanted answers about the mysterious events surrounding him but hesitated to ask due to his fierce reputation. He leaned against his Pontiac, waiting for Devin to finish his class, unsure if Devin and Valerie planned to ride with him.

As Eric waited, an unsettling feeling crept over him. He glanced at the road and locked eyes with a short, older woman who was observing him intently. She stood by the crosswalk, waiting for the signal to cross. As the traffic halted, she hurried towards the school parking lot.

The woman wore Jordache mom jeans, a yellow floral blouse, and oversized prescription glasses. Her frizzy hair danced in the wind as she waved energetically at Eric, trying to get his attention. Uneasy, Eric moved to the driver's side of his car as the woman shouted, "I know you! Please wait, I need to talk to you!" Devin and Valerie emerged from the school, pausing their conversation to watch the bizarre encounter.

The desperate woman cried out, "I heard about what happened to you. It was an animal that hurt you, wasn't it?! My daughter and husband died because of an animal attack, just like that boy!" Her voice trembled with torment as she appealed with Eric.

Trying to defuse the situation, Eric gently pushed her away, asking, "I'm sorry, lady, but what do you want me to do about it?" Devin intervened, questioning her motives. The woman insisted Eric harbored the beast within, as depicted in books and shows. Desperate to free herself from the pain, she began to undress, provoking the supposed beast within Eric.

Growing agitated, Eric tried to stop the woman from exposing herself in front of the high school students. She grinned manically, her disheveled appearance revealing the toll of sleepless nights fueled by fear. The onlooking students buzzed with curiosity, wondering what Eric had done to provoke such a reaction.

Devin calmly intervened, leading the woman away. She claimed to have been watching him and warned him to keep an eye on his friend, suggesting Devin possessed the same dark essence. Pushed away, the woman straightened her blouse, delivering a haunting message before departing to the street.

Laughing maniacally, she ripped out her curly hair, declaring one of them had to die to set her family's souls free. Valerie, sensing the woman's intentions, ran after her, with Devin and Eric in pursuit, shouting, "No! Don't do it!"

In the middle of the street, the exhausted figure stood as a macabre centerpiece amidst the bustling chaos. The trio, immobilized by dread, observed in stifled horror, their breaths catching in their throats.

The woman's hands shook uncontrollably, betraying the facade of composure she attempted to maintain. Her eyes widened, reflecting the dim glow of the streetlights as they flickered overhead, set to match the overcast season.

As they watched, the trio's hearts pounded in unison with the erratic rhythm of passing cars, their gazes darting between the woman and the relentless flow of traffic. The distant wail of sirens mingled with the woman's tired voice, each syllable dripping with impending doom.

The wind swept through the busy street, carrying with it the stench of decay and despair, tangling the woman's hair into a disheveled mess. Her frantic movements mirrored the frantic beat of their hearts, a desperate dance on the precipice of oblivion.

Suddenly, a gruesome presence materialized behind the unsuspecting trio, its form a grotesque parody of life, adorned in tattered rags stained with the blood of its countless victims. The air grew thick with the suffocating weight of fear as the trio's pleas for the woman's safety went unheard.

Unknown to them, the spirit of a young girl, twisted and tortured in death, screamed out in silent anguish for the woman's salvation. The woman, lost in her own delusions, waved at the spectral apparition, a futile gesture of recognition and resignation.

With mounting dread, the woman came to a grim realization, her trembling hands clutching at the fabric of her fate. It was not just fear that gripped her; it was the chilling certainty of what she believed had to be done to find peace.

The blare of horns shattered the silence as the woman, driven by despair, hurled herself backward into the path of oncoming traffic. The world slowed to a surreal crawl as the semi-truck barreled toward her, its headlights piercing the darkness like accusing eyes.

In a gruesome inevitability, the truck collided with the woman's fragile form, sending her hurtling through the air in a grotesque ballet of death and despair. Valerie's horrified scream echoed through the empty streets as Devin and Eric bore witness to the woman's lifeless body crumpling against the unforgiving asphalt, her skull shattering like porcelain against the cold concrete.

Her body lay sprawled across both lanes, bringing traffic to a standstill. Onlookers gasped, some rushing to help, but it was too late. The police identified her as Maria Blake, mother to the deceased Anna and wife to the recently deceased Phillip Blake—a family brutalized by a large animal weeks prior. The Blake family tragedy would echo through the communities for years, a tale of one set free and two remaining, haunting her. Little did Maria know, despite her futile sacrifice, her family's souls remained ensnared in limbo, neither in Heaven nor Hell, but cursed apparitions haunting and unsettling Layla Hatcher.

CHAPTER FOURTEEN

YOU MIGHT THINK

Ryan perched on the arm of an old beige sofa nestled in the woods under the shade of ancient trees. The sofa had found its place there, undisturbed for years, offering Ryan a secluded spot for some peace—well, almost peace, considering the company of Scott and Colin. They were engrossed in flipping through an aged Playboy issue from several years back, featuring Justine Grenier from February 1984—*a classic*, in their opinion.

Ryan's mind wandered; the tale spun by his brother about Maria Blake on the day she passed lingering like a dark cloud. His suspicions about the peculiar occurrences he had witnessed lately were growing. Scott, noticing Ryan's despondency for several days, had become rather tiresome with his jabs. On the other hand, Colin, never having seen a naked woman before, had claimed dibs on the magazine and was thoroughly captivated—one of the small blessings Ryan had bestowed upon him.

"What's the matter with you there, Mopey-MaGoo?" Scott teased, a customary practice of adding "MaGee" or "MaGoo" to someone's mood, occasionally throwing in a "McPouty" for variety. Ryan, gazing into the woods and uninterested in the exposed women, replied with a nonchalant, "Nothin'." Scott snatched the magazine from Colin to highlight a specific page, but unfortunately, the Bunnies had suffered from fading over time due to the elements and who knows what else. While the boys kept the pages safeguarded under the cushions, it couldn't prevent the inevitable color bleeding.

Scott playfully hurled the magazine at Ryan's head. Startled, Ryan juggled it in his hands, ensuring it didn't land on the damp leaves below. When he looked down, a pair of bare breasts greeted him.

"Look at those chug jugs and tell me you don't feel better," Scott grinned. Unfazed, Ryan shook his head and retorted, "Yeah, yeah. Seen those a bunch of times already." Perplexed by the idea that someone could see a pair of breasts too many times, Scott raised an eyebrow and questioned, "You goin' funny on me?" Ryan glanced over, shaking his head, "Guess I'm just not in the mood." Colin eagerly grabbed the magazine from Ryan, his tongue sticking out, anticipating seeing more nudity.

It was a brisk day; a couple of days post the traffic accident involving Maria Blake. Ryan wasn't entirely sure why he decided to enter the woods. After what happened to Eric in those woods, fear should have gripped him, but it didn't. *After all, there isn't a full moon tonight.*

"Hi boys!" a voice behind a tree exclaimed. "Jesus!" they all shouted, startled by the unexpected presence. They scanned the surroundings, with Ryan leaping from the arm, Colin rushing to a nearby tree, and Scott collapsing onto the ground in a fetal position.

A light cackle resonated from behind a large oak tree as Christina emerged, holding her sides. "That was too good!" Ryan shook his head, initially in disbelief at the scare but then smiled, glad to see her. "That's not funny!" Colin's voice echoed from a distance.

"Oh, it was very funny! The look on your faces!" she laughed, trying to catch her breath. The boys composed themselves, retaking their spots on the couch, with Ryan now on top, Colin on the arm, and Scott on the cushions. "Whatcha lookin' at? Naked girls?" Christina asked with a mischievous grin, already knowing where guys stashed the goods.

She shook her head, reached under the cushion, and pulled out an issue of Hustler. The guys exchanged uncertain glances, caught off guard by the unexpected turn of events. Eyes wide open, they looked at each other, unsure of how to respond without sounding like perverts.

Scott theatrically placed a hand on his chest, his voice dripping with mock indignation. "I, for one, am appalled by this. To think such people would hide this…." He struggled to maintain a semblance of moral outrage, but the gleam in his eyes betrayed his act.

"Cut the shit, Donovan. It's not exactly a secret," Christina retorted, her tone slicing through Scott's pretense. She opened the magazine, her fingers flipping through the pages with casual ease. Ryan watched her unflinching eyes scan the explicit content, impressed by her nonchalant attitude. Most girls would have giggled nervously or called them perverts, but not Christina.

Christina's gaze lingered on the voluptuous models, a flicker of insecurity crossing her face. She glanced down at her own chest, comparing herself to the women on the glossy pages. Would anyone appreciate her as much as the guys envied those models? Unlike the magazine's models, she didn't have large breasts. She looked over at Ryan, lost in thought, and wondered if size truly mattered—*am I good enough?*

"You realize most women don't look like this, right?" she stated, breaking the silence. Scott swiftly swiped the magazine from her, flipping through it with a smirk. "You know, it's amazing how little I care right now," he replied sarcastically, prompting laughter from Ryan and Colin. Christina, however, turned her attention to Colin, realizing a sixth grader was being exposed to such explicit content.

"You guys! What the hell are you showin' him?" she exclaimed, her voice sharp with disapproval.

"Oh, what difference does it make! He's going to see this stuff sooner or later if he hasn't already!" Scott declared. Colin chimed in, supporting his new friend, "Yeah, my older brothers keep this stuff in their room. No big deal." Ryan thought, *That was a lie. He wouldn't be nearly as excited if that were the case.*

Christina shot a skeptical look at Colin, who nervously averted his gaze. Scott turned to Ryan, observing Christina shuffling leaves around with her feet. "Speaking of smutty stuff, could you diddle Hatcher's pickle to help him lighten up? He's been in a mood all week. Longer—probably." Offended, Christina stomped and huffed. She brought her fist back and punched Scott on the shoulder, calling him a creep and a slew of other names.

Still, Christina acknowledged Scott's point. "You noticed that too, huh?" she eventually agreed. "He won't tell me what's bothering him." They both began discussing Ryan as if he weren't there. *Do they realize I can hear them?* Colin watched them gab, oblivious to the fuss. To him, Ryan was the perfect friend right now, not noticing his recent change in demeanor.

Ryan's patience wore thin, anger bubbling up as they continued to prod at his mood—*screw it!* "I think there is more than one werewolf living in the neighborhood," he shouted, desperate to halt their endless gossiping.

They all fell quiet, staring at their friend, the magazine forgotten. After close to a minute of stunned silence, Scott bit his lip and said, "Okay…explain."

***

Meanwhile, Devin Hatcher was meticulously painting Mr. Craggs' floorboard trim. The garage door remained open, letting in the frigid air Melvin preferred, and leaving Devin shivering. Melvin, settled in his recliner, rubbed his bald, age-spotted head. He flipped through a National Geographic while keeping an eye on his neighbor's son. "You done good, boy. Gettin' all dat shit out of mah house," he complimented. Devin hadn't anticipated that working for Melvin Craggs would involve clearing out magazines and books from every corner of the house—not just the living room.

This had better be worth it, Devin thought, his breath visible in the cold air.

Footsteps echoed from the garage, drawing the attention of both Devin and Melvin toward the door. A figure stood silhouetted against the sunlight, her blonde hair glowing like a halo.

"Valerie?" Devin called, squinting.

"Yeah. It's me. Your mom said you were over here. Sorry," she replied, stepping into view. Devin quickly stood and walked over to the screen door. "You all right?" he asked, noting the rare insecurity on her usually confident face. As he opened the door to step outside, he assured Melvin he'd be right back. The acrid smell of cigar smoke made Valerie cough as she moved away from the entrance. Despite Devin's cleaning efforts, the house's stench remained stubbornly embedded.

"I can't stay long, but there's a party this Saturday night at a friend's house in Wadsworth. Do you want to go with me?" she asked. Devin's heart leapt. Valerie Donovan, the girl he'd adored since childhood, was inviting him out.

"Wait," Devin said, a sudden realization hitting him, "What about Eric?" Valerie averted her eyes, mumbling, "We broke up." Disbelief washed over Devin. "Say what?" he asked.

"He called me yesterday and said he wasn't feeling good about the relationship anymore. Thought it would be best to end it," she explained. Devin frowned, thinking, doesn't sound like Eric. I thought he'd be, well, less considerate.

"It was just weird," Valerie continued, her voice tinged with confusion. "It came out of nowhere. It's like he's different now. Like the attack…it changed him." Devin couldn't argue but felt the weight of the unspoken bro code: friends shouldn't date each other's exes. But Norton was a small place—if everyone followed that rule, no one would date at all.

"Yeah, um, let me see if I have anything going on," he told her, grinning. Valerie tucked her blonde hair behind her ear, smiling as she backed away. "That sounds awesome!" she said, beaming. "Just let me know." Devin nodded, watching her walk away, her hands in her back pockets, rocking a purple off-the-shoulder sweater.

Devin practically danced back inside. "What's wrong with ya? Ya look like you're havin' a spasm—brain damaged even," Craggs groaned. Devin's enthusiasm couldn't be dampened, not even by his crotchety old neighbor. "Let me guess. You like her," Melvin observed. "Tryin' to escape the torture area? The friend zone dat is?"

Devin stopped and looked at Melvin, biting back a sarcastic reply. "You mean her?" Devin pointed outside. "That beautiful angel who just came to your door? Yeah. Yeah, I do."

"Liked her for a while then, have ya?" Melvin asked.

"How'd you know?" Devin replied.

"She asked for somethin', and you fell over yourself to please her. Sounds like a crush if I ever saw one." Devin bristled, "Her boyfriend just broke it off with her."

Melvin looked away, uneasy. "You mean da Flanagan boy? I'd watch out for him if I was you. So much rage in dat family, in dat house even. He sees you with her, may go off the deep end. But maybe dat's what she wants."

"I don't think you know enough to make that assumption," Devin snapped.

"Oh, really? She just got left, and she comes crawlin' to you magically. Think I proved my point."

"If anything was proven, it's that girls don't like the rank smell of old cigars mixed with black mold! They have a type," Devin shot back, using air quotes. Melvin smiled wryly, "If ya say so." An awkward silence settled between them, one young and naïve, the other old and full of cantankerous wisdom.

Despite his rough exterior, Melvin Craggs was a wealth of knowledge, something his neighbors failed to appreciate. He glanced at his freshly cleaned mantle, where antique frames displayed old photographs.

"Who is that with you in those pictures?" Devin asked, attempting to bridge the gap.

Melvin stood and walked over. "Dat, boy, mah Sally, mah wife," he shared, sadness clouding his eyes. Devin had never seen her, so he assumed something had happened. He didn't have to ask; Melvin filled in the blanks.

"Came back from the war in '45 and married her. We had been datin' before I shipped out, but I made sure she didn't go nowhere. Had nine years together before she passed."

"How'd she die?" Devin asked.

"Polio. Got it in 1952, during the pandemic. It was hard on both of us. Her bein' crippled was one thing, but she was one of the few where the disease affected the muscles. She suffocated in her sleep one summer night. Weren't nothin' I could do but watch her go. She just stared at me until her eyes closed. Always wondered if I gave her some kind of relief by bein' next to her. Maybe I'll never know," Melvin continued.

"I'm sorry."

"Don't be. We had a good life together. Some years were better than others, and even with her needing a wheelchair, we ended on a real good one. Da real kicker was a year later when the cure was available. Dat's what gets me the most. I can't say I know much about people anymore, but if there's one thing I can tell you…people will say life is short, which it is, but it can also be long, especially if you don't waste it like me. It's the people who have regrets—the ones wishing for more time have the shortest days. So go and hang out with dat girl you like and just live. You never know how things will turn."

***

Ryan's supernatural secret was out now.

Instead of laughing, Ryan's friends exchanged glances; their expressions were all the conversation needed. Without a word, they gravitated indoors, descending to the bottom floor of his house. All four stormed through the front door and slid down the banister, a ritual they'd established, except for Colin, who hesitated at the perceived risk. After some coaxing, he reluctantly joined, sliding down belly-flat and emerging somewhat awkwardly on his feet. Amidst a brief celebration, Ryan retrieved a chalkboard from the coat closet and hastily scribbled notes.

Having already recounted his encounter while recovering from the mace's sting, Ryan detailed the sight of the colossal wolf towering over the transformed adults, its life fading from Melvin Craggs' shotgun blast to its snout. None of them could refute his tale, but skepticism lingered, as natural as breathing.

What followed would be the most uncomfortable part for Ryan. With a worn-down piece of pink chalk, he wrote, "The Suspects."

"Let's just pretend you ran into a werewolf, not a wolf…a werewolf. What does it matter now?" Scott asked.

"What kind of wolf was it?" Christina asked. Ryan put his board down onto his lap, curling his lip, not understanding what they were getting at. "What do you mean, what kind of wolf?"

"Are you talking like *American Werewolf in London* or *The Howling* type?" Colin helped clarify. Ryan, stupefied he knew those films, looked over to Colin and began to speak until Scott interrupted, asking what was on Ryan's mind. "How do you know anything about those movies?"

"Because I've seen them," Colin answered sarcastically. Wide-eyed, he shook his head with his mouth open to point out how dumb the question was. Uh-duh. "How? You have like a thousand kids in that place, and most of them are younger than you," Ryan added.

"I watched them with the older ones at night. It's fine! Nothing was bad in them," Colin assured his overconcerned friends, acting more like parents than buddies. Ryan scoffed and leaned forward, "What do ya mean there is nothing bad? One of them has a conversation in a porn theater, and the other has Elisabeth Brooks going full boobs and bush!"

"I bet he saw an edited version. Yeah, those blow," Scott nodded, understanding. Colin shrugged his shoulders, not fully understanding the difference between a movie on VHS and one on television or why. "What difference does it make? It was a freakin' werewolf!" Ryan shouted loud enough only his mother could hear.

Christina put her finger in the air. All three boys shut up, hating she had power over them. She grinned, knowing her control, and proceeded to get to the point of the question. "Does it use all four legs, or just two?" Ryan went over all accounts of Halloween night he could remember. "Both, I guess. It was running on all fours when it bit into Eric, but it was standing when I got to the cornfield."

"Did Craggs have a silver bullet or somethin'?" Scott interjected. Ryan rolled his eyes and pointed out a couple of things, "One. It was a shotgun, so probably not. Second, thinking a bullet needs to be silver is dumb. How would a silver one go through a body any more than a regular one?"

"You ever see that flick? *Silver Bullet*?" Scott ignored Ryan, focusing on the other two.

"Yeah, it's the one with the vampires near the beach, right?" Colin asked.

"No. That's *Fright Night*. It's a vampire one," Christina wrongly stated.

"Uh-uh. That's the one with the vampire neighbor. Lost Boys is the vampires on the beach with an oiled-up saxophone guy with the big pecs. But the kid in that one was in *Silver Bullet*." Christina and Colin both realized the mistake and nodded, now understanding. "But he was in *Stand By Me* too, right?" Christina asked, continuing a conversation, attempting to remove Ryan's concerns.

Ryan, fed up with the conversation he would generally love to have, became frustrated and slammed his fist onto the blackboard, setting the movie facts straight. "Corey Haim was in *Silver Bullet* and *The Lost Boys*. The guy in *Stand by Me* is Corey Feldman, who was also in *The Lost Boys*, both of which, by the way, has nothing to do with werewolves except for *Silver Bullet*!"

"What's wrong?" Colin naively asked. Christina and Scott whispered about Corey Feldman now, trying to remember if he was in *Gremlins*, as Ryan shot them a look, bringing down the conversation.

"What's wrong is that I have werewolves on my mind, then you bring in vampires along with an oiled-up, beefy saxophone man, and now I'm all over the place! Can we please get back to the point? If you don't mind!" Ryan's voice rose, his eyes wild. His friends took a step back. "Let me get to my point!"

"Then what is it?" Scott asked slowly, trying to calm him down, his patience thinning. Ryan grabbed a chalkboard and began scribbling names. His friends leaned in, curious. When he finished, he turned it around to reveal three names: Eric Flanagan, Valerie Donovan, and Calvin Hatcher—his father.

"I think one or more of them may have taken on a werewolf curse, and next week during the full moon, they will change and hurt people."

Scott frowned, seeing his sister's name in pink, unable to imagine how Ryan felt about writing his father's name. "You actually believe this, don't you?" Christina asked, the fun of the conversation fading. She had known Ryan to be imaginative but not to this extent. Ryan had always been honest, not one to fabricate stories. Her conclusion: Ryan was on the verge of a breakdown, yet she knew his belief was sincere. Ryan conveniently left out the part about seeing ghosts—werewolves were one thing, but spirits would be too much, especially for Colin, who was still younger.

Christina and Colin remained silent. They could see their friend was at his breaking point and feared saying anything which might push him further.

The names on the list didn't directly involve Christina and Colin, but Scott was confused about his sister's inclusion. Rubbing his temples, Scott groaned, "Please explain." Ryan stood, sighed, and began to elaborate. "These are the people I saw with scratches on their bodies afterward. Eric is obvious; he had the most injuries but recovered remarkably fast. That's suspicious, right?" Ryan's friends nodded in agreement.

"Your sister had cuts on her leggings. I saw blood." Scott protested, "That doesn't mean a wolf did it." Ryan nodded, "True. The cuts looked like claw marks, but it could've been something else. A thorn bush maybe." Despite his words, Ryan was convinced the markings were from an animal.

"What about your dad? Why him?" Colin asked.

"I saw cuts on his arm before I walked Valerie home," Ryan replied. "He's also changed. He doesn't look the same."

"How? Does he look bad?" Christina asked. Ryan shook his head, "No, he looks good, but it's happened so quickly. The cuts he said were from a thorn bush healed fast, and he's lost a lot of weight."

"Maybe he's been dieting. If he quit drinking, the weight could drop off. Saw that on *Donahue*," Christina suggested. Ryan sat back in an old plaid chair, contemplating his insinuation—his father becoming a monster in less than a week. "I shouldn't have said anything."

Christina moved over to Ryan and perched on the arm of his chair. He avoided her gaze, embarrassed. She wrapped an arm around him. "Can you guys come Saturday and just, well, spy on him? He's supposed to be rebuilding the shed that day."

"Usually, people do that in spring or summer. Why now?" Scott asked, puzzled.

"Yeah, exactly!" Ryan agreed.

***

Evening settled in, and Ryan's friends either rode their bikes or walked home, while Devin finished his work at Melvin Craggs' house. His mind buzzed with mixed emotions: excitement about his crush inviting him to a party, and anxiety about seeing Valerie so soon after his breakup with Eric.

Devin entered the house through the garage, his father Calvin sitting downstairs, eyes glued to the flickering screen of channel seven—one of the few clear channels they got. They exchanged awkward glances, both unsure of what to say. Calvin considered starting a conversation but decided against it as Devin headed upstairs.

"You missed dinner," his mother had called from the kitchen. "Leftovers are in the fridge." Devin shifted direction, finding her at the sink, her shoulder blades pressing against her denim shirt with each scrub of the pans.

He wrapped his arms around her from behind, hugging her tightly. "I'm sorry I'm such a little shit sometimes," he murmured. She smiled, patting his arm. "You're a teenage boy. It's what ya do. I forgive ya as soon as it happens because I know you're a good lad."

She turned to face him, noting the confusion and loneliness in his eyes. "What is it? What's the matta?" she asked gently.

Devin leaned against the counter, searching for words. "I don't know. Something seems off. People are acting strange. Even Layla is being, well, reserved. Everything feels different." Rebecca nodded, understanding.

"Yeah, but it happens. It will happen. Different doesn't have to mean bad, though, does it? It just means different." Devin shook his head slowly. "No, I suppose not." An uncomfortable silence settled between them; the unspoken tension thick.

"You need to give your father a break," Rebecca said bluntly. Devin looked away, his stubborn streak surfacing. "No, Mom, I really don't. I'll be out of here in a little over a year, and Ryan and Layla will have to deal with his bullshit." Rebecca threw the dish towel onto the counter, her patience wearing thin.

"He's a good man, your dad. People just lose their way sometimes," she insisted.

"Maybe. Or some men never change," Devin retorted.

Rebecca studied him, forming a hypothesis. "If you think about it, if you thought your father was truly bad, you wouldn't be so eager to leave. Explain that." she challenged.

Devin frowned. "What do you mean?"

"I think you believe he's okay, or you wouldn't feel comfortable leaving Ryan and Layla with him when you go off to college. Don't pretend it's about them just to make your point," she explained.

Devin scoffed, unable to argue. Rebecca continued, "I think you're frustrated because there's no one to blame for my cancer, and you're taking it out on your father more than he deserves."

For once, Devin didn't argue. He couldn't find a rebuttal. Rebecca giggled, satisfied with herself. "That's very astute of me, ain't it? What do they call that?"

"Projecting?" Devin questioned.

"Maybe."

Devin's feelings began to surface. He turned his face away, struggling to fight back the rising tide of emotions. "I don't...want you to go anywhere," he mumbled, his voice breaking, tears threatening to spill over.

Rebecca walked over, gently running her fingers through his hair. "Oh, my baby boy. Please don't feel bad for yourself or me. I will get to see the great things you will do and the man you will be. I can't do that cooped up in a bed, in pain. I will be around, just not the way you think I should, that's all." She hugged him tightly, his tears soaking into her shirt, holding him longer than she had since he was twelve.

"Do you believe that?" Devin asked, his voice shaking.

"I do, even if you don't. I can have enough faith for both of us. Fair?" Devin averted his gaze, feeling slightly embarrassed.

"Please give your dad a break—it wasn't him," Rebecca pleaded before Devin left the kitchen. He tightened his lips, offering his mother a pitiful smile before heading towards his room.

As he wandered toward his room, Devin noticed Ryan standing outside Layla's door, peering in. "What are you doing?" Devin asked. Ryan put a finger to his lips, signaling for silence.

Peeking inside, they saw four dolls arranged upright in Layla's room—some by her bed, others near her dresser, a mix of baby dolls and stuffed animals. Layla emerged, closing the door behind her, then looked at her brothers. "Hello, gents," she quipped before moving on.

Devin and Ryan exchanged puzzled glances. "I don't know, man. She's your sister," Devin joked, distancing himself from Layla's odd behavior. Weird, they thought, shrugging it off, but Ryan stayed to observe what Layla did next.

Layla gazed at the front door as she descended the stairs, one step at a time, reaching for the doorknob. The door creaked open, and she glanced back at her room before shutting it and running back upstairs. She reentered her room to find one doll, the kind whose eyelids shut when laid flat, toppled over. "That's not the right way," she whispered, setting the doll upright again before exiting and closing the door.

She descended the stairs again, this time reaching the bottom. Ryan listened as her footsteps moved towards the garage. "What are you doing, Layloo?" their father asked.

"Nothing," she replied sweetly.

"Alright. Why don't you go up to bed, sweetie? Don't let the Tickle Man come out. You know how it can take me over," Calvin chuckled. Layla giggled and agreed, hopping back upstairs. She glanced at Ryan when she reached the top.

"What are you doing exactly?" Ryan inquired.

"Playing a game," Layla answered. Intrigued, he asked, "What's the game?" Layla hesitated, twisting her mouth. "I have to find the right exit. The dolls fall over if I don't. No dolly falls if I pick the right one. If I pick a wrong one, then one or more fall over. If I pick the worst one, then they all fall over."

Ryan nodded, somewhat understanding. Layla opened her door to go to bed but stopped, looking at the floor. Ryan peeked around the door to see three of the four dolls had fallen over. "What does that mean?" he asked.

"It means I picked a really bad exit."

Ryan knelt and looked up at her, wrestling with a question he had avoided for so long— "You see them, don't you?"

Layla nodded.

"How often?"

"The one in the pink dress mostly, the one looking for her kitty. She tells me things—shows me where to go. The others stand in one

A whisper of wind rustled the curtains, though no window was open. The figures pressed closer; their shapes undefined but undeniably menacing. "I don't know what you want," Rebecca continued, her voice gaining strength, "but if you're here for evil, I cast you out! You are not welcome, and you must leave."

With a quick glance back at the window, she found only her kitchen table in view, relief washing over her as she saw the figures had vanished. The oppressive weight lifted, leaving her shaky but resolute. She had commanded them to depart, though she couldn't be certain if they were capable of heeding her words.

Maybe it has nothing to do with wickedness, she thought, trying to rationalize the eerie encounter. Yet, deep down, she knew these shadows brought more than just cold air and fear. She feared they brought a darkness seeping into the corners of her home, threatening to overtake the light she fought so hard to maintain. If only she knew the truth.

CHAPTER FIFTEEN

HEAD OVER HEELS

It was about eleven in the morning on Thanksgiving Day when the telephone rang, summoning Ryan to the receiver. Calvin entered Ryan's room, lifted his legs by the ankles, and playfully smacked him on the bottom, mimicking the antics of Foghorn Leghorn. Such teasing was typical in the Hatcher household, with Calvin often finding amusement in his playful pranks on the kids over the years.

The Hatchers hadn't upgraded to a portable phone yet, relying instead on the cream-colored rotary phone in the kitchen or the standard brown one downstairs. Ryan preferred the downstairs phone for its privacy. He dragged himself out of bed, groaning as he made his way to the door. The aroma of coffee and strawberry Pop-Tarts filled the air, but Ryan had no appetite. He hadn't felt hungry for the past few days.

Barely managing to produce a tired "hello," Ryan answered the phone, his mind foggy from a restless night haunted by ghosts he couldn't understand. "*Good morning!*" came the sweet, familiar voice on the other end. It took a moment for Ryan to realize it was Christina. "Hey, Christy?"

"*Of course it's me. Who else would it be?*" Christina replied with faux offense, her playful tone lightening Ryan's mood. Her cheerful voice helped wake him up a bit more. "*I caught you while you were still asleep, didn't I?*" Ryan nodded, momentarily forgetting he needed to speak. "Yeah, but that's okay. I need to get up anyway." He suddenly remembered Christina wasn't supposed to be in town. "Where are you?"

There was an unusual pause for Christina, who loved to have a chat. "*Plans didn't work out,*" she finally said.

"So you didn't get to go to South Carolina to see your cousins and all that?" Ryan asked.

"*No. My parents decided to go somewhere else, by themselves,*" Christina replied with a hint of disappointment.

"Do you want me to come over? No, wait. What are your grandparents going to do today?"

"*Um, to be honest, I don't know. I don't think they made plans because I was supposed to be gone,*" Christina admitted. Ryan had an idea and asked if he could call her back. She agreed, and Ryan rushed upstairs to ask his mother if Christina and her grandparents could come over for Thanksgiving. Rebecca didn't hesitate to agree, as Calvin had gone overboard with the food shopping the night before. "There's more than enough," she assured Ryan, excited to have company.

Ryan hurried back downstairs and called Christina. She answered confidently, expecting his call. "*Hello, Ryan,*" she greeted.

"What if that wasn't me calling?" Ryan teased.

"*Then I wasted my sexy voice on a total stranger or one of my family members. Yeah, that could have been really gross,*" Christina realized. They both snickered before Ryan properly invited her and her family to dinner around four o'clock. "It won't be normal, just to warn you. It's Kentucky Fried Chicken with a metric shit ton of sides," he explained. The kids didn't enjoy traditional Thanksgiving dishes like many others, finding turkey tasted like paper. To Ryan, if you had to put gravy and stuffing with something to make it taste good, it wasn't worth it in the first place. "*I'll ask and let you know,*" she replied. They said goodbye, and Ryan waited patiently for the phone to ring again.

Maybe some alone time would be nice, he thought as he waited for the call.

It didn't take long.

Ryan eagerly lifted the receiver from its base, his pulse quickening in anticipation.

"*They said that would be nice, so I guess we will be there around four!*" Christina exclaimed with excitement from the other end of the line. Ryan mirrored her enthusiasm, a grin spreading across his face.

"Great! See you then," he said, feeling a warmth in his chest.

Before ending the call, they indulged in their playful "couples game."

"You hang up... no, you hang up— you didn't hang up either!"

The game was the kind that made others cringe whenever they overheard new couples do it. But for Ryan and Christina, it was endearing, even though they weren't technically a couple.

With a final laugh, they both hung up, leaving Ryan in a buoyant mood as he replaced the receiver.

Time dragged on as Ryan and Devin sat on the couch, their eyes glued to the Minnesota Vikings facing off against the Houston Oilers. The droning commentary of the game filled the room, blending with the distant clatter of pots and pans from the kitchen above. Their mother had banished them from the kitchen to focus on desserts and attempt to teach Layla how to bake. Calvin's restlessness was undeniable; his leg bounced with pent-up energy, eager to tackle the shed in the backyard. The task of replacing its wooden sides wasn't overly complex, but the thought of organizing the interior filled him with apprehension.

Neither brother relished being there; Thanksgiving always stretched into an endless day of boredom. Devin occupied himself with his portable Coleco Donkey Kong game, while Ryan awaited Christina's arrival, his stomach fluttering with anticipation.

"I need your help with the shed tomorrow," Calvin directed at Devin, his voice cutting through the game's noise.

Devin glanced up, his expression a mix of irritation and defiance. "Can't. I'm still helping Melvin with his house."

Calvin's eyes narrowed; incredulity etched across his face. "Can't you go another time? Didn't he give you a deadline?"

"Nope, and yep. Supposed to be today, but couldn't get the place clean in time," Devin replied bluntly.

"I need this done Sunday," Calvin asked, his tone a notch softer.

Devin shot back, "That sounds like a you problem."

Calvin's jaw tightened; his lips pressed into a thin line. He rose abruptly, his shadow looming over the boys. Ryan instinctively shrank into the corner of the couch, his heart pounding. He had never seen his father so angry before.

"Please don't test me," Calvin said, his voice trembling with suppressed rage.

Devin stood, his posture rigid, his chin jutted out defiantly. "Do it," he taunted. "I dare you."

Calvin's eyes softened, a flicker of desperation breaking through his anger. "I just wanted some time with you, you know? That's all. You don't have to be a little shit about it."

Devin paused on the stairs, his back turned. "I don't understand why I'm so terrible. Why choose old man Craggs over your dad?"

"You know why. And what difference does it make? Get Ryan to help," Devin replied, his voice rising.

"Because you're my goddamn son, not his!"

A heavy silence fell over the house. The blender upstairs ceased its whirring, and the faint sound of air passing through the old windows filled the void. Devin had countless thoughts he wished to articulate but engaging in a shouting match felt pointless. With resolve, he ascended the stairs past his mother, who had heard the entire exchange.

"What da hell was that?" Rebecca whispered, as Calvin returned to his chair, deflated. Ryan watched his father closely, noting how his body swelled with anger before returning to its normal size. It didn't mean he was turning into a wolf, but the possibility lingered in his mind. Parents always appear larger when they were angry, but he had never seen anyone so furious before. If his father's rage was any indication of how he might change, Ryan finally understood what fear truly meant.

The doorbell rang, snapping Ryan out of his thoughts. He sprang to his feet, momentarily forgetting the argument, and dashed up the stairs to answer it. His excitement waned when he realized Layla had beaten him to it. She had wanted Christina all to herself, to play with her dolls in her room. He recognized her game and wasn't going to play it, not letting her have her way this time. As he approached, Layla turned around with a mischievous grin, daring Ryan to back off.

Layla swung the door open to reveal Christina, her curly blonde hair cascading around a black coat draped over a red dress with black pantyhose. Her grandparents, Jo and Carl, stood beside her, dressed elegantly. Ryan always had a soft spot for Christina's grandparents;

their kindness made him call them grandma and grandpa. The Hatchers, in contrast, were more casually attired—jeans and long-sleeved t-shirts for the boys, a nice polo for Cal, and a blouse for Rebecca. Layla, always aiming to outshine, wore one of her many dresses.

"Hello! Come in!" Layla beamed, stepping aside. The Hatchers and their guests exchanged pleasantries, with the men reintroducing themselves just in case. Jo, her eyes glistening with tears, hugged Rebecca tightly. "It's been too long," she whispered, noting Rebecca's frailer appearance since her diagnosis. The poor dear, Jo thought, her heart aching as she discreetly removed her coat.

The group gathered around the kitchen table, the adults occupying most of the space. The kids stood, eventually drifting to the family room, chatting while nibbling on the feast laid out: the Colonel's original recipe chicken, mac and cheese, mashed potatoes, green beans, and potato wedges for the carb enthusiasts. The adults discussed various topics, while the kids delved into music, movies, and school gossip.

Mid-conversation, Rebecca remembered something important. "Hey, guys!" she called out, her voice cutting through the chatter. Despite her frailty, her voice retained its commanding presence. "Come here for a sec. We need to tell you something." The kids groaned, reluctantly setting aside their plates and trudging over.

"Next week, your dad and I will be out for a bit," Rebecca announced. It was rare for them to go out alone, let alone for multiple days. "What do you mean?" Devin asked, puzzled by the idea of his parents needing time to themselves.

"On Tuesday, we'll be going to Cleveland for the Philharmonic Orchestra holiday concert and staying overnight," Rebecca began. Calvin interjected, "That one was your mother's idea."

"Anyway, we'll stay there through Wednesday, come home Thursday morning, and then we are going to a party that night with people from your father's work," Rebecca continued.

Ryan's interest piqued. The dates sounded familiar, but he couldn't place why. "That's kind of weird," Devin remarked. It was unusual, but given the circumstances, they wanted to make the most of their time.

"I'm sorry if your father and I want to be alone, away from you kids. God forbid!" Rebecca said with mock indignation. The adults laughed, while the kids exchanged glances, contemplating what they could do in their parents' absence.

Ew, yuck...blech! The thought of their parents having alone time was almost too much to bear.

"Devin's in charge. I'm trusting you all with this. No parties, don't burn the house down, be civil," Calvin instructed, his finger pointing at each of his kids, even Layla, who looked indignant at the implication she could be a troublemaker.

Jo interjected, "You know, they could come with us to the Fall Festival. We're going on Wednesday, so if you all want to tag along." Christina turned her head towards Ryan, her eyes hopeful, waiting for his response. Ryan nodded but said, "We'll see," instead. The weight of something unknown pressed on him, and Christina sensed it. She decided she would get him alone later to find out what was bothering him. Ryan quickly remembered that Colin was planning to go to the festival the same day with his foster siblings.

Layla watched her brother sink back into the couch, placing his plate on the table beside him. She sensed something was wrong. Although she didn't know much about life, she could tell when her usually laid-back brother was tense; she had seen it for several days now. Ryan felt her eyes on him and turned to meet her gaze. They stared at each other, understanding they needed to talk. *But how do you start a conversation with a child about something that nobody else believes?*

Layla finally broke the silence, her voice soft but firm. "Ryan, what's wrong?"

Ryan hesitated, glancing around to make sure no one else was listening. "It's just... there's been a lot on my mind," he admitted, struggling to find the right words.

"Is it about the ghosts?" Layla asked, her innocence cutting through the tension.

Ryan nodded slowly. "Yeah, it's about them. I don't know how to explain it, but something doesn't feel right. And now with Mom and Dad going away, I just... I don't know."

Layla reached out and squeezed his hand. "We'll figure it out together, okay?"

Ryan managed a small smile, grateful for her support. "Yeah, sure."

The wine glasses continued to fill as the parents chattered on, their voices blending into a lively hum. Ryan threw his trash in the overflowing bin, feeling excluded from the adult conversation. Devin had no interest either, so they went their separate ways as Christina joined Ryan outside.

***

A bit of rain dampened the ground, making it hard to find a dry spot. Nevertheless, the pair made their way down the stairs, passing Calvin and Carl, who were both passed out on the chair and sofa as the Lions and Cowboys played. Christina walked alongside Ryan as they headed to the shed his father would fix the next day. They moved the chopped wood Calvin kept behind the shed to use in their fire pit, arranging it so they could sit comfortably without getting their rear ends too damp.

Ryan needed to get out of his head. He glanced at Christina, who looked lovely despite the dampness. The dreary weather suited her, complementing her sense of style and pale skin. To him, she was beautiful, and this moment, with colored leaves adding a vivid backdrop to her black coat, would be etched in his memory forever. Her recent admission of romantic thoughts gave him a warm, fuzzy feeling whenever she was around.

"I'm sorry you couldn't go down South with your folks," Ryan said, trying to shift his focus from his anxieties to her.

"Yeah, well, I shouldn't have been too surprised. It's not like they haven't made plans and canceled on me before," she replied, her tone tinged with resignation. He nodded, unsure how to comfort her. Christina didn't need him to say anything; she just needed him to be there.

"What happened? I know it's not really my business, but we've known each other for a long time, and I've always wondered," Ryan ventured cautiously. "I didn't want you to hate me for asking."

Christina, surprised that Ryan had taken so long to ask about her parents, looked away, blowing cold air from her mouth. "I could never hate you," she assured him. Shifting to get comfortable on the woodpile, she began her story.

"So, my parents were drug addicts when I was born, and afterward. There was a lot of abuse from both. They would yell at each other, beating each another, and it wasn't an uneven fight. They both held their own, from what I remember. When I was four, about a year before you met me, I was sent to live with my grandparents."

Ryan listened intently, feeling sadness and admiration for her resilience. Christina continued, her voice steady despite the painful memories. "Living with my grandparents was the best thing that could have happened to me. They gave me a stable, loving home. I owe them everything."

Ryan reached out and squeezed her hand, offering unspoken support. Christina smiled faintly, grateful for his presence. The rain continued to fall gently around them, but in that moment, they felt a sense of warmth and connection weather couldn't touch.

"That sucks. Did they ever get better?" Ryan asked. Christina took a deep breath, bracing herself for the difficult conversation ahead.

"Yeah. They got better, I think. I mean, my parents say they are. But why haven't I gone back to them if they were, you know? Why am I still living with my grandma and grandpa? I thought they would want to have me, but they don't." Her nose began to run as her eyes swelled, fighting back tears. "We always make plans, ya know? But there's always something. I go with them on weekends around town, but nothing that really matters." Ryan nodded, feeling her heartbreak.

"But I matter, don't I? They were the ones hurting themselves and each other, but it's like I'm the one they are afraid of. I think they hate me. They do. They hate me! I'm the reason they fought!" Christina sobbed into her black fabric gloves, hiding her face from Ryan. He had never seen her cry like this before.

It was the first time he needed to comfort someone who wasn't his own family. Gently, he put his left arm around her while she cried, unsure if she wanted to be touched. Christina moved into the pit of his arm, unknowingly wiping her nose against his sleeve. Ryan knew he had to find the right words. These next words needed to mean something. *I need to be articulate now*, Ryan thought, searching for what to say—*what I say and what I mean always seem to disagree.*

"I don't know your parents. They always gave me dirty looks when I saw them," Ryan started. Christina snickered through her sobs. "But I don't think they hate you. I think, maybe, they're ashamed. Maybe they hate themselves? They don't know who you are now because they missed out on the best parts, ya know? That's on them. I'm afraid to tell you, but you are not someone anybody can hate," Ryan explained before ending his heartfelt thought, "It's impossible!"

Christina looked up at Ryan, her face stained with tears and a runny nose. If he didn't know better, which he didn't, Ryan thought she wanted him to kiss her. Her eyes, red and glistening, held a vulnerable longing making his heart race. He moved his face towards hers, then hesitated. *Not now. It's not the right moment.* He watched her beautiful face draw closer, but he froze, unsure of what to do next.

Christina closed the small gap between them, her forehead resting gently against his. Her breath mingled with his, warm and shaky. Ryan's heart pounded in his chest, each beat louder than the last. He could feel her raw emotions pressing against his own.

"I'm sorry," he whispered, his voice barely audible over the sound of the rain.

Christina shook her head slightly, her tears mingling with the raindrops on her cheeks. "Don't be. Just... be here with me," she murmured.

Ryan nodded, wrapping his arms around her in a protective embrace. He felt her body relax against his, her sobs subsiding into soft sniffles. The moment was heavy with unspoken words, yet it felt right in its own imperfect way. They remained holding onto each other as the world around them blurred into the background.

Closing his eyes, Ryan's uncertainty clawed at him as he hesitated, then reopened them to behold Christina, frozen in the same pose, now peculiar as her complexion was drained of life. Leaning back, Ryan's gaze penetrated her partially agape grinning mouth, witnessing the horror within: teeth coated in a sickly gray hue, blood oozing from four savage lacerations etched into her brow. He watched the unthinkable—Christina's once wide and beautiful smile twisted, contorting her features as the wounds elongated, rending her tissue apart. A grotesque frown replaced her smile, her jaw unhinging unnaturally wide, revealing a gaping maw of emptiness where teeth, tongue, and tissue should be. From the depths of her void-like cavity, blood gushed forth, cascading down her disintegrating form, exposing vicious claw marks beneath the crumbling flesh.

In Ryan's embrace, Christina's body disintegrated, consumed by an unseen force, leaving only ashes clinging to his hands and clothes. A murky silhouette materialized, kneeling before him, its dark orbs fixating on him with an unsettling intensity. Before Ryan could summon a scream, the apparition, its teeth stained crimson, bellowed in Christina's voice, accusing him, "Why did you let me die!"

Clutching his fists to his eyes, Ryan yearned to awaken from the nightmare, but warm fingers grazed his knuckles, sending a shudder through his body. Recoiling from the touch, Ryan tumbled from the woodpile, his heart pounding with irrational fear. Yet, as he felt Christina's presence once more, he struggled to ground himself, to dispel the surreal dread enveloping him.

Wiping his eyes, Ryan recoiled at the imagined residue of human remnants, only to be met with Christina's gentle inquiry, her voice tinged with concern, "What happened? What's the matter, Ryan?" Desperate for solace, he reached out, seeking the tangible reassurance of her existence amidst the surreal nightmare threatening to consume him.

"What happened? What's wrong?" Christina's soothing voice broke through the tension, her eyes wide with concern as she knelt beside Ryan. The dilapidated shed loomed behind her, devoid of any spectral presence. Ryan grasped her hand tightly, struggling to catch his breath amidst the suffocating dread gripping him.

"You could have just told me you didn't want to be near me," Christina quipped, attempting to mask her underlying worry with humor. Ryan managed a weak smile as they emerged from behind the shed, his mind racing to find a semblance of sanity amidst the chaos.

"I've been having these dreams lately, maybe visions. I'm not sure what to call it. They just happen out of nowhere. They last for a few moments, then reality comes back," Ryan confessed, his words laden with uncertainty. Christina furrowed her brow in contemplation.

"Well, there is one explanation—you are cuckoo for Cocoa Puffs," she teased, trying to lighten the heavy atmosphere. Ryan chuckled nervously, "Is there a pill I can take for that?"

Christina's expression shifted, her concern deepening as she recognized the gravity of Ryan's mental state. "It sounds like something I heard on a show on PBS. Sleep paralysis? Maybe not. Could be something else I'm forgetting the name of," she suggested. Ryan struggled to comprehend.

"But I'm not asleep," he protested, his confusion evident. Christina paused, reflecting on what she knew.

"Sure, but you told us you haven't been sleeping well. What if you are nodding off?"

"Would it come on that quick?" Ryan questioned, seeking validation. Christina shook her head.

"I don't think so."

Ryan surrendered with a dramatic gesture; flinging his arms into the air in a gesture of defeat. "Then I am either a lost cause or a weirdo. Probably both!" The wind howled, tugging at Christina's hair, which billowed across her face, obscuring her mouth and brow. Despite the chaos, her eyes, those captivating orbs, twinkled with amusement beneath the tangled strands.

With a gentle sweep, Christina brushed her nearly white, blonde hair from her face, revealing a playful grin. "Let's just go with weirdo. I can work with that. Lost cause means we should just give up," she quipped, her lighthearted tone a balm to Ryan's troubled soul.

Christina looked above Ryan's head towards his house. Ryan turned his head and saw Layla staring at them in the yard, not blinking or waving hello like she usually would when she saw Christina.

In her dimly lit room, Layla's gaze drifted beyond the couple, drawn inexorably to the decrepit shed looming in the distance. As she watched, a shiver crept down her arms and legs, for nestled amidst the shadows, the spectral figure of the ginger-haired girl materialized, her eyes fixed on Layla with an intensity sending a chill through her veins.

With a suddenness that made Layla's heart leap in her chest, the girl darted out from behind the shed, her movements jerky and disjointed, like a marionette controlled by unseen hands. Each twitch of her limbs, each crack of her neck echoed in the silence of the night, a macabre dance that filled Layla with a primal dread. The entity had visited Ryan and Christina, prompting a vision of his deceased friend in his arms. Messages were being sent in the form of visions and there was little doubt to Layla it was the visitors doing it.

Never before had Layla witnessed such unnatural contortions, such a grotesque display of movement. Panic surged within her as she realized the extent of the horror unfolding before her very eyes. That scares me! Layla's thoughts screamed silently, her plea echoing in the recesses of her mind—please don't do that again.

***

"Yeah. Something feels off," Ryan sighed, his conviction growing that the entities haunting his home were demonic tormentors. They lurked alongside Colin's family, inhabiting the children in his visions, and now haunting images of Christina crumbling between his fingers haunted him. *What are their intentions? Is there a message behind it all?*

"Why did you seem so worried when your parents mentioned they'd be away next week?" Christina had been pondering this since dinner, unable to find an explanation. Ryan glanced towards his house, about to delve into his probable delusions. With a seriousness that startled Christina, he replied, "Because—that's when the full moon happens."

CHAPTER SIXTEEN

EVERYWHERE

Ryan opened his eyes after a fitful sleep to find another pair of eyes staring back at him. Rebecca crouched on the floor, peeking just above the edge of the mattress with only her nose and eyes visible. The eerie feeling of being watched settled over him, more intense than he'd ever imagined. He blinked hard and saw his mother's wrinkled, crow's-feet-framed eyes. She was smiling, her mouth hidden below the mattress.

"Jesus Christ!" he yelped, flinging himself towards the wall. His mother stood up, laughing heartily—it was the first time he'd seen her laugh in ages. Her cancer usually made laughing painful, but not today. *I'll take what I can get.*

"What is wrong with you people and waking me up in the morning? You're as bad as Dad!" Ryan gasped, catching his breath. He glanced around the room; the sun hadn't risen yet. "What time is it?"

"It's about six o'clock. I need you to get moving and watch the blasphemy," Rebecca teased. Ryan rubbed his eyes, curled his lip, and asked, "Why?" Rebecca's sly grin appeared. "It's the day after Thanksgiving. We are going shopping!"

Ryan groaned, burying his face in his pillow. "Why do I have to go?" Rebecca opened his closet, like she used to when he was in elementary school, only to find a mess of clothes on the floor. "Ryan Hatcher, I swear!"

Trying to lighten the mood, Ryan quipped, "You shouldn't. It's not very nice."

Rebecca gave him an unamused look as she gathered his dirty clothes. "You're going because I invited your friends. It will be fun, I promise." Ryan, puzzled, asked, "Who did you invite?"

"The usual rogues; Scott, Colin, and Christina," she smiled. "Oh, and your sister."

"How are you going to fit all of us in the Turbo?" Ryan asked, getting out of bed to help with the clothes. "Just put Layloo on one of your laps. It's just down the street," she replied.

"What if you get caught?" Ryan's concern about being stopped by the cops was clear.

"What are they going to do? Put me in jail? I'll be dead before I get a court date," Rebecca said, not noticing the impact of her words. Ryan shook his head, opening his mouth to yell but stopping himself. "That's not funny," he muttered, dropping the clothes and walking out. Rebecca watched him go and decided to focus on the day ahead with Layla, Ryan, and his friends.

The other teenagers walked over to the Hatcher's house, except for Colin, who rode his quasi-new bike. As he coasted down the driveway, Rebecca pointed at the bike. "Hey! I recognize that thing!" she playfully shouted. All four stood around the garage, waiting for Rebecca to signal them to hop in. Christina broke the awkward silence first.

"So, why are we all going to the mall today? And why did your mom want us all to come?" she asked Ryan.

He shrugged with a slight smile. "I've learned to never question or try to understand. Just do what Rebecca Hatcher wants, and everything will be fine."

Scott nodded in agreement while Colin hung on to every word. Christina pouted and replied, "Fair enough."

They packed into the car, uncomfortably squeezing in. A few minutes later, Rebecca snapped her fingers and shouted, "Let's go!" As they struggled to fit, Scott asked, "What are we doing first?" He was always the one to ask about the day's schedule, especially if free food was involved.

"Well, I thought we'd start with an early lunch," Rebecca answered, glancing at Scott in the rearview mirror. Scott pouted his lip and nodded, liking the idea, waiting for her to look away before doing a quiet fist pump. "Then what?"

"You'll just have to see," Rebecca answered mysteriously.

The Rolling Acres parking lot was packed. Ryan never understood the Black Friday craze—it was crowded, and people were rude. Plus, he was highly claustrophobic in overcrowded areas. They squeezed out of the car and headed to the mall's entrance on an unseasonably warm day. Realizing they'd be hot inside, they threw their coats and jackets into the back seat. Ryan looked out onto the main road and across at the businesses along Romig Road. They lived near one of the largest shopping areas in Akron, but today, they were about to rule it, with Layla as their princess.

Inside, Layla's eyes were glued to the large water fountain, as always. The tall pillars spewed water from the tops, endlessly fascinating her. Rebecca reached into her purse and handed each of them a nickel. "Make a wish," she told them, and they all did. Ryan flicked his coin with his thumb, watching it ricochet off the red tiered tiles around the cascading water pillars. Layla and Colin threw theirs like they were pitching in the World Series. Scott aimed his coin, trying to land it on one of the pillars creating a waterfall that reminded him of Nakatomi Plaza from his new favorite movie, *Die Hard*.

Christina paused to watch the children playing around the fountain, illuminated by the glass roof above the decorative scaffolding. Before tossing her nickel underhand, she mouthed her wish, careful not to let anyone hear—otherwise, it wouldn't come true. The coin landed on the second tier of bright red tiles. Satisfied, Christina nodded to Rebecca and stood beside her, with Layla following as usual.

They headed to The Picnic Place Food Court, where they could pick from several eateries or mix and match if feeling bold. Scott, Colin, and Christina rummaged through their wallets and purses, coming up short for lunch money, as if hoping a magical money fairy had filled their pockets. Rebecca, shaking her head at their obvious ploy, sighed. "It's fine, you lot. I got it. Just tell me what you want."

Colin and Christina chose Orange Julius, opting for their signature drink and a hot dog. Colin devoured a Pepperoni Cheese Dog, while Christina, looking starved, wolfed down a Bacon Cheese Dog. Scott made a beeline for the Philly Steak eatery, partly for the taste and partly because it gave him horrific gas. The thought of making the others suffer with his farts made him chuckle—yes, Scott Donovan was that kid.

The Hatcher clan settled on Sbarro for a slice of New York-style pizza and pasta salad. The kids preferred pepperoni, while Rebecca opted for sausage. Her appetite had waned due to illness, but today she felt better and ordered a giant meatball.

Rebecca sat back, watching the kids blow straw covers at each other, laughing and getting along. Ryan and Layla, relieved to be away from their haunted house, relaxed for the first time in a while. The fun was just beginning for them.

***

Meanwhile, Devin was preparing to do some final work on Mr. Craggs' home. He decided to skip a shower, figuring he'd sweat and stink anyway. Around noon, he walked into the kitchen to find his father sitting there, looking lost as he stared at the table. The house felt empty without Rebecca, and Calvin wondered how he'd cope when she was gone for good.

Devin couldn't imagine his mother not being around, but the thought of losing a spouse was foreign to him. His anger towards his father overshadowed any sympathy he might have had.

"Are you going to do anything productive today or just let psoriasis of the liver set in a little more?" Devin asked harshly, not caring about the consequences. Calvin sucked in his teeth, deciding to play along. "I stopped drinking, but maybe it's already lingering there." Devin shook his head slightly, rolling his eyes, not expecting an answer. Deep down, he craved confrontation.

"You going next door again?"

"Yeah, a couple more days, and I think I'll be done," Devin replied, searching for his coat.

Calvin stood up and walked toward Devin, looking different than before. He stood straighter, his head now full of hair. His shirts fit better and no longer rose when he sat and drank in front of the television.

"Can we talk civilly, like men?" his father asked. Devin took a deep breath, knowing this conversation was inevitable. "Fine. Let's talk. What should we discuss?" he said sarcastically.

"Oh! I know! Let's talk about how you beat Mom that night."

***

"Here's money for each of ya," Rebecca said, handing out envelopes. "Do whatever you want with it. Spend it. Keep it. It doesn't matter to me. Just have fun today." The kids opened their envelopes to find one hundred dollars in tens. They exchanged surprised glances before looking at Rebecca. "Mom, this is too much. How can you do this?" Ryan asked, concerned.

"Ain't none of ya business how! It's mine, and I'll do what I want wit it. Got it?" she scolded, then smiled again. "Make good decisions with it and have fun. Remember today for as long as you can."

I think I will remember it forever, Ryan thought.

"I'm going to do my own shopping. We meet here, at the food court. Got it?" Layla looked up at the ceiling, focusing on the pink and green neon lights. "Got it," she said.

Rebecca made everyone promise to keep Layla close, no matter who she shopped with. Layla quickly announced she and Christina would be doing girl shopping. "That sounds fine to me," Scott agreed, relieved the little ankle-biter wouldn't be tagging along with the boys. He was eager to spend his newfound fortune, sniffing and rubbing the bills against his face.

"Do you realize how many people probably had their hands on that money?" Christina asked.

"Yeah, some lady probably changed her kid's diaper and forgot to wash her hands," Colin quipped, understanding Scott's humor. Scott looked down at the bills and then examined his hands. "Need to go to the bathroom first." Ryan elbowed Colin and smiled before sighing. "Now we have to wait longer because he's a bit obsessive-compulsive." Yes, that Scott Donovan. The same guy who ate a steak sandwich with cheese and onion just to pass gas near them later was also the one who despised having a speck of dust on his hands. Colin and Ryan sat back down, knowing it might take a while before Scott emerged from the restroom.

***

"It was wrong of me, I know," Calvin admitted.

The memory of that night was vivid. Rebecca and Calvin were arguing in the office next to the laundry room. It was shortly after Rebecca's diagnosis, and Calvin had started drinking heavily. His bitterness spread to everyone, including his kids. Medical bills piled up, and their lifestyle was no longer sustainable.

Devin, listening to records in his room above the laundry room, could hear the fight through the vents. The shouting escalated, his mother's high-pitched screams blending with his father's deep yells. He crept downstairs, avoiding the creaky spots, and peered around the open door. He saw his father strike his mother, the sound of the blow echoing through the room—a sound Devin would never forget.

"It wasn't just a slap! Your fist was in a ball!" Devin yelled, starting the confrontation. "I know. You don't have to do a play-by-play," Calvin replied calmly.

"How do you excuse that?" Devin pressed. Calvin knew there was no defense. "I can't. Nothing justifies it. After that, I knew I didn't want to be that person anymore. I can't take it back."

Devin's anger flared. He wanted his father to fight back. "I've had a lot of wrong moments. Haven't you had bad moments when you talk back to your mother or hurt your brother's feelings?" Calvin asked.

"Don't even compare those to what you did. And she was already sick!" Devin screamed.

"What do you want from me?" Calvin yelled. "Do you want to hit me? Come on, then. Take your shot!" His chest expanded, making him look larger. Devin saw the intensity in his father's eyes—wide, black, dilated pupils.

Devin backed away, scared of what he might do. He realized he was ready to hit his father, realizing he might not be any better than him. Calvin backed down, leaning against the wall, breathing deeply to calm his racing heart. He remembered techniques from an anger management tape he'd listened to. *You did good*, Calvin thought. "I'm sorry it happened, but your mother forgave me. Can you?"

Devin put on his shoes and jacket and headed to work. "She forgave you because she had no other options. Don't act like you'd be here if she was healthy." Calvin was hurt by the comment. Devin didn't believe it, knowing his mom was just forgiving. "I don't know. Maybe," he said, walking away.

Before reaching the front door, Devin turned back. "I never thought my dad would be just like every piece of white trash in this town. Drunk and abusive. My best friend deals with it, and no one cares. I'm tired of being the only one who does."

Calvin watched his son walk away, realizing Devin no longer saw him as a perfect father but as a flawed human. This realization broke Calvin in a way only a father could understand—a truth he hoped to keep from his other two kids a little longer.

***

Ryan, Scott, and Colin did what any red-blooded American boys with some money would do—spend too much at Aladdin's Castle Arcade, of course. They agreed to limit themselves to ten dollars each. Colin, never having been to an arcade, admitted this excitedly. Scott, flabbergasted, said, "I have much to teach you, young one."

As they passed the Chess King men's clothing store, they approached the dark storefront of the arcade, illuminated by demo screens flashing and demanding coins. The arcade was alive with bleeps and bloops, bodies jerking around joysticks, and fingers mashing buttons. Colin's eyes scanned the entrance through the dense cigarette smoke. The sights and sounds made him hesitate. Ryan and Scott turned to see their friend staring in awe. With grins plastered on their faces, they knew Colin was in for a treat.

"What are we going to play?" Colin asked in wonder. Scott put his arm around him and replied, "The question isn't what we're going to play, but what aren't we going to play."

Inside, the arcade cabinets lined the walls and the middle of the space, with a coin machine to change their money. Realizing the device only took one and five-dollar bills, the boys flagged down a staff member to break their tens.

They walked around, deciding what to play first—*Pac-Man, Burger Time, Donkey Kong, Outrun, Double Dragon, Contra, The Goonies II, Tron,* or maybe even *Centipede.* The options were endless. Ryan decided to explore one end of the arcade while Scott and Colin looked for a machine. Scott was relishing his role as arcade sensei to Colin, who gravitated towards *Space Invaders* first.

Scott decided it was the perfect moment to unleash the pent-up gas rumbling inside him. As the noxious cloud spread, players stopped, covering their mouths and noses. The room filled with the sounds of game over screens, players losing lives, and disgust.

***

Christina and Layla made their rounds, bouncing between clothing stores—Wet Seal, Contemporary Classics, Gadzooks, Limited Express, and Merry-Go-Round. After picking up some tops on sale, Christina looked down at Layla, grinning. A trip inside Higbee's for some makeup was next on her list. Layla, though young for makeup, enjoyed the excitement in Christina's eyes. Sensing Layla's boredom, Christina bought her a clearance dress and a Fresh n' Fancy pink makeup kit made for girls her age. "This is probably something her mother should be doing with her," Christina thought.

Then, like any book lover, Christina guided Layla into Waldenbooks. They wandered through the aisles until Christina reached the Stephen King section. She picked up *The Tommyknockers* and *Misery*, torn between the two. Books were a rare luxury, and choosing just one was tough.

"Why not just get both?" a small voice of reason asked. Christina looked down at Layla, who was staring at the book covers. She had a point; why not get both? Christina succumbed to the power of suggestion, choosing both novels. Layla picked up a book from the same shelf and flipped through it.

"What about this? Would I like *IT*?" Layla asked. Christina took the colossal book, glanced at the cover, and put it back, knowing its content. "That book is not for you. Not yet anyway," Christina told her. "Maybe when you're older." She tugged on Layla's coat and headed toward the register. Layla looked back at the cover, depicting a paper boat heading towards a storm drain with a reptilian-looking hand emerging.

"But I want to read it," Layla exclaimed. Christina knelt down and gave her some advice. "Read it? You can barely lift it. Rule of thumb: If you can hardly pick up the book, chances are it's probably not made for you."—that and the underage sex scene, she thought.

"But I want to read something scary," Layla whined. Christina hesitated, but sensing Layla's determination, she guided her to the kids area and let her pick a smaller book. After what felt like hours, Layla finally chose *The Cave of Time*, a Choose Your Own Adventure book. She wanted what she thought may be scary, thinking it would prepare her for what was coming next.

Layla sensed something imminent. The dead had been preparing her, showing the way, but she wasn't sure why. Only her big brother saw them and was equally puzzled by their attachment to their family. Layla didn't want to ask for help; she was stubborn like her mother. But maybe it was time to tell him—no—show him, she wondered.

***

Scott spent more than initially agreed upon. "How much in quarters did you use?" Ryan asked, already sensing the absurdity.

Scott's head hung low. "Thirty."

"Thirty!" Ryan and Colin yelled in unison.

Scott pointed towards the arcade's center. Ryan's eyes locked onto the screen with the distinctive Bluth animation style. "*Dragon's Lair*? Did you beat it at least?" he asked knowing full well Scott was in it for the well animated breasts on the damsel in distress, Princess Daphne.

Scott's face flushed. "No."

Laughter burst from Ryan and Colin. Scott shot Colin a glare. "I don't know what you're laughing at. You didn't even know what an arcade was before today!"

"I did too! Just never been in one. Only saw one in *The Last Starfighter*," Colin muttered defensively.

Ryan checked his Casio watch and his eyes widened. "Oh, shit! We need to go!" They quickly exited Aladdin's Castle, moving briskly through the corridor past Casual Corner and Hickory Farms.

They found the girls waiting by the exit. Ryan's gaze settled on his mother, noticing the slight sag in her shoulders. "You okay, mom?" he asked.

Rebecca nodded, a smile masking her weariness. "I hope ya didn't use too much of your money because I'm going to Children's Palace next."

Layla's eyes sparkled with excitement, and Colin mirrored her enthusiasm. Ryan, Scott, and Christina exchanged knowing smiles. Despite their age, the allure of the most fantastic toy store lingered. They crammed into the car and drove towards the castle-shaped store on the horizon.

Before the company with the giraffe as a mascot reared his head into the Akron area, there was Children's Palace. Forget Kay-Bee toy stores with their tight aisles; —the 'palace' was where it was at. Children's Palace was a dimly lit store with colored halogen lights animating neon lit animals around the border of the sales floor. The store aisles were so wide four friends could spring down them with Sit 'n Bounce Balls. Every once in a while, Peter Panda, the store mascot, would walk around, giving kids a pat on the head or a hug if the child wanted it.

After walking through the entrance where a person met Layla in a Peter Panda mascot suit with a red balloon, Rebecca pulled Scott and Christina to the side. "I need you to keep Ryan and Layla busy. I'm going shopping for them." They both smiled and nodded, understanding what Rebecca would do—she was Christmas shopping.

Colin and Layla darted up and down the aisles, their voices animated as they chattered about their favorite shows, matching toys in hand. Scott and Christina had no trouble keeping up with their excitement. Meanwhile, Ryan trailed behind, disinterested. The colorful toys that once held magic were now mundane. If he were younger, he'd be clamoring for a new Ghostbusters or Transformers toy. A sting of disappointment flashed across his face as he remembered never owning any Transformers, just the knockoff Go-Bots his dad insisted were just as good—*they weren't. Go-Bots. The off brand that was not more than meets the eye.*

Scott grabbed Ryan by the arm, steering him toward the electronics section. "You know you want to look," he teased.

Ryan dug in his heels, shaking his head. "No. Nope. There's no point. I won't get it anytime soon."

Scott laughed maniacally, pulling him harder. They arrived at a glass display case showcasing the holy grail of gaming: the Nintendo Entertainment System with Super Mario Bros and Duck Hunt. Scott's eyes gleamed as he leaned closer. "You have to make this happen, Ryan. It's time to ditch the Atari and ColecoVision. This is your destiny—*The Legend of Zelda, Mike Tyson's Punch-Out, Final Fantasy,* and… *Contra.* Up, up, down, down, left, right, left, right, B, A, Start—the thirty lives code. Oh yeah, it needs to happen."

Ryan glanced at Scott and asked, "Why is this on me?"

"Because your family has the scratch. You think my podunk family can afford this? I have to eat knock-off Sugar Smacks. I need to live vicariously through you. By denying yourself, you are making me go without. Is that what you want?" Scott explained, his tone a mix of humor and desperation.

"You're an idiot. Why am I even friends with you?" Ryan joked.

"Two reasons, Ryan, my boy. Because I am so damn exciting, and because you lack options. I'm a realist. It's okay."

Ryan considered it for a moment, then nodded. "You didn't have to agree so fast," Scott muttered, feigning disappointment.

Ryan grinned to show he was just teasing. "You know what the real tragedy is?" he asked. Scott shrugged, curious. "It's Black Friday, and these Nintendo systems aren't sold out yet."

Scott nodded, "Times are tough all over, I guess." The unspoken reality hung in the air: Akron was still reeling from the shutdown of industrial plants, which had cost thousands of jobs over the past few years.

Rebecca approached them, eyebrows raised. "What's going on here? What's all dis then?"

"Just fantasizin'," Ryan sighed.

Rebecca glanced at the glass case and the displayed games, knowing her sons had been eyeing the Nintendo for a while. "So, if you had this thing, what three games would you want with it if you had a choice?" she asked.

Ryan and Scott exchanged thoughtful looks. "Legend of Zelda, Contra, and… Punch-Out. —Yeah," they spouted with a sigh.

"Good to know. Okay, guys, get everyone out to the car for me. We are going to The Ground Round for dinner."

Ryan and Scott, thrilled, dashed off to gather the others. They loved that restaurant. The food was great, and "They let you throw peanut shells on the floor!" Scott squealed.

Rebecca treated them to a feast they would later take for granted. She savored seeing her kids happy, laughing, and chatting, absorbing every moment as she nibbled on bread. Finally, they all piled into the car, their stomachs full from the early dinner, making the ride home even more cramped. Everyone thanked Ryan's mom as they exited the car and headed into their homes.

The ride home was strange for Ryan. He sensed something was off with his mom. Rebecca had spent way too much money for the day, and she was typically more frugal than his dad. Ryan stepped out of the car and headed to the swing attached to the tree by a rope in the backyard. Lost in his thoughts, he didn't say anything to his mother or Layla.

After settling down from the day, Rebecca walked into the kitchen to make her evening tea. She noticed Ryan sitting on the swing, facing the sunset beaming through the trees. She thought to herself, he is perceptive, knowing she would need to talk with him.

Rebecca walked barefoot through the grass and dying leaves on the ground. She came up behind her son, not wanting to startle him, and waited until he acknowledged her presence. Ryan knew she was there but didn't know what to say.

"I know why you did what you did today," Ryan spoke softly. Rebecca put her hands to her sides and nervously patted her legs. "You're going to go away soon, aren't you?"

Rebecca walked over to his side and looked at the orange sun going down over the horizon. "Yeah. I think so. I'm not sure." Ryan nodded, already knowing the honest answer.

"I was supposed to die today, son," she confessed with quivering lips.

He hated the idea of anyone seeing him get emotional, so he turned his head away, aware his mother would easily see through him. "Today was a gift, so I guess I wanted it to be for you too," he murmured. "I think my friends had a good time," Ryan joked weakly, trying to hold back his tears.

"Did you?" his mother asked, her voice full of concern.

Wiping his eyes, Ryan nodded and said, with fractured words and a broken heart, "Yeah, but not if…it means…losing you."

His mother gently grabbed the back of his head, pulling him into her chest. "I'm on borrowed time now, love. Let's do what we can with it. Does that sound fair?"

They both cried for one another as the sun finally set in the west, casting long shadows over their shared sorrow, the sky ablaze with hues of orange and pink, a beautiful yet heart-wrenching backdrop to their sadness.

CHAPTER SEVENTEEN

SOMETHING ABOUT YOU

The clan gathered around noon on Saturday to indulge Ryan's theory that his father was a werewolf. Ryan waited for them in the garage, where he helped his dad bring out supplies to rebuild the shed—long sawed-off wood, wood panels, insulation, and a nail gun.

Colin arrived first, followed by Scott, and finally Christina. As they entered the garage, Scott dropped his book bag filled with four walkie-talkies, three binoculars, cans of orange Crush, and snacks for when hunger struck. "What's all this?" Ryan asked, curious.

Scott grinned, ready to educate the group. Ryan recognized this smile—it meant Scott was about to show off. "These, my out-of-touch friend, are TRC-217 CB walkie-talkies and binoculars. Not the plastic ones with orange antennae from our childhood," he proudly explained.

Unimpressed by the display, Ryan glanced at an imaginary camera on the wall, channeling Ferris Bueller. "Let me rephrase—why do you have them?" Christina smirked at Ryan's sarcasm, enjoying his snarky side.

"I swiped them from the garage. My dad never uses this stuff, so why not?" Scott replied. Ryan couldn't argue; he wanted to spy, and Scott delivered.

"I have to say… I'm impressed," Ryan admitted, earning a smile from Scott. "Thanks. If only my dad would appreciate it like you do," Scott joked.

Christina struggled with the walkie-talkies, so Colin showed her how to use them. "Press the button to talk, then release it when you're done," he instructed. She nodded, getting the hang of it. "So, what's the plan?" she asked.

The truth was, there was no plan. "Just make sure Dad doesn't get too suspicious," Ryan improvised. They split up around the house and into the woods behind. Colin found a pile of leaves near the shed and crawled inside. Christina hid under a tarp on the deck, while Scott went the extra mile and climbed onto the roof using the patio furniture. The wood creaked under his weight, causing concern for Christina. "How much do you weigh?" she whispered, annoyed.

"More than you can handle, baby," Scott joked, out of breath. Rolling her eyes, she raised her walkie, ready to report.

Ryan found a more straightforward hiding spot under the deck, behind an old, covered hot tub no one used. He peered through the cracks in the wood above him to see Christina had made herself comfortable. "What's everybody's location?" Ryan spoke into the mic, causing audible feedback that caught his father's attention.

Calvin paused his hammering and glanced towards the patio deck. Scott lay flat on his stomach, hoping his grey hoodie would camouflage him against the roof shingles. Everyone else froze, hands clamped over their ears. The hammering resumed, breaking the tension.

Ryan let out a breath, turning down the volume on his walkie-talkie. "Turn yours down too," he instructed the others. Silence followed. Ryan's eyes darted around, worry creeping in. "Hello?" he whispered urgently into the mic.

A rustling sound broke the silence. "I'm here. By the shed," Colin's voice came through, barely audible.

Christina, peeking from under her tarp, added gently, "Under the deck. All clear."

Scott, still flat on the roof, grumbled, "Trying not to fall off here. What's the plan?"

Ryan sighed; the pressure of leadership heavy on his shoulders. "Just keep an eye on Dad. Report anything suspicious," he said, trying to sound confident. He squinted through the cracks in the wood, watching Calvin's every move, hoping they wouldn't get caught.

"*You have to say 'over'—over*," Scott whispered.

"*Yeah. That's true, over,*" Colin added. Ryan was becoming annoyed by the sticklers he called friends.

"*Even I know that—,*" Christina tacked on before Ryan interrupted, "Okay! I get it!" There was another pause between the four.

"*If you're going to be obnoxious about it, then I don't want to play anymore,*" Scott snobbishly said. He was trying to get Ryan's goat and was successful.

Good grief.

Colin poked his binoculars out of the leaves to watch Calvin work. "*Why am I the only one away from y'all?*" he asked. Ryan looked around, realizing he, Scott, and Christina were all on the same side, just different height levels. "He's right. We need to get on other sides," Ryan realized, finally preparing a plan.

"*How do you plan on that, genius? There are only so many sides before we venture into Craggs' yard. Even then, it's wide open—over,*" Scott pointed out. Ryan looked around the yard and into the woods and found other hiding areas behind the shed. "I'm going to the back of the shed by the woods. I'll go left and circle to the back. Christina. Colin. I need you two to be my eyes, over."

"*You can't! The noise of the crackling leaves and branches will alert him. It's too risky. It's suicide, I tell ya! Over.*" Scott desperately told Ryan.

"My God, man! What would you have me do? It's the only way! Over." Ryan quietly yelled into the mic, putting on a performance.

"*You son of a bitch! Ya got big balls, Ryan.*" Scott sighed.

"That's what your mom said last night, over," Ryan laugh inwardly.

"*Overdramatic much? Over,*" Christina raised an eyebrow, her playful smirk hinting at her thoughts on her taste in guys. She watched Ryan with a mix of amusement and curiosity. His playful energy was something new to her, and despite its dorkiness, she found it endearing.

"I'm going in, over," Ryan announced with a disingenuous serious tone, crawling out from under the deck. With a quick, enthusiastic glance back, he sprinted towards the woods.

"*I salute you, soldier,*" Colin chimed in, "*...over.*"

Calvin heard a rustling come from the woods. He poked his head out from the side of the shed, thinking it was a squirrel.

"*Get down!*" Christina whispered urgently. Ryan dropped flat onto the ground, holding still, eyes wide and attentive, waiting for the signal. Calvin emerged in front of the building, his gaze scanning the woods, oblivious to the three sets of eyes fixed on him. He frowned, puzzled by the noise, then turned back towards the shed.

"*He's going back. Go now and be quiet,*" Colin instructed, his binoculars still poking out from the leaf pile.

"*What's it like under there?*" Scott whispered, his curiosity evident.

"*Pretty sweet, actually,*" Colin replied with a grin.

Ryan began his careful crawl towards the back of the shed, his movements slow and deliberate. He was nearly there, on the verge of reaching his destination, when his best friend suddenly appeared beside him.

"What's up, man?" Scott said casually.

"How did you get over here so fast?" Ryan hissed, keeping his voice low.

"I just cut across the yard. Your dad didn't see me. I was good and quiet," Scott answered nonchalantly while chewing on a red Twizzler.

Ryan sat up, his back against the shed, a look of annoyance crossing his face. "Did you bring me one at least?" he asked, pointing to the candy in Scott's mouth.

Scott reached into his hoodie pocket and handed Ryan a Twizzler. Picking off the lint, Ryan quickly ate it, a small smile of satisfaction creeping onto his face.

"*You guys, he just went inside the shed with some wood. I think you're good to go,*" Colin communicated. Ryan and Scott crawled to the back of the shed, where they found a hole to look inside.

"Radio silence," Scott whispered, turning off his and Ryan's walkies. Christina and Colin, unaware of what he meant, kept theirs on.

Ryan's left eye hovered over the hole, careful not to get too close to the splintered wood, wary of a potential tetanus shot. He watched his father carefully place pink insulation against the newly installed wall, safety goggles and mask on. Calvin adjusted his goggles and mask, trying to get them more comfortable.

"Why wear a mask?" Ryan whispered to Scott.

Surprised, Scott replied, "Protects against the fiberglass." Scott marveled at Ryan's lack of basic knowledge about tools and materials, everyday things men traditionally knew. But it was a trade-off—Scott could teach him how to fix things, and Ryan could be the sensible one.

Calvin examined two sets of panels to nail over the insulation. One of them was off. He pulled the wood outside to compare it with the others and realized he had cut one of the panels too short, making it impossible to nail into a stud.

"God fuckin' dammit, piece of fucking crap! God!" he bellowed, startling Christina and Colin. Ryan and Scott flattened themselves against the back of the shed, terrified of being discovered.

"What do we do?" Scott mouthed.

Ryan stared blankly, unsure of what to do next.

Ryan and Scott peered through the hole in the shed, their eyes widening as they witnessed Calvin in front of the shed, kicking and punching new drywall, his curses growing louder and more furious. Calvin's rage was unlike anything Ryan had ever seen. Previously, his father would yell, but now, he was hitting and throwing objects. Calvin stormed into the shed and began hurling glass jars full of nails, screws, and washers—it wasn't enough to quench his anger.

Christina watched from above, her worry mounting as she saw Calvin stomp into the house with hatred in his eyes, slamming doors along the way. She pressed the button on her walkie-talkie and began to yell for Ryan and Scott to get away. *"Hello? Hello!"* she called, but there was no answer from Ryan or Scott. Panic set in, and she turned to Colin. *"Do you see them anywhere?"*

"No. I hid when his dad got mad. Sorry!" Colin replied, his voice shaky.

The garage door slammed shut again, jolting Christina's nerves. Her heart raced, but what she witnessed next halted her. Calvin strode back to the shed, a pistol gripped tightly in his right hand.

No! That's where they are! Don't shoot! The words screamed in her mind, but fear choked her voice, leaving her breathless.

Calvin reached the shed's entrance and let out a primal scream, unleashing a flurry of gunfire into the wooden structure. Bullets tore through the air, shredding the already splintered wood. Six shots echoed, then another six after he reloaded. Christina prayed, hoping her friends had escaped the violent onslaught. Colin covered his ears, desperate to block out the chaos, while Christina stifled her gasps, dreading what she might see next.

In the deafening silence that followed, Christina cautiously opened her eyes. Smoke and dust hung in the air, obscuring her view. Then, movement in the bushes caught her eye. A sickening realization dawned on her—her friends might be lying lifeless behind the shed, victims of Calvin's fury. Helpless, she waited for Calvin to leave before she could act.

Calvin glanced down at his weapon, taking a deep breath as he struggled with his emotions. Unaware of his son's presence just beyond the wreckage, he retreated into the garage, then the house. In solitude, he collapsed onto the couch, tears cascading down his cheeks, the weight of a desolate future settling heavily upon him.

Emerging from cover, Christina dashed down the patio stairs, her senses on high alert, unsure if it was safe. As she reached the yard, a mound of leaves stirred, revealing Colin, who had wriggled out from beneath the pile, concern etched on his young face. She instinctively raised her hand, urging him to halt. He shouldn't witness the potential horror lurking behind the shed. No child should see a dead body and neither should I, she thought, scared of what she would find.

Approaching the side of the building cautiously, Christina poked her head around the corner, her heart pounding with dread. She closed her eyes briefly before taking another step, praying it wasn't true. Please, let it be something else, she begged silently. When she opened her eyes, relief flooded her as she spotted a large branch resting atop a cluster of bushes.

"That tree branch didn't stand a chance," a voice remarked from behind her.

Turning around, Christina saw Ryan beside her, peering down at the bushes with the same mixture of concern and relief. Her eyes widened, and she threw her arms around him. "Oh, thank God!" she exclaimed, pulling Ryan into a tight hug. After a moment, she released him and started to rant. "I thought you were still there! I thought you were going to be full of holes!" Christina sighed, hugging Ryan once more, her fear still evident in her nervous hands. "I didn't mean to make you worry," Ryan muttered, feeling awkward and guilty.

Meanwhile, Scott, with another Twizzler hanging from his mouth, waved his arms in the air. "I'm fine, by the way!" he announced. Colin approached Scott from behind, placing a reassuring hand on his shoulder. "I was worried about you too," he admitted sincerely. Scott nodded appreciatively, "Thanks, man."

Then, true to form, Colin bombarded them with questions. "Were you scared? Where did you go? How did you escape? What kind of gun do you think that was? Was it too loud? I thought it was too loud. Can I have a Twizzler? I don't like the black ones. Do you like the black ones?"

Scott, grumbling, retreated, "Sweet Jesus, I wish I had gotten shot."

Agreeing the day's events were too overwhelming to process, Ryan's friends left to find solace at home for the rest of their Saturday. An undeniable truth lingered: Ryan's father was not himself, not in any recognizable way. Something needed to be addressed, but Ryan was at a loss for where to begin. The only certainty was his father's volatile outburst earlier must not happen again.

Entering from the garage, Ryan found his brother engrossed in playing *Enduro* on their Atari 2600, a household staple their dad had acquired years ago. Moving through the house, Ryan entered the laundry room and then his father's office, where Calvin kept his firearms. Opening the closet door, Ryan retrieved the shoebox housing his father's pistol—the Astra Terminator. The warmth lingering on the muzzle unsettled him. Ensuring it was unloaded, Ryan tucked the gun into the waistband of his jeans, concealing it beneath his red hoodie. He pocketed a handful of bullets, feeling a meager sense of defense against any lurking threat. Though other guns were locked away, one was better than none.

A draft swept through the office, causing a spine-chilling dread seizing Ryan. He felt watched, a sensation he had grown all too familiar with. Scanning the room, he spotted a shadowy mass hovering in the laundry room, its gaze fixed on him from outside the house. Another draft stirred the air, this time from the office window with its faulty lock. Calvin's negligence had left it vulnerable, a fact Ryan now regretted.

Turning to close the window, Ryan froze as the head of a figure with blue-tinged skin appeared outside, its vacant, milky eyes locking onto his. The eyes, empty and soulless, pierced through him, paralyzing him with fear. Panic surged through his veins as dark, viscous blood oozed from the figure's gaping mouth, the thick liquid dripping onto the windowsill with a sickening splatter.

The figure, once a teenager, moved in grotesque, jerky motions, its limbs bending at unnatural angles as it dragged itself away. Each movement left a streak of blood in its wake, a grim, visceral reminder of the life it once had. Ryan's heart pounded in his chest, each beat louder than the last, as he watched the macabre scene unfold before him. The air grew thick with the scent of death, mixing with the stale office air, creating a nauseating feeling.

In the ensuing silence, Ryan's breath came in ragged gasps. He struggled to calm himself, the dread gripping him like a vice. Just as he began to steady his breathing, a tapping at the window jolted him back into a state of panic. The undead teenager had returned, its bony fingers tapping rhythmically against the glass, each tap echoing like a death knell.

The teenager's mournful moans seeped into the room, filling it with a haunting, otherworldly sound. Its eyes, still locked onto Ryan's, pleading for acknowledgment, for some form of connection. Ryan recoiled, his body vibrating with a mix of fear and revulsion. The sight of the figure's twisted form, with its dark, viscous blood still oozing, was more than he could bear.

Shaking his head, Ryan forced the ghastly vision from his mind, his legs feeling like lead as he retreated from the office. The haunting moans lingered in his ears, a chilling reminder of the horror he had just witnessed. Each step away from the window felt like a struggle against an invisible force pulling him back to the nightmarish scene.

Finally, Ryan reached the living room, where the familiar sound of his brother's video game provided a stark contrast to the terror he had just experienced. The cheerful bleeps and bloops of the game was almost surreal in comparison to the grotesque reality outside.

Ryan stood there for a moment, his heart still racing, as he tried to anchor himself in the normalcy of the living room.

"Devin?" Ryan ventured, his voice barely above a whisper, seeking his brother's attention amidst the game's frenetic action.

"Yeah?" Devin responded, absorbed in his gameplay, oblivious to the horrors Ryan had just encountered.

"I think there's something wrong with Dad."

CHAPTER EIGHTEEN

WEST END GIRLS

"Hello?" Eric answered the phone, forgetting that few still cared.

"Hey, man! It's Devin. Where have you been? It's like I have to make plans to see you."

"Sorry. Got a lot on my plate with school and stuff."

Devin anticipated the awkwardness of the conversation. Asking for permission to go out with Valerie after their breakup felt inherently wrong. "Hey, um, so there's this party tonight hosted by some rich kid from Wadsworth. Valerie invited me, but I wanted to check with you first because, you know, you guys used to date."

There was a pause, and Devin could hear Eric's hesitation on the other end of the line. The faint chuckle that followed appeared forced, a thin veil over deeper emotions. Devin could imagine Eric's reluctant expression, the way his brows might furrow slightly in discomfort.

"Yeah, I figured as much, man. Just thought I'd run it by you anyway. Don't want anything to mess with our friendship and all," Devin added, joining in the laughter to ease the tension. He could picture Eric's forced smile, his eyes not quite meeting his own in an attempt to downplay the situation.

As he waited for Eric's response, Devin shifted uncomfortably, his mind racing through memories of Eric and Valerie together. He could almost see the way they used to hold hands, the smiles they exchanged. It made the silence on the other end even more pronounced, an acknowledgment of the history lingering between them.

"Dude, it's fine. I'm an adult, and I think I did the right thing. Have fun, but not too much fun. Chick can be a real man-eater. I'm just putting it out there," Eric replied shockingly. Flustered, Devin fumbled around his room, needing to find something to wear to the party.

"It's really cool, man," Eric finally said, his tone carrying a hint of resignation. *"Don't worry 'bout me. Go have fun. Just... you know, be careful."*

Devin felt a mix of relief and guilt wash over him. "Thanks, Eric. I appreciate it." He knew this conversation would linger in the back of his mind, a small shadow over the night's festivities.

"If it's all cool, then I'll go with her?" Devin reiterated.

"Have fun. Maybe I'll see you there."

They hung up after exchanging a casual "later." Devin struggled to catch his breath; excitement surged through him like never before. The thought of being alone with Valerie sent a thrill through his body. He eagerly picked up the phone again, nervously dialing Valerie's number to confirm it was on.

Meanwhile, in his now immaculate room, Eric turned towards the mirror. His reflection stared back at him; eyes shadowed with the weight of unspoken feelings. He studied his transformed appearance, a stark contrast to the turmoil within. Those affected by the wolf's bite, who struggled to accept the gift or curse, saw their human bodies diminish, weakened by their internal conflict. Only by embracing the wolf within could one unlock their true potential, becoming resilient, balanced, and formidable.

Eric ran a hand through his hair, the tips of his fingers brushing against his temples where the first signs of change had begun. He recalled the nights spent wrestling with the beast inside, his body racked with pain and confusion. But tonight was different. He had begun to understand, to accept the duality of his nature.

His muscles, once taut with resistance, now felt strong and purposeful. His senses, heightened by the wolf's essence, detected the faintest sounds, the slightest changes in his surroundings. The room, once a chaotic mess, now reflected his newfound clarity and control.

As he stared into the mirror, Eric saw not just a reflection, but a merging of identities—a harmony between man and wolf. The thought of Devin with Valerie stirred something primal within him, but he pushed it down, channeling the energy into focus and determination.

With a final deep breath, Eric turned away from the mirror, his mind set on the challenges ahead. He knew embracing the wolf wasn't just about physical transformation; it was about finding balance, about becoming the person he was meant to be. And as he walked out of his room, he felt a sense of resolve he had never known before.

You have done well.
You have created order in your life.
You are rejecting the chaos and filth, pushing it away.
You, we, will hunt in three days for three nights when the moon is whole.

Eric nodded in acknowledgment of the inner voice guiding him, fully grasping the task lying ahead and the necessary steps he must take. Yet, he understood that attaining peace, for both him and others, would demand patience. The hardships he had endured should not be inflicted upon anyone else—a reality he had witnessed too frequently. Despite his noble intentions and well-devised plan, Eric remained acutely aware of the unpredictable nature of the wolf in its entirety.

His reflection in the hallway mirror caught his eye again, and he paused, seeing not just the man but the beast beneath the surface. The golden flecks in his eyes glimmered, an indication to the duality within. Eric's senses sharpened, catching the faint rustle of leaves outside, the distant hum of traffic. Every detail of his environment spoke to him, a symphony of the living world he was now more connected to than ever before.

Eric inhaled deeply, the cool air filling his lungs helping ground him. The wolf's presence was a constant hum in the back of his mind, a reminder of its unpredictability. He knew taming it required more than just strength; it demanded wisdom and restraint. Each day was a test of his resolve, a balancing act between human and beast.

With a final look at his reflection, Eric accepted the challenge ahead. His path was clear, but the journey was fraught with uncertainty. He embraced the inner voice, the guiding force promising balance and resilience.

***

Devin rummaged through his clothes, tossing aside anything not fitting the party vibe, adding to the mess in his room. Shirts and jeans flew onto the bed and floor as he searched for the perfect outfit. After much deliberation, he settled on a pair of dark blue jeans, a red button-up shirt left untucked, and a sleek black jacket paired with his favorite Doc Martens. Now came the crucial part.

Knocking lightly on his parents' bedroom door, Devin entered to find his mother, Rebecca, flipping through a Cosmopolitan Magazine. Her elegant, relaxed demeanor contrasted sharply with his nervous energy. "You look nice. Where are you off to?" she inquired casually, brushing a strand of hair from her face, her eyes scanning him with mild curiosity.

"Can I use the car? There's a party. Valerie invited me to go with her," Devin replied, his voice tinged with excitement and anxiety. He shifted his weight from one foot to the other, awaiting her response with bated breath.

Rebecca paused, considering for a moment before nodding. "Sure, why not," she consented, causing Devin to pump his fist in triumph prematurely.

"But," she added, flipping a page in her magazine, "you'll have to take your brother and his friends along."

Devin's elation deflated instantly, the realization hitting him like the sound of The Price is Right soundtrack when a contestant loses. *Bumbum bum bum…bwowww.* "Mom, are you serious?" he protested, hoping it was just a joke. The excitement drained from his face, replaced by a look of pure disappointment.

"Absolutely. They could use something to do, and they'll be in high school soon. It'll be good for them to socialize," Rebecca explained with a shrug, her logic unwavering. She met his gaze with a look that said her decision was final.

He slouched, feeling defeated, and stormed out of the room with a muttered "Fine!" His steps were heavy with frustration, each one echoing his thwarted plans.

As her son left with an attitude, Rebecca couldn't help but sip her tea with a satisfied smile. She knew the balance of responsibility and freedom was a lesson he needed to learn.

To distract himself from his frustration, Devin headed downstairs and powered up the Atari, hoping to lose himself in the game before he had to leave to pick up Valerie and the others. The familiar beeps and boops of the console filled the room as he immersed himself in the pixelated challenges of Enduro. His concentration was soon broken by the sound of the front door opening with a loud bang, followed by his father's heavy footsteps stomping through the house. Devin didn't need to see him to know he was agitated—likely about something related to the shed. Moments later, the door slammed shut again, and Devin's grip tightened on the joystick.

The sudden crack of gunshots outside startled him, causing his heart to skip a beat. He paused, eyes wide, but then dismissed the noise, attributing it to hunters in the woods. It was a common enough occurrence in their area. He quickly refocused on his game.

Soon after, he heard lighter footsteps entering the house and moving towards the laundry room. Assuming it was his father returning, Devin paid little attention until the person spoke, and he recognized Ryan's voice. Without acknowledging Ryan, Devin continued to focus on the game.

"Devin?" Ryan's voice cut through his concentration.

"Yeah?" Devin responded, still engrossed in the game, his hands maneuvering the joystick with practiced ease.

"I think there's something wrong with Dad," Ryan stated, drawing Devin's attention from the screen with the seriousness of his tone.

Setting aside the controller, Devin powered off the Atari, recognizing the gravity in his brother's voice. Their interactions were often minimal, but this time felt different, like a conversation between equals. Devin turned to face Ryan as he approached and took a seat on the couch.

"What's going on?" Devin asked, fighting the urge to call his brother a silly name. Trout sniffer would have been a good one. Wait. Did I use that recently? Devin started mentally listing the names he could jokingly call his brother later, but then he remembered they were supposed to have a serious discussion.

Ryan hesitated, finding it tricky to start the conversation he dreaded. He knew he had to begin with the events of Halloween night, getting through it without becoming overly emotional—he didn't want to seem weak in front of his brother. So, he took a deep breath and laid out everything that had happened after Eric was pulled away by the giant wolf. He described reaching the cornfield and witnessing the transformation of the werewolf back into a human, the shooting, the eerie presence of ghosts, and finally, his theory about the curse spreading to Eric, Valerie, and their dad.

As Ryan spoke, Devin's eyes widened, the color draining from his face. The vivid descriptions painted a terrifying picture in his mind, making his earlier frustrations seem insignificant. He listened intently, his initial skepticism giving way to concern as the weight of Ryan's words sank in. When Ryan finished, Devin realized they were dealing with something far beyond their understanding—a reality they had to confront together.

"So let me make sure I understand this. Setting aside the werewolf stuff, are you saying our parents, Rick Donovan, and Melvin Craggs, shot someone and hid the body on Halloween?" Devin asked, incredulous.

"Well, Melvin shot him with a shotgun, so yeah," Ryan confirmed.

"You understand what you're saying? Our parents are accessories to murder?"

"What did you expect them to do? If that guy was a werewolf and they only found out after he died, how would they explain it? Who would believe them?" Ryan argued, hoping Devin would see his point. "I think they did the smart thing. They had us to think of."

Devin crossed his arms, processing his brother's revelations. He didn't want to argue about what Ryan saw or thought he saw, but he didn't have to acknowledge it either.

"Dad has had anger issues before, Ryan. You just never saw it," Devin admitted.

Ryan, skeptical, responded, "If that's true, it can't be like this. He was punching and kicking holes in drywall and wood panels."

"It's not hard to do," Devin said.

"You didn't see it. Not like this," Ryan countered, standing up to emphasize his point.

"I saw Dad hit Mom! Okay?" Devin yelled, cutting off Ryan's argument. Ryan sat back down, shaking his head in disbelief. "It was around the time they found out about her cancer. They were arguing about money and bills. She said something, probably being defiant like she does, and he punched her. She fell, holding her face. That's why he moved out."

"Was he drunk?" Ryan asked. Devin nodded, "Yeah. Definitely."

Ryan threw his arms up, exclaiming, "Well, that's why! Not that he should have done it, but he wasn't drunk today. Dad hasn't been drinking since he's been back—he's getting worse without the alcohol. His rage is building up, and I'm scared of what happens when it explodes."

Devin didn't want to debate his brother's werewolf theory. Instead, he shifted the focus. "Let's talk about it later. You need to get ready."

"Ready for what?" Ryan asked, confused.

"A party."

As Devin fiddled with the buttons on his shirt, he side-eyed Ryan, annoyed. Before Ryan could take a step, Devin muttered, "You're kind of an asshole. You know that?"

Ryan stopped, looked over his shoulder, and asked, "What did you just say?"

"You heard me. I tell you our dad hit our dying mother, and you use it to justify your ridiculous werewolf theory. You made it about you."

Exhausted and fed up, Ryan began to yell, "That's rich. You calling me self-absorbed when all you do is mope in your room, trying to forget the rest of us exist? You think it's going to be easier when Mom's gone?"

"Shut your face!" Devin shouted.

"Pushing us out of your sight. Out of sight, out of mind, right? Trying to get those reminders of her away?"

"That's not what it is, okay?" Devin shot back.

"Then what?"

"I can't stand watching her fade away! I'd rather she have something else! Something she can live with! She's my mom!"

"And I'm your brother! We're your goddamn family too! It's not about you either! Hypocrite! Asshole!" Ryan retorted.

After a moment of tense silence, Ryan started up the stairs. Devin looked away, seething, trying to justify his anger.

Ryan turned back and said, "Believe me or don't. I'm so tired. I can't sleep because of this crap. Too much weird stuff is happening that you can't see. The mother of the kids killed by an animal almost a month ago stood in front of Flanagan and then threw herself into traffic. That's weird in this little town. I used to think nothing exciting ever happened here, and now I wish it didn't. Help me or not. Don't care anymore. Can't make you care. Maybe I'll just wipe my hands of you like you have with us."

Ryan continued up the stairs, preparing for a party he didn't want to attend, while Devin stewed in his thoughts.

Devin slumped as he and Ryan climbed into their mother's Dodge "Turbo" Daytona to pick up Christina, Valerie, and Scott. Colin, they had unanimously decided over the phone, shouldn't attend this kind of party. According to Scott, Colin's sixth-grade mind wouldn't handle it. Devin and Valerie knew what this shindig entailed and anticipated the surprise awaiting the others.

Christina emerged from the house in a blue V-neck sweater, a Debbie Gibson hat, a white skirt, and Keds. Ryan's eyes lit up, taking in her beauty. Devin elbowed his brother, eyebrows raised and nodding subtly, acknowledging Ryan's successful interaction. "Why don't you two get in the back? Valerie is going to sit up front." Ryan hopped out, almost colliding with Christina. Their faces came close, prompting nervous smiles and mumbled "excuse me" and "sorry." Devin turned, laughing, "Congrats. That was the most awkward thing I've ever seen."

They drove to the Donovan residence, Devin blaring the horn to alert Valerie and Scott. Ryan thought it was rude, believing you should go to the door. He didn't realize Devin might be avoiding Rick. Scott emerged first, dressed in a black sweater and faded jeans, his hair slicked back—a new look for him. Valerie followed, wearing a low-cut, fuzzy pink sweater, black leggings, and a thick white belt. Devin noticed Valerie's accentuated curves. They exchanged hellos, ready for the high school party in the neighboring town.

The route to Wadsworth was straightforward. Wadsworth Road lay just outside Holiday Heights; a left turn and a straight drive. Devin preferred his brother and friends to stay behind, but Valerie was excited for them. She turned in her seat, grinning, finding it cute her little brother and his friends were attending their first real party.

"Are you guys excited?" Valerie asked, hoping for enthusiasm. They shrugged, uncertain, especially Ryan and Christina, who felt awkward in their own skins.

"I'm surprised! I remember how excited I was for my first big party," Valerie reminisced.

"And I'm surprised you can even talk with your tits all the way up to your throat," Scott quipped, ever the annoying little brother.

Christina, annoyed, repeatedly slapped Scott's arm. "You are such an asshole!" Valerie, amused, joined in, playfully beating her brother. Ryan cowered in the corner, trying to avoid the female warpath.

"Was it something I said?" Scott laughed before Christina landed one last punch, making him yelp in pain.

They arrived at a large, two-story house, nestled away from neighbors by at least half a mile, with a serene pond in the back. Teenagers' cars crowded the street, making it challenging for Devin to find a spot close to the house. Eventually, they parked on the side of the road and walked up to the residence.

The front door stood wide open, inviting anyone inside. Drunk high schoolers wandered in and out, seeking fresh air or a smoke. Inside, what was likely once an immaculate home now showed signs of wear and tear from rowdy parties. They stepped into the living room, where a girl in a purple t-shirt with a sloppy sidetail belted out "We Don't Have to Take Our Clothes Off" by Jermaine Stewart.

Scott scanned the room, noticing the girl's off-key performance. "Sounds like someone is choking a constipated yak," he joked, aiming for laughter. His quip succeeded, drawing laughs from Ryan, Christina, and a couple of guys leaning against the wall leading to the kitchen.

As the night unfolded, Devin and Valerie found themselves on the back porch, enjoying the view of the pond. Meanwhile, Ryan, Christina, and Scott mingled in the family room, where older kids were engrossed in a game of Seven Minutes in Heaven. Intrigued, they decided to join and dropped their names into the bowl.

A slender Black student, sporting large shades and denim overalls with one side of the front flap left unbuckled, effortlessly commanded the microphone as the master of ceremonies. Christina moved to the girls' side, where they exchanged the names they had drawn. The party's rule exempted participants more than a grade apart from entering the closet together. Unfortunately, Stephanie Melker, Ryan's supposed stalker with her pearls, had drawn Ryan's name and was determined to cheat.

Ignoring Christina's attempts to intervene, Stephanie stubbornly clung to Ryan's name. Frustrated, Christina boldly pulled Stephanie aside. "Alright, Steph! What's it going to take for you to give up his name?" she demanded.

Amused, Stephanie laughed, "You're out of your mind if you think I'm giving up Ryan and that pretty mouth of his."

Meanwhile, Scott, having grown impatient with waiting, wandered off to another part of the house, where some guys were attempting keg stands. Despite being an eighth grader, Scott's height and demeanor earned him acceptance into their group. One hour into the party, Scott was already buzzing. Ryan noticed and shook his head, knowing he'd have his hands full with Scott during high school.

The MC's voice boomed over the microphone, calling out Scott's name. Initially oblivious, Scott was jolted into attention by the high schoolers' cheers. Realizing he had forgotten about his participation, Scott found himself being pushed toward the closet. "There he is, everyone!" the MC exclaimed, urging Scott to select a name from the bowl as the girls eagerly awaited their turn. Caught off guard by the sudden attention, Scott waved awkwardly, unsure how to handle the spotlight.

"And... Ramona...Dankworth?" the MC shouted, reading the name from the paper.

Scott looked around for the lucky lady. Ramona, taller than he was, with black hair in braided pigtails and headgear, made her way through the crowd. Scott's smile turned into a frown of concern. This girl is massive, he thought, and could cut my face open with her braces with one sudden tilt of her head.

"You know what? I'm not feelin' so hot," Scott muttered, crafting an excuse to avoid his first kiss with Ramona Dankworth. Glancing over at Ryan, he quietly asked for assistance in escaping the Seven Minutes in "*Hell*" closet with her. Ryan, chuckling, approached him, placing a reassuring hand on his shoulder.

"Look. Take the metal off her face and lose the pigtails; you don't have it too bad. She's tall, and trust me, in a few years, Ramona will be a total babe. Get in now while you can!" Ryan advised with a grin.

"I don't know, man. Ramona's got a lot goin' on with that grill. And she's got a wide face. It's goin' to be like makin' out with a Jack o Lantern," Scott protested.

"Maybe. But if you're good...word travels fast in these towns," Ryan wisely countered, raising his eyebrows. Although Ryan wasn't entirely convinced by his own words, Scott bought into them, and that's what mattered most. With a shrug, they both entered the narrow closet, and as the MC closed the doors, the crowd erupted into cheers. Ryan flashed Scott a huge smile, accompanied by a sarcastic thumbs up.

"What do you want?" Christina confronted Stephanie, frustration coloring her tone.

"Please. Like you have anything I could possibly want," Stephanie retorted, her words dripping with contempt. She leaned in closer, a malicious grin spreading across her face. "What would he want with some poor girl from a trash home whose parents want nothing to do with her? Let him be with someone with a future. Not some would-be orphan if her parents made the right decision."

"Seven minutes is up! Get those two out!" the MC announced, stirring up the crowd. Stephanie waved mockingly. "Uh-oh. Looks like I'm next." She sauntered to the front of the room, relishing the attention. Pretending to rummage in the bowl, she theatrically pulled out a slip of paper and revealed Ryan's name. "Ryan Hatcher and Steph Melker!" the MC declared, prompting cheers from the crowd.

"Looks like someone's playing my song. I'll make sure we make beautiful music," Stephanie remarked with a wink, heading towards the closet. Christina seethed, her fists clenched as her fingernails cut into her palms, fighting the primal urge to lash out. She spotted Ryan approaching and felt her heart sink, convinced she wasn't what Ryan wanted. Tears welled up as she pushed through the crowd, the grating teenage banter about school mascots filling the air.

Scott noticed Christina storming off into the backyard and urgently called out to Ryan, "Dude!" Ryan glanced over, catching sight of Christina's curly blonde hair bobbing as she retreated. She was clearly upset at the prospect of him entering the closet with another girl. Stephanie grew uneasy, sensing Ryan's hesitation.

"Don't you leave me like this and embarrass me! You'll ruin the best shot you ever will have with me," Stephanie warned, clutching his arm tightly. Ryan recoiled, his upper lip curling in disgust at her arrogance.

"The best chance I have ever had just ran outside. Excuse me," Ryan spat out bitterly, wrenching his arm free as he made a beeline for the back door, desperate to escape the suffocating air of the party.

CHAPTER NINETEEN

NEW SENSATION

Devin and Valerie reclined on the grass near the dock, where Akron's privileged residents parked their small boats and kayaks. The cool night air brushed against their skin as they watched the moonlight dance on the water's surface. "You sure you don't want to go back in?" Devin inquired tenderly. Valerie edged closer, her eyes shimmering with the moon's reflection. "Honestly, not really. I just wanted an excuse to hang out with you." A bashful smile crept onto Devin's face. He glanced away, feeling the warmth of her words like a gentle breeze. "You never need an excuse to hang out with me. Just ask."

The soft strains of "All through the Night" by Cyndi Lauper drifted through the open windows of the party behind them, adding to the ambiance. Valerie nervously bit her bottom lip, then gathered the courage to voice the question lingering in her heart. "You like me, don't you?" His smile spoke volumes, but Valerie wanted to hear the words. "Why didn't you say anything?" Devin's cheeks flushed, and he averted his gaze. Valerie, sensing his vulnerability, tenderly cupped his face and guided his eyes to meet hers before leaning in for a gentle kiss.

It was everything Devin had imagined and more.

"Have you ever, ya know, made it with a girl?" Valerie whispered seductively into his ear. Devin chuckled nervously, feeling the weight of her question. "What? Like right now?" he joked, trying to lighten the mood. Valerie laughed softly, her warm breath teasing his skin. "No, you weirdo! Not in the backyard," she teased, glancing around to ensure their privacy. "Have you? Ya know?" she asked again, her curiosity evident. Devin felt the familiar dilemma of teenage boys—

admitting inexperience or risking being labeled a prude. "No," he confessed.

Unfazed by his response, Valerie took his hand, her touch reassuring. "How come?" she inquired gently, genuine curiosity in her eyes. Devin narrowed his eyes, pondering her question. "Well, believe it or not, I'm not exactly beating off girls with a stick," he quipped, hoping to ease the tension. Valerie's expression softened into a sympathetic smile. "Surprises me! It really does."

"Not many people look my way," Devin explained, his tone tinged with self-deprecation. Valerie's features softened further, her heart aching for him. "Girls can be so dumb sometimes," she remarked ruefully. "We get used to going for the ones who are bad for us, thinking that's how it's supposed to be."

Devin considered probing into Valerie's personal life, sensing a shared understanding. "You think your folks being like that influenced your idea of relationships?" he ventured. Valerie's eyes clouded with thought as she mulled over his question, the gears in her mind turning. "I don't know. Maybe. I guess I thought Eric would save me because of his dad and mine…" Her voice trailed off, uncertainty threading through her words. She turned to face him, her gaze searching. "Would you save me if I needed it?"

"Anytime," Devin vowed earnestly, his eyes steady and sincere. "But I don't think you need anyone to save you from anything." Valerie rested her head on Devin's shoulder, the warmth of his presence soothing her. For the first time in a long while, they soaked in the tranquil silence, finding solace in each other's company. Devin's heart swelled with a newfound contentment, realizing someone was finally at ease with him.

"So you've never been with a girl?" Valerie asked again, her tone incredulous. "No. Why does it matter so much?" Devin wondered, feeling the weight of her scrutiny. Valerie shrugged, a mischievous glint in her eye. "It's just kinda rare for a guy your age to still be… untouched," she declared, her voice laced with amusement. Struck by inspiration, she gasped dramatically. "You're like a unicorn! A sexy high school unicorn!" Devin felt his cheeks flush as he glanced around, aware of the curious stares directed their way. "Okay! I think the entire western side of Akron knows now," he muttered, feeling a blush creeping up his neck as Valerie giggled and pulled him back towards her.

"Why does it matter?" she questioned, her curiosity piqued. "I don't know. I guess I always felt like I wouldn't measure up," Devin confessed, his voice tinged with uncertainty. Valerie rolled her eyes playfully. "It's sex, Dev. Not like trying to poke a straw into a Capri Sun packet on the first try," she quipped, her words bringing a smile to Devin's lips. He couldn't help but marvel at her wit and charm. Is she even more incredible than I thought?

"If we're going to do this, we have to keep it between us," Valerie insisted, her tone serious. "Why?" Devin asked, puzzled by her request. "You know how it is. I'm popular, and you're... well, you," Valerie explained awkwardly, her gaze shifting away. "Are you trying to Breakfast Club me? Keep me hidden away until it's convenient for you?" Devin snapped, his frustration boiling over. "Shhh! Lower your voice. People can hear," Valerie hissed, placing a finger to her lips in a hasty attempt to silence him.

"You want to be with me, then do it! I'm not your backup plan. I'm not some second-rate option. If you want a fling, go find someone else," Devin declared, his voice rising with indignation. He stood up abruptly, fists clenched, ready to storm away. The whispers of the crowd outside grew louder, a symphony of murmurs discussing Devin's confrontation with Valerie, one of the most popular girls at Norton High School. Valerie's cheeks flushed with embarrassment, a pang of uncertainty twisting in her chest. For the first time, she felt out of her depth, the arbitrary rules of high school social hierarchy slipping through her fingers like sand, their importance fading.

Eric Flanagan, leaning against a nearby wall, watched the scene unfold with keen interest. His sharp eyes tracked Devin's every move as he stormed away, the words of their exchange echoing in his mind. The crowd's murmurs filled the air, a backdrop to Eric's racing thoughts. His predatory instincts sharpened, sensing an opportunity. A slow, calculating smile spread across his face as he prepared to make his move.

You have an intelligent colleague.

You should make him one of us.

You two could be unstoppable, not allowing trivial things like connections to hold you back.

"Here I was thinking the same thing," Eric murmured to his alter ego, a faint smile playing on his lips as he stared into the distance. His eyes narrowed, scanning the room with calculated indifference. A burly varsity football player from Barberton, clad in a purple and white letterman jacket, downed his makeshift screwdriver—a potent mix of Sunny Delight and Everclear. Catching sight of Eric's internal dialogue, the jock, fueled by alcohol and bravado, took offense and approached with aggression. "What did you say, ginger?" he slurred, clearly spoiling for a fight.

Eric turned slowly to face the imposing figure, secretly relishing the chance to assert his dominance. He felt a surge of primal energy coursing through him, goading him into the confrontation. With a deliberate, almost casual motion, he adjusted the cuffs of his long sleeve Billabong shirt. "I was just wondering how you manage to drown out the taste of Everclear with so little orange juice. Are you trying to set a new record for alcohol consumption?" he retorted, his voice dripping with sarcasm.

The football player, towering over Eric and most others at the party, was caught off guard by Eric's audacity. He stumbled over his words, trying to save face. Eric's eyes gleamed with amusement, sensing the opportunity to press further. "I see you've been hitting the tequila hard tonight," he taunted, his tone biting. "But let's be real here, big guy. Your steroid abuse isn't doing wonders for your manhood. Maybe that's why you're overcompensating with the booze."

The player's face reddened with anger as he slammed his cup onto the kitchen counter. His friends, sensing the brewing conflict, began to gather around, rallying to his side. The tension in the room thickened, charged by Eric's unyielding stance and the player's wounded pride.

Oh. Yes, please.

Eric tuned into the quarterback's internal turmoil, sensing the tumultuous clash between stomach acid and tequila. He detected the unsettling churn, the telltale sign of impending upheaval. Yet, the football player's stubborn pride and ironclad self-discipline managed to suppress the rising tide within him. "Ah, there it is," Eric remarked with feigned disgust, simulating retching motions in an attempt to trigger the jock's gag reflex.

The player began to convulse, clutching his abdomen in agony. His disheveled blonde hair fell over his face as he writhed, struggling to contain the roiling storm within. Eric's manipulative ploy was taking effect. He anticipated the inevitable outcome and skillfully exploited it to humiliate the Barberton player through the power of suggestion. "Come on, big guy. Let it out. You'll feel better," Eric goaded, his voice dripping with malice. As the pressure built, he urged the player on, taunting him to release the pent-up turmoil.

With a final heave, vomit spewed forth, splattering onto the kitchen floor. Audible disgust erupted from the onlookers, who then proceeded to mock and ridicule the football player. Amidst the laughter and jeers, Eric remained unfazed, his smirk never faltering as he observed the scene with his piercing green eyes. While the crowd reveled in the jock's embarrassment, Eric relished the chaos he had incited.

Sensing the player's mounting fury, Eric welcomed the impending violence, his golden eyes ablaze with anticipation. With a predatory grin, he braced himself for the confrontation, ready to embrace the primal instincts others dared to suppress. This exhilarating sensation was uncharted territory for Eric, but he welcomed it with open arms, embracing the darkness within as others recoiled in fear.

Before the altercation with Eric Flanagan began, Ryan dashed out of the back door in search of Christina, who had hastily exited the house, visibly upset, fearing Ryan might kiss someone else in a closet. His eyes scanned the vast backyard, finding no sign of her, prompting him to venture further. Navigating through the shrubbery dividing properties, he emerged into another area. There, under the moonlight, he spotted Christina. Her hair shimmered white, and her legs dangled over the side of the dock. He halted, taking a deep breath, preparing himself to talk to her.

"What's wrong?" Ryan inquired, feigning ignorance. He knew Christina well, having shared countless moments of laughter and tears with her, more than he ever did with Scott. Though he would never admit it, Ryan recognized Christina as his closest friend. Yet, amidst this sudden spark of romantic interest, Ryan feared it could all vanish.

"Why aren't you with Stephanie?" Christina asked snidely, her tone laced with bitterness when she mentioned Stephanie's name.

"Because I saw you leave," Ryan replied, closing the distance between them. His footsteps echoed on the boardwalk, prompting Christina to spring to her feet. "You should go back. She's pretty. I get it."

"Is that what you really want to say to me?" Ryan's voice rose with anger, an unfamiliar tone towards Christina. She had never heard him raise his voice like this before.

"No," Christina's voice quivered, "It feels like whenever we're alone and close, I expect you to make a move, and you never do. And the one time I wanted to kiss you, some other girl took my place!"

"I'm sorry, okay? I've never done this before. I thought I was just shy, but not with you. I never have," Ryan explained, his frustration spilling over.

"Then what is it?" Christina sincerely asked.

"I'm scared! Okay? Don't tell Scott, but you're probably my best friend, really. What do I do if it goes away and never comes back? How am I supposed to face you? What if you hate being in a relationship with me and everything goes downhill?" Ryan poured out his fears.

Christina struggled to find the right words. "I don't know what to say to you. I'm not sure how to make you feel better about it. All I know is I would be lost without you. I have this feeling when I'm around you I've never had with anyone else. I wish maybe you felt the same. I wish I could tell you how it will all end. I hope I won't have to." She looked at him, her eyes reflecting the moonlight and a flicker of hope.

His arms enveloped her waist, and he rested his chin on her shoulder. She felt his breath on her neck, relishing the new and thrilling sensation. Christina's hair smelled as wonderful as it did the last time he was near her. His natural musk made him irresistible, and she fought to control her hormones from doing things she knew she shouldn't. She closed her eyes, anticipation building for something she had desired for longer than Ryan would ever know.

"When I kiss you, it's not going to be in a closet with a bunch of people waiting outside. I hope that's not what you wished for because it's not what I want. It will be when it's just us, alone. Somewhere we will remember no matter what or when," Christina declared, her eyes fixed on the pond. The lights from the houses across the way illuminated the small waves. The water was calm, and the breeze light—the perfect setting.

"I think the right time is now," she whispered. Ryan gently turned her around, looked into her eyes, and leaned in to kiss his new girlfriend, Christina White. Their lips met in a tender, exploratory kiss, the world around them fading away. They practiced making out for what seemed like hours but was only several minutes. When they finally pulled away to look at one another, they giggled, knowing how weird but fantastic it was. Christina began to walk away with a smile on her face.

"What? What is that smile?" Ryan asked, concerned she might have hated the way he kissed her. Christina turned around, revealing a calm, relaxed, almost playful look. She looked him up and down and answered, "Not bad, Mr. Hatcher. Not bad at all. There may be hope for you yet." Ryan, relieved, smiled and ran up behind her to tickle her. Christina screamed and ran away, trying to avoid his fingers—he knew how ticklish she was.

Ryan caught up to her, pulling her close again, this time spinning her around in a playful dance. They stumbled, laughing, and fell onto the grass, the moonlight casting a silver glow over them. Christina looked up at him, her eyes sparkling. "You know," she said lightly, "I think this is the start of something really special."

Ryan gazed back at her, his heart pounding with a mix of joy and excitement. "I think so too," he whispered, leaning in for another kiss, sealing the promise of what was to come.

Ryan and Christina strolled back to the party, relishing each other's presence. As they approached the tall bushes delineating the property, piercing screams and shouts erupted from the party house. Everyone in the backyard rushed toward the windows to glimpse the unfolding chaos. Squeezing through the shrubbery gap, they beheld a scene of turmoil emanating from the kitchen area.

Ryan's eyes scanned the crowd, catching sight of Valerie ascending a small hill, her face flushed, and her pace hurried. His stomach churned with unease as he failed to spot his brother nearby. Navigating through the mob, they entered the house, the air thick with tension.

A boy from another school sat on the floor, propped against the kitchen island, clutching his wrist and grimacing in agony. His face twisted in pain, his eyes wide with desperation. The cacophony of voices gradually hushed as Ryan homed in on the distressed high school athlete, who was lamenting, "I can't play anymore. It's all over... No one will recruit me... I've lost my scholarship. It's finished!"

Ryan maneuvered through the crowd, his heart pounding as he sought to discern what had transpired.

Murmurs and gasps floated through the crowd—It was that red-haired kid. Did you see how fast he was? Where'd he go?

The boy cradled his right wrist, his gaze fixed on his hand, fingers hanging limp from the knuckles once anchoring them. Each shake of his fist caused the bones in his digits to sway loosely, held in place only by skin and stretched ligaments. Amid his wails of agony, he tested his thumb, ensuring it still retained some functionality. Several upper-classmen who had rallied behind the Barberton player now sprawled on the kitchen floor, some nursing bloody noses while others lay unconscious, creating crimson pools from the cracks in their heads. The level of violence enacted spoke volumes, resonating with undeniable force.

Ryan and his cohorts recognized the aggressor from eyewitness accounts; there remained no doubt. Eric Flanagan had undergone a profound change, both mentally and physically, providing Ryan with ample evidence to support his suspicions—at least in his own mind.

Devin approached Ryan from behind, whispering urgently, "We need to leave." Ryan nodded in agreement, acknowledging his brother's assessment. As the boy in the letterman jacket cradled his crushed hand, crying out in despair over his shattered dreams, Ryan departed to find Scott and Valerie. Amidst all the trials and tribulations Ryan would face in his life, the haunting sound of hopelessness emanating from the boy was one he knew he would never forget. Subsequently, they learned the unfortunate, inebriated individual in the letterman jacket was the quarterback for Barberton High School.

All five teenagers who had anticipated a night of fun and cherished memories now sat in silence as they drove home. Scott, Devin, and Christina couldn't shake off Ryan's story about the events of Halloween night. They all sensed something was off with Eric Flanagan, but none were willing to confront it just yet. Ryan glanced over at them, catching their gaze before they quickly averted their eyes. Tonight wasn't the time for the conversation.

Devin pulled into Scott and Valerie's house to drop them off. Valerie glanced at Devin, hoping for reassurance, but instead, she asked, "Call you tomorrow?" Devin nodded in response. As Scott stepped out and exchanged knowing smiles with Ryan and Christina, Ryan grinned subtly. Scott, recognizing the unspoken understanding, smirked and headed home. Next was Christina's home, and although the new couple was coy, their affection was evident. In the rearview mirror, Devin noticed Ryan reaching for Christina's hand, using only his pinky to gently rub it. Despite the unfortunate turn of events later in the night, there was no denying the positive impact it had on them.

Ryan walked Christina to her door, admiring how her blonde hair bounced with each step. "Sorry the night didn't end on a high note. It was going so well," Ryan remarked apologetically. Christina turned around, disagreeing, "It's one to remember, but not because of what happened to that guy. I'll remember the pond more, sweetie." Without kissing Ryan goodbye, she shot him a playful, almost seductive glance as she closed the door behind her. Ryan couldn't help but smile, excited about what the future held for them as he lingered by the front door.

"Hey, loverboy! Let's go!" Devin's voice snapped Ryan out of his thoughts, and he quickly hopped into the front seat with a goofy grin. Devin glanced at his brother, pleased to see him happy with Christina. "It's about time. I was starting to think you'd never get the hint," Devin teased. Ryan scoffed in response, "Yeah, right! Like you pay attention to anything I do." "You might be surprised, little brother. You might be surprised," Devin said with a smirk, relieved to see Ryan's love life blossoming. "I'm glad things are going well for you," he added, hinting at his own troubles with Valerie. Ryan felt a pang of sympathy for his brother. All he could offer was a simple, "Sorry."

Devin nodded, hoping things would eventually work out. Sometimes it just sucks, he thought

Around midnight, both brothers cautiously entered the house, their senses heightened by the faint murmurs emanating from their father's office. The atmosphere felt heavy and foreboding, as if the very air itself held secrets. Tiptoeing into the adjacent laundry room, they spotted Layla standing there, her figure silhouetted against the dim light filtering through the narrow window. It was the same window that had once kept away a chilling specter—a poltergeist that had smeared its gruesome tale upon the glass, haunting Ryan's memories.

"What are you doing, Layla?" Devin's voice cut through the tense silence. Layla turned to face her brothers with a solemn expression, almost otherworldly. "I think this might be the way," she murmured cryptically. Devin, the skeptic, pressed for clarity, "The way where?" His question hung in the air, unanswered, as Layla's gaze shifted to Ryan, who felt a frosty fear coursing through him. "The way to escape when darkness descends," she whispered, her words dripping with an ominous weight. "That's what she says…Anna sees the end."

Ryan's heart skipped a beat as he clenched his jaw, a sense of impending dread settling over him like a suffocating shroud. He knew, with a primal certainty, something wicked loomed on the horizon—something that would coincide with the first full moon in two nights' time.

As they exited the laundry room, the Hatcher siblings were greeted by a haunting figure looming over them from the staircase landing above. Lightning briefly illuminated the house, casting frightening shadows dancing upon the walls, revealing Calvin in his disheveled state, clad only in his boxers and an open robe. Ryan and Devin exchanged uneasy glances; their perceptions of their father forever altered by recent events. Eric's transformation had shattered their illusions, leaving them to ponder the depths of their father's newfound capabilities.

Calvin drew in a sharp breath, his eyes ablaze with an intensity sending shivers through his body. Devin glanced at his watch, realizing they were fifteen minutes overdue. Breaking the tense silence, Calvin's voice, low and menacing, commanded, "Go to bed." His words were laden with unspoken implications, hanging heavily in the air.

CHAPTER TWENTY

INBETWEEN DAYS

Sunday's gray skies mirrored the somber mood. The night's violence haunted everyone's thoughts, casting fear and doubt in their minds. Ryan's theory of a paranormal influence on Eric Flanagan weighed heavily on them, an unspoken fear. They hadn't witnessed the brutality firsthand, but the tales and rumors were enough. The strange events of the past three weeks were too connected to be mere coincidence. Devin had always said Norton, Ohio, was the dullest place in the Midwest. Recent happenings proved him wrong, though "interesting" wasn't the word Ryan would choose for the chaos of the past month.

Devin's mop glided over Melvin Craggs' floor, revealing the rich grain of hardwood beneath layers of grime. The floorboards creaked gently, as if sighing in relief. After two weeks of relentless cleaning, the end was in sight. Devin didn't expect any compensation beyond the satisfaction of a job well done—a favor to Melvin and his mother, who had enlisted his help.

"You could actually entertain guests now, Melvin," Devin said, finishing the cleaning with a flourish. Melvin grumbled something incoherent, drawing a smile from Devin, who imagined the choice expletives. The air smelled faintly of bleach, mingling with the musty scent of old wood.

"No one cares about this place anymore," Melvin said, pushing himself up from his threadbare chair. His joints cracked audibly, a reminder of his age. "Burned too many bridges, and I'm too old to make new friends. No one gives a damn about what this old geezer has to say."

Thanks to Devin, photos of Melvin's life now adorned the walls, breathing warmth into the old house. Devin leaned against the kitchen table, which had once been piled high with unread books. The table's surface, now clear and polished, reflected the dim light filtering through the window. "That's a stellar attitude," Devin quipped, forcing a smile. Melvin's eyes narrowed, sensing the sarcasm. "Because now you have an excuse to keep pushing people away. Life is short—or long? Especially if you waste it. Those who regret and wish for more time end up with the shortest days, right?" Devin retorted, echoing Melvin's own words.

Melvin sighed deeply, a sound filled with years of weariness, and motioned for Devin to follow him to the garage. Sunlight streamed through the open garage door, illuminating dust motes dancing in the air. Melvin pointed to a covered object. "Take that cover off," he instructed. Devin revealed an old motorcycle, its chrome accents gleaming despite the layer of dust. "Looks like it's hardly been ridden," he said, impressed.

"Haven't taken it out in ages. Fire it up, let it run. It's time it saw some real action," Melvin said. Devin, inspecting the bike more closely, traced his finger along the AJS emblem. He admitted he knew little about motorcycles. "Why don't you take it for a spin?"

Devin's excitement mixed with apprehension. He had never ridden a motorcycle before. The thought of it filled him with a mix of anticipation and anxiety. "I'm not sure how to ride this," he confessed. Melvin waved dismissively. "It's like riding a bike, just heavier." Devin's skeptical eyebrow suggested he doubted it was so simple.

Soon, Devin found himself straddling the motorcycle, its leather seat cool and firm under him. The scent of gasoline and metal filled his nostrils. "Start it up like I showed you!" Melvin yelled over the sound of the engine roaring to life. Devin ignited the motorbike, feeling the powerful vibrations through his legs. He released the clutch too early, causing a slight wobble but managing to keep his balance. Melvin shook his head, realizing teaching Devin might be a challenge. The motorcycle rumbled beneath him, a beast waiting to be tamed, and Devin's heart raced with the thrill of the unknown.

After several wobbly attempts, Devin finally managed to mount the motorcycle. He cautiously rode it up the road, maneuvering through the adjacent cul-de-sac and back, nearly tipping over at one point. As he steered into Melvin Craggs' driveway, a triumphant grin spread across his face. Melvin, rarely one for visible emotions, offered a thumbs up.

"What do ya think?" Melvin asked.

Devin's eyes sparkled. "It felt really nice with the wind in my face, you know?"

Melvin's gaze grew distant, memories of past rides flickering in his eyes. "You wanna ride it around for the day?"

"Are you serious?" Devin's excitement was intense; he couldn't wait to flaunt the bike around the neighborhood.

"Why not? I'll let you use it whenever you want, but you gotta stay in the neighborhood and fill it up. Not that you'd need to. It's got pretty good gas mileage," Melvin replied. "Oh and wear a helmet. Your momma will give me hell if ya don't."

Devin agreed eagerly, shaking Melvin's hand before fetching the helmet from the garage. As he strapped it on, he already knew where his first destination would be on his semi-new ride.

Valerie felt isolated, barricaded in her room. Her father's wounded ego and fragile masculinity were like oppressive weights pressing down on her. The walls pulsed with the echoes of her parents' incessant arguing, a relentless cycle of turmoil. Silvia Donovan, her mother, bore the brunt of it, enduring both verbal and physical abuse. Their children pretended ignorance, avoiding confrontation, though they heard every word.

Her school friends were physically present but mentally distant, their laughter and chatter a hollow comfort. Over the school year, Valerie realized she didn't quite fit in. Despite her outward appearance—pretty, popular, trendy—her life behind the scenes was starkly different. The stigma of being labeled "white trash" by their peers, particularly because of her father, weighed heavily on her. Even Eric had deserted her. While everyone else seemed to be evolving, her world remained stagnant.

Frustration and fear consumed her. Tired of feeling deprived of life's pleasures, she directed her resentment towards her environment— "My parents, this house, this damn town!" she seethed, her voice deep with anger.

A sudden urge for liberation surged within her. Gazing out the window, Valerie spotted a familiar figure on a motorcycle—a neighbor who had always cherished her. The sight sparked a glimmer of hope, a chance for escape.

Devin Hatcher pulled up to the curb outside her house and caught sight of Valerie peering out the window. Removing his helmet, he flashed a warm smile at the enchanting figure behind the glass and waved. She appeared excited. Feeling relieved, he donned his helmet again as Valerie hurried to the garage to retrieve hers, eager to join him. She dashed toward him, Devin, her knight in shining armor, rescuing her from her dark thoughts—and he relished the role.

"Where do you want to go?" Devin inquired as Valerie settled onto the back of the motorcycle, disregarding Mr. Craggs' advice to stay within the neighborhood. She positioned herself on the seat and replied, "Anywhere away from here, where we can be alone." Devin nodded, thinking, I have no objection to that.

As they drove past Norton's only four-corner intersection and turned right, they found themselves on a dead end road known as The Curvy Swervy. It was a spot frequented by high schoolers seeking solitude for various reasons, often leaning toward intimacy. It was Valerie's suggestion to visit there, and she directed Devin as he drove. Devin trusted her choice of location and went along for the ride.

Upon reaching the end overlooking the highway, Valerie made her way toward the fence, erected to prevent people from accidentally falling forward and tumbling down the hill into oncoming traffic. "Have you ever been to a high place, like the roof of a house or a small building and wondered if the fall would kill you?" she asked Devin. He walked up behind her to peer at the busy road below, pondering her question before responding, "No. I think about how much it would hurt if I survived."

Valerie took hold of Devin's hands and guided his arms to encircle her waist. "Are you okay?" he inquired, concern etched in his voice.

She shrugged, a soft moan escaping her lips. "I don't know," she said, reaching behind her and running her hands through his hair. "I just want to feel good again. Can you do that?" She turned and nuzzled her nose against his neck, her breath warm against his skin. Devin's eyes rolled back as Valerie placed his hands on her breasts, enveloping him with an eerie chill. "Don't be afraid of me," she whispered with a sly grin, her eyes closed, "I won't bite."

Devin kissed her hard, and she loved every moment of it. It was a dream come true, his teenage dream, making out with Valerie Donovan. She became overcome with excitement as she put her tongue down his throat and began to moan, hurting Devin's face. As his bottom lip began to leave from between hers, she bit down hard, causing it to bleed.

Stumbling over his feet, Devin pulled away, frightened. He had never imagined Valerie, who always came off as so sweet, could be this insatiable. The more she tried to grab onto his body, Devin became convinced the girl next door wasn't her anymore. This wasn't how he wanted to lose his virginity, and it wasn't going to be. Not on a dead end road in the middle of the street; a popular sex hangout—an area that could illuminate the sky if someone ran a blacklight over the ground from all the bodily fluids no doubt covering it.

"What is wrong with you?" he asked, concerned. Valerie began to unbutton her blouse and answered, "I just want to feel good. Just for a little while. I'm so tired of being alone." She wanted validation and the only way she knew was for someone to reciprocate her advancements.

You need to be aggressive! Guys like that, she told herself.

"I don't like this part of you. This isn't the person I know. What happened to you?" Devin asked, wiping the blood from his mouth. Valerie grew angry as tears rolled down her now red, windburned face, not understanding why Devin would reject her. "What are you? Some kind of faggot!" she yelled at him. Devin looked at her with wide, open eyes, seeing Valerie Donovan for who she was right now—a pit of insecurity and self-hate. He scoffed at her, cementing his rejection. Devin walked toward the motorcycle and began to put on the helmet.

Valerie's anger began to fade into shame. She wasn't sure what made her do and say such harsh things. She knew Devin wouldn't look at her the same anymore. The admiration and respect had disappeared, at least for now. "Get on the bike," he ordered her. She wiped tears from her face, and the rage within began to vanish, allowing her natural skin tone to return.

She wrapped her arms around him, but not as tight, placing her face against the back of his jacket, dreading the return home. Devin stopped in front of Valerie's house and let her climb off. She looked at him, waiting for him to say something—anything. She placed her hands in the air, shrugged her shoulders and scoffed at her own ridiculousness, and asked with humility, "How do you like me now?"

Devin turned to her, unsure if he was upset at himself for not realizing who she was. He placed her on a pedestal, naïve and love struck, disappointed she acted like someone else because it was easier than coping with her own self-worth. "I don't know what's happening. Everything is different," Devin explained. She agreed, noticing as well, even with herself.

"Look. I'm sorry. Come over Wednesday, and we'll hang out. My parents are going to the festival thing like everyone else that night. We can hang out and watch a movie or go if you want...I'll be normal, I promise." Devin, attempting to be unflappable, sighed, asking, "Does that mean you're not embarrassed about being around me by yourself?" Valerie shook her head aggressively, "Of course, I'm not."

"Not sure if I can. May have to stay home and feed my pet," he joked. Valerie smiled and decided to play along. "What pet?"

"My sister keeps looking for a cat. So there may be one in the house when I get home."

"What kind?" Valerie wondered.

"Not sure."

"You don't know what kind of cat your sister is looking out for?" Devin slowly shook his head and joked, "No. Didn't want to be nosy—respecting their privacy."

They both laughed.

Valerie watched as the light gently haloed Devin's figure, the sun casting a golden glow around him as another day drew to a close. She couldn't deny he was handsome, more so than she had ever really noticed before. And he was a better person than Eric, she reflected silently, her thoughts mirroring his own.

"I'm sorry I called you...ya know," Valerie apologized sincerely, her voice carrying genuine remorse. "If I had a buck every time somebody called me that in front of my face or behind my back, I wouldn't have to worry about paying for my first year of college."

Devin nodded, understanding her meaning, and watched as she turned to walk away, heading towards a home she clearly didn't want to return to. With a wave goodbye, she reminded him to come by Wednesday night. He lingered for a moment, watching her disappear through the door, wondering if he was being naive or hopelessly falling in love.

Returning the bike to Melvin Craggs, Devin braced himself for the expected scolding from the old man. True to form, Melvin gave him an earful for taking the bike out of the neighborhood after explicitly being told not to. Devin didn't argue, instead explaining about the girl. Melvin listened, his gruff demeanor softening slightly.

"Men always want to be someone's Superman, not realizin' they already are. Sometimes looks are deceivin'," Melvin mused. Devin nodded thoughtfully, grateful for Melvin's understanding. He knew he had acted on impulse, driven by a desire to help Valerie, but hearing it framed in a way made him realize there was more to his actions than simple chivalry.

CHAPTER TWENTY ONE

DON'T STAND SO CLOSE TO ME

Rebecca and Calvin Hatcher spent most of Sunday working on the shed, carrying items from the garage to their new storage space. From his window, Ryan watched his parents move back and forth. Calvin's deliberate pace allowed Rebecca to keep up, and though she took more breaks than he did, she managed to stay on her feet for most of the day. Ryan's eyes narrowed when he saw them carry wire fencing into the shed. *Why would they need fencing inside there?*

"I'm bored," Layla whined, her voice pulling Ryan's attention away from the window. "Nobody wants to play with me."

Ryan glanced at her with a smirk. "Not even the girl in the pink dress?"

Layla shook her head, but Ryan didn't notice; his focus was back on his parents. He couldn't shake the uneasy feeling gnawing at him. *A three-day trip, a new shed, and now this strange addition of wire fencing?* It all seemed too coincidental. *I hope I'm wrong,* he thought, sending a silent plea to any deity that might be listening.

Ryan forced himself to turn away, taking a deep breath. "What do you want to do?" he asked Layla, who was now holding up a small, pink rubber ball with a mischievous grin. *Man! We haven't played that in years!*

Layla skipped down the hall, her feet barely touching the ground, and plopped down in front of the linen closet. Ryan followed more slowly, sitting cross-legged outside the kitchen entryway. Their game had no official name, but as soon as one of them produced a bouncy ball, they both knew it was on like Donkey Kong. It was their special thing, a bond forged when Devin was too old to care.

The goal was simple: throw the tiny ball to the other person, letting it bounce only once. They had to remain seated, shifting their bodies to catch it but keeping their legs crossed unless the ball went rogue. If it bounced off a wall, the bounce was fair game and didn't count towards the one.

They began tossing the ball, laughter erupting as it went astray, bouncing wildly down the hallway. Ten feet apart, they challenged each other, trying to make the other tip over onto their sides. Giggling, they continued their game, the tension of the morning momentarily forgotten in the joy of their shared play.

Thunk! Ryan bounced the ball off the wall, causing Layla to lunge forward. Her fingers just barely managed to snatch it from the air. "You just barely caught it!" he exclaimed, eyes sparkling with excitement.

Thump-thump. Layla frowned as the ball slipped from her hand, bouncing twice before rolling towards Ryan. He scooped it up effortlessly. "I'll get you next time," she declared with a determined glint in her eye.

Ryan's arm cocked back, a mischievous smile tugging at his lips. He aimed for the ground, hoping the ball would rebound off the ceiling and back towards her. Layla, anticipating his move, braced herself. She knew the look all too well—this throw was going to be a wild one.

As the ball hit the floor and shot up towards the ceiling, Ryan realized with a pang of disappointment it would fall short. The ball ricocheted off the ceiling and descended toward the hardwood floor. Both siblings crawled forward, eyes fixed on the ball, ready to pounce as soon as it landed.

Wait for it.

Layla glanced at Ryan, expecting him to seize the ball like he always did. *That darn Ryan*, she thought, *he only gets it first because he's bigger!* But Ryan hesitated, still watching the ball's descent. They exchanged a worried glance, realizing the ball was heading towards the stairwell—the very place where one of the five ghosts lingered in their home.

A chill swept through the hallway, making the hair on the back of Ryan's neck stand up. The usual warmth of the house retreated, replaced by an icy stillness. Shadows lengthened unnaturally, creeping along the walls as if drawn by an unseen force. Layla shivered, wrapping her arms around herself instinctively.

Then came the smell—a putrid, suffocating odor clawing at their throats. It was the stench of decay, heavy and unmistakable, like something long dead and forgotten. Layla wrinkled her nose, her eyes watering as the foul air filled her lungs.

Ryan's gaze darted to the stairwell, the darkened corner where the light refused to reach. The ball should have bounced by now, but there was only silence, an oppressive quiet pressing down on them. Layla's heart pounded in her chest, each beat echoing in the eerie stillness.

The air grew heavier, thicker, as if saturated with dread. Layla's skin prickled with an invisible threat, a sense something was watching them from the shadows. She looked at Ryan, her wide eyes mirroring his fear.

A faint, almost imperceptible whisper slithered through the air. He swallowed hard, forcing himself to stay still, his eyes never leaving the darkened stairwell. The atmosphere pulsed with tension, the weight of unseen eyes bearing down on them.

Layla's hand reached out, seeking the comfort of her brother's presence. Their fingers brushed, and she clung to him, both of them rooted in place by the heavy, foreboding air. The game was forgotten, replaced by the suffocating presence of death that seeped from the very walls of their home. Their breaths caught as they waited for the ball to land, knowing it was now in haunted territory.

Ryan looked up, dreading what he would see.

The ball was levitating, suspended in the shadow of the nearly beheaded man lingering outside Layla's room. His eyes were hollow, staring down at the piece of rubber as maggots tumbled from his decaying body. Ryan froze, his breath caught in his throat as he stared at the older man in a tattered suit, surrounded by an aura of darkness.

But Layla was unfazed. She rose to her feet, her small fists clenched, and stomped over to the apparition. "Give us back our ball!" she demanded, her voice unwavering. Undisturbed by her words, the man's ethereal form floated.

"Did you hear me? I said, give me the ball back. It's not yours!" Layla's patience with the apparitions had worn thin. "Say something!"

She reached out, her hand trembling but determined to retrieve her toy. "No! Layla! Don't!" Ryan's urgent scream echoed through the hallway as he watched her step closer, her arm extending into the ghoul's shadowy figure.

Layla grabbed the ball, but as she pulled her hand back, the entity's icy grip closed around her arm. A scream tore from her lips as a chilling sensation shot through her. The spirit twisted to face her, its grotesque, decayed visage more horrifying up close. With a violent motion, it flung Layla across the hall. She flew towards a sitting Ryan, who caught her just before she hit the floor.

As the entity turned back around, its head lurched forward and fell with a sickening thud, rolling towards them. The siblings stared in horror as the decapitated head came to a stop, its eyes wide and bloodshot. A guttural voice emanated from the severed head, filled with fear and confusion—*You can't go this way! Not this! You'll pay if you go…the wrong way!*

A cold dread clutched their heart as the head's warning echoed through the hallway, its eyes locking onto theirs with a haunting intensity. The siblings screamed; their panic magnified by the ghastly sight before them.

Ryan quickly covered his sister's eyes with his hands, squeezing his own shut as the eerie voice faded into the walls. When they finally dared to look again, they saw the rubber ball bounce once more before coming to rest near the stairs. Exhausted, they stayed on the floor, their hearts pounding, minds racing, trying to make sense of what had just happened.

Devin entered the room, his face a mix of confusion and concern. "What's happening?" he asked, looking down at them sprawled on the floor.

"It's nothing you'd want to know," Ryan replied, still breathless. Layla, her face a storm of frustration, stood up and marched away, muttering, "Grown-ups never listen anyway."

Devin's eyes followed her before turning back to Ryan, puzzled. Ryan shrugged, knowing explaining wouldn't make a difference. "There's something strange in our neighborhood. Something's off, and somehow, it involves us. But for some reason, only Layla and I seem to notice."

Devin extended a hand, helping his brother up from the floor, a skeptical look on his face. *He won't believe me. I should just drop it.*

"Have mom and dad been at the shed all day?" Devin asked, wrinkling his nose at the foul stench in the air, eager to shift the conversation. Ryan shook his head wearily. They made their way to Ryan's bedroom, ready to delve into their ongoing discussions. The brothers conversed as equals, with Ryan even sharing details about him and Christina. When the topic shifted to girls, Devin opened up about Valerie and her recent changes.

"Just promise me you'll stay cautious. I hope I'm just paranoid, but if not, you need to keep watch—on Eric and on Valerie," Devin urged, his tone serious. Ryan nodded solemnly as they continued discussing the events of the past few weeks.

Their conversation meandered to their favorite movies when they were interrupted by music wafting up from downstairs. It was late for their parents to still be working in the backyard. Ryan stealthily crept downstairs while Devin ventured into the kitchen to inspect their revamped shed. Peering through the vertical blinds, Devin was pleasantly surprised to see the renovation complete, no longer an eyesore.

Devin wondered where his brother had disappeared to. Following the sound of the familiar music, he made his way back toward the stairs. The scent of freshly cut wood mixed with the earlier foul odor, creating an unsettling atmosphere. As he approached the stairs, the music grew louder, pulling him closer to the source. The U2 lyrics from *With or Without You* echoed through the house as the record played on.

Devin found Ryan perched at the top of the second flight of stairs, observing their parents as they danced together. Their mother appeared weary and fragile, while Calvin appeared revitalized, a stark contrast. Devin felt a sting of injustice. The woman who had always been their rock was now the one suffering, while the man who had often been absent was granted a second chance. Though neither of them were particularly religious, Devin couldn't help but wonder if there was some greater purpose to it all.

Ryan watched their parents with a sense of melancholy, pondering if this would be their final dance together. The brothers observed their parents sharing a moment unlike any they had witnessed before—not merely as mom and dad, but as two individuals, connecting in a fleeting moment until the song's end not knowing when their life together will—*with or without you.*

Layla sat on her bed, clutching her tiny rubber ball, scrutinizing it for any signs of alteration, but finding none. With a shiver of fear, she tossed the ball out of her room, hearing it thud against the front door after bouncing down the stairs.

Frustrated, Layla abandoned the ball and turned to her dolls for comfort before bedtime. She arranged them in a circle, with Teddy Ruxpin at the center, ready to recount one of Layla's favorite stories, The Airship. As the animatronic bear began to speak, Layla listened attentively, propping herself up on her elbows.

Unexpectedly, the room filled with the eerie sound of bouncing. The pink rubber ball had returned, landing with a soft thud within the circle of dolls. Layla's heart raced as she cautiously approached the edge of her room, peering into the darkness beyond. There, on the stairs, stood another ghostly figure—a young boy, his face contorted in anguish. But unlike the previous apparition, this one was horrifically mutilated, with gaping wounds and entrails spilling out onto the steps.

As Layla recoiled in horror, Teddy Ruxpin's soothing voice abruptly ceased, replaced by a low, guttural growl. The mechanical bear's eyes glowed with an otherworldly intensity, fixating on Layla with a malevolent gaze. "You can't go this way! Not this! You'll pay if you go…the wrong way!" The toy's warning echoed through the room, each repetition becoming louder until Layla covered her ears.

In the dim light, the toy dolls surrounding Teddy Ruxpin moved their heads, their plastic eyes gleaming with malice as they teetered on the edge of the circle. With a sense of impending dread, Layla frantically searched for Anna and her pink dress, realizing she was no longer alone in the room.

"I don't like this. This isn't fun anymore," Layla whispered, her voice barely audible over the growing raucousness of malevolent whispers and ghostly moans.

CHAPTER TWENTY TWO

BLUE MONDAY

The day was draped in darkness and solemnity. Overcast skies bore heavy clouds, and rain cascaded in a steady rhythm, its pitter-patter echoing through the leaves that clung desperately to the trees. Ryan trudged to school on Monday morning, each step heavy, his mind burdened by a lack of sleep. The atmosphere on the bus mirrored his mood, the air thick with unspoken thoughts, except for Colin, who prattled away, oblivious.

At home, breakfast was a silent affair. Devin and Layla exchanged wordless glances over their cereal. When their parents inquired about their somber demeanor, the Hatcher kids remained mute, the weight of the previous day's events evident in their silence. A shared, unspoken burden hung over them.

The dreary weather deepened Ryan's sense of foreboding. He couldn't shake the impending dread, knowing the full moon loomed near. The thought of his father turning into a werewolf filled him with a helpless fear, an inescapable fear gnawing at his sanity.

Even Christina, usually a beacon of energy, was worn out. She attempted to lighten the mood with a joke, but the exhaustion in her eyes betrayed her. They all struggled with the uncertainty of what lay ahead.

Colin, ever curious, bombarded Ryan with questions, while Scott clung to his bravado despite the swirling gossip. Amidst the high school drama, Ryan felt a darker presence lurking beneath the surface.

The spirits haunting him and Layla grew more aggressive, their presence more ominous. Ryan sensed Layla held a crucial piece of the puzzle, her silence laden with secrets. *She knows more than she lets on*. As the day dragged on, his anxiety intensified, a suffocating weight pressing down on him.

"Do you want me to come home with you?" Christina asked, sensing his reluctance. Despite the temptation, Ryan shook his head. "No. Whatever's going on there, I need to figure it out. I don't want you mixed up in all the crazy stuff."

Confused, Christina probed, "What stuff?"

Ryan sighed, "I'll tell you after this week. I promise. There's a chance I'm losing it, and I need to be sure before I say anything weirder to my girlfriend."

"Because declaring werewolves exist isn't weird already?" Christina retorted sarcastically, prompting Ryan to offer a disingenuous smirk as they held hands. She had a point. Adding ghosts to the mix would only complicate things further. The term 'girlfriend' had slipped out naturally in his thoughts when referring to Christina, and Ryan laughed to himself, leaving her puzzled. "Nothing. Just a moment of clarity," he reassured her, then leaned in to kiss her hand.

Christina tugged at his collar, drawing him closer before resting her head against his chest. The scent of citrus and lavender emanated from her blonde hair, and Ryan gazed down at her blue cardigan, draping his coat over her shoulders while she ran her fingers along his back. Despite the dropping temperature outside, neither of them minded. These quiet, secluded moments on the deserted roads and in the surrounding woods had become their sanctuary, though they hadn't fully realized it yet.

"Call me later," she whispered before pulling away to head home. "Remember, nothing in life is to be feared. It is only to be understood. My grandma used to say that, quoting some writer or something." Ryan flashed her a thumbs up, eliciting a smile from Christina as she walked away. It was sage advice, but Ryan couldn't shake the thought: delving too deep into understanding could lead to danger.

Later that evening, Ryan sat across from his sister, poking at his quarter pounder meal, an unspoken conversation hanging heavily between them. Layla's pointed looks urged him to speak, but she hesitated, unsure how to explain the situation herself. Anna, the ghost girl in her room, had warned her to stay silent, but another presence lurked, one which had always intertwined with Ryan's fate. Layla had spent most of her time in her room, a sanctuary from the harsh realities of the outside world, never fully realizing the connection.

Their parents, engrossed in their meals of chicken nuggets, burgers, and piping hot fries, oblivious to Ryan's intense gaze. The sound of their chewing grated on his nerves, each bite amplified in his mind, reverberating off the walls. Watching the meat disappear between their teeth, he couldn't shake the unsettling image of raw human flesh. With every swallow, he half expected his father's face to contort into a snarling werewolf.

Ryan?

The voice echoed ominously in the background. Ryan's gaze shifted from his father to the strange, animalistic noises around the table. He gasped, recoiling in horror, sinking back into his seat as his family members transformed into grotesque, snarling werewolves. They tore through the remnants of their meal, driven by primal instincts to scavenge for any remaining scraps of meat.

These creatures didn't sound like wild beasts; their growls and snarls were disturbingly human, a twisted mockery of their former selves. Each howl carried the familiar timbre of his family's voices, a desperate request for sustenance. His parents and brother, now towering werewolves with demonic features, loomed over him menacingly, their forms reminiscent of the unfortunate man they'd encountered on Halloween night.

Only Layla remained smaller, resembling a wolf cub. Her innocent appearance was betrayed by the menace in her bared teeth as she glared at Ryan, poised to strike.

As the food dwindled, the werewolves ceased their scavenging, their hungry gazes turning towards him. With a collective growl, they clambered onto the table, their limbs and fingers unnaturally elongated. They slowly encircled their prey. Paralyzed with fear, Ryan willed himself to move, tears streaming down his cheeks. But it was futile.

They descended upon him, their claws ripping through his clothes and slicing into his skin with savage abandon. Ryan's screams were choked, his throat tight with fear as he watched his own blood splatter across the table. His mother's face, distorted by the snarl of a beast, snapped at his arm, her teeth tearing through muscle and sinew. The pain was excruciating, every nerve ending ablaze as his flesh was rent asunder.

His father, a towering monstrosity with glowing eyes and demonic fangs, tore into Ryan's leg, the bones crunching under the powerful jaws. Ryan's vision blurred with tears, but he could not look away. He watched in horror as his brother, his features twisted and grotesque, clawed at his chest, the sensation of his ribs cracking echoing through his mind.

Layla, her innocent face now a mask of feral hunger, bit into his side, her smaller teeth just as merciless. The sound of human meat being ripped and the warmth of his own blood pooling beneath him were a gruesome symphony. Each bite, each tear, sent waves of agony through his body, the pain so intense it was almost blinding.

Ryan's cries for mercy were swallowed by the cacophony of growls and snarls. He could feel the life draining from him with every savage bite, his body growing weaker, his vision dimming. The world narrowed to the pain and the monstrous faces of his family, their eyes alight with a predatory gleam.

Helpless, he surrendered to the nightmarish reality. His thoughts became a fractured montage of fear and pain, each second stretching into an eternity. He knew there was no escape, no salvation from the clutches of his evil kin. As the darkness closed in, he felt the final, searing bite at his throat, and then, mercifully, the agony faded to nothing.

"Ryan!" His mother's voice sliced through his thoughts. Startled, he blurted, "What?" Rebecca recoiled at his tone, her expression stern. "Watch yo tongue, young man. I asked ya a question."

"Sorry, what?" Ryan mumbled, his mind still foggy from his daydream. Calvin shot his wife a glance, concern flickering in his eyes as he noticed Ryan's distracted demeanor. Devin's worried gaze mirrored his father's. Ryan's obsession with things only seen in movies had taken its toll on him. He had lost his appetite and started muttering to himself, becoming increasingly lost in his own world. The family had noticed his behavior, but they had chalked it up to typical teenage angst.

"Are you going to the festival with everyone on Wednesday night?" Rebecca asked, a hint of impatience creeping into her voice. Ryan had completely forgotten about the festival and his friends' plans. "Your brother is going to the Donovans' for dinner, and they're going afterward. Isn't Christina and Colin going too? I thought I heard you mention it," she continued. Still shaken from his unsettling daydream, he shrugged, muttering, "I don't know."

"You should go. It might be fun," Calvin chimed in, trying to coax Ryan out of his funk. "It'll be getting cold soon, and you won't want to go out as much."

"I'll think about it," Ryan said vaguely, not wanting to make a big deal out of attending the festival. "I think I'm going to lie down. Excuse me," he announced, leaving the kitchen. His family watched him leave, puzzled and concerned.

Only Devin and Layla sensed something deeper was wrong, while their parents remained clueless— that they knew of. Alone in his room, Ryan stared at the ceiling, his thoughts a chaotic whirl. The wallpaper, adorned with vintage cars from the thirties, mocked him, a reminder of his family's lack of understanding of who he is. He felt more isolated than ever, regretting having voiced his fears about werewolves and the eerie presence in their home.

"Why do you want me to make these pictures?" Layla's voice echoed through the vents, reaching Ryan's ears as he lay in bed. The muffled conversation stirred agitation within him. The spirits, the looming threat of the werewolf curse, and Layla's silence about her own struggles gnawed at his sanity.

With a surge of frustration, Ryan stormed down the hall to Layla's room, ignoring the comforting glow of the television downstairs where his parents were engrossed in ALF. He burst into Layla's room without warning, startling her. Wide-eyed, Layla glanced nervously at her dresser before meeting his gaze.

"Where is she?" he demanded, his voice a low growl filled with urgency. Layla hesitated, unsure of how to respond. "Did I scare her off?" Ryan pressed, his tone intensifying. Her fearful nod only fueled his frustration. His eyes fell on her Lite Brite set and the sheets of black paper, and his impatience boiled over.

Snatching the papers, Ryan flipped through them, his mind racing to decipher their meaning. They weren't drawings but mere holes in black paper. "Give 'em back!" Layla's voice trembled as she reached for the papers, but Ryan kept them out of her grasp.

"What are these?" Ryan's voice was cold, demanding answers. Layla insisted they were just pictures, but he knew better. These are more than just pictures. Determined to unravel the mystery, Ryan seized the Lite Brite set and dismantled it, revealing the bulb beneath. Layla's protests fell on deaf ears as Ryan directed the light toward the ceiling, illuminating a pattern of puncture dots created on the sheets of thin construction paper.

"What is this?" Ryan's voice sliced through the tension, his eyes narrowing in concern. Trembling, Layla lifted her gaze and whispered, "That's the hallway outside."

"Is that supposed to be the stairs next to it?" His tone softened, sensing Layla's fear. Layla nodded, her hands still, relinquishing her struggle to retrieve the picture. "And what about this circle with the line below it?"

Ryan's curiosity was tinged with apprehension. "That's the man in front of the hallway," Layla explained quietly, her voice barely audible.

"You poked holes making an X. How come?"

"Because that way isn't the way to go," she said, gently pulling the paper from his grasp. Ryan pulled out another sheet, revealing three stick figures under a platform.

"What about this?"

"That's us under the deck," Layla explained, her eyes reflecting her fear. He glanced back at the picture above, confusion knitting his brow. "Why are we under the deck?" Layla hesitated, her gaze flickering with uncertainty. "I think we're hiding."

"You made it! How can you not know what you made?"

"I don't make these for me! I do it for Anna! She tells me, and I make it!" Layla cried. Feeling guilty for his outburst, Ryan pulled another sheet from the pile. He noticed two stairs resembling their home and the landing between an X over the front door made with colored pegs.

"Is going through the door not the way?" he calmly inquired, a chill creeping over him as he remembered the dolls toppling over when Layla attempted different routes days prior. She shook her head, her voice barely above a whisper. "I think one of us will get hurt if we do."

Examining one last picture, depicting them in front of the blue spruce tree in the yard, Ryan's expression softened. "What are they telling us? What will happen if we don't do what they're telling us?" he asked, his voice filled with concern.

Layla nervously chewed on her fingers, her eyes wide with fear. "I think something is going to want to hurt us really bad, Ryan! I'm scared! They don't want to hurt us. They're here to warn us…to tell us where to go!" Layla cried, her voice breaking.

"Why are they telling us to stay away from those doors?" Ryan's voice was gentle as he tried to calm his sister's fears. Layla's eyes darted around her room, her breath shaky. "Because when they died…it wasn't right! No one told them which way to go yet!"

THE
COLD
MOON

CHAPTER TWENTY THREE

OWNER OF A LONELY HEART

"You need to talk to Dad while you still can," Ryan urged his brother, glancing at their parents hurriedly packing for an overnight trip. His eyes flickered with concern.

Devin scoffed, crossing his arms. "I think you are paranoid—nothing's going to happen to them...or him," he retorted confidently, the smirk on his face unwavering. "Even if I believed in your wolf idea or any psychic ability, I don't have anything to say to him."

Ryan turned to leave Devin's room, but a memory of his mother's words resurfaced, something she had said a week prior when he debated going to Colin's party. Her voice echoed in his mind, reminding him about priorities. He paused, the weight of her words settling in his chest. "Maybe you need to realize it's not all about you," Ryan said, his voice laced with frustration.

"The hell did you just say to me?" Devin snapped, his tone sharp enough to cut through the air, hoping their parents would overhear.

Ryan shook his head, undeterred. "Mom won't be around forever," he said. His voice was steady, yet the gravity of his words hung in the room like a heavy fog.

Devin tossed his headphones onto his bed, the loud thud emphasizing his irritation. "Don't talk like that!"

Ryan stood his ground, his patience fraying. "It's true, and you know it! I'm tired of tiptoeing around the truth. Why am I the only one trying to come to terms with this?" His eyes bore into Devin's, searching for a flicker of understanding. "Let's assume I'm wrong, and Dad is normal. Then what? He's still going to be around. Can you at least acknowledge he's trying? Can you do something to make Mom feel a little better? Can you be a man for a moment?"

Ryan's voice cracked slightly, the pressure of unspoken truths weighing heavily. "I shouldn't be the one to do it, but you're so wrapped up in yourself, avoiding everything!" His final words lingered in the air, a challenge and a prayer intertwined.

Ryan clenched his jaw, the realization hitting him like a cold splash of water. *If dad is a threat, and they have to stop him? We could lose both parents.*

Devin took a step back, shifting his weight uneasily. "I've been busy!" he protested, his voice lacking conviction.

Ryan scoffed, turning away. "Yeah, busy avoiding your responsibilities. You spent weeks cleaning out an old man's house for nothing. It wasn't out of the goodness of your heart."

"I did it because Mom asked me to!" Devin shouted, his face flushing.

"You did it to get away from us!" Ryan shot back, his eyes narrowing with accusation.

Exhausted from the argument, Ryan left Devin standing there and headed downstairs. He flopped onto the couch and turned on the TV, the flickering screen doing little to distract him. As he watched reruns, his mind kept returning to his parents' departure. *What if dad turns and hurts mom?* The thought gnawed at him, a scenario he had never seriously considered before. *Maybe I have been too preoccupied with werewolves and ghosts.*

Calvin brought down the luggage, the heavy thuds of the bags breaking Ryan's reverie. "Seems like a lot for a couple of days," Ryan commented, trying to keep his tone light.

Calvin paused, glancing upstairs before looking at Ryan. "It's your mom. She's always been like this. Thinks she's going to need everything. High maintenance, I tell her, but she just shrugs it off."

Ryan smiled faintly, wondering if he had been wrong about his dad all along. *Maybe they were just going away for some quality time together—one last time.*

Around four in the afternoon, Calvin and Rebecca called their kids downstairs to say goodbye. Layla bounded down the stairs first, her cheerful facade masking her true feelings. Ryan reluctantly rose from the couch, his feet feeling like lead as he approached. The embrace with his parents lasted longer than usual, each second amplifying his anxiety.

Struggling to contain his emotions, Ryan's eyes welled up with tears, his throat tightening. "What's wrong, bud?" his dad inquired, concern etched on his face. Using his long-sleeved shirt to dab his eyes, Ryan shook his head, fabricating an excuse. "It's just you guys have never been away for so long. I mean, I know it's not long, but it feels like it to me…to us."

Layla clung to Calvin's leg, her small hands gripping tightly as she tried to delay his departure by playfully dragging herself across the floor. Unaware of her brother's concerns about the wolf curse, she simply knew there were lingering presences in the house. "Why do you have to go?" Layla whimpered, her voice a mix of confusion and sadness.

"Married people need time alone together," Rebecca explained gently, crouching down to Layla's level. "We'll be back before you know it. Be good for your brothers while we're away, alright?" Layla reluctantly agreed, her usual good behavior not being a concern.

Calvin glanced upstairs, his eyes searching for any sign of Devin coming down. However, the floors remained silent, the air heavy with his absence. "Alright then," their father sighed, disappointment shadowing his features, "I guess we're off."

After a final hug, they left, but it wasn't enough for Layla and Ryan. They followed their parents outside, watching as they started the red Mazda and pulled out of the garage. The car's departure left a sinking feeling in Ryan's stomach, an unease he couldn't shake.

A noise echoed from above, signaling Devin's change of heart as he dashed from his room to the garage. He rushed past his siblings and approached the car on the passenger side where his mother sat. Rebecca rolled down the window, waiting for her oldest child to speak. There was a tense silence before Devin finally spoke up. "So, when will you be back on Thursday?"

"Probably around noon, if I had to guess," Calvin replied, his eyes softening.

Devin nodded, then continued, "Are you sure you've got everything you need?" They exchanged smiles, recognizing Devin's attempt to be helpful and mature.

"There's money in an envelope on the kitchen counter and some lasagna in the fridge for you to heat up and buy a pizza for yourselves," Rebecca told him, her voice warm with reassurance. Devin nodded again, giving a thumbs up to the meal plan for the next two nights.

"Are you alright?" Calvin asked, his gaze piercing.

Devin pondered Ryan's theory about the curse and their mother's potential fate. He felt the pressure to be strong and reliable, but he began to question whether it was necessary anymore. A heavy sigh escaped him as he met his father's eyes. "Yeah, I'm alright," he said, forcing a smile.

"Just, ya know, be careful. Cleveland and all…ya know?" Devin's voice cracked, betraying his attempt to mask his worry as he offered his caution as an excuse to talk to them. They both nodded in response, offering crooked smiles in appreciation of his concern. With a heartfelt nod and teary eyes, Rebecca rolled up her window, and they drove away.

Calvin and Rebecca Hatcher made their way down Greengate Lane, their car's headlights cutting through the early evening shadows. Just before they turned onto Wadsworth Road, Rebecca's mouth quivered, her efforts to hold back tears evident. Calvin rubbed her back reassuringly before making the turn, his touch a unspoken promise. He stole a brief glance at her, aware seeing his wife cry would only stir his own emotions. However, Rebecca's tears weren't solely for herself or him; they were tears of relief, signaling the rekindling of communication among everyone, even if only to a limited extent. It was a small step, but at least Rebecca harbored the hope that it was possible before she departed this world. Now, she had to attend to matters with her husband.

What did you say to them?" Ryan wondered, watching as his brother walked past him and Layla.

Without pausing to look at either of them, Devin replied, "Told them goodbye." His footsteps were heavy, each step a mix of regret and determination. He never knew if taking the time to see his parents off was a sign of respect. He wanted to let them know, in his own way, he would do better. Then he began to wonder if Ryan's theory might have been correct. They wouldn't know until the news came tomorrow if another person had died from a vicious animal attack.

All three siblings remained indoors, a thick silence settling around them like a fog. There was nothing more Ryan could say; all he could do was flip through the thin, punctured pages Layla had created alongside an entity hiding in her room. Placing the papers next to one another, he hoped to understand and follow the path revealed to them if the time came. This would have been the night to cut loose and break some rules, but they had no plans for hijinks. Simply getting through the nights, waiting for their parents to come home, was enough.

They settled on a pan pizza from Pizza Hut accompanied by breadsticks and a two-liter of Pepsi for the evening. Devin, true to his solitary nature, retreated to his room with his share of the meal, the muffled sound of rock music drifting through the door as he engaged in conversation with Valerie. They discussed her suggestion of inviting him over for dinner at her place before heading to the fair the following night. Their conversation also drifted to Eric's whereabouts, who had been missing since the party on Saturday. They wondered if he would ever resurface. Eric Flanagan had become a mere shadow of his former self since Halloween, lending further credence to Ryan's theory. He had grown calmer, less volatile, and surprisingly invested in school, but there remained a darkness within him. Before ending their call, they reminded each other to be cautious.

Hours passed, and Layla finally succumbed to sleep, her head resting on her brother's lap. After attempting to decipher the cryptic pictures to the best of their ability, her exhaustion got the better of her. Ryan gently lifted her, tucked her into bed, switched off the Tinkerbell lamp, and whispered a soft goodnight. As he stepped out into the hallway and prepared to close the door, a spine-tingling fear took hold of him. He noticed a figure standing by Layla's dresser, shrouded in darkness.

Though dimly lit, Ryan could discern the pink dress described by his sister and the burning red hair, streaked with dried blood down her leg. He closed his eyes momentarily, hoping when he opened them again, the apparition would vanish as it had in the past. To his dismay, she remained. With a heavy sigh, Ryan maintained his gaze on the ghostly figure, unmoving, lingering in the shadows. "I hope you're right," he whispered to the spectral presence before closing the door. *I hope to God you're right.*

CHAPTER TWENTY FOUR

MIRROR IN THE BATHROOM

Recompense.

Following his brutal attack on Saturday, the local authorities began searching for Eric Flanagan, though their efforts were lackluster, typical of the Akron police assigned to suburban areas. Unbeknownst to anyone, Eric slipped into his house once a day while his father dozed off in his favorite lounger in the mornings. Despite the urgency of his situation, Eric's adrenaline surges, which negated any immediate need for sustenance. While it would have been simple to grab a bag of Doritos or some prepackaged cheese slices, nothing appealed to him except the slab of steak thawing in the refrigerator. A voice urged him to consume it raw, but his civility rebelled. He was well aware his body was undergoing changes, but it wasn't until the day of the first full moon that the extent became apparent.

His heart raced, and his muscles throbbed, yet he couldn't remain still. An insatiable hunger gnawed at him, urging him to feed on food he had no desire to eat. Surprisingly, surviving in the woods for the past three days hadn't been as challenging as anticipated. The only real inconvenience was the persistent dampness of his body and clothes, saturated with sweat.

Occasionally, woodland creatures darted in front of him, capturing all his attention. His focus narrowed on the animal, blocking out the surroundings. A bunny hopped nearby as he attempted to relax. Its ears perked up at the rustling bushes from where it emerged, and

Eric's senses heightened, detecting the blood coursing through its veins. He listened intently to its rapidly beating heart, observing the pulsating veins throughout its diminutive frame. Slowly, he crawled on all fours toward it, his breath shallow with anticipation. Just as he was about to pounce, the bunny darted away. Eric growled in frustration, his eyes flashing with primal hunger, vexed by his instincts and the relentless hunger pains

You will get what you need.
You will hunt and feed as you have never known.
You will be fulfilled.
You will learn patience.
You will change.
You will become apex.

Eric tugged at his shirt, feeling as though it were suffocating him, his muscles straining as if he had overexerted himself. "It hurts so bad!" he yelled, but the voice that had spoken earlier remained silent for the rest of the day. Desperate for any comfort, Eric was driven by his instincts back to the familiarity of his home, his bed. He sprinted through the woods, his breath ragged and heart pounding. Crawling through his bedroom window, he discarded his clothes onto the floor and collapsed into bed, wrapping himself in the quilt his mother had crafted before her passing. Shivering uncontrollably, he endured the discomfort until his father's movements in the living room signaled the start of his nightly binge drinking.

Conor Flanagan's shadow flitted back and forth beneath Eric's door as Conor aimlessly wandered the house. A man who believed he had nothing left in his life, Conor had become weary of television and alcohol but continued to indulge out of habit. Communication with his son had ceased long ago, convinced Eric's attitude could never be rectified after his wife's death. Resorting to physical violence had become Conor's only means of asserting control over his disobedient son.

When the police arrived at their house in search of Eric, Conor saw an opportunity to rid himself of his son's presence. He hoped they would handle the situation so he wouldn't have to. Unemployment had rendered Conor lazy and self-absorbed. He believed Eric's absence might be the best outcome for both of them. As he watched Conor's shadow, Eric prayed his father would not enter his room.

The sound of a soda can tipping over echoed through the silence, catching Conor's attention in an instant. Eric, parched from days of neglecting his body's basic needs, grabbed the old Pepsi can, desperate for any liquid, even if it meant drinking his own backwash. Conor's ears perked up at the noise while scrounging for a snack, settling on a forgotten stick of beef jerky tucked away in a cabinet. His paranoia heightened without the numbing effects of alcohol, especially after reading about the recent deaths in the area. Gripping his double-barreled shotgun from hall closet, Conor cautiously approached Eric's room, his senses on high alert, prepared to defend his home at all costs.

As the sun began its descent, Eric's discomfort intensified. Beads of sweat formed on his brow, and he felt a sense of urgency. Hastily dressing, he silently slipped back into his sweaty clothes, his mind racing with thoughts of seeking medical help. Unbeknownst to him, an infection far more insidious than any physical ailment ravaged his body—a sickness consuming not just flesh, but mind and soul.

Conor grappled with the decision of whether to approach his son's room, torn between caution and aggression. Should he open the door slowly, risking detection? Should he opt for a swift entry, hoping to catch the intruder off guard? Resolving to trust his instincts, Conor counted down, his grip tightening on the shotgun. Two... One...

Meanwhile, Eric hastily buttoned his jeans, opting to layer up with a sweater and jacket, his only protection against the encroaching chill of the night. Before he could finish dressing, the door exploded inward, the top hinge splintering under Conor's forceful kick. Frozen in shock, Eric found himself staring down the barrel of his father's shotgun, his heart pounding in his chest as he raised his hands in surrender.

"The hell have you been, boy?" Conor bellowed in anger, his gaze narrowing on his weakened son—a prime target for his pent-up frustrations. "The police were here, asking questions about you and some damn party. Said you hurt some kid, crushed his hand."

Struggling to maintain composure, Eric fumbled for his sweater, his movements sluggish from exhaustion. "Nothing. I'm leaving," he murmured, his voice barely audible above the chaos unfolding around him. Ignoring his father's inquiries, Eric pushed past him, his mind set on escape.

But Conor wasn't about to let him off easy. "Where the hell do you think you're going?" he demanded, bewildered by his son's erratic behavior. With a combination of defiance and resignation, Eric finally turned to face his father, his frustration boiling over. "Why do you care?" he spat, his tone laced with bitterness. "Tell me, Dad, why should I believe you give a fuck about me?"

Conor's grip on the shotgun loosened slightly as he scoffed at his son's audacity. "You've been growin' a spine, haven't you? Maybe you soaked up too much of your mother's nonsense. Maybe I underestimated you." Eric's chuckle was laced with pain, sweat trickling down his face as he grimaced and clutched his side.

"Wrong since Mom died, huh?" Eric's words lingered in the air, each syllable a dagger aimed straight at Conor's heart. Father and son locked eyes, a noiseless battle raging between them. Conor licked his lips, steeling himself for the verbal onslaught he was about to unleash. "Should've been you," he spat, the venom in his voice cutting through the tension like a knife. "Your mom was a saint. She kept me in line, and now I'm stuck with an ungrateful brat. Big goddamn disappointment."

Eric's eyes blazed with anger and hurt, his body shivering as he fought to hold back tears. He took a deep breath, his resolve hardening. "Maybe you're right," he said quietly, "but I'm not staying here to find out." With that, he turned and walked out the door, leaving Conor standing alone in the hall, the weight of his words hanging heavy in the air.

Eric's response was swift, his nostrils flaring with rage as he bared his teeth. "I know you do. I know you wish it was me," he retorted, each word dripping with contempt. "You wasted everything she worked for, Dad. You stopped giving a damn. She'd be ashamed of you. A worthless, drunken, abusive waste of space. I wouldn't even use your face to wipe my ass." Each insult was a cathartic strike against his father's ego.

The room crackled with tension as father and son faced off, their words hanging in the air like a toxic cloud. The shotgun wavered in Conor's grip, the barrels inching upward towards Eric's head as his scowl deepened. "Get out of my house before I do something I regret," Conor growled, his voice laced with menace.

"I thought you already did," Eric retorted, his tone dripping with disdain as he limped past his father, his body wracked with pain. He refused to let Conor see him any more vulnerable, refusing to give him the satisfaction.

With a violent motion, Eric flung open the bathroom door, the sound of it slamming against the counter ringing through the house. He slammed the door shut in his father's face, the click of the lock a final barrier between them. Conor rattled the doorknob furiously, his fists pounding against the wood. "Open the door, Eric!" he bellowed. "When I get in there, I'm gonna make you regret it!"

Eric leaned against the counter, forcing composure, his hand slamming flat against the surface as he struggled to contain the agony coursing through his body. He dry heaved into the sink, bile rising in his throat. Glancing at his reflection in the mirror, he froze, horror spreading across his features as he watched his eyes change. His pupils narrowed, elongating into ovals, as jade-colored shards crystallized within his green irises. Hair sprouted from his skin, his hands contorting and elongating before his eyes. With a primal scream of agony, Eric realized something was happening to his body, his cries reverberating through the house, a harbinger of the transformation to come.

Conor froze, his heart pounding in his chest as he listened to the conversion unfolding behind the bathroom door. Eric's agonizing cries turned into guttural moans. He fumbled for his shotgun, his hands shaking with fear and anticipation. Each thud against the floor sounded like a death knell, echoing through the house.

With bated breath, Conor pressed his ear against the door, straining to hear over the pounding of his own heartbeat. He caught the heavy panting, the scraping of claws against tile, and then... silence. His heart lurched as he whispered, "Eric, are you alright?" Genuine concern laced his voice, a rare moment of vulnerability amidst the chaos.

The bathroom door burst open with violent force, hurling Conor against the wall. The shotgun discharged, its deafening blast echoing through the room as the spread pierced the ceiling. As Conor fought to regain his bearings, he was confronted with a sight chilling him to the core.

In the doorway stood not his son, but an animal brimming with hatred and rage. Towering over him, it bore little resemblance to the boy Conor once knew, save for a few strands of red hair. With menacing teeth and shining fur, it radiated a terrifying presence, sending waves of dread coursing through Conor's veins.

Tears streamed down Conor's face as he realized the truth of what had become of his family. "This isn't you," he argued, his voice breaking with sorrow. But as he met the creature's amber eyes, he knew his words fell on deaf ears. The beast before him was a manifestation of his failures, a reminder of the darkness lurking within. And as it loomed over him, Conor could only pray for forgiveness for the sins that had brought them to this moment. *The kindness comes out when the filth is faced with death.*

...Yes, it is, Eric thought as the animal took over.

The enormous beast loomed over Conor, its snarls echoing through the darkened hallway as it bore down on him with relentless fury. With each swipe of its razor-sharp claws, it shredded the door above Conor, slicing through the wood like butter and gouging deep wounds into his skin.

Conor's screams pierced the air, a symphony of agony and dread. He fought desperately to free himself from the creature's grasp, but each attempt only drove the beast into a frenzy, its bloodlust fueled by his fear and pain.

"Stop it, Eric! Stop!" Conor yelled. As tears and snot streamed down his face, his voice choked with anguish and desperation.

The giant wolf nipped at Conor's right hand, piercing through the skin to bone, craving the taste of human blood and meat for the first time. Conor yanked his hand away, but the beast's tooth ran through the flesh between his pointer and middle finger, leaving a deep, jagged wound.

Mustering all his strength, Conor kicked the door off him and scrambled to his feet, only to fall repeatedly. "Leave me alone!" he screamed; his voice hoarse.

Eric's werewolf form stood back on its hind legs, stalking Conor with a menacing slowness, watching him stumble and scream for mercy. "What do you want from me?" Conor shouted, backing away from the advancing creature.

The wolf was not frail like the one who had scratched him weeks ago. It was more prominent, heavier, and muscled, making it an even more terrifying and lethal predator.

Conor began to piece it all together—the attack, his son's recovery—something straight out of the movies, he thought. His heart pounded as he dashed to the front door, hands shaking as he grabbed the dusty baseball bat he'd kept for years. It was meant for father-son games, but it had gathered dust in the corner, forgotten along with old umbrellas. Conor had often thought about playing with Eric, but he always dismissed the idea, thinking he was too old, and that Eric wouldn't want to spend time with him. Now, facing the grotesque creature his son had become, Conor wished he had seized those moments while he still could.

The wolf's eyes gleamed with hunger as Conor swung the bat, trying to keep the beast at bay long enough to escape. Strands of saliva dripped from the werewolf's gaping jaws, splattering onto the furniture and floor as it growled menacingly, driven by primal instincts to hunt its prey.

Conor's bat connected with a piercing crack against the creature's left arm, but it barely flinched. It retaliated with a swift swipe, slicing open Conor's left arm, spraying blood onto the walls. Stumbling backward, Conor was seized by the beast and hurled against the bay window, shattering the glass.

Pain coursed through Conor's body, silencing any shout he might muster. Knowing his fate was sealed, he struggled to stand, locking eyes with the creature. There were no words left to say, no apologies to mend what had been broken between them. The inevitability of his demise loomed.

The werewolf lowered its massive head, its snout inches from Conor's face, licking his cheek with a grotesque mix of saliva and blood, a chilling gesture of twisted empathy—I'm sorry you failed. Conor tasted his own tears mingling with the creature's foul breath, a bitter reminder of the love and loss that had brought them to this moment.

Margery Garrett, Flanagan's next door neighbor, dragged her aluminum trash can to the end of the driveway when she noticed something unusual. Shadows danced ominously in the Flanagan's window, a stark contrast to the usual silence following Conor's nightly drinking. Margery, ever the nosy neighbor, approached cautiously. She kept her distance but strained to see what was happening inside.

As she peered through the window, horror gripped her heart. Conor Flanagan's contorted body was pressed against the glass, his screams piercing the stillness of the evening. With a sickening lurch, she watched as claws tore open his rib cage. Crimson spattered against the windowpane in a grotesque display of violence.

Frozen in terror, Margery could only watch helplessly as Conor's body was ripped apart, his organs sliding down the glass, spilling onto the floor as the creature within him feasted. The sight was too much to bear, and with a strangled cry, Margery turned and fled, her mind reeling with shock and disbelief.

Racing back to her own home, Margery frantically screamed for her husband to call the police, her voice carrying through the night air like a banshee's wail. "Something's killing him! A large beast, like a big dog!" she shouted, her words ringing out in desperation as she sought help from anyone who would listen.

Meanwhile, the werewolf within the Flanagan's house heard Margery's cries and sensed danger approaching. With a final, savage snarl, it cast aside Conor's mangled body and crashed through the shattered window, disappearing into the darkness of the wilderness, leaving behind a scene of unimaginable gore for those who dared to witness it.

You must be elusive.
You must not be greedy and feed when you like.
You need little to be known about us.

Minutes later, Ryan Hatcher stood by the living room window, transfixed by the chaotic scene outside. The flashing red and blue lights of the police cars illuminated the darkness, casting eerie shadows across the neighborhood. He didn't need confirmation from anyone; he could already sense the weight of the tragedy unfolding.

Someone died tonight, and Ryan couldn't shake the feeling this was just the beginning. The searchlights of the police cars swept across the area, their beams cutting through the night as a wave of dread washed over him.

Eric Flanagan had murdered his father, that much was clear. The lone witness would recount a horrifying tale of a large animal attacking Conor, but Ryan knew the truth was far more sinister. No investigator could believe an animal could inflict such deliberate, calculated violence, tearing open a human rib cage with such precision.

As the reality of what had transpired sank in, Ryan felt a chill. This was the moment when Eric crossed the point of no return, descending into darkness with no remorse for the carnage he had wrought. And Ryan feared they were all just pawns in a much larger, more malevolent game.

CHAPTER TWENTY FIVE

ONE THING LEADS TO ANOTHER

Turkey farmer Gary Jersyk sank into his lime-green Barcalounger, a monstrosity of comfort his wife, Betty, had rescued from obscurity. The fireplace crackled, its warm glow driving back the chill while helping to save on the electric bill. Gary was on a mission to slash their power expenses, constantly flipping off switches and unplugging anything with a cord. But with winter approaching, he knew their resolve would be tested.

Fresh off a triumphant Thanksgiving season, they had sold premium turkeys to customers eager for quality beyond supermarket standards. Word of mouth had propelled their business, ensuring a steady stream of buyers. With Christmas on the horizon, they looked forward to even greater profits. Still, the pervasive scent of turkey manure clung to the air, a pungent reminder that success didn't come without its challenges.

Betty entered with decaf coffee and a slice of pecan pie, a small comfort for her hardworking husband. They settled onto their velour couch, decorated with autumnal patterns, and savored a quiet moment by the fire.

Just as they began to nod off to the gentle crackling flames, the peace was shattered by the clamor of agitated animals outside. Bleating sheep and whinnying horses jolted Gary from his drowsiness. Betty, sensing his tension, asked, "What's happenin', pa?"

"Just something spookin' the animals. Nothing to worry about, probably," Gary reassured her, though the sudden clamor from their typically calm horses gnawed at him. He grabbed a flashlight and rose from his seat, casting a quick look at Betty which told her he would investigate. She sighed, knowing these gestures only amplified her anxiety.

The screen door burst open, slamming against the house with a deafening creak—a clear warning to any would-be intruders. Gary had become a local legend in western Akron, his name wrapped in tales of violence and retribution. Some whispered he had killed a man in his barn for seeking shelter on a cold winter's night, while others spun yarns of him driving vandals into the woods to face a savage bear.

In reality, the Jersyks were just an elderly couple seeking solitude, living off the grid in remote Nowhere, Ohio. Gary, clad in his red and black flannel hunting jacket, cast his flashlight beam towards the chicken coop, the light casting eerie shadows against the coop's weathered wood. He brushed a hand across his nose, his breath forming frosty clouds in the chilly night air. Aside from a scattering of feathers, nothing appeared amiss.

Behind the house, the turkeys were unusually agitated, their frantic gobbling cutting through the howling wind. Gary frowned, a sense of unease creeping over him. Turkeys were typically most active in the afternoons. Sounds like…fowl play—he loved that joke, but tonight, it failed to lift his spirits as the nervous humor of his own suspicion lingered.

Gary rounded the corner, his flashlight beam slicing through the darkness as he aimed it toward the extensive fencing enclosing the turkeys. He approached the gate with an easy stride, his demeanor unaffected by the possibility of intruders. The rumors surrounding him no longer fazed him; he had embraced the false reputation with a shrug. As he swung the gate open, he swept the beam of light around the pen, scanning for any signs of disturbance.

Stepping carefully to avoid the turkey droppings coating his boots, Gary watched as the birds parted, creating a clear path for him. But amidst the scattered fowl, something caught his eye—three turkeys lying motionless in the muck. Squinting, he tried to discern the cause of their distress when a menacing figure emerged from the shadows. The flashlight revealed piercing green eyes, framed by sleek black fur with hints of grey and white.

Instinctively, Gary turned to retrieve his gun, his movements deliberate but swift. From the bedroom window, Betty observed her husband's actions with growing concern. "Why are you moving so slowly?" she called out, her voice cutting through the night air. Ignoring her, Gary quickened his pace, hoping to avoid provoking the creature lurking in the pen.

But Betty's persistent questioning only served to escalate the situation. "Why aren't you talking?" she pressed, her voice rising in volume. Frustrated, Gary shot her a glance and muttered, "Betty! Shut the hell up!"

As Gary hastened his steps, the squelching sound of the creature's approach grew louder. Sensing the impending danger, Betty leaned out of the window, her gaze fixed on the looming threat. With a gasp, she warned her husband, "Gary, watch out!"

Responding to her cries, Gary's pace quickened, his heart pounding in his chest. But before he could reach safety, the beast lunged forward, sinking its teeth into his arm with a vicious snarl. With a sickening thud, Gary was thrown into the air, his body careening towards the huddled turkeys. Betty watched in horror as the scene unfolded, her screams echoing through the night as her husband's severed arm fell to the ground, creating a bloody puddle.

With his face buried in turkey waste, Gary desperately lifted his head, calling out for his wife's help. The wolf, however, had other plans. It moved with chilling precision, pressing Gary's head back into the muck with its paw. Gary gasped for air, suffocating under the weight, as the werewolf tore at his clothes with its teeth, ripping flesh from his back and sides.

The beast's hot breath seared Gary's neck, its growls reverberating through his bones. Each bite was a savage reminder of his helplessness, the pain shooting through his body like lightning. Mud and blood mixed beneath him, the ground becoming a macabre canvas of his struggle. Gary's fingers clawed at the dirt, seeking anything to grip, to fight back, but the werewolf's relentless assault left him powerless. The creature's eyes, glowing with a predatory gleam, reflected the sheer horror in Gary's wide-eyed gaze as darkness began to close in around him.

Betty stood frozen, paralyzed by the gruesome scene before her. She watched helplessly as her husband was devoured, unable to comprehend the horror. Snapping out of her trance, she reached for the olive green rotary phone beside their bed, her trembling arthritic fingers dialing the emergency number.

The phone felt cold and heavy in her hand, the rotary dial clicking ominously with each spin. Her breath hitched, coming in shallow, rapid gasps, as the operator's voice crackled through the receiver. She could barely form words, her voice a quivering whisper, "Help... my husband... a wolf is attacking him." Her eyes flicked back to the window, where the dim light of the flashlight cast flickering shadows on the blood-soaked ground. The sight of Gary's body, motionless under the monstrous creature, seared into her mind. The line between reality and nightmare blurred as she watched the beast gnawing, its fur matted with blood and shit.

Through tears and frantic gasps, Betty continued begging for help, describing the nightmare unfolding in their backyard. As the dispatcher instructed her to stay on the line, Betty glanced out of the window, her heart pounding as she searched for any sign of the beast. It was gone.

When the authorities arrived, they found Gary's lifeless body lying face down in the filth, his head submerged. His spine protruded grotesquely through his back, chewed and loose, evidence of the brutal attack. Though he had long since succumbed to asphyxiation, the sight was no less harrowing.

In the end, Betty could only offer a silent prayer of gratitude for the small mercy her husband had been spared the agony of feeling his flesh and bones being torn apart.

CHAPTER TWENTY SIX

THIS MUST BE THE PLACE

Ryan opened his front door at eleven in the morning to find his trio of friends standing there, their faces a mix of concern and anticipation. It was clear they had urgent news. As they stepped inside, Ryan's stomach tightened in apprehension.

"Did you hear? They found Mr. Flanagan in his home," Scott began, his voice trailing off as he looked at Ryan, eyes wide with expectation.

Ryan's nod was slow and heavy, already burdened with the grim details. The recent spate of attacks had left the community reeling, fear spreading like wildfire. Another victim only deepened the collective anxiety.

As his friends detailed the latest developments, Ryan kept his face a mask of calm, though inside, a cold dread spread. His eyes flickered around the room, half expecting the ghostly apparitions that had plagued him in recent weeks. To his relief, they remained unseen.

While Scott, Christina, and Colin continued their discussion, Ryan's thoughts drifted. A hollow feeling gnawed at him, a testament to the relentless violence claiming lives.

When the conversation finally lulled, Ryan seized the moment to escape the stifling air indoors. He headed to the garage, the familiar clutter offering a brief refuge.

His friends followed, their voices becoming a distant murmur as Ryan sifted through his father's belongings, searching for a distraction from the grim reality. Colin's discovery of a few baseball gloves and a ball sparked an unexpected suggestion.

"Can we play catch?" Colin's eyes sparkled with excitement.

Scott looked puzzled, but Colin's enthusiasm was infectious. Christina glanced at Ryan, seeking his approval.

Surprised but eager for a diversion, Ryan nodded. "You know what? I think it sounds like a good idea right now."

With a newfound sense of purpose, the four friends made their way to the front yard, where the towering blue spruce stood sentinel. As they began to play catch, the weight of recent tragedies momentarily lifted, replaced by a fleeting sense of normalcy.

Devin lingered in his room, experimenting with various outfits and assessing himself in the mirror, cursing his lanky frame. Each change of clothes felt like a futile attempt to look more confident, more presentable for his visit to Valerie's house later that evening. The strained dynamic between their families weighed heavily on him, especially since Valerie's father had a longstanding grudge against his own family after a falling out. Despite a tentative reconciliation during Halloween, Devin remained skeptical about its longevity.

Devin's concern for Valerie gnawed at him. He had noticed unsettling signs of potential abuse within the Donovan household, though Valerie and her brother Scott kept quiet. The suspicion lingered in his mind, compelling him to check on her, despite the familial tensions.

Unaware of the attacks from the previous night, Devin's thoughts were also consumed by concern for his friend, Eric. Although disapproving of Eric's reckless behavior on Saturday night, he couldn't shake the worry for his friend's safety. Eric's abrasive demeanor often made him difficult to like, but their longstanding friendship made Devin unwilling to abandon him.

Now, as Devin finalized his outfit, he steeled himself to speak with Valerie, attempting to mask the nervousness simmering beneath the surface. His reflection stared back, a blend of determination and anxiety etched into his features, as he prepared to navigate the complicated web of family animosities and unspoken fears.

***

The corpse of a high school student stared back at Eric Flanagan when he opened his eyes. The boy looked familiar, and Eric quickly sat up, heart pounding and confusion swirling. He found himself in a wheat field near the main highway, naked, cold, and terrified. Instinctively, he covered himself with his hands, scanning his surroundings. The teenager's eyes and mouth were open, dried blood streaked down his face, and flies buzzed around.

They lay on a blanket, one nude and the other with most of their clothes torn off. Panic and confusion gripped Eric as he tried to piece together what had happened. Did he have an experience he couldn't remember? He shifted, popping his back, and saw an almost-naked girl beside him. She had brown hair, a purple sweater, and no bottoms. Her throat was ripped out, and parts of her left breast and side were eaten down to the ribs. Recognition struck him: these were his classmates, Ben and Julie.

Eric's stomach churned as he remembered the attack. He imagined the horrific scene: them consummating their relationship, clothes and flesh torn apart. Their lifeless eyes seemed to accuse him, silently asking why they had to die.

A wave of nausea hit as he thought about what he'd done. Images of consuming their insides flashed in his mind, leaving him unsure if it was reality or just his imagination. He pictured himself, a cannibal, relishing their skin flapping between his teeth. The revulsion was overwhelming. Eric began to retch, horrified by his actions. This was not what he had wanted.

You have done what was necessary.
You are whole, strong, and able.

Eric paused; his gaze fixed on the ground as he tried to collect himself. The voice guiding him no longer felt as unsettling as it once had. Accepting his transformation was a monumental task, but he had to confront the reality that he was now something different. His new lupine instincts offered him a path filled with purpose, resolve, and self-assurance—a chance to rise above the mediocrity of his surroundings and escape this wretched town.

Amidst the swaying wheat, Eric turned his attention to the sun, struggling to pierce the thick veil of dark clouds. The scent of impending snow hung in the air, urging him to flee from the lifeless bodies of the young lovers. An inexplicable certainty enveloped him: his father was no more, the memory of their violent confrontation the last clear recollection before his awakening. As he retrieved the crimson stained clothing belonging to Ben, a fellow student from Norton High School, fragments of the previous night's events flooded his mind.

Inspecting the garments, Eric found the long-sleeved shirt beyond salvaging, but the pants and undershirt were relatively intact. He pulled them on, the jeans slightly loose but manageable with Ben's belt—a small stroke of luck amidst the chaos.

Laying low, Eric reflected on his father's abusive behavior and the torment he endured growing up under his roof. The saying "you can never go home" rang true for him, but solace could be found elsewhere. Others shared his plight—people who, like him, had never known the warmth of a loving home. If there was a silver lining to his monthly Lycan transformation, it was his newfound ability to confront abusers threatening those too afraid to stand up for themselves. He made it his mission to protect the women and children trapped in the clutches of abusive, unemployed blue-collar workers—a heavy commitment as those were a dime a dozen in Akron.

He dashed through the field and into the woods, his purpose clear, eagerly awaiting the onset of nightfall. His destination was somewhere close to home. In his fervent quest to be a savior, Eric overlooked the consequences of his actions and his inability to rein in his impulses. Everyone yearns to be a hero, yet few acknowledge the harm good intentions can inadvertently cause.

The trees closed in around him, their shadows growing longer as the day waned. The crisp air filled his lungs, fueling his resolve. However, with each stride, Eric's thoughts flickered with memories of his uncontrolled rage, the faces of the innocent mingled with the guilt. He yearned to protect, to make a difference, but his monstrous nature cast a dark cloud over his noble aspirations. As the sky dimmed, the line between savior and destroyer blurred, reminding Eric that even heroes must grapple with their own darkness.

***

"I think we need to address the elephant in the room," Christina began as the four friends tossed a tennis ball around in the Hatcher's yard, next to the giant spruce tree. Not knowing what the term meant, Colin looked around for a pachyderm before realizing the metaphor when Scott replied, "Oh, please. Sorry, bud, but I'm still not buying your werewolf theory has any legs."

"You can't, or you won't?" Ryan deadpanned. He knew he was onto something and grew tired of the coincidences everyone refused to acknowledge. "I mean, without shooting one, how can you prove it's a human without seeing someone change in front of you?" Ryan caught the baseball Scott threw to him and pondered the question.

Colin asked, "What do you think you would do if one changed in front of you?"

Scott answered honestly, "I'd probably run towards the fuckin' hills!" They all, including a melancholy Ryan, laughed at the delivery of his answer.

"Hey! Knob gobbler!" a voice from above called out to Ryan. He lifted his head towards the living room window, where Devin shouted. Ryan looked up at his brother, who laughed because Ryan responded to his insulting name, then asked, "Have you seen my blue button-up?" Ryan threw up his hands and shrugged, not wanting to put up with his brother's crap. "Well?"

"Oh! Um…I don't care…(whisper) fuckin' dickhead," Ryan hissed.

"I heard that," Devin said before he closed the window.

Ryan turned and looked at Scott, who had a goofy grin with his arms out, delighted his friend was beginning to stand up for himself. "I'm so proud of my little boy! His balls have gotten bigger and hopefully dropped." Before taking another step, Scott tripped over his own feet and landed face-first in front of Colin. The standing three looked at one another, holding in their laughter.

Their tree had been part of too many supernatural happenings for Ryan not to notice. He recalled the corpse of the jogger, endlessly repeating the same motions, the eerie picture Layla had created with her Lite Brite set, and Layla mimicking the ghost's movements. Unbeknownst to him, his mother had also been pushed by something in the same spot. There were too many coincidences. Ryan's mind lingered on the man in black jogging attire, replaying how he moved and ultimately put his arms out as if to block an invisible attacker.

"Did you see that?" Scott asked, pulling dried leaf fragments from his mouth and lips. Though they hadn't seen it, Scott believed enough to experiment further.

Before long, Colin stood in front of the tree, an old football helmet on his head and pillows tied around his torso to lessen the impact. The others stood back, waiting and timing the phenomena. "What am I supposed to do?" Colin asked nervously.

"Nothing. Just stand there and tell me if you feel anything," Ryan instructed. They waited, anticipation hanging in the air. After a few minutes, Scott sighed, "I don't think it's going to happen again. Maybe it was just some weird thing… like the Bermuda Triangle."

Just as he finished his thought, Colin fell forward, hitting the ground hard but unscathed thanks to the helmet and pillows. "I felt something," Colin gasped, staring at the dying grass from inside the helmet.

They rushed to Colin, lifting him and brushing off the pillows and his clothes. "That was weird," Christina stated the obvious. Colin bent over to dust his jeans when he noticed Ryan walking away from the group. Concerned, he decided to follow his first real friend.

Ryan's thoughts churned with frustration. *I'm not fine. I am so tired of this secret bullshit*, he thought.

In just one month, Ryan felt as though he had mentally aged five years. No one understood him like they once did. Once the quiet one of the group, he had become brooding, outspoken, and for the first time, surer of himself than ever before, even if the company he kept wasn't. Ryan was determined to find something to prove he, at least, could be justified in his thoughts.

"Where are you going?" Christina yelled. Ryan owed her, them, an answer. He had debated bringing it up again for days, fearing the possibility of losing his friends. But then a realization struck him: *I don't owe them anything! I am the one dealing with this shit, not them!* He had become conceited. His resolve turned into a crusade to prove he was right, forgetting his concern for others and how much danger they could be in. Ryan stomped through the garage toward his father's workbench, a place normally off-limits.

Ryan's father was obsessive-compulsive about his tools, parts, and bench. Every jar contained a different type of nut or bolt. Wrenches, pliers, and screwdrivers were meticulously arranged by size and type in his red Craftsman toolbox drawers. Under the bench were milk crates full of books and magazines, ordered by issue and release date. With all the tools and self-help books in the garage, if Ryan had a dollar for every time his dad built something, he would probably have a buck. He doubted anything substantial would be in the drawers, knowing his dad was too afraid of messing them up himself.

To everyone's surprise, Ryan unearthed a grey plastic bin filled with nothing but toys from his childhood days with Devin. Sitting down on the cold concrete, he carefully examined each item, memories flooding back with each toy he picked up. There were plastic spaceships, action figures from Masters of the Universe, and Captain Power ships with video cassettes. He recalled the thrill of battling imaginary foes on screen, the cockpit deploying in response to the show's action, firing infrared light from the white ship.

As Ryan and his curious friends delved into his childhood treasures, the anger and confusion began to dissipate. Colin examined the toys with wide-eyed curiosity, while Scott reminisced about their past adventures. Memories resurfaced, old and new, as they found a portable Pac-Man arcade cabinet with a blue ghost illustrated on a yellow and black sticker. Christina shared stories of playing dolls with Ryan when no one else was around. Ryan watched Colin playing with the toys, feeling a pang of jealousy and possessiveness.

In a moment of impulsivity, Ryan reached out to grab the toy from Colin. Colin flinched and pulled the toy back, puzzled by Ryan's sudden action. Ryan withdrew his arm, realizing these toys were no longer his to claim. They remained in his possession, but he had outgrown them, moving on from the world of make-believe long ago. Time had a way of making people forget the things that once shaped them, but the memories and sentiments always had a way of resurfacing.

Though his toys held sentimental value, Ryan recognized they no longer belonged to him in the same way. They needed to find new owners who could appreciate them, if only for a little while longer. It was hard to let go—hard to move on.

Ryan sank down, feeling ashamed of his selfish impulse to snatch the toy away. He realized Colin, being younger, might not have had the chance to play with such toys before. However, Colin didn't seem unwilling to return the game. "Do you mind if I play with this?" he asked tentatively. Ryan shook his head lightly, saying, "It needs batteries, but you can take it home and play with it. Just... um... let me have a turn when I come over to your place, okay?" Colin agreed, his eyes fixed on the small arcade game. Now, he could relive the arcade experience in his own way, thrilled at the thought, uncertain if he'd ever get to go back.

Meanwhile, unnoticed by the others, Christina's fingers traced the spines of the books near the workbench. Her touch paused on one seemingly out of place, its cover slightly askew. She pulled it out, hesitated, and then started flipping through its pages in rapid succession. Her brow furrowed with each turn, eyes darting from front cover to back cover and back again, a mix of disbelief and uncertainty clouding her expression.

Ryan sensed Christina's unease, setting down the Ghostbusters Ecto-1 plastic car he had been examining. "What's wrong?" he asked, rising to his feet. Christina met his gaze briefly before walking over to him with the book in hand.

Without a word, Ryan glanced at the cover and began scanning through the pages, discussing poltergeists, spirits, possessions, vampires, and the historical contexts surrounding these phenomena. Intrigued, their friends watched as Ryan stopped at a folded page, skipping past the introduction to a marked section. Drawings of mythical creatures adorned the pages, illustrating their imagined forms in vivid detail.

Christina read over Ryan's shoulder, absorbing the first paragraph before he abruptly closed the book. The realization that his father had kept such a book in the garage, nestled among others, and had marked a chapter about Lycan lore, made his gut rumble, unsettling him deeply.

He tossed the book to Scott, who fumbled but managed to catch it. Opening to the folded page corner, Scott began to read, Colin leaning in close beside him, eyes fixed on the text.

Meanwhile, Ryan stepped outside into the crisp fall air, Christina trailing behind. Her silence spoke volumes—her reluctance palpable. The events of the previous night, the full moon, and the convenient absence of Ryan's parents all conspired to plant unsettling thoughts in her mind.

"It's not just a possibility anymore," Ryan declared, his words echoing Christina's unspoken fears. "Halloween. Eric Flanagan is missing. Four killings last night. There were maybe a couple each night when it started a month ago."

Listening to Ryan, Scott felt a pang of regret for not taking his friend's concerns more seriously. As he scrutinized the book's cover and back, disbelief etched on his face, he realized there was more to uncover.

"You won't believe this," Scott said, approaching Ryan and tapping the inside cover. Taking the book from Scott's outstretched hand, Ryan saw it—a signature in the upper right corner: M. Craggs.

Ryan glanced towards his neighbor's house, the book confirming his suspicions. The adults—Ryan's parents, Scott's parents, and Melvin Craggs—were all involved in the events of Halloween night, burying the body of the man who had transformed into a werewolf. They had kept it hidden; a secret burdened by the curse threatening anyone harmed by it.

"Ryan," Scott began solemnly, catching his friend's attention, "I don't think there's any way to doubt it anymore. Your neighbor gave your dad this book just in case he was going to turn." Christina recalled Devin mentioning their neighbors extensive collection of literature, saying, "He had so many magazines and books. Owning this wouldn't be unusual."

"Do you think your parents know about him—the marks on his body from that night?" Ryan asked, glancing back at Colin, who was still seated in the garage, listening intently.

"They've been acting weird. I mean...they're always weird, though. But if they are covering up a murder, then it makes sense, I s'pose," Scott answered.

"Is it murder?" Christina asked. "I mean, if the man was attacking, it's more like self-defense, right?"

"But he wasn't human when the attack started. He was a werewolf," Scott interjected.

"So what? What difference does that make?"

"It makes all the difference," Ryan interrupted their potential debate. "How would they explain why they shot a naked man in the face? Because he was a monster? I hate that they buried the body and covered it up, but at the same time, I can't say I wouldn't have done the same thing." Ryan huffed, watching his cold breath leave his mouth. "They did what they had to do."

"Only...the police probably think it's the same animal because they never found the body. Be-cause it was human," Christina thought out loud. Ryan and Scott nodded as they walked into the garage from the cold. "There isn't just one anymore," Ryan pointed out again. "There are probably at least two, and the suspects are the same: My dad, Scott's sister—Valerie, and Eric Flanagan, which I think at this point is the most obvious."

"How do we know the last wolf didn't scratch someone else? Like on the other nights?" Christina logically asked.

"We don't," Ryan shrugged. "But this book my dad borrowed, or old man Craggs gave to him makes me think my dad is in danger. No. Anyone near him will be in trouble. But you're right. Maybe there are others out there."

Scott became concerningly thrilled over the possibility of monsters in Norton. "This is the most exciting thing this town will ever be a part of, and we're in the middle of it!" Colin stood up, angry at Scott for saying such things. "People are dead, and Ryan's dad might be part of it. Maybe it shouldn't be something to get excited about!" Scott shamefully looked down at his feet, forgetting people he knew were involved. "Sorry," he told everyone.

"It's fine. You get excited. I get it," Ryan reassured him before voicing his concern, "Did you see your sister this morning?"

Scott pondered for a moment before replying, "No. I passed by Valerie's room, and her bed wasn't made, which is unusual for her. I assumed she must have gone out early. Come to think of it, I thought maybe she was here with your brother, since they've been hanging out."

Ryan shook his head, adding, "I haven't seen her all day." The others exchanged concerned glances, realizing no one had seen or heard from her.

Curiosity sparked by the equipment he had glimpsed in the garage days ago prompted Ryan to inquire further, glancing over at Scott. "What else does your dad have hidden in the garage? Think he'd mind if I borrowed some of it? It might come in handy, maybe even save a life or two."

"Okay, butt nugget," Devin interrupted as he strolled into the garage, ready to head to Donovan's house for dinner and then to the festival. Ryan found it odd that school had been canceled due to animal attacks, yet the festival proceeded as planned for public amusement. *Maybe they assumed it wouldn't be an issue with so many people gathered in one place.* "I'm going to your house," Devin informed Scott.

"Can you give us all a ride?" Ryan asked, eager to raid Donovan's garage for supplies. Devin shook his head, his tone cocky as he replied, "Nope. I'm taking Craggs' motorcycle over." Ryan's irritation with his brother's attitude flared. He tossed the book of paranormal entities at Devin, his voice sharp, "Give this back to Melvin while you're at it." Devin glanced at the cover, puzzled. "What is this?"

"Someone borrowed a book. I'm returning it. He'll know what it is, and you can tell him I found it. He owes me," Ryan retorted with disdain. Scott punched Ryan lightly in the arm. "Come on. We'll walk there."

"Can't. Have to look after Layloo."

"I'll stay!" Christina volunteered.

Ryan smiled gratefully at his girlfriend and mouthed, "Thank you." The boys gathered and hurried to Scott's house, hoping to beat Devin. Surprisingly, they did, quietly sorting through boxes so as not to alert Rick, who was likely a few bottles deep already. They found walkie-talkies, handcuffs, duct tape, a crossbow with arrows, and a functioning taser. After piling everything on the garage floor, Ryan looked at his friends, all wearing red bandanas, including himself, and declared, "I need to borrow these."

"Why all of them?" Colin asked. Ryan gave him a knowing look and replied dramatically, "Because you never know."

Devin pulled up on the motorcycle. Scott realized he still hadn't seen Valerie and wondered if she was home. "How'd you all get here so fast?" Devin asked. Ryan glanced at his friends and fibbed, saying they ran. Colin rode his bike leisurely as Ryan and Scott walked, while Devin took his time.

"Wait. Who's watching Layla?"

"Christina is."

"Don't make your girlfriend suffer. She's probably making her play dolls or something," Devin scoffed.

"Well, my girlfriend is pretty awesome," Ryan retorted with a grin. Devin shook his head, "Whatever; just get home." Ryan agreed, starting to pack up the supplies Scott and Colin had helped gather.

Valerie stepped out of the kitchen garage door, greeting Devin. Scott sighed with relief, knowing his sister was safe. Ryan felt glad for his friend but couldn't shake the worry she might have transformed the previous night.

Carrying a box full of supplies ready to walk home, Ryan looked at Colin, who was getting on his bike, and at Scott, Valerie, and Devin. They were all heading to the Winter Festival, and Ryan felt compelled to say, "Please be careful tonight. I hope I'm wrong, but maybe I'm not." His friends nodded, and Devin stared at him blankly, pondering if werewolves were the least of their town's worries. Valerie's odd behavior lately made Devin dismiss the idea of her being possessed or cursed, unaware of how her strange moods intensified nearing a full moon.

Ryan walked into his garage with tools which might prove crucial tomorrow night. He hoped fervently that they wouldn't be needed after all. Christina walked from inside his house and joined him, eyeing the weapons and bindings with curiosity. Ryan understood her unspoken question and assured her, "Just in case."

She nodded and informed him that his little sister was asleep, taking a nap. Ryan thanked Christina, giving her a kiss goodbye. As she headed towards the driveway, Christina paused, unable to suppress her concern. "Are you okay?" she asked.

Ryan smiled; his expression uncertain. "Don't know, but please be careful tonight. In case you haven't heard, we might have werewolves."

"I hope not," she nervously giggled, beginning her walk home to prepare for the town's festival. Ryan watched her go, praying everything he feared wouldn't come to pass tonight.

CHAPTER TWENTY SEVEN

MANIAC

Ryan felt like everything from here on out was beyond his control. Lying on the blue couch, staring at the ceiling, he replayed the recent events, the various theories, and the messages the ghosts had tried to convey through Layla's Lite-Brite pictures. The feeling of helplessness gnawed at him, making him anxious and irritable. Fate had taken the reins, and all he could do now was wait and see what the night would bring. He had never fully grasped the meaning of 'too close to home' until now. What once felt like a safe, little town now harbored lurking entities, possibly even within his own house.

His sister stayed quiet, playing in her room while listening to the radio. Ryan assumed she was occupied with her dolls until he noticed scattered circles of colored light on the wall near the stairs. *Layla is making another picture.* He wasn't interested in what she was creating this time—he had seen enough and doubted there would be anything new.

The house was quiet, usually a preference for Ryan. But tonight, he craved distraction from his spiraling thoughts. He considered going downstairs to watch one of his VHS movies, recorded by Calvin. But he dismissed the idea. He needed to stay alert and prepared for the worst, not get lost in *The Wrath of Khan*.

No. I have to be ready.

***

Meanwhile, Rick kept giving Devin the stink eye every time he talked, laughed, or made any noise. At one point, Devin shifted on the brown leather couch in their living room, creating a flatulent sound sending everyone into fits of laughter, especially Scott.

Despite Devin's insistence the noise wasn't what it seemed, Rick's glare was intense, like someone scraping fingernails across a chalkboard. The idea of his daughter being involved with a Hatcher felt wrong to Rick. He wanted to dislike Calvin and his family, but deep down, he knew his only reason was jealousy, which he masked with contempt.

The Donovans didn't have much money due to Rick's layoff, but they managed to set aside some for the festival rides. Silvia decided it was best if everyone stayed in for dinner, so she made her famous tacos. Silvia Donovan was known for bringing a crockpot of seasoned hamburger meat and large tortilla shells to community events. It was cheaper than hard shells, and the residents of all three townships devoured them, always leaving none behind. No one could ever figure out her secret, and Silvia never revealed it.

After dinner, Rick decided to ease up on Devin. Normally, he would bombard a boy with questions to unsettle him. However, compared to Eric Flanagan, Devin was a much better choice for Valerie, so Rick restrained himself.

They all sat and ate as the kids chatted about music and movies, excitedly discussing upcoming releases like the new Batman movie. Silvia and Rick listened to their kids speak with passion, something they hadn't heard in years. Usually, the kids stayed in their rooms or went out; tonight, they were reconnecting. Rick realized he was mostly to blame for pushing them away. He had been too busy wallowing in self-pity and being harsh, forgetting how to be a dad. Beer and the occasional prescription drug had convinced him he was invincible. But the damage was done, and everyone knew it. Tonight, however, they enjoyed each other's company, and both Devin and Rick thought, *this is nice.*

Suddenly, the doorbell's chime rang throughout the house. Everyone glanced at one another, eyes wide with curiosity and a hint of concern. Scott, always the brave one, hopped up from his seat and made his way to the front door. The clock read five in the evening, but the sky was already losing its light. As Scott opened the door, a man stood with his back turned, leaning casually against the brick exterior. The red hair pulled back into a ponytail was unmistakable.

Eric Flanagan turned around, his smile not reaching his eyes. Scott's heart pounded in his chest, and he could feel his words sticking in his throat. "Wha...what do you...you need?" Eric's grin widened, sensing Scott's fear. "Hey there, champ," he said smoothly. "Folks around?" Scott's frown deepened. "We're eating," he replied, trying to keep his voice steady.

Eric's nostrils flared as he inhaled deeply, savoring the scent of dinner wafting through the door. "Mmmm. That smells good. Mind if I talk to the family? It's been too long! Know what I mean?" His tone was light, but his eyes were dark. Scott moved to close the door, but Eric's hand shot out, catching it with unnerving strength.

Eric leaned in, his eyes now a sinister green, darting erratically as sweat beaded on his forehead despite the cold. "Let me in, and you might live through this, big boy," he whispered menacingly. Scott's blood ran cold. Ryan was right—Eric Flanagan was turning into a werewolf.

"Who is it?" Silvia called from the dining room, her voice breaking the tense silence. Scott turned his head towards her, fear written all over his face. He knew something terrible was about to happen.

"Just me, Sil," Eric smiled as he pushed through the doorway. Sil? He never called her that, Scott thought. "I could smell those famous tacos of yours from outside. Are they delicious? Mmmm. I bet they are! Are they, Scott?" Shifting his eyes between his mother and Eric, Scott finally nodded.

Valerie stood from the table, her face pale. She had heard how they found Eric's father in their house, brutally murdered. "Val...you look great!" Eric grinned, wiping sweat from his brow. He is too happy, Scott noted, his demeanor off. Too happy for a guy whose dad died. Maybe he is crazy? "You shouldn't be here," she told him, feeling weak in the knees. "The cops are looking for you. They want to know what happened to your dad."

Eric shrugged, "Don't know." He bit his bottom lip, glancing at everyone at the table. "But let's be honest, though. Do you really give that much of a shit?"

His human side faded, the amber eyes of his wolf nature taking over. The Donovans sat frozen, except Scott, who lingered by the front door, readying to escape. He eyed the poker near the fireplace, knowing it was their only defense.

"Would you like some tacos?" Silvia asked, her voice nervous as she held a shaking plate.

"No thanks. Don't have the appetite for tacos right now, but I'll tell ya, you could make a killin' selling 'em. They are to die for, I'm sure!" Eric proclaimed, standing straight and stretching his back. "Hey, man!" Eric shouted to Devin. "It's been a bit, hasn't it?" Devin, unamused, nodded, "Where you been?"

"Out and about. You know me."

"Yeah, I do, and 'out and about' isn't something you do. Where you been?"

Eric sighed, irritated. "I've been getting by."

Rick, silent until now, stood from his seat and ordered, "Get out of my house! I never liked you. You're nothing but a punk-ass nuisance in this town, and everyone knows it, even your dad!" Scott inched closer to the door, mumbling, "Oh, shit," under his breath. Eric's fake smile turned into a frown as he sucked his teeth, readying for a clash. "Oh, I bet he did. Seems like you two have a lot in common—dolin' out the discipline, right?" Rick turned to his daughter, knowing what Eric was insinuating. "The fuck is he on about?"

"Hey, Devin! Did you know my old man loved beating the shit out of me? Berating me? Putting out lit cigars and cigarettes on me?" Eric asked intensely. Devin shook his head, shocked. Eric never invited anyone over, embarrassed by his dad for good reason. "Yeah. Whenever I went to school with a shiner, it wasn't from a fight with punks like I told you. It was from that fuckin' asshole!"

Devin, taken aback by Eric's confession, became distraught and confused. "Why didn't you say anything?" Eric wiped sweat from his face, pulling at his shirt collar, burning up—his human side pushing through to explain, shoving the wolf back. "I don't know. I was embarrassed—didn't want to put my problems on you. I thought if you knew, you wouldn't want to hang with me, ya know? I knew you wouldn't."

"You don't know that!" Devin exclaimed, saddened by his friend, realizing he was better than anyone gave him credit for. Eric often acted out, ran his mouth too much, sometimes too far. "You made that decision for me, man."

Eric began to cry. "No one else ever talks about it! Why should I?" Rick watched as Eric began to twitch, hoping he wouldn't reveal his secret. "People just take it. This whole goddamn world is full of abusive assholes! You're in a room with one right now. Ain't that right, Mr. Donovan?"

Valerie looked from her father to her mother, knowing the truth she kept to herself was about to be spoken. "I know you've seen it, man. The bruises she hides under makeup, hoping none of her hoity-toity friends realize she and her family are nothing but white trash. It's all about appearances, ain't it? I know you've seen it, Devin, or at least wondered about it even if you weren't sure," Eric hoarsely yelled before the beast's gruffness took over.

Falling to his knees, Eric began to writhe in pain, panting. Rick thought it was the perfect time to retaliate. "You shut your face! You don't know what the hell you're talkin' bout, boy!" Rick shouted, stomping towards him, ready to pull him by the shirt and throw him out.

Scott watched with his mouth hung open. He could only imagine what would happen to Eric Flanagan now, wondering if he would do what Ryan said he would—turn into a werewolf. Eric lifted his head back, jumping to his feet just as Rick threw his fist back to strike. Eric swiftly ran past Devin and punched Rick in the throat, causing him to fall onto the dinner table. He choked on his breath, pushing taco meat and saliva-softened shell onto the carpet as Silvia and Valerie scattered.

Placing his right hand over Rick's throat, Eric picked him up with a strength he had forgotten he had now, moments before the full moon would appear in the sky. "Put him down!" Valerie screamed, not knowing what to do as her stomach began to turn. Silvia made her way over to Scott, ready to protect him at all costs.

"Get! Out!" Eric hissed as his voice croaked, turning into a howl. It glared at Rick. The wolf would take care of him, the abusive father who liked to hit his daughter. Hyperventilating, Rick watched as Eric grew, looming over him. His eyes were becoming greener as his pupils thinned.

Grabbing the poker as the rest ran out of the house to get help, Scott, with his morbid curiosity, stopped and watched Eric, hoping to see how he would turn. From extensive horror film viewings, he knew this would be the point when the audience would scream for him to run. Valerie reached inside through the front door threshold, and took her brother by the arm, pulling him outside. Silvia screamed for someone to call the police. Neighbors shifted their blinds, peeking through to view what was happening outside. Valerie ran to the side of the road, waving down anyone who could save Dad. Several cars drove by, rubbernecking the scene, not wanting any part of violence happening mere feet away.

They were scared; everyone was.

The sound of agony made everyone halt, including the neighbors who had walked outside. Devin couldn't make out if it were Eric or Rick, then a second human scream came from the house. "What the hell is happening to you?" they heard Rick shout from inside the house. Grunts from an animal were heard. Everyone looked at one another, wondering what was happening at the Donovan house.

Valerie clutched Scott tightly, her eyes wide with fear. Silvia, still holding Scott's arm, began to tremble, unable to tear her gaze away from the house. The street was eerily soundless except for the muffled sounds occurring from inside. Scott's heart pounded in his chest, his mind racing with the horror unfolding within their home. The thought of what Eric was becoming sent chills down his spine. He glanced at his neighbors, their faces pale, reflecting his own terror. The tension in the air was thick, everyone frozen in place, anticipating the next horrific sound or sight.

As the moon slowly ascended in the night sky, its light casting an eerie glow over the neighborhood, the full extent of the horror they were about to face became all too real. The transformation was imminent, and they could do nothing but wait in helpless dread.

The front door burst open. Rick stumbled out, eyes wild, yelling for everyone to flee from the monster inside. The scene that unfolded would haunt the residents of Holiday Heights forever. Emerging from the house, a monstrous figure with the head and torso of a giant, rabid dog walked on hind legs, snarling and drooling. Men stepped back, their faces pale, while women stifled screams. Scott and Devin stood rooted to the spot, horror struck, as Rick reached out, desperate for aid.

The truth was undeniable—Ryan Hatcher had been right—Eric Flanagan was a werewolf.

Eric's transformation had occurred this night and the previous one. No one dared imagine the horror he had unleashed upon his father. Witnessing the brutality Eric had inflicted on Conor Flanagan would have sent them running far from the Donovan home.

Rick, panting and terrified, shouted for his family to seek help. The wolf bared its fangs, saliva dripping as it savored the scent of fear, extending clawed hands, ready to strike again. Valerie edged closer; disbelief etched on her face. She had tried to dismiss the previous month's events as a hallucination. Examining the creature's fur, she noted hints of Eric's red hair, hoping to find a trace of the boy she knew. Deep inside, Eric was fighting, but the wolf's dominance overwhelmed him.

Scott's gaze flicked to his sister, relieved she hadn't transformed, confirming she wasn't cursed. Ryan's suspicions about her injuries being unrelated to lycanthropy provided a small solace amid the chaos.

The wolf's hand shot up, claws gleaming, poised to tear into Rick. As Rick braced for the attack, he noticed a flicker of recognition in the beast's eyes. The wolf, momentarily restrained by Eric's will, hesitated. Eric, struggling from within, fought to protect Valerie and Scott, his resentment toward Rick paling against the abuse he had suffered from his father.

The werewolf's eyes glinted with hunger, surveying its options. Eric managed to hold back the beast, unwilling to let it harm those he cared about, despite the rage and hurt he carried. The internal battle raged, but for now, Eric's humanity clung to control, protecting his friends and family from the monster within.

You wanted this!
You want vengeance!

You cannot play vigilante and grow a pathetic human conscience!

Eric's heart sank. The wolf was right. This was exactly what he had feared, what he had secretly anticipated. The futility of resistance dawned on him once more. His friends' safety hung by a thread, a consequence of his own actions.

You will leave my friends and their families alone! Eric's voice trembled with resolve as he confronted his other self.

No. I will not.

The wolf's claws tore through Rick Donovan's chest, the rending sound of flesh and bone drowned out only by the wet slap of its saliva mingling with his blood. As Rick crumpled to the ground, gasping for air, the wolf's howl of triumph reverberated through the air, causing fear to envelop the horrified onlookers—family members and neighbors alike. Their screams joined the frantic dissonance, a chorus of fear and despair filling the night air. Amidst the tumult, another voice rose above the chaos, growing louder by the second, a desperate plea for help hanging in the air like a fleeting hope against the darkness.

"Get off my dad!"

Scott Donovan charged forward, wielding the fireplace poker like a weapon forged in fury. The iron hook crashed down with the force of vengeance, tearing through mange. The wolf recoiled with a pained yelp, rising onto its hind legs in a display of monstrous strength. Scott held fast to the poker, suspended in a fierce battle against gravity and adrenaline. The iron continued its relentless assault, drawing crimson rivulets from the creature's wounded hide.

In a final, desperate effort, Scott released his grip, tumbling to the ground beside the wounded beast as it struggled to reach for the weapon lodged into it. He glanced at his father, agonized yet grateful for his son's valiant attempt to save him, mouthing the word, "Run."

Enraged and wounded, the wolf tore the weapon from its back with a feral snarl, fixing its predatory gaze upon Scott. "Oh, shit!" he exclaimed, scrambling to his feet as panic surged through him. With primal survival instincts guiding him, he fled from the monstrous threat, knowing his family's lives depended on his escape. The wolf hesitated, poised to give chase, but then realized it was being observed—a werewolf's nightmare, an audience to its bloodlust.

You have let too many people witness.
You must leave now.

We must leave now.

The wolf's hulking form crouched low, blending into the shadows as terrified bystanders scattered, anticipating another onslaught. Silvia dashed to her husband, pressing her hand urgently against his chest to staunch the bleeding. Across the chaos, Valerie turned to Devin, her voice laced with urgency.

"Where is he going?" she demanded.

Devin's brow furrowed in uncertainty. "I'm not sure, but Ryan might have an idea."

CHAPTER TWENTY EIGHT

SWEET DREAMS

Ryan found himself in the midst of Norton Fall Festival, surrounded by a bustling crowd of families, children, high schoolers, and college students. The Ferris wheel and various attractions cast a festive glow over the modest fairgrounds, resembling a lively shopping center parking lot. Among the throng, he spotted Christina walking with Colin. Tonight, they were accompanied by their respective families—Colin with the other foster kids from his house, and Christina with her grandmother. There was no sign of his brother, Devin, or Valerie and Scott—they hadn't arrived yet.

The radio blared out popular hits, contributing to the vibrant environment. Children giggled while grabbing cotton candy, oblivious to everything around them. Couples stole kisses discreetly behind the funhouse and house of mirrors. The festival appeared just as Ryan had imagined—rides, food, and a lively crowd.

Yet beneath the surface, unease gnawed at Ryan.

The night air should have been chilly, but Ryan realized he was only wearing socks on his feet. As Colin and Christina approached, Ryan noticed their animated conversation, but their voices sounded distant, like a silent film unfolding before him. Christina waved with a smile, and Colin followed suit, their laughter echoing strangely in Ryan's ears.

Time slowed, the rides pausing and the background talk fading into silence, leaving only the faint strains of Hall & Oates' *Maneater* playing from the radio. Christina and Colin continued to smile at him, unaware of the eerie stillness enveloping them.

Ryan struggled to respond, to join in their laughter, but his voice failed him. Panic surged as he realized he was trapped, unable to warn his friends of the impending danger. A shadow loomed nearby, and before Ryan could react, a werewolf sprang toward Christina and Colin.

Frozen with terror, Ryan watched as the beast's jaws closed around Christina's head, freezing her smile in place. Blood sprayed in a grotesque display as the creature savaged her before his eyes. Colin stood motionless, his accusatory stare piercing Ryan, until the wolf pounced on him too.

Face to face with the werewolf, Ryan screamed, his voice swallowed by the void. Then, a gentle touch on his shoulder shattered the nightmare, pulling him back from the brink.

***

"Ryan!" a familiar voice called out.

He blinked awake to find his brother, Valerie, and Scott looming over him in the living room. Startled, Ryan nearly tumbled off the couch. The remnants of his vivid dream clung to his senses, blurring with reality as he struggled to grasp the present moment.

"What!" Ryan exclaimed, trying to steady himself. They had startled him awake, the last vestiges of his dream lingering. Dreams, especially nightmares, often intertwined with reality, and it took a moment for him to ground himself.

"It happened! Eric turned into... into a monster, and he almost killed my dad," Scott stammered, his voice trembling with raw emotion. Ryan saw an intensity in Scott's eyes he had never witnessed before. For weeks, Ryan had borne the weight of hopelessness and anxiety alone, believing he was the sole bearer of a terrible truth. Now, with Scott's revelation, the gravity of their situation was laid bare. His friends and family were now fully aware of the danger lurking in Norton, and it was time for them to unite and confront the darkness haunting his family.

Scott recounted the events that had unfolded barely twenty minutes ago, confirming Ryan's worst fears. Yet now was not the time for Ryan to revel in being right or to offer hollow consolations of "I told you so."

"Where do you think he would go?" Valerie's voice quavered with desperation.

Ryan didn't have an answer.

How can I predict where an animal might go next, especially if the werewolf had taken control of Eric's mind? How am I supposed to know any of this? Ryan pushed himself up from the couch and began to pace. "I need time to process. I can't just make up answers out of thin air. I'm not some psychic. I'm just a guy trying to piece together clues from Halloween night, not decode the workings of an animal's mind!"

As Ryan spoke, his gaze drifted towards Layla's room, drawn by the colorful lights spilling out. The others followed his line of sight, watching as Ryan hesitated at the doorway. Inside, Layla sat beside her Lite-Brite set, quietly waiting for Ryan to acknowledge her creation.

Memories flooded Ryan's mind, overwhelming him—

He was transported to Colin's birthday party at his house, gathered around the dinner table devouring pizza. Vivid memories resurfaced—the spirits lurking behind his friends, Colin, Alicia, Luis, Isaiah, and Alex. Their bodies torn apart before his eyes haunted him, accompanied by urgent voices echoing in his mind: *Help them! Save yourself! Save them! Save us!* As these haunting recollections wrestled for his attention, the scene collapsed around him, folding in on itself like origami, revealing another moment from Thanksgiving.

Now, he saw himself holding Christina behind the shed after dinner, a memory etched vividly in his mind. She cried about her parents; a vulnerability she had hidden from everyone else. Ryan remembered the moment distinctly; she was so lost in his embrace. Then, inexplicably, Christina stilled, and as Ryan looked on, her body began to disintegrate, crumbling into ash. This had happened, *but how did it connect?* It felt surreal, an out-of-body experience as he stood there, hands shuddering, desperately trying to piece her back together. Christina's remains slipped through his fingers, crumbling into nothingness like fine soot. The sensation of helplessness engulfed him as he stared at the empty space where she had been, grappling with the cruel reality of her sudden disintegration.

Ryan found himself back in his house, momentarily distanced from the haunting memories that had plagued him. His gaze fixated on the mesmerizing lights in Layla's room as Devin and the others approached from behind.

"I know where it's headed. I should have pieced it together sooner. They've been trying to warn me!" Ryan exclaimed, urgency gripping his voice.

Valerie exchanged a puzzled glance with Devin, unsure of her younger brother's cryptic remarks. Devin shrugged, equally baffled, and turned to Scott, who mirrored their confusion.

"I need to grab my things. We have to act before it's too late!" Ryan's urgent call echoed down the hallway as he hastily retrieved his coat and shoes.

"Who's in danger?" Scott demanded, his voice rising as Ryan prepared to depart.

"Christina. Colin. And some of the kids from his house. At least them. I should have connected the dots. Nothing's a coincidence anymore! I should have seen it coming!" Ryan muttered to himself, his gestures betraying his growing agitation, prompting concern from those around him.

Devin and Valerie entered Layla's room, drawn to the soft glow of the Lite Brite. As they approached, they saw Layla's creations illuminated on the ceiling—a Ferris wheel, peanuts, and various structures represented by boxes.

"I'm not sure why I made this. They just seemed important," Layla explained with uncertainty.

Ryan listened intently to his sister's words, a realization dawning upon him—the spirits within were not malevolent; they were issuing a warning.

"Let's go! We need to get to the festival!" Ryan's urgency reverberated through the room.

Devin swiftly scooped up Layla and headed towards Melvin's house, the unspoken agreement clear among them. The consequences of their actions on Halloween night were catching up, and now it fell upon the younger generation to set things right.

Scott's fear emanated palpably. For the first time, Ryan saw his usually steadfast friend rendered speechless, gripped by terror at the prospect of confronting Eric. "I can't do it," Scott confessed, his body tensed on the couch.

"Please, man. I need you there with me," Ryan implored, his voice tinged with urgency. "You're the bravest guy I know."

"It's too much," Scott protested, curling into himself.

Ryan hesitated, contemplating whether to leave Scott behind, until a mischievous idea crossed his mind. "If you don't come, I'll spill the beans about you and Ramona Dankworth's make-out session with her headgear and how it gave you a big 'ol floppy one," he threatened, a sly grin playing on his lips.

Scott shot Ryan a glare, a mix of anger and resignation in his eyes. "God, I hate you sometimes," he muttered.

"No, you don't," Ryan retorted, pulling Scott from the couch.

With trepidation gnawing at them, they rushed out of the house and piled into the Turbo. The usual flutter of nervous butterflies in their stomachs felt more like razorblades carving out ulcers as they headed toward the festival. Ryan stole a backward glance at his home, noting the eerie glow of Layla's Lite Brite upstairs. It served as a chilling reminder of the danger they were about to confront, guided by innocent art inspired by the whispers of the departed.

CHAPTER TWENTY NINE

THE KILLING MOON

Little Justin Davis clutched his father's hand tightly as they entered the festival grounds. It was his first time here, and the dazzling array of flashing lights promised an unforgettable experience. At five years old, Justin wasn't tall enough for the roller coasters, but that didn't bother him. There were plenty of other attractions to explore and enjoy with his father, Charlie. Like the Tilt-a-Whirl, or even better yet, The Gravity Rush—that one spins you around really fast! He had been eagerly anticipating this day for weeks, and he was determined to ride that particular attraction.

Then, Justin spotted it—the festival ride known as The Mambo. Similar to The Gravity Rush but with even more thrilling flips and spins, it towered above the grounds, seemingly reaching dizzying heights. Though he knew he was too small to ride it now, Justin couldn't help but set it as a future goal, even if it appeared out of reach for the time being.

The tempting aroma of festival foods caught Justin's attention, especially one that looked like long strands from his Play-Doh factory, coated in sugar, cinnamon, and other delicious toppings. Corn-dogs, drinks, and other treats beckoned to the attendees. Amidst the screams of thrill-seekers and the pleas of those eager to disembark from the rides, the chilly November air wrapped around them. Parents hurried their children along, their faces adorned with hardened snot from the cold. As Justin and his dad paused to take in the scene, a group of rowdy kids caught their attention, weaving through the crowd.

Devin's authoritative voice cut through the commotion, urging the youngsters to quiet down and avoid drawing unwanted attention.

Valerie's gaze drifted toward the nearby woods, a potential hiding spot for any lurking dangers. Ryan couldn't shake the feeling that once news of Rick Donovan's animal attack spread, a curfew would swiftly follow. Yet, for now, the night remained eerily quiet, with an unspoken sense of danger lurking just beyond the festivities.

Scott stayed close to Ryan as they searched the festival grounds for their loved ones. Thoughts of his father weighed heavily on his mind, especially considering the state Eric had left him in before vanishing into the night on all fours. The fact that his father was moving offered a glimmer of hope, but Scott couldn't shake the worry gnawing at him. All he could do was cling to the sight of his father's movement and convince himself everything would eventually be okay.

A teenage couple began making out around the other side of the shopping plaza where the local grocery store stood. Things were heating up between them, but the young lady had no interest in having sex behind a shopping center near a set of dumpsters.

Her boyfriend didn't give a shit.

The bushes next to them began to shake as twigs snapped. The girl turned her head to see what was making noise as the guy took her movement to mean she wanted a little neck action. "You hear that?" she asked him, only to get, "Sorry. Something's not agreeing with me." The girl curled her lip and slapped him on the top of his head. "Not that! Don't be gross!" Her boyfriend rubbed the top of his head, disappointed the mood had been spoiled.

"I want to go back," she told him. He began to walk towards her with his arms out, ready to put them around her waist again. "Not yet, babe. I want to stay a little longer."

"I don't like this. I want to go back and listen to the live band," the girlfriend demanded. "I want to listen to the music." Her boyfriend approached her with a cheesy smile, raised eyebrows, and replied with a tacky answer, "We can listen to music, or maybe we can just listen to our own." The girl looked at her dumb boyfriend and muttered, "That is the worst thing I have ever heard."

"You love it," the boyfriend implied, and with a smile and a sigh, the girlfriend said, "I do. Dammit. I do." They both laughed, readying their mouths to French kiss again.

A large body leapt towards the couple. They felt animal fur against their faces before realizing anything had lunged at them. The boy looked his fate in the eyes. He heard its snarl and saw its face wrap around his, chewing his cheeks off. The girlfriend managed to let out a quick scream before the wolf took its claw, slicing the sides of her mouth and causing her to choke on her own blood.

The couple's mutual, goofy friend left the festivities to find them—and by finding, he wanted to catch them in makin' it behind the building. He tiptoed around the premises for a couple of minutes before coming upon a black figure moving on the grocery store's pavement. It peered at him as the friend believed his friend was *gettin' some* and was on top.

"Hell yeah! Get it!"

The shadow halted its movement. "Don't let me interrupt," their friend quipped as he approached. Circling around a dumpster, he stumbled upon his friends sprawled on the grimy pavement, their bodies battered and their clothes in tatters. Emerging from the darkness, the ominous shape of a large wolf poised itself for an imminent attack.

Everything felt eerily familiar to Ryan, the scene unfolding before him echoing the dreams that had stirred him earlier when Devin woke him. Standing amidst the bustling festival crowd, he closed his eyes briefly, seeking guidance from Layla's spectral guides, hoping they would illuminate his next steps.

Ryan and Scott weaved through the throngs of festival-goers, their eyes scanning the scene for Colin and Christina. The lines for the rides were shorter in the chilly night air, dissuading many from venturing out. Passing by the shooting gallery and various food stalls, Scott spotted Colin in line with his foster siblings, preparing to board The Gravity Rush. Across from them loomed the larger thrill ride, The Mambo, with eager riders waiting their turn. Colin, acting as the responsible elder, ushered his younger foster siblings—Alicia, Luis, Isaiah, and Alex—onto The Gravity Rush for an adrenaline pumping experience. *All the kids from that dream, the vision I had at the party*, Ryan reflected.

Just a few feet away, the Ferris Wheel towered above them. Scott nudged Ryan, pointing out Christina boarding it with her grandmother, Jo. Ryan watched as Christina gracefully entered the swaying carriage, assisting her grandmother to settle in. With their friends securely seated, they awaited the exhilarating ride, anticipating the wind tousling their hair as they ascended into the night sky.

Something feels off.

Ryan's vision blurred once more as he scanned the festival grounds, desperate to locate his friends among the bustling crowd. A pounding headache gripped him as the grating of grinding metal and screeching gears assaulted his senses. The source of the dreadful metallic clamor became evident—the Mambo. Though no expert in machinery, Ryan instinctively knew the unsettling noises from the ride spelled danger for its occupants.

One by one, the rides lurched into motion: the Mambo first, followed by the Ferris Wheel carrying Christina, and finally the Gravity Rush with Colin and the other kids. Images of clanging metal and loose bolts invaded Ryan's mind, intensifying his agony. He sank to his knees, reaching out for anyone to heed his frantic warnings.

"Run! It's here! It's killed my friends!" a voice cried out in the distance. Security personnel rushed towards the commotion, urging the panicked individual to calm down and explain. Pointing towards the shopping center, the young man bolted away, fully aware of the imminent danger pursuing him.

Yellow-jacketed security guards exchanged uncertain glances, unsure of how to respond. Before they could react, a shadowy figure darted between them, knocking them off balance. It was Eric—a werewolf.

Exposed to the crowd, the beast prowled the festival grounds, snapping and snarling at those who dashed past, desperate to flee. It was Ryan's first glimpse of Eric's altered state. Pointing in horror, Scott shouted, "That's him! That's him!" Despite his transformation, traces of Eric's humanity remained—the fur bore a hue reminiscent of his fiery red hair, and a familiar scowl adorned the creature's face.

Panic swept through the crowd, sending people scrambling over one another, disregarding injuries in their frantic bid to escape the creature's wrath. Some stumbled over rail guards meant to corral visitors, focused solely on survival. The werewolf, however, targeted those who strayed from the safety of the crowd.

As people sought refuge near the active rides, the creature focused on those who had fallen, savagely tearing at their bodies. A woman in a red hat and scarf thrashed in desperation as the creature tore chunks from her face, savoring the taste of blood spilling onto the concrete below.

The operator of the Mambo seized a bat, prepared to confront the menacing beast. With determination, he descended the metal ramp, confronting the creature with a defiant shout. "Come on, you ugly mutt!" he bellowed, his voice echoing above the chaos. The wolf paused in its attack, its growls resonating in the night air. In the operator's stout figure, it saw a resemblance to Eric's father, triggering a primal response.

We want him!

Without a hint of resistance from either persona, the werewolf rose to its full height, looming menacingly over the man who dared to challenge it.

The ride operator brandished his bat, retreating up the ramp he had just descended, his warnings falling on deaf ears as the wolf advanced steadily towards him. It relished the operator's fear, toying with him as he backed away, his retreat halted only by the control unit for the ride at the path's end which began to spark as the level moved upward. Meanwhile, The Mambo continued its relentless rotation, the screeching of metal grinding against metal intensifying.

As one of three massive metal arms carrying eight riders per side wobbled, Colin and his foster family above on The Gravity Rush were oblivious to the chaos below. To them, it was a moment of fleeting joy, an escape from their troubles. But beneath them, pandemonium reigned.

Something bad is going to happen.

The ride operator's bravado crumbled, replaced by desperate sobs as he clung to his bat, hoping the menacing beast before him would relent. His dreams of heroism shattered; he whimpered like a frightened child on the verge of surrender.

With a swift motion, the wolf swatted the bat aside, plunging its claws into the operator's chest, tearing through bone and smoke-stained lungs, extracting chunks of his still beating heart. As the operator's life ebbed away, he collapsed onto the control panel, inadvertently triggering a cascade of sparks and metal.

Ryan watched in horror as The Mambo accelerated to a dizzying speed, screams of terror echoing through the air. His heart pounded with dread as he prayed fervently for some safety mechanism to halt the chaos. Yet, if such a mechanism existed, it remained stubbornly inactive.

The Mambo's metal groaned, and bolts sheared off, hurling a bench carrying eight people into the air. Their screams abruptly halted as their airborne seats careened violently, colliding with the nearby Ferris wheel before hurtling towards The Gravity Rush. With each collision, havoc ensued as the pieces of the attractions became entwined with one another. The metal of two sets of bucketed containers of The Gravity Rush, each capable of holding four people each, tore from their unmaintained bolts on the steel arm that once supported them, causing several to fall.

Horror gripped Ryan's heart as he cried out in anguish, overwhelmed by the unfolding tragedy before him. He could only imagine what was going through his friend's minds now.

I didn't do it right! This is my fault!

Time stretched, each moment elongating into what seemed like eternity as the townsfolk stood frozen in shock. Cries of panic mingled with the cacophony of destruction, their echoes rebounding off the shattered remains of amusement rides. Some fled, their frantic footsteps echoing through the chaos, while others remained transfixed by the unfolding catastrophe, their faces etched with horror and disbelief. In a cruel twist of fate, Ryan was forced to bear witness to the grim spectacle of death.

The Ferris Wheel, once a beacon of joy, now twisted and buckled under its own weight. Ryan's breath caught in his throat as he watched in horror. The structure collapsed with a sickening groan, its metal supports splintering and snapping like bones. People trapped in their seats struggled futilely against the safety restraints, their cries drowned out by the grinding of metal and the sharp snap of cables. The wheel toppled onto its side with a deafening crash, maiming those caught beneath its crushing weight. The air filled with the sickening crunch of bones and the visceral splatter of viscera, a symphony of agony and despair piercing Ryan's soul.

Driven by desperation and consumed by dread, Ryan dashed towards the wreckage. His heart pounded with fear and hope, adrenaline coursing through his veins. Scott followed close behind, his face a mask of anguished determination. They hurdled over twisted metal barriers, ignoring the requests of security guards who tried in vain to restrain them. Their minds raced, searching for any sign of their loved ones amidst the twisted carnage. But before they could reach the epicenter of destruction, festival security intercepted them, their firm grips halting their frantic advance.

As they argued with the guards, Scott's gaze drifted upwards, his expression crumbling with defeat. Ryan felt a pang of helplessness as he watched his friend's spirit seem to wither before his eyes. Following Scott's line of sight, Ryan's heart plummeted as he beheld the horrifying sight ahead—a scene of devastation that left him reeling, his legs giving way beneath him as despair washed over him like a suffocating tide.

Strands of platinum blonde hair danced in the brisk wind, entwined with fragments of debris and the faint scent of oil and fear that permeated the air around the twisted remains of the Ferris Wheel. Ryan's heart lurched as he recognized the familiar shade that framed Christina's face since their early school days. It wasn't just her hair; it was a part of her, something he'd grown accustomed to noticing even in passing moments.

The wind, now relentless in its fury, whipped Christina's strands about, some daring to escape the mangled metal that had entrapped them moments ago. Ryan watched helplessly as they fluttered like delicate wisps of memory, carrying with them echoes of laughter shared and secrets whispered under the guise of childhood innocence.

He remembered those times vividly, how Christina would playfully accuse him of having a keen nose for her perfume whenever he mentioned catching a whiff of her hair. It was these small, mundane details that now felt hauntingly precious amidst the chaos unfolding around him.

Each strand which floated towards him carried a weight of its own—a reminder of the person Christina was, and now, the tragedy that had befallen her. Ryan felt a lump form in his throat, the bitter taste of despair mingling with the metallic tang of blood and machinery.

In that moment, amidst the wreckage and the howling wind, Ryan clung to the strands of hair caught in the air, as if holding onto them could somehow bring Christina back, could rewrite the horrific scene playing out before his eyes. But all they offered was a fleeting connection to a life lost, a symbol of the innocence and joy now shattered and strewn across the carnival grounds.

As he stood there, frozen in grief and disbelief, Ryan realized that amidst all the chaos and destruction, it was these small, personal details—the strands of hair, the memories—piercing through the numbing shock, reminding him of the individual lives torn apart by fate's cruel hand.

People scattered in fear as the wolf prowled through the carnage, hunting. Ryan fell to his knees, tears streaking his face, but no sound escaped his lips. The weight of the night's horror settled heavily upon him—his friends were gone.

To Ryan's left, The Gravity Rush screeched to a laborious halt, its usual cheerful melody of whirling seats now a somber noise of metal against metal. The operator strained against the controls, his efforts evident in the sporadic jerks and sputters of the ride. Above, the seats continued their mechanical dance—parents clutching their children tightly, their faces etched with fear and confusion. Nearby, lone children wailed for their absent guardians, their cries lost in the turmoil.

On the ground lay two bucket seats, torn from their mounts, their frames twisted and gnarled like the remnants of a once vibrant life. Beneath them, victims lay trapped, pinned by protective beams meant to shield but now condemning. Colin's outstretched arms draped over the others; a final act of courage frozen in time. His foster siblings, Alicia, Luis, Isaiah, and Alex, lay still beside him, their small forms eerily calm amidst the chaos surrounding them. Their eyes, closed in peaceful resignation, belied the horror of their fate.

Ryan's gaze swept over the scene, his heart heavy with sorrow and disbelief. Each detail etched itself into his mind—the bent metal, the limp bodies, and Colin's valiant stance even in death. The show of protection and sacrifice spoke louder than any words could, evidence of Colin's unwavering commitment to those he loved.

Amidst the wreckage, Ryan knelt beside his fallen friends, his hands trembling as he reached out to touch Colin's shoulder. He could feel the cold of death lingering in the air, mingling with the acrid scent of oil and fear. With each breath, Ryan struggled to comprehend the enormity of their loss—a loss no amount of bravery or sacrifice could undo.

Ryan's hands trembled as he pressed against the heavy beams, trying in vain to lift them from his friends. Weakness overtook him, and he collapsed, crawling to each fallen form. He brushed aside hair and clothing, searching for signs of life, only to find blood and the stench of fear. *They died because I wasn't fast enough!* He stared at his bloodied hands, desperate to cleanse them of guilt, yet knowing his cries would go unheard amidst the rush for survival.

The werewolf approached from behind, its presence a grim inevitability. Ryan felt it looming, but he no longer cared. Eric, the boy transformed into a tragic creature, seized Ryan's neck and tore into his jugular without resistance. Ryan's eyes closed as life slipped away, his final gaze witnessing his own entrails spill onto the blood-stained ground.

I deserve this.

***

…No, you don't…Just breathe…

***

Ryan gasped, his lungs burning for air as he stood amidst the concrete path leading to the fair's entrance, Scott a steady presence by his side. An unsettling sensation lingered, not merely a physical touch but a whisper in his mind—an ethereal presence, *maybe it is the one Layla talks to.* He glanced at his hands, their cleanliness a stark contrast to the impending chaos he sensed would soon stain them.

"I'm not sure," Ryan murmured, his thoughts still grappling with the encounter. "But we can't stay here." Unsure of who he was talking to, they resumed their hurried walk, Ryan's mind racing with thoughts of the mysterious voice and its urgent plea to return.

She sounded young, Ryan thought to himself, the memory of the voice haunting him.

"Eric's around," Ryan said abruptly, urgency lacing his voice as he shared his concerns with Scott. "We need to alert everyone before something terrible happens." Scott nodded grimly, immediately springing into action. He waved his arms wildly, shouting at the top of his lungs, "The creature! It's here! Get out while you can! Protect your children!"

Security responded swiftly to Scott's frantic warnings, diverting their attention as Ryan sprinted past towards The Gravity Rush. His heart pounded harder as he spotted Colin and the foster kids lining up for the ride. Determination etched on his face, Ryan knew he had to intervene, even if it meant physically stopping them.

"Colin!" Ryan's voice pierced through the chaos, desperate to reach his friend. "We have to leave, now!" Colin looked bewildered; confusion etched on his face as he processed Ryan's urgency. "What's happening?" Colin shouted back, his concern growing.

"It's here! Trust me, we need to go!" Ryan insisted, urgency seeping into every word. Colin hesitated, scanning the tumultuous scene around him and the frightened younger kids under his care. He could sense the gravity of Ryan's warning, realizing the ride wasn't worth risking their lives.

Scott, meanwhile, weaved through the crowd, eyes locked on Christina near the Ferris wheel, moments away from boarding with her grandmother. "Christy!" Scott's voice cut through the clamor, desperation dripping from every syllable. Christina turned, puzzled by the urgency in Scott's tone, uncertain of the danger he insisted lurked nearby.

"Ryan's here! The werewolf's here!" Scott shouted, his words an urgent declaration in the chaotic night. Jo, Christina's grandmother, turned to her, concern furrowing her brow as she sought an explanation amidst the rising panic. Christina hesitated, torn between observing Colin's frantic attempts to save his siblings and heeding Scott's desperate warnings.

As Colin continued to persuade his foster siblings away from the ride, Christina held her breath, her heart torn between loyalty to her friends and the mounting fear of the unseen peril Scott insisted hovered over them all.

The ride operator forcefully intervened, shoving Colin back into the line despite his urgent shouts. Colin's frustration was apparent, etched deeply into his furrowed brow as he watched helplessly while his foster siblings boarded the ride against his vehement warnings. Sensing the escalating danger, Christina tugged at her grandmother's arm, urgency in her voice as she urged Jo to leave. Jo, never one to enjoy the rides herself, nodded in acquiescence, sensing the gravity of Christina's concern.

Meanwhile, Ryan's eyes scanned the fairgrounds with a growing sense of dread. Despite his frantic warnings, most fairgoers continued to queue up for the rides, oblivious to the impending peril. "You have to get off the rides! It's not safe!" Ryan shouted desperately, his pleas drowned out by the laughter and chatter of those around him. He gritted his teeth in frustration, searching for another way to break through their indifference.

In the midst of this chaos, Ryan's eyes caught sight of a young man sprinting towards the festival from the direction of the shopping center. "Run! It's here! It killed my friends!" The young man's voice carried over the crowd, punctuating the air with fear.

Here we go. This happened in my thoughts. How?

Security guards, already busy attempting to detain Scott, turned towards the commotion. Scott, frozen in disbelief, watched as a massive wolf emerged from the darkness, its eyes locking onto him with an unsettling intensity. Ryan recognized the young man as the one who had stumbled upon his friends behind the store.

Scott broke free from the guards, his voice reaching a pitch Ryan had never heard before—a desperate, piercing shriek that cut through the chaotic noise like a warning bell. He dashed towards the crowd once more, arms flailing, intent on alerting everyone to the imminent danger stalking them.

This is it! Have to do this right!

Ryan's heart sank as he watched the events unfold, realizing with a sinking feeling they mirrored the vision he had experienced earlier, albeit with slight variations. While some individuals had heeded the warnings and left, the rides continued to operate unabated. He knew it was up to him to divert the creature's attention away from the unsuspecting operator of The Mambo.

As Scott sprinted towards him, Ryan felt a surge of relief knowing his friend had managed to evade the pursuing werewolf. Eric's massive form paid no heed to Scott, the crowd now captivated by the urgency in the teenager's voice as he warned them of the imminent danger.

"Typical," Scott muttered, reaching Ryan's side with frustration etched on his face. "Adults ignore a kid, but when a high schooler speaks up, suddenly everyone listens." The irony of the situation hung between them as they prepared to confront the looming threat head-on. They shared a knowing look, understanding the unfortunate truth of how perceptions shaped responses.

Ryan shot Scott a wry glance, his tone sharp as he retorted, "Causing a scene isn't exactly the smartest move right now. Maybe calmly approaching security could've worked." Scott bristled at the sarcasm; his frustration evident. "I was trying to get their attention. Do you honestly think they'd evacuate just because I said so?" It was a valid point; one Ryan couldn't argue against. While Scott's efforts had prompted some to leave, it hadn't triggered a mass evacuation.

Amidst the panic stricken crowd surging towards the exit, a formidable figure emerged on the horizon, moving with purpose towards the rear of the festival grounds. Its predatory gaze swept the area, hunting for its next prey. People scrambled over guardrails, desperate to escape the advancing creature. Sensing the impending danger, Scott pulled Ryan aside, uncertainty etched on his face.

"We need to keep Eric away from The Mambo. Something's not right about it," Scott insisted, scanning their surroundings anxiously. He turned to Ryan, pressing, "How do you know?" With time ticking away, Ryan could only offer a vague reply, "I just do." Christina's voice cut through the chaos, pleading for them to leave. Ignoring her reasoning, Ryan knew he had to stay, even though Christina and Scott failed to grasp the urgency.

"Stay back!" the man near The Mambo's control board shouted, his voice echoing with resolve. For Ryan, it felt like déjà vu, a haunting familiarity with chaos unfolding before him. Spotting a metal chair nearby, Ryan grabbed it, his mind racing for any makeshift defense—*like those circus performers facing lions*. It wasn't a well-planned strategy, but he knew he had to act. Rushing onto the grass, he hoisted the chair, positioning it with its legs outward.

"What the hell are you going to do with that?" Christina's voice cut through the tension, surprising Ryan. "Yeah, I'm with her. What's the plan here?" Scott added with concern. Ryan shot them both a defiant look, his mouth curling in frustration. "I don't know! You got a better idea?"

"Yeah, I do! It rhymes with 'let's get the hell out of here'!" Scott's fear-laced retort rang out, but Ryan stood resolute.

"I can't do that. I couldn't live with myself if something happened and I could've stopped it," Ryan replied firmly.

Heart pounding, Ryan surged forward, his footsteps pounding against the grassy ground. The ride operator, eyes wide with dread, huddled near the control panel, gripped by the imminent threat of machinery gone awry. The air crackled with tension as the werewolf, muscles coiled for attack, loomed over the scene.

With a primal roar, Ryan launched the metal chair, every ounce of strength propelling it towards the creature's head. The impact reverberated through the night air, a deafening clang that briefly stunned the beast. But as it staggered back to its feet, its eyes fixed on Ryan with a newfound fury.

Defenseless now, Ryan's mind raced. His eyes darted around frantically, searching for anything—a weapon, an escape route—anything to fend off the advancing monster. Panic seized him, each heartbeat thundering in his ears as fear drove him backward, step by terrifying step.

"Come on, Eric, you ugly hound," Ryan muttered through gritted teeth, his voice strained with determination. He edged backwards, calculating his next move, desperate to outmaneuver the creature now hunting him.

But the werewolf closed the distance swiftly, its intent unmistakable in its predatory stance. Ryan's resolve hardened. With a final glance over his shoulder, he bolted towards the exit, the pounding footsteps of the beast echoing ominously behind him. Yet, even as he fled, the realization dawned that his struggle was far from over.

Another caught the mongrel's attention.

Amidst the chaos, a child's cry pierced the air. Whirling around, Ryan's blood turned cold as he saw Eric fixated on a young boy, poised to attack—a boy from his vision moments ago.

You know the morsels are the tastier of all options. You should have a tiny one before the night ends.

Eric's transformation into a werewolf had unleashed a primal force within him, intoxicating in its raw power. Beneath the beastly exterior, he lost touch with his human identity, consumed by urges he couldn't quell—the thrill of the hunt, the rush of the kill, the primal desire for human sustenance.

As he prowled through the shadows of Norton, Ohio, Eric felt a bitter disconnect from the townsfolk. They had never shown him an ounce of care or concern. Despite his rebellious spirit and outward defiance, no one had bothered to delve beneath the surface, to inquire about his struggles or offer a hand in understanding. To Eric, they were self-absorbed, wrapped up in their own lives without a thought for others like him.

No. Not a child! Eric's thoughts raged against the primal instincts driving him. *We're survivors, but this is outright murder! There's no honor in hunting the defenseless.*

Yet, despite his protests, the werewolf within him hungered, indifferent to his begging for restraint. The conflict within Eric grew as he battled against his feral instincts, struggling to reconcile his humanity with the relentless hunger threatening to consume him.

You know nothing!

You will feed because size and maturity have nothing to do with it!

Little Justin Davis found himself adrift amidst the pandemonium of fleeing crowds, separated from his father for the first time. Fear gripped him tightly, his small frame shivering with sobs and desperate cries for his daddy, his lip bitten in anguish.

"Stop!" Ryan's voice sliced through the chaos; a desperate cry aimed at diverting the advancing werewolf's attention away from the terrified child. He scanned the ground urgently, seeking anything that could serve as a weapon against the beast. Suddenly, a barrage of objects pelted the creature—empty beer bottles, assorted debris—hurled by none other than his brother Devin and Valerie.

Devin brandished a metal pole adorned with decorative flags, while Valerie wielded a makeshift arsenal of bottles scavenged from a nearby booth. "Stop, Eric!" Devin's voice thundered, confronting the monster with unwavering resolve. The werewolf, heedless of their identities, turned to face them with a menacing snarl.

Scott and Christina joined Ryan, standing steadfast beside him, united in their mission. It was a rare moment of solidarity amidst the chaos, and Ryan hoped it wouldn't be their last.

"Come for us! Come on!" they shouted in unison, still trying to draw the wolf's focus away from the child. But like Eric, the creature saw through their distraction. It hunkered down, preparing to strike. Devin was the first to sprint towards the little boy. Justin wailed at the sight of the monstrous canine, yearning for his dad, bewildered by his absence. The wolf growled, crouching on its hind legs, poised to pounce on Justin Davis, its intent clear—to split apart his tiny body.

Charlie Davis located his son amidst the chaotic backdrop of The Gravity Rush, accompanied by a police officer he had urgently called for help. As he dashed towards Justin, his focus was not on the lurking werewolf but on the perilously swinging metal seats threatening his son. Vaulting over the barrier, Charlie tackled Justin to the ground, shielding him from imminent danger.

Meanwhile, Devin charged towards the wolf, wielding a metal pole salvaged from nearby debris. With swift determination, he swung the pole at the creature, aiming for its snout. The impact reverberated through the air, causing the wolf to yelp in pain as its face contorted from the blow. Struggling to regain its footing, the beast momentarily diverted its attention from Justin and Charlie.

Devin landed on the ground beside them, relief flooding his expression as he watched Justin rise to his feet, unharmed and reunited with his father. Charlie managed a reassuring smile at his son, mustering strength amidst the chaos. "I think we've had enough adventure for one night, don't you, spor…?"

Silence.

Everyone involved—Ryan, Scott, Christina, Devin, and Valerie—watched as one of the metal seats from The Gravity Rush collided with the back of Charlie Davis's head, decapitating him, his blood sprayed onto his little boy's face. Justin choked on his breath not knowing what had just happened to his father. Trying not to swallow the blood pouring from his father's wound, Justin ignored his father's severed head and patted his own back, hoping his father was merely choking like he used to do for him. The metal alone would have killed Charlie, but something else slammed against his skull.

A piercing scream cut through the air as The Gravity Rush continued its frenzied motion. The sudden halt of the ride caught everyone off guard. Amidst the confusion, a teenage girl's anguished cry rang out, breaking through the chaotic scene. "I didn't see him. I couldn't move fast enough!" she wailed, her voice laced with shock and guilt.

Responding swiftly, the operator and bystanders rushed to her aid, drawn by her distress. As they approached, the grim reality unfolded before their eyes. The girl clutched her injured leg, her cries piercing the tumultuous ether. It was only upon closer inspection that the severity of her injury became apparent — the lower part of her left leg hung limply, shattered from the impact with Charlie Davis's head.

Meanwhile, Justin Davis stood in stunned silence, trying to process the sudden turn of events claiming his father's life. Red streaks stained his hands, a chilling reminder of the violence that had unfolded. Valerie, leaping over the fence, enveloped Justin in a protective embrace, guiding him away from the heartbreaking scene of his father's lifeless body lying on the grass, a tragic casualty of the carnival ride's unexpected calamity.

There was no simple fix. There were going to be casualties no matter what I did. Why did it have to be that little boy's burden to bear? Ryan remembered little Justin from the beginning of his vision, understanding more of the cause and effect of his actions.

The werewolf regained its composure, looming over Ryan as he scrambled desperately to escape. His hands searched for purchase on the unforgiving concrete, but an unseen rock sent him tumbling to the ground, his heart racing with terror. This was the monster's doing, and it knew it, relishing its dominance. Standing tall on its hind legs, the creature cast a chilling shadow over Ryan, who gritted his teeth against the urge to ask for mercy, even as the distant flicker of police lights danced in the night. Tonight, he wouldn't yield.

The eerie glow of the approaching police lights highlighted the werewolf's sleek fur and the menacing gleam of its blood-stained claws, poised to strike.

Suddenly, the sharp crack of gunfire shattered the tense silence, each bullet finding its mark in Eric's body. The creature convulsed in agony with every hit, and despite his fear, Ryan couldn't suppress the sympathy he kept for the boy trapped within the beast. As Eric collapsed to the ground, writhing in pain, Devin and Valerie rushed forward, hoping against hope to salvage some fragment of humanity.

Valerie hesitated; her hand nervous as she approached the fallen creature. Gently, she placed her palm against Eric's fur, her heart heavy with sorrow. Tears streamed down her face as she caressed him, grieving not for the monstrous form before her, but for the tormented soul within.

"Hey, buddy," Devin choked out, his voice thick with emotion. "It hasn't been a great day, has it?" Though Eric could not reply, he heard his friend's words, sensing the weight of their shared grief. Tears welled in his eyes as pain coursed through his body, and in that moment, a flicker of Eric's true humanity began to emerge from the darkness.

As police officers approached cautiously, ordering Devin and Valerie to step away, Valerie rested her head on the wolf's chest. "I'm so sorry for everything you've been through," she whispered softly to Eric, her heart aching for her friend and the tragic life few understood. It could have been different for Eric—*it should have been.*

Scott and Christina hurried over to Ryan, conveying their support as he slowly rose from the ground. Together, they stood in solemn silence, witnessing Devin and Valerie's grief stricken farewell to their fallen friend. The werewolf's eyes closed for the final time, its monstrous form gradually reverting back to Eric Flanagan's human state. A palpable unease settled among the officers who had fired the fatal shots, their expressions reflecting a mix of confusion, relief, and apprehension.

As the crowd dispersed, only the Akron police and the five friends remained, lingering amidst the aftermath of the Norton Fall Festival. They averted their gazes from Eric's lifeless body sprawled naked on the ground, surrounded by remnants of the festive chaos. Despite Eric's animosity towards Ryan and his friends, they felt no satisfaction in the tragic outcome that had befallen him—or anyone.

Turning away from the grim scene, the group moved towards their trusted—The Turbo, pausing briefly as an officer intercepted them for witness statements. They responded evasively, reluctant to divulge the full scope of the surreal events they had just witnessed—a truth too extraordinary and bizarre for the authorities to fully comprehend, mirroring the disbelief that would inevitably ripple through the local community.

Ryan contemplated the evening's events on the ride home, his mind swirling with thoughts about his vision and the tragic loss of the young boy's father. Though relieved his friends were safe and casualties were minimized, he couldn't shake the feeling he could have done something differently to prevent the father's death.

Amidst the turmoil, two thoughts brought him a measure of solace. One was the wisdom of Mr. Spock, whose words echoed in his mind about sacrifice for the greater good. The other was a vision of his mother, her comforting advice about acceptance and navigating life's uncertainties lingering in his thoughts.

A single tear rolled down Ryan's cheek, a silent tribute to his dearly missed mother and the fallen father from tonight's chaos. Devin caught sight of the sorrow reflected in his brother's eyes through the rearview mirror, acknowledging their shared grief. They all yearned for the reassuring presence of their mothers, but for now, they had to return home and await the dawn.

Upon learning of their father's hospitalization from their mother's call, Valerie and Scott decided to spend the night at Ryan and Devin's house. Christina, dropped off at her house, awaited her grandmother's arrival. Overwhelmed by the night's events, Christina found it hard to focus, her mind still grappling with the chaos and tragedy they had witnessed.

Devin made his way to Mr. Craggs' house to fetch Layla and take her home. "What happened?" Melvin inquired as Devin prepared to leave. With a heavy sigh, Devin turned to face Melvin, weariness evident in his voice. "You wouldn't believe it. You'll hear more tomorrow, probably," he replied, weighed down by the night's events.

As Devin headed towards his driveway, Melvin followed closely, urgency in his voice. "I need to know what's goin' on! Strange things are happenin'," Melvin insisted.

Devin paused, frustration and exhaustion washing over him. Running a hand through his hair, he turned to Melvin, irritation coloring his tone. "Melvin, it's late, and I've had a hell of a night. I lost my best friend tonight. It's been a really crappy night, so if you don't mind, I'm going home now. Goodnight," he said tersely, bitterness seeping into his words.

Just as Devin began to walk away with Layla, realization struck him like a sudden revelation. He halted in his tracks, turning back to face Melvin, his expression hardening. "You knew somethin' was wrong with Eric and chose to shut up 'bout it. My little brother is a wreck because of all this—exhausted and filled with fear and anxiety," he accused, his voice sharp with disappointment.

In the dim light, Melvin met Devin's gaze with guarded eyes. "Your parents didn't say anything either?" he asked, admitting his role in the charade reluctantly, guilt tainting his voice.

"No, they didn't. But why did nobody speak up?" Devin retorted bitterly before adding, "Stay alert. There's one more moon tomorrow." Melvin didn't respond overtly, instead fixing Devin with a steady gaze and cryptically replying, "I hoped everything would turn out fine."

***

Later that night, Scott made hot chocolate for everyone before they retired to bed, hoping fervently for a better day to come. They walked down the hall, Valerie settling in with Devin while Ryan's room became the gathering spot for the others.

Upon opening Layla's bedroom door, they were greeted by a surprise—a bright, colorful picture she had created with her Lite Brite set. Three stick figures stood in front of trees, two boys and a girl, with small white triangles and red highlights creating a dramatic scene. Off to the side, a full moon loomed large.

Ryan glanced at his sister, his chest swelling with pride as he asked delicately, "It's not over yet, is it?" Layla shook her head solemnly, her eyes serious as she replied, "She says she's really sorry, but there's still one left." Ryan felt the known cold that came when the dead girl in the tattered pink dress lingered among them.

The triangular shapes on the artwork resembled menacing teeth descending upon the three figures—the Hatcher children caught between impending danger.

CHAPTER THIRTY

SEND ME AN ANGEL

Everyone woke up earlier than they should have, given the night they had. The adrenaline from the previous evening made it difficult to find restful sleep, but some managed a few hours before waking around eight. It was Wednesday, November 29th, the day after the last full moon. Ryan's mind raced, trying to find a reason to avoid his plan for tonight. If the memories of the Norton Festival hadn't disturbed their sleep, the ringing telephone would.

Devin stumbled to the phone while making coffee for anyone who wanted it. "Hello," he greeted groggily.

"*You sound worse for wear,*" Rebecca commented, her voice immediately gaining Devin's full attention and sparking a hope they weren't already on their way home from the hotel.

"Mom! Everything all right?"

"*All right, then, calm down. Everything is fine. We're going to be late coming home because I wanted to get some Christmas shopping in. I thought maybe we'd pick up some Swinson's hamburgers and shakes for an early dinner before heading back out to the party. Sound good?*"

Relief washed over him, knowing they wouldn't be home immediately, giving him more time with Valerie. If his mother came home and found her there early in the morning, questions would arise. "*What's wrong? Got a girl there or somethin'?*" Rebecca teased nervously.

"Yeah, I mean, no. Just take your time," Devin replied, hoping his parents wouldn't return too soon. He knew what Ryan had planned and wasn't looking forward to his role in their overnight scheme. The brothers had discussed it while their friends slept, keeping their sister, Layla, out of the loop. They understood her ghostly visitors used her to relay information, and they wanted to shield her from knowing more than necessary.

"*Okay, love. Tell your brother I love him, and I will see you soon.*"

Devin's mouth quivered, contemplating what lay ahead. He wanted to talk to his dad but couldn't bring himself to reach out. "Hey, mom…"

"*Yeah?*"

"I miss you guys."

A long pause came from the other end. "*We miss you too. See you in a bit.*" Devin stayed on the line until the receiver clicked on her end. He hung up, staring out into the woods where this journey began—this tale of fear and loss.

As he turned to the coffee machine, he caught a glimpse of figures standing on the patio, staring at him through the glass door. Shadows loomed just beyond the glass; their outlines barely discernible in the dim morning light. Devin's breath hitched, his heart pounding in his chest. He froze, refusing to look directly, a cold sweat breaking out on his forehead. The eerie stillness of the figures, unmoving and silent, cast fear and anxiety.

The world around him held its breath, the only sounds being the faint hum of the refrigerator and the ticking of the kitchen clock. Devin's eyes darted around the room, trying to focus on anything but the ghostly shapes outside. His mind raced, conjuring images of phantom onlookers and malevolent spirits, remnants of the night's horrors still fresh in his memory.

Valerie's voice broke the spell, jolting him back to reality. "What's wrong?" she asked, poking her head around the corner. Devin forced a smile, his muscles stiff with tension. "Nothing. Just tired, I think. Seeing things," he replied, his voice barely steady.

As Valerie's presence filled the room, the figures outside dissolved into the morning mist, leaving Devin to wonder if they had ever been there at all. She sniffed the air, relaxed by the aroma of coffee in the crisp morning. The house was cold, as Calvin preferred to keep the heating bills down during fall and winter.

Devin noticed Valerie's bare feet and asked, "Aren't your feet freezing?" She laughed, taking a sip of coffee, and replied, "Colder than a witch's tit." The Hatchers had an overabundance of slippers—raccoon head, pink, black leather, brown. With all the hardwood floors on the top floor, they needed them in the cold. Devin went to the hallway closet and picked out a pink pair. Returning to the kitchen, confident she'd like them, he handed them over.

"So, like, because I'm a girl, I would just love the pink ones?" she said expressionlessly. He began to justify his choice until Valerie started giggling, "Relax. I'm just messin' with you."

Devin managed a weak smile but felt the weight of the previous night's events pressing down on him. Valerie noticed his lack of amusement, coughed awkwardly, and began to pour a cup of Sanka coffee. "I'm going to wake Scotty up soon. We need to go home and wait for mom to call or see if she is even home. Maybe go and see dad if we can. But first…coffee," she said, raising her mug with a small, comforting smile.

Devin agreed. "You can call, you know."

"I know. I just think it's time to walk home and let her see we're okay."

They both nodded uneasily, the silence between them heavy and awkward. The new couple hadn't yet reached the phase where they could be quiet together. Devin, fidgeting slightly, broke the silence. "Do you want to talk about last night?" he asked. Valerie sat down at the kitchen table and sighed; her gaze distant. "Werewolves exist, and our friend was turned into one and went on a rampage. What else is there to say?"

Devin looked away, struggling to find the right words. "There's a lot to say. We just don't know how to yet. This isn't normal. These things don't just happen."

"But they do, don't they?" Valerie's voice was tinged with frustration and disbelief.

"What do you mean?" Devin asked, his brow furrowing.

"Things like this have probably happened before. If you told me werewolves existed a week ago, I'd think you were nuts. Look at us now. We don't even know how to be sad for our friend! Just think of what we don't know and what we might discover tomorrow—we don't know anything."

Devin nodded, a heavy silence settling over them as they sipped their hot beverages. The reality of the paranormal hung in the air, altering their understanding of the world. Trying to lighten the mood, Devin forced a smile. "I just hope vampires aren't real." Valerie shot him a sharp look, clearly not amused by the attempt at humor.

***

"Do you think my dad is one now?" Scott's voice trembled as he turned to Ryan, the weight of the question hanging heavily in the air. Christina, who had been pacing in the garage, stopped abruptly, her eyes wide with dread. "If he doesn't die, I mean." Ryan hesitated, not wanting to be the bearer of more bad news.

"I don't know," he said, trying to soften the blow. But Scott wasn't having it. He jabbed a finger in Ryan's direction, his voice rising in anger. "Stop that!"

"Stop what?"

"I've never lied to you about anything! So don't start with me now!" Scott's eyes blazed, his frustration boiling over. Their friendship had always been built on brutal honesty, and now was no time for half-truths.

"Fine," Ryan snapped, ready to confront the issue head-on. Scott straightened up, arms crossed, bracing himself for the truth. Christina edged towards the other side of the garage, her anxiety on high. Confrontations always made her nervous, especially when it involved choosing sides between friends. But this time, there was no side to pick—only the harsh reality to face. "It's a good possibility. Is that what you want to hear?"

Scott began to pace, his agitation mirroring Christina's earlier movements. "Yeah. That's what I wanted to hear, dickhead." Ryan threw his hands up in frustration. "What exactly do you want me to say? I have my own shit to deal with today. I warned everybody in this damn house! It's not my fault no one wanted to believe me!"

"How could you expect us to believe something like that, Ryan?" Christina interjected; her voice tinged with disbelief. "You're talking about things you only see in the movies." Ryan walked away, shaking his head at the irony. "The things I see in the movies are the only reason I put anything together."

"And they said watching TV would make us dumb," Scott joked, trying to lighten the mood. They all smiled uneasily, the weight of the situation still pressing down on them. "You know this all starts again next month if you're right. So what do we—what do I do then?" Ryan's heart sank, knowing the burden his friend and Valerie would have to bear.

"Would you rather he died?" Christina's blunt question sliced through the air. Scott's eyes widened, shocked by her directness. "What? Why would you even ask me that?"

Ryan leaned against the garage wall, understanding the harsh logic behind Christina's words. "I mean, assuming he's got it in his blood, he's going to change and probably hurt people. Is it better than death just because he's your dad?"

"I don't want to answer that! It's a shitty answer one way or the other," Scott retorted, his voice filled with anguish. Christina crossed her arms, her expression one of grim contemplation. "How?"

"If you have to ask, you haven't put yourself in that situation," Scott ended the conversation, opting for restraint over losing his cool, which he was known to do from time to time. His passive-aggressive reply lingered in the air, but Christina didn't mind. She knew it was insensitive to bring it up so soon after the attacks.

Ryan's thoughts drifted to Devin and Valerie, remembering how they had to watch their friend die. He worried the same might happen to Scott if his dad attacked or bit him. The thought of Scott turning into a monster caused him internal grief. Could he kill a friend he had known most of his life? Ryan hoped he would never have to find out.

"What happens when it does? When it, you know, happens," Scott asked, finally voicing the question he dreaded.

"Then we'll deal with it as best we can," Ryan assured him.

Scott reached into his camouflage coat pocket. His dad, Rick, made him wear it when they went hunting. Scott didn't like it then, but now, he would have to protect people from another kind of monster. He pulled out a cigarette, an item pilfered from his dad's dresser.

"Swear it," Scott said, holding up the cigarette.

"What's it for?" Ryan asked.

"You snort it... it's a cigarette, idiot! You smoke it," Scott joked.

"I know, but what does it have to do with what you're talking about?"

"We'll smoke it to finalize the promise. I was thinking of doing the whole blood pact thing, but my mom said there are too many possible diseases in it."

"So lung cancer is better... awesome," Christina interjected. Scott scoffed, accusing her of being overdramatic. "It's just one, and we're going to share it! Can't get cancer from one cigarette, jeez! Right?"

Ryan took the initiative, grabbed the cigarette and lighter, lit it, and took a deep drag. He coughed violently as he exhaled, the acrid smoke burning his throat. "Why do people like this?" he muttered, passing it back to Scott, who eyed it skeptically after seeing Ryan gag.

Scott took a tentative drag, released the fumes with less enthusiasm, and shrugged. "Not that bad," he said, holding it between his fingers and thumb, mimicking scenes from movies where people passed joints. Christina curled her lip, disgusted at herself for participating in this makeshift pact. She barely put the filter to her lips, took a tiny puff, and immediately exhaled the smoke without inhaling. "You didn't even inhale!" Scott pointed out, disappointed.

Christina extinguished the cigarette with her shoe, her expression defiant. "Take it or leave it."

Given the circumstances, they all fell silent, looking out into their neighborhood. The usual quiet now felt oppressive, with the stillness and cloud covered sky casting a dreary pall over the day.

"Do you need us to come back later?" Christina's voice cracked with guilt, secretly hoping for a "no" from her boyfriend. Scott glanced at Ryan, who pondered his answer. He already knew his response but needed a moment to affirm it.

"No, there's no sense in you all getting yourselves in danger. It's my, our, problem now. We'll take care of it."

"What if you can't?" Scott questioned, raising an eyebrow. "It's your dad. Will you be able to do what you have to in the end?"

Ryan felt a surge of anxiety at Scott's words. He hated that his friend had planted a seed of doubt, but the question was valid. The reality of potentially having to confront and possibly harm his own father was a terrifying prospect.

I don't know. Will I?

"I don't know," Ryan admitted, his voice low and uncertain. "I think I can do what's best for everyone, no matter how hard it is. My dad wouldn't be able to live with himself if he knew he killed his family… and I couldn't live knowing I did nothing to stop it."

Valerie was the first to walk out into the garage, calling out, "Scott! We need to go." Devin followed her outside, glancing back at Ryan with a look indicating they needed to talk. Ryan knew what his brother wanted but wasn't eager for the conversation.

"You gonna be okay?" Scott asked one last time. Ryan glanced over at the box of materials and weapons Scott had brought from his garage. "I'll be good. It'll be fine," Ryan reassured both Scott and Christina.

"By the way, why does your dad need three sets of handcuffs?" Ryan asked, curious.

"Hell if I know, dude. Don't go there. I know your mind went somewhere filthy," Scott replied, pretending to puke.

"I didn't say a word," Ryan playfully defended himself.

Christina kissed Ryan on the cheek. "Please be safe," she said, her voice filled with concern.

He smiled at his pretty girlfriend, relieved she was alive. "I'll figure it out," he promised, though it didn't make Christina feel any better. It was the best reassurance she would get from him.

Their friends walked up the driveway, dispersing in different directions as they approached the first road on the right where Christina lived.

Devin walked to where his little brother stood, eyes distant and filled with worry. Neither knew if they would see their friends again after tonight. The weight of the world pressed heavily on their shoulders, both wishing this was a nightmare they'd yet to wake from.

"What do we do now?" Devin asked his little brother.

Ryan looked back at the box and replied, "We get ready. I have an idea."

"Aren't you afraid you're wrong?"
"If I'm wrong, it'll be the best mistake I'll ever make."

***

Calvin and Rebecca Hatcher arrived home to find their children already gathered. Rebecca's longing for affection surged as she enveloped them in hugs, her need intense after their time apart. The kids, accustomed to her exuberance, endured her embrace before heading upstairs, leaving Ryan and Calvin lingering awkwardly in the foyer.

"So, what did you guys bring back?" Layla probed; her curiosity piqued.

"Nothing you need to worry about right now. And don't even think about going off to snoop," Rebecca cautioned with a playful sternness.

Calvin, typically reserved with his sons, initiated a rare hug with Ryan. It felt meaningful, as if it might be the last. Normally brief, this one lingered. "You okay?" Calvin asked quietly, feeling Ryan nod against his chest, avoiding eye contact to hide his emotions. "It's been a strange week, Dad," Ryan mumbled.

Once settled in, Ryan and Devin recounted the recent events, careful to omit their direct involvement. They recounted the animal attacks, Rick's encounter, and the chaos at the festival, omitting any mention of Eric's fate. The truth of Eric's death weighed heavily on them, unspoken and unresolved.

"These animal attacks have me thinking we should consider moving somewhere more populated," Rebecca remarked nervously. Lost in thoughts sparked by his sons' stories, Calvin barely registered her words, murmuring, "Yeah, maybe."

As the evening wore on, Ryan noticed his father's distraction, sensing his unease grow as thoughts raced through his mind, elsewhere despite being present.

Devin quietly made his way to the garage, retrieving the box Scott had loaned them for the evening. With the plan now poised for action, all they needed was the right moment.

"Let's eat before it gets cold!" Rebecca's voice rang out, prompting everyone to dig into their greasy Swinson's bags, grabbing burgers, fries, and milkshakes.

The boys watched their parents and Layla eat steadily, their own appetites waning as anticipation grew. It had been a while since they'd seen their mother eat so heartily, even finishing a kids' meal—a change from her recent habits.

"You gonna eat those?" Layla nudged Ryan about his fries, though he didn't respond, allowing her to take them.

Across the table, Ryan and Devin exchanged glances, communicating that it wasn't yet time. Calvin sat with his back against the wall, Rebecca and Layla opposite him—positions easy to move from when the moment came, as it soon would.

"What's up with you two?" Calvin asked, noticing their unusual behavior since their return.

"We're fine, dad," Ryan murmured.

"Just tired," Devin added flatly.

As the sun dipped below the horizon, Ryan nodded to Devin, signaling the start of their plan. "Hey, dad, Scott showed me this cool trick. Mind if I show you?"

"Sure thing, buddy. Go for it," Calvin agreed, glancing at the time. Ryan pushed his chair back, heading for the box and bringing it into the kitchen. A white sheet from the linen closet covered the contents—a collection of tools and supplies. "I'm going to make something disappear," Ryan declared cryptically, prompting Devin to join him in unveiling their scheme, capturing Rebecca and Layla's curiosity.

"Will this take long? We need to leave soon," Rebecca's voice quivered with nervous urgency, eyes darting to the kitchen clock. Devin noted her timekeeping vigilance since they arrived home, reassuring, "No, it won't be long."

A white bedsheet draped over Calvin; his grin hidden in anticipation. Ryan retrieved handcuffs, slipping the key into his pocket and tossing another pair to Devin, who secured one side around their father's wrists and the other to the armrests.

"Is all this really necessary for your trick?" Calvin asked, perplexed.

"Don't worry, Dad," Devin said, producing a rope. "It's part of the act."

Calvin felt the rough fibers of the rope against his neck tightening. "I don't think this is safe. I don't like this," Rebecca interjected, concern etched in her voice, but Ryan dismissed her with, "Trust me, Mom. This is the safest way."

Devin secured Calvin's feet with a bungee hook as Layla's joyful expression shifted to concern. Under the sheet, Calvin's face contorted, struggling for breath. "What are you doing?" Layla exclaimed.

"Yeah, boys, let your father go," Rebecca demanded, her patience wearing thin. "This isn't fun anymore."

"Yeah," Calvin's muffled voice came from under the sheet. "Can't breathe too well. You tied it too tight around my neck."

Ryan and Devin left the table, arming themselves from the box—Ryan with a crossbow and Devin with a baseball bat and taser.

"Can you see yourself, Dad?" Ryan asked.

"No."

"Then it's like you've disappeared," Ryan said through gritted teeth, pride mixing with a disturbing urge.

"This isn't funny! Untie me now!" Calvin's anger boiled, his desperation growing. Ryan wished they had something to calm him down, doubting their plan's viability in the face of potential disaster.

Rebecca's heart raced, clutching Layla tightly as fear and confusion overwhelmed her. "Have you lost your mind?" Her voice quivered with disbelief. Ryan's gaze narrowed as he aimed the crossbow at his father's head. "Trust us, Mom. This is the only way," Devin explained, his voice filled with resolve.

"To make sure he's not a werewolf and to stop him if he is, so he can't hurt anyone," Ryan added solemnly, his determination evident. Rebecca bit her lip, anger bubbling as she struggled for words. "This is insane! Let me go!" Calvin demanded, straining against his bonds.

"No, Dad. We can't," Ryan replied firmly, his grip on the weapon unwavering. "You've lost it! We need to leave now. Untie me!" Calvin's desperation tinged his voice.

Rebecca gently pushed Layla towards the living room, her mind racing with fear and uncertainty. "Ryan, don't be foolish!" Calvin's voice cracked, trying to reason with his son.

"I know what I saw that night. Don't pretend otherwise!" Ryan snapped; his gaze unwavering. "How Craggs shot the creature and found a man underneath. I saw the marks on you! You all conveniently left during full moons. Do you think I'm stupid? Layla's shown me things!"

"Layla's shown you? Ryan, you're imagining things. We can help you! Just let us go, and we'll talk about this tomorrow," Calvin begged desperately, but Devin intervened firmly. "No, Dad. We've seen too much. Eric's gone because of those... things! Ryan's not crazy. Stop blaming him!"

Ryan's arms grew tired holding the crossbow, adrenaline coursing through him. Swiftly, he slung it onto his back and withdrew his father's Astra Terminator pistol, his expression grim and resolute.

Rebecca gasped, "Don't do this!"

"I won't do anything unless he turns," Ryan reassured his mother, his voice steady.

Night had fallen when Layla began crying in the kitchen doorway. "It's okay, sweetie," Rebecca comforted, placing a hand on her stomach. "They're just confused."

"No, I'm not!" Ryan yelled.

Calvin's frantic struggles intensified, the chair creaking and groaning under his forceful attempts to break free. Rebecca, thrown from her seat, clutched her stomach in agony, her cries piercing the tense atmosphere.

"It hurts so much!" she screamed; her pain palpable. Wide-eyed with fear, Layla contended with her brothers. "Stop it, Ryan! Devin! You're upsetting Mom! You're hurting her stomach!" Tears streamed down her face, her small body shaking with distress.

But the boys remained unmoved, their focus fixed on their mother as she crawled under the table, determined to free their father. "Mom, no! Don't do that! He could be dangerous! We can't take that risk!" Devin's voice rang out in desperation, as Layla's cries went unheard.

Ryan glanced under the table, his grip on the pistol tightening. "Mom?" His voice faltered with uncertainty. "Are you...?" Fear gripped him as he loosened his hold on the weapon, his hand trembling with the weight of what he began to witness.

He was wrong—this whole time.

I was so wrong.

"Get away from me! Get out of the house!"

Ryan staggered back, his eyes fixed on his mother's newly transformed blue eyes, her voice deepening as she trembled beneath the table. Shame and fear mingled in her expression as her children witnessed her transformation into a monster.

"Devin! Untie Dad, now!" Ryan's voice echoed through the kitchen, urgency propelling him across the linoleum.

"What? Why?" Devin's confusion was evident.

"It's not Dad. It never was! It's Mom! She's the one who's the wolf!"

She had a coat on that night. Dad put it on her, so I couldn't see any marks. It's not a scratch that turns a person—it's the bite!

Rebecca painfully crawled out from under the table towards Ryan, her hand shifting violently as she reached out, yearning to touch her son. Her eyes desired forgiveness, unable to articulate her words, only emitting distorted human screams mingled with harrowing howls as her body continued to transform.

Devin wrestled with the rope around Calvin's feet, urging him to stay still as he struggled to untie the knots. He wanted to comfort his mother, but all he could do was listen to the bones in her fingers elongate, snap and bubble, causing him to retch. Her hands and feet stretched, skin breaking as her enlarged veins burst through, falling onto the floor. Claws emerged from the tips of her fingers, ripping through her human nails until they dropped to the ground.

"Where's the key? I need the key!" Devin screamed.

Layla began to chew the ends of her fingers, a habit whenever she was upset or scared. "What's going on? What's happening to Mommy?" she hollered, her voice muffled by her distress. The boys had no time to comfort her. Their father was tied down, helpless, and if the wolf inside their mother found him bound, it would be an easy kill. Rebecca was no longer the mother they knew, and now the boys needed to save their dad from their own misguided actions.

Canine hairs erupted from Rebecca's pores, tearing her skin as they pushed through, dark and coarse. Her body convulsed violently, each jerk causing her clothes to rip further, the fabric unable to contain her expanding form. Muscles bulged and shifted beneath her skin, which split open in jagged lines, revealing the sinew and bone beneath. Blood oozed from the tears, running down her body in rivulets mingling with the growing fur, turning it a gruesome, sticky red.

Rebecca's fingers elongated, the bones cracking and stretching, her nails blackening and curving into claws. Each extension brought a sickening pop, and the flesh of her hands tore open, releasing a nauseating stench of iron and decay. Her limbs stretched and distorted, her legs snapping into new angles, forcing her to inch out from under the table in a grotesque crawl.

Her face was a battlefield of transformation. The skin around her nose and mouth split with a wet, tearing sound, blood and strands of tendons hanging like macabre curtains as her muzzle pushed forward. Her eyes, once filled with human sorrow, now flickered with a predatory glint, narrowing as the wolf took over. Blood vessels burst in her eyes, turning the whites a vivid red against the emerging sapphire irises.

Rebecca's spine elongated, vertebrae popping audibly as her back arched unnaturally. Her ribs expanded, each one snapping into a new position with excruciating slowness. She let out a deep howl, a sound that was part human agony, part animal rage. The cry was filled with such pain that it shook the walls, reverberating through the room.

Strands of flesh and congealed blood sloughed off her face, splattering onto the floor in thick, wet chunks. The fur underneath was matted and dark, the remnants of her human skin sticking to it before drying and cracking away into dust. Her jaw elongated, teeth pushing out of her gums, growing long and sharp. They snapped into place with a final, gruesome clack, her new maw filled with deadly, glistening fangs.

Ryan and Layla watched helplessly as their mother's transformation completed. The creature before them was no longer their mother but a monstrous hybrid, her human features twisted into something nightmarish. Rebecca's last semblance of humanity faded from her eyes, replaced by the cold, predatory stare of a wolf.

Calvin had experienced the disturbing sounds of bones snapping and muscle tearing before. He remembered the night they drove out to the desolate wilderness, trying to protect their children from the horror. Watching from a distance, he felt helplessness and dread as his wife's body underwent its hideous alteration. The memory haunted him, and he vowed never to witness it again.

After that night, he took precautions. He administered tranquilizer darts to Rebecca, ensuring she slept through the tumultuous nights of her transformation. The first night had been the worst, the tranquilizers barely enough to subdue her savage instincts. Calvin still shuddered at the memory of finding her naked in the woods, her primal hunger unleashed upon unsuspecting prey.

Rebecca had awakened disoriented and ravenous, her instincts driving her to a nearby turkey farm. Mr. Jersyk had paid the ultimate price for his unexpected encounter with the transmuted beast. Calvin knew he should have ended it then, put an end to the nightmare consuming his wife. But he couldn't bring himself to do it, held back by a mixture of love and fear.

As the nights passed and the tranquilizers took effect, Rebecca grew accustomed to their sedative embrace. Yet Calvin knew their luck would eventually run out. The tranquilizers were a temporary solution, a fragile barrier holding back the primal forces within his wife. One day, the barrier would fail, unleashing a terror which could not be contained.

Ryan swiftly retrieved the handcuff keys and tossed them to Devin, urgency pulsating through the air. The sharp scent of Rebecca's transforming body filled the room, mingling with Calvin's urgent shouts. Devin's hands shook as he grabbed the keys, fumbling with the locks while Calvin squirmed in his restraints. Layla's panicked screams echoed through the chaos, a symphony of fear and confusion.

Devin's heart raced as he struggled to free his father; his mind clouded with images of his mother's transformation. He knew the terror awaiting them, having witnessed it with Eric. Ryan slid beneath the table; desperation etched on his face as he attempted to unlock Calvin's handcuffs. Each attempt was met with frustration—the keys didn't fit.

Frantically, they exchanged keys, their hearts pounding with each click of the locks. Finally, success—a simultaneous click signaled their liberation. Calvin wasted no time tearing away the sheet concealing him, his movements fueled by a primal instinct to protect his family.

Amidst the chaos, Layla's screams intertwined with Rebecca's tortured grunts as the change continued. The werewolf's form took shape, its coat a symphony of dark hues, reminiscent of Rebecca's striking features. Despite the fear, there was a twisted beauty in the creature's shape—a grotesque allure that belied its horrific nature.

Calvin's gaze shifted between his wife's beastly form and his sons, a silent command passing between them. With cautious steps, Ryan and Devin edged towards the living room, their movements deliberate and calculated. Layla, her breath hitched in fear, followed suit, her fingers gnawed raw in her distress.

Their mother loomed over them; her eyes gleaming with malevolence. Calvin issued a stern directive—run. With grim determination, Ryan and Devin nodded, their resolve unwavering even in the face of unspeakable horror. Each step toward the door was measured, their breaths shallow and controlled. They clung to the semblance of a plan, grasping at straws in a world unraveling at the seams.

First, we can't go to Layla's room. I remember for sure. Second, we can't go down the hall to any other bedroom. Instead, we go down the stairs.

"Go, now!" Calvin yelled, causing the werewolf to bark at the children.

Ryan surged forward, adrenaline coursing through his veins, every muscle tense with urgency. Devin's footsteps echoed behind him as he scooped up Layla, her fingers desperately stretching towards their mother. The wolf's thunderous pursuit filled the house, a relentless predator closing in on its prey. A chair splintered under its weight, eliciting a pained whine, but Calvin's defiant yell only fueled its rage.

With a chilling snarl, the beast turned its attention to Calvin, eyes gleaming with primal hunger. It loomed over him, and in a swift, brutal motion, backhanded Calvin, hurling him towards the sliding glass door with bone crunching force. The sickening impact reverberated through the room, glass fracturing ominously around his crumpled body. As Rebecca struggled against the primal instincts surging within her, the chaotic scene descended into a frantic battle for survival.

You shouldn't concern yourself with the old one. The younger ones taste better.

He managed to get his knees under him, struggling to stand and face his wife's other self. The wolf roared, thick saliva landing on his face and body. "You don't want to do this, Becs," he implored. The werewolf lifted the dinner table with its massive hands and hurled it at Calvin. It flew over his head, crashing against the sliding window, shattering the glass. The wolf dropped to all fours, its ears twitching as it honed in on Ryan's voice nearby.

The three Hatcher children made their way towards Layla's room. Before Devin could move inside, Ryan yelled, "No! Down the stairs, into Dad's office!" Ryan struggled to remember what came afterward from the black pages he had viewed with Layla, doubting his memory. Devin carried Layla down the stairs, ready to open the front door. As Ryan ran down, he glanced back and saw spirits—a girl in a pink dress and a balding man in a suit—watching them. He then turned to see Devin turning the knob to the front door, the middle of the split-level house.

"No! Go to the office!" Ryan screamed again. Devin looked over Ryan's head to find their mother, the werewolf, looming above them, shaking its rear, readying to attack. "Come on!" Ryan urged, pulling Devin by the shirt and forcing him to descend the second flight of stairs.

The werewolf launched itself towards them, crashing headfirst into the front door, creating a massive dent in the wood and shattering the glass above. It shook its head, regaining its focus to hunt the children. They burst into the laundry room, then their dad's office, with Ryan slamming and locking each door behind them.

They had bought some time, but not much. The wolf began scraping through the laundry door, slamming its body against it. It wouldn't be long before the monster started breaking down the office door, so Ryan had to think quickly.

He thought about the front door, the warning on the paper, and the fallen dolls when Layla evaluated the path and how the dolls fell every time she failed. If Devin had continued to try to get out through the front, he would have died—they all might have. *Can't think about that now!* "Layla, where do we go next? Do you remember?"

Layla, with determination, stopped crying to scan the room, finally pointing at the only window in the confined space. Ryan looked at the small rectangular window, wondering if they could all fit through. He remembered a young man wearing a bloody letterman jacket lurking about—the thought of the poor student's insides sliding across the glass when he crawled past sickened him. But then the image of another Lite Brite page with three stick figures below a narrow opening appeared. "Okay, Layloo, let's get this thing open!" Their mother's brute strength had nearly destroyed the door to the laundry room, and she would soon break into the office and tear them apart.

"Are you sure?" Devin questioned, not realizing there was nowhere else to go now. The monster's bark grew louder and more intimidating as it grew frustrated.

"Yeah, this is it!"

"Then where?" Devin asked, unsure his brother knew what he was doing. Ryan flipped through those pages again in his head, and the only one he could recall was the one with the deck and the figures lying underneath it. "After this, we hide behind the hot tub under the deck. Got it?" Layla agreed, wiping away the snot from under her nose. Devin reached for and unlatched the window that hadn't been open in years. "It's stuck!" he screamed, striking it with the side of his fist. Outside the office, a loud crash echoed.

She's gotten through the first door. You have to fight this, mom!

Ryan didn't know what to do for her. Talking to her wasn't helping. Rebecca had no control anymore.

With adrenaline coursing, Ryan hopped onto the desk and began to push the window open alongside his brother. Layla grasped the bottom of their jeans, watching the door splinter apart, listening to her mommy growl and bark. Layla couldn't understand why she wanted to hurt them.

The office window creaked open as Ryan and Devin exerted all their strength to widen the gap, desperate to create an avenue of escape. But their efforts were thwarted by the stubborn hinge, leaving the window stuck halfway. Panic surged as they realized only one person could squeeze through.

"Layla, it's your turn! We need you to get outside," Devin urged, his voice strained with tension. "Once you're out, lift the window so we can follow. Do you understand?" he implored; his words punctuated by the thunderous growls of the approaching werewolf.

Glancing anxiously between her brothers and the front door, where the mucus coated snout of her transformed mother protruded through a small hole, Layla hesitated. Despite the danger, the sight of the canine nose evoked a sense of innocence and longing in her young heart.

Approaching the wolf cautiously, Layla reached out and tentatively placed her hand on its snout, her small fingers trembling. Mommy just needs to be petted, she thought. With childlike naivety, she began to stroke it gently, oblivious to the ferocity lurking behind the animal's facade.

The wolf calmed, and Rebecca, trapped within the animal, watched her children, hating herself for putting them through such fear and torment. *Maybe there is hope after all*, Ryan thought to himself. For a few moments, all was tranquil until Devin pushed the window out further, prompting the beast to snap at Layla's hand. She was quick to pull away, running over to Devin, who picked her up and put her through the window.

Layla scooted from the opening onto her knees, staining her Rainbow Bright pajamas, and began pulling on the window with all her strength. The hinges creaked loudly, making all of them wince. Ryan was the next to escape from the office. The bottom of the office door had come apart, allowing the wolf to grasp it from underneath, lifting it and causing the hinges to tear off the splintered wood.

Devin stood face to face with the wolf, its gaze piercing through him. In those eyes, he could no longer see his mother. The realization dawned on him that their plan to restrain the wolf, regardless of the shape it took, would have been ineffective. It was too intimidating, too powerful to be contained by mere restraints.

With Ryan's and Layla's help, they dragged Devin through just as the monster charged. *It should have been able to grab him. Something is holding it back.*

They dashed around the back corner of the house, their hearts pounding as they reached the deck, their designated hiding spot. Every footstep echoed loudly in their ears, a stark contrast to the horror gripping them. They bit down hard on their lips, fighting to stifle any involuntary shivers from the biting cold. Silence was their only ally now, their survival hinging on it. Above them, the wooden planks of the deck quivered, signaling the wolf's imminent arrival outside. *How? The only explanation I can think of was that Dad must have escaped through the kitchen and didn't close the sliding glass door behind him.*

The beast descended the deck's stairs with calculated stealth, its movements slow and deliberate as it sniffed the air for their scent. Layla watched in fearful fascination as the wolf prowled around the side of the deck, drawing closer to their hiding place. She could see the steam of its breath in the chilly night air, evidence of its exhaustion from the relentless pursuit. Pausing in the grass, the wolf tended to its wounded paws, chewing away splinters and shards of glass from the debris left in its wake. With renewed focus, it scanned the yard, its senses alert and honed.

Layla couldn't help but admire the strange beauty of the creature her mother had become, recognizing familiar features amidst the primal visage. Even as Ryan fought the urge to reveal himself, hoping for her to remain calm, he knew deep down the beast's instincts would always override any semblance of humanity.

The wolf shifted its massive body, eyes fixated on the children as its predatory instincts kicked in. Layla's scream pierced the tense air as the beast bared its sharp teeth, poised to strike. A gunshot rang through the frigid night, drawing the creature's attention. Devin peered through the gaps in the wooden slats to see his father standing in the yard, brandishing a gun. Calvin lowered the barrel, signaling it was a warning shot to ward off the approaching danger.

"Come on, Rebecca. Come towards me! Come and get me!" Calvin's voice echoed with urgency, a desperate attempt to reach the woman trapped within the beast. The wolf, undeterred by his pleas, focused its predatory gaze on the children once more.

"Stop it!" Calvin's voice cracked, raw with desperation, as he fired another shot. The bullet struck the ground beside the wolf, causing it to briefly glance back at him. It growled, baring its teeth, hostility radiating from every bristling hair as Calvin took a step closer. The beast hunched, releasing a haunting howl chilling Calvin and the children to their cores.

Unseen by them, Rebecca fought with every ounce of her strength, straining against the curse that transformed her. The howl was a cry of anguish, not aggression—a sign of Rebecca's struggle against the werewolf curse, her body weakened by cancer.

As the mournful cry filled the night, Ryan, Devin, and Layla scrambled out from under the deck. They sprinted across the narrow lawn, leaves crunching and twigs snapping underfoot, each sound a beacon to the lurking werewolf.

The wolf's gaze shifted from Calvin to the fleeing children, a predatory gleam in its eyes. Ignoring the easier prey before it, the beast focused on the rapidly disappearing figures of Ryan, Devin, and Layla. It knew the surest way to break Rebecca's resolve was to eliminate her children. It bolted after them without hesitation.

"No!" Calvin shouted, chasing after it. "I'm here! Come after me! Leave them alone!"

Layla lagged behind her brothers, her heart hammering in her chest. She glanced over her shoulder, her breath hitching as she saw the wolf closing in. The beast's hot breath grazed her neck, causing her tiny hairs to raise.

Tears blurred her vision as dread tightened her throat. She realized with gut-wrenching clarity that if she didn't act quickly, her own mother, consumed by the primal urge to hunt, would be her killer.

Taking a hard left, Layla veered the hound off course. It slid in the grass, struggling to regain balance. The blue spruce tree loomed ahead. She just needed to hide behind the trunk.

Ryan and Devin skidded to a halt, breathless. They realized their mother wasn't chasing them but targeting Layla. Calvin emerged from behind the house, confusion etched on his face as he scanned the unfolding scene. Layla stopped in front of the spruce tree, eyes locking onto her father. *Daddy can protect me*, she thought.

It was too late.

Layla froze, shock visible as the werewolf leaped through the air, ready to strike. Her father and brothers shouted desperately, urging her to flee. Suddenly, an unseen force propelled her forward, just as the wolf landed, bewildered and searching for its vanished prey. *The pusher*—the constant entity since this all began, had intervened.

Ryan quickly realized everything was unfolding according to a plan. Layla was meant to stop in front of the tree. The lingering spirit had intervened, leading her from harm's reach. The victims of the werewolf's curse had orchestrated their actions meticulously. Yet Ryan couldn't shake the unease; he had no memory of Layla needing to be positioned in front of the spruce in her drawings. *Maybe she knew.*

The wolf loomed above Layla, who had collapsed onto the ground, poised for one final assault. Layla swiftly rolled onto her back and locked eyes with the towering beast, her mother's eyes staring back at her. In that moment, she yearned, clinging to the hope somewhere deep within the creature's ferocious exterior, her mother still existed.

You need the food!
You let the human man hold you back.

You will see how the smallest are the most delicious.

No...Not my Layloo.

The werewolf paused.

It released a pained whine, the anguish evident in its eyes as the tension in its snarling features began to soften. In a fleeting moment, recognition passed between Layla and Rebecca, a glimpse of the loving mother buried within the wolf. Yet, the inner turmoil surged forth once more, the growls and snarls signaling its readiness to strike one last time.

Calvin dashed forward, desperation driving him to reach out toward them, even as headlights abruptly bore down upon the scene. The wolf's eyes widened in dread as the oncoming truck approached, a harbinger of imminent danger. With a sickening thud, the vehicle collided with the werewolf's body, pinning it against the sturdy blue spruce tree in the Hatchers' yard.

The impact shattered ribs and crushed the vertebrae, holding the creature in place. As the wolf let out pained yelps, its breaths grew shallow, realizing the futility of resistance. Trapped and immobilized, it lay still, the realization sinking in that escape was hopeless.

The Hatchers stared at the mustard-yellow truck, devastated. A man emerged from the driver's side, clutching his head, sporting a large gash from the impact of colliding with the steering wheel upon hitting the wolf. Melvin Craggs stepped in front of the headlight beams.

Calvin's eyes grew wide, rage boiling within him.

"What did you do?" he demanded before screaming, "What did you do!" Calvin lunged at his neighbor, shoving the old man to the ground. He balled his fist, ready to strike, but Melvin, his eyes brimming with sorrow, rose and grasped Calvin's arms. With a depth of sincerity Calvin had never heard from him before, Melvin said, "It was the only way I could think of." Calvin recoiled, his desire to harm fading as Ryan and Devin rushed to the front of the truck, where their mother began reverting to her human form.

"We need to move this truck!" Devin's voice cracked with urgency, but Melvin, shaking his head, knew it would only hasten her demise.

Despite the commotion, the neighborhood remained still. Ryan observed only the billowing clouds of their breath and the dark expanse of the night sky. No one emerged from their homes, and no lights flickered on. With rumors of the festival and the recent attacks, the neighbors had chosen to keep to themselves. Perhaps they silently watched, opting to let things unfold without interference. After all that had occurred in the past month, maybe the neighbors could keep this secret. *No, they will.*

"We have to move it! Move the goddamn truck!" Ryan yelled.

"It's fine," a weak voice said. "It won't help." Rebecca lay naked across the hood, her head resting on the cool metal surface as the engine sputtered to a stop. Blood trickled from her mouth, her arms hung limp, partially immobilized from her shattered spine. She gazed at her home, memories flooding her mind—the laughter and love shared with her husband and children, a bittersweet comfort amid the agony of her torn body.

Melvin removed his coat, and gently draped it over Rebecca's shivering body to shield her nudity. Turning to Layla, who remained frozen where she had fallen, he saw the shock etched on her face, the horror of witnessing her mother transform back into a dying woman. With tender care, Melvin lifted Layla into his arms as she began to sob, her fingers gnawed raw with anxiety, tears streaming down her cheeks and mingling with her running nose.

"Momma!" she shouted.

"It's okay, baby girl. You shouldn't have to see this," Melvin murmured through his tears, shielding her from the heartbreaking scene. Layla stretched out her hand toward her mother as Melvin carried her away, guiding her to a safe distance where she wouldn't witness the sight of her mother pinned against the tree, her body broken. Rebecca, with a weak wave of her finger, bid her daughter farewell, her gaze lingering on Layla for a moment before she disappeared from view behind the billowing exhaust smoke.

Ryan, attempting to ignore his sister's sobs, tenderly stroked his mother's head. "It's ironic, yeah?" Rebecca whispered with a faint laugh, "I thought it would be cancer that got meh." Her attempt at humor brought a bittersweet warmth to the somber moment as they stood together, a family united in grief.

"What can we do, Mom?" Ryan whispered gently, though deep within, he knew there was little they could do. Their presence and words were all they had to offer Rebecca in her final moments. After everything they had endured—the warnings, the nightmares, the haunting visions—it all seemed inconsequential now.

In the end, someone had to endure pain, but no one circling Rebecca Hatcher in her final breaths could have ever believed it would be all of them—not like this.

Ryan failed to comprehend why the spirits had intervened to protect his friends but not his own family. Then, like a sudden revelation, he understood—the curse of the wolf needed to be broken to free the souls of the departed, allowing them to find peace. "I'm so sorry I couldn't protect you, Mom," Ryan sobbed, his voice thick with anguish.

Rebecca mustered the strength to move her left arm, reaching out to caress her son's hair, a gesture reminiscent of their tender moments together when he was younger. "My brave boy, always trying to be the hero. But you don't have to be. Just be good. That's all I ever wanted," she whispered tenderly.

"Tell us what we can do, Mom," Devin interjected, his voice tinged with a mix of determination and grief.

Calvin leaned in close, pressing his lips against her forehead, his words barely audible as they quivered with emotion. "Is there anything you need?" he murmured, yearning to provide his beloved wife with some comfort.

Rebecca Hatcher mustered a gentle smile, her eyes shining with love for her boys. "Oh, there's nothing I need... but if ya can, maybe keep meh in ya hearts... you know, from time to time. Okay, my loves?" she requested, her voice trailing off as she drifted into a final peaceful slumber.

"It will be. Every moment, Mom. I promise," Ryan vowed, his voice choked with emotion as tears ran down his cheeks.

As the weight of their loss settled over them, the Hatchers clung to each other, the night air heavy with sorrow. The stillness of the neighborhood only amplified their grief, the absence of prying eyes or concerned neighbors creating a void around their tragedy. The promise Ryan made echoed in the quiet, a vow to carry his mother's memory with them, ensuring her love and sacrifice were never forgotten.

Rebecca's peaceful expression in death offered a small measure of comfort to her family. Her pain had ended, but the ache of her absence was just beginning to set in. They stood there, united in their grief, knowing they had to find a way to move forward while keeping her memory alive.

Ryan, Devin, and Calvin held each other close, their tears mingling with the cold night air. As they whispered their final goodbyes, they felt the presence of the spirits lingering nearby, a silent acknowledgment of the curse lifted, and the souls freed. The night was filled with both loss and a glimmer of hope. Their family forever changed yet bound together by an unbreakable love.

As their wife, mother—and friend—slipped away, snowflakes began to descend from the sky, as if nature itself acknowledged the end of the wolf's curse. Layla gazed at the falling snow, feeling her mother's presence in the gentle flakes. Tears welled in her eyes, tracing a path down her cheeks, mingling with the melting snow beneath her.

In her grief, Layla wondered if Anna, the girl in the pink dress, and the other spirits had finally found peace and a path forward. She looked up at the cold night sky, feeling a connection to her mother and the departed souls.

Unbeknownst to them, the souls of the wolf's victims stood in the woods behind them, watching over their saviors. With the curse broken, they were finally released from their purgatory, free to move on. As the Hatcher children wept for their mother, the spirits departed, their whispers of gratitude lost in the night.

Melvin backed his truck, gently guiding Rebecca's body onto the ground. In solemn silence, Devin fetched clothes for his mother while Calvin tenderly carried her inside, laying her on a blanket. Together, they dressed her before calling for an ambulance, crafting a story of a hit-and-run to explain her injuries. Melvin, leveraging a favor owed to him, arranged for his truck to vanish at a local scrap yard, ensuring it would be crushed into anonymity, concealing the truth of that night. Their pact bound them in secrecy for life.

After the ambulance departed with their mother, Ryan retreated to his room without a word. He offered his sister an embrace, assuring her things would be alright. In the solitude of his bedroom, he found a peace he hadn't felt since his mother's diagnosis. As he drifted into sleep, it felt as if the weight of worry had lifted, promising one of his best nights of rest in weeks—finally.

Reflecting on the night's events, Ryan found solace in their restraint from violence. They could have used the gun, the bat, or any means, but they chose not to. It wasn't much, but it was a small comfort as he grew older. Looking back, he understood the spirits lingering around their home had guided them, even amidst sacrifice and sorrow.

In the end, that had to be enough.

EPILOGUE

PICTURES OF YOU

It was Christmas Eve, and the Hatchers and Donovans gathered under one roof, basking in the warmth of the holiday spirit. Silvia Donovan had a brilliant idea the previous week and reached out to Calvin to discuss it. Together, they decided their two families shouldn't spend the holidays alone. Calvin then suggested to Ryan that they extend the invitation to Christina and her family. Ryan happily agreed, eager to see his girlfriend and Scott's best friend, knowing Devin would be equally pleased with Valerie's company. However, when Ryan invited Colin, he respectfully declined, opting to spend the holiday with his own family.

Though disappointed, no one would dispute Colin's sentiment.

Christina's relationship with her parents showed signs of improvement. They made plans for her and Ryan to stay with them for the latter part of the holiday break, a step towards reconciliation which should have happened long ago. It wasn't perfect, but it was progress.

As for Rick Donovan, he didn't transform into the werewolf Ryan feared; he had only been scratched. However, Silvia had finally reached her breaking point after months of abuse and kicked him out of the house. Rick now lives near Cleveland, working to rebuild his life. Silvia made it clear he could return one day, but she doubted he would ever be the man she married.

Remarkably, Scott and Valerie were coping well with their parents' separation. With their father out of the picture, they found a new sense of peace and began to communicate with each other in a way that resembled family. They now spent every other weekend with their father, gradually increasing the duration of their visits as Silvia grew more comfortable with the arrangement. When Rick protested, Silvia stood her ground, asserting. Valerie couldn't help but feel proud of her mother's strength and resilience.

The voices of people speaking behind Ryan faded as he stared at the new shed in the back. All this time, he had wondered about the significance of rebuilding the shed and why it was so important. Ryan had thought it might be where their father kept their mother trapped during the full moon, but it wasn't. Devin was tired of wondering. So, acting nonchalantly, he turned around and smiled at everyone he passed on his way to his parents' room.

Making sure no one was looking, Devin took his father's keys from the dresser and headed down to the garage. As his foot touched the last step of the staircase, he looked up to find Ryan staring at him. "Where are you going?"

"I was just going to get some fresh air," Devin mumbled, knowing there was no talking his way out of this one. Unfortunately for him, Ryan was too smart for his own good.

"Let me ask that another way...Where are you *really* going?" Ryan pressed.

Devin looked away and sighed. "Aren't you curious about the shed and what's in it?"

Ryan's eyes widened with excitement, relieved he wasn't the only one curious. "Hold on a sec! I'll come with you!" He calmly walked to his room, hoping not to attract attention. He met Devin in the garage, and they trudged through six inches of snow from the driveway to the far end of the yard.

Devin fumbled through his father's keys, searching for the one to the padlock while Ryan kept watch. Finally, Devin found the matching key with the name of the padlock etched into it. "I think this is it, Ryan!"

They swung both doors open, pulled the light chain, and found the last thing they ever expected to see. Devin covered his mouth in shock as Ryan walked in behind him. Boxes lined the walls, wrapped in colored, decorated paper with holiday and birthday designs.

They're presents. All of them are.

Fencing, installed by their dad, encircled the inner shed, safeguarding the gifts from prying eyes, including curious children.

Insulation ensured the interior remained insulated from extreme temperatures, protecting the presents from the elements. Devin and Ryan walked quietly along opposite sides of the shed. Tags marked each gift, detailing whether they were for Christmas or birthdays, the recipient, and the appropriate age or year for opening. Layla had the most gifts, being the youngest.

Devin, taken aback by the sight, overlooked the '53 Model 20 500 Melvin Craggs owned, now rightfully his. Rebecca had purchased it from Melvin in secret, known only to their father. The tag read, "For Devin on his 18th Birthday." Overwhelmed, Devin struggled to contain his emotions. Ryan, too, retreated toward the open doors, not wanting to confront the reality of their mother's absence.

They stood together, shoulders tense and eyes shimmering with unshed tears, attempting to compose themselves before rejoining the holiday gathering. The weight of their mother's absence hung heavy around them. From the shadows behind them, a pair of familiar arms enveloped the brothers, drawing them into a comforting embrace. Startled, they turned to see their dad's weathered face nestled between theirs, a faint smile tugging at the corners of his mouth despite the sadness in his eyes.

"I figured curiosity would get the better of you," Calvin chuckled softly, his voice tinged with both relief and melancholy. He gently bit his lip, a habit he always had when trying to hide deeper emotions. It wasn't anger he harbored towards his sons, but a quiet gratitude they had found the shed, unraveling a secret he had carried alone for so long.

"How?" Ryan asked, wiping away tears. Calvin snickered gently, explaining, "Your mom applied for a credit card and maxed it out, saying, 'What are they going to do, come after me?' We all laughed because we knew that's exactly what she'd say."

"I miss her," Devin admitted quietly. Calvin squeezed them tighter, reassuring, "I know you do. It was tragic how she was bitten, but maybe the curse gave her more time than she should have had. Part of me believes that, but another part wished for her peace. Does it make me selfish?"

Ryan and Devin shook their heads. "Maybe thinking of it the first way is better," Ryan offered, unsure himself. Devin wiped tears from his face, embarrassed to cry in front of his father and brother.

Calvin took a deep breath, showing a vulnerability they rarely saw. "They say at AA it's okay to be sad and cry when bad things happen, or when you lose someone you love. There's no shame in it. I wish I'd realized that sooner." They stood together in the cold silence, reflecting in the shed.

"Well, I can tell you she loved that little day out with your friends last month. Maybe that makes it all worthwhile," Calvin added with a hint of lightness, hoping to lift their spirits momentarily. They stood before the gifts, reminiscing about Rebecca—the sweet and feisty woman she was. They wouldn't have had her any other way.

"Since it's Christmas Eve, maybe we should open one present tonight, all of us together," Calvin suggested. "Really?" they exclaimed nervously. Calvin pointed to a rectangular box, prompting one of them to grab it. Ryan eagerly tore off the red and gold wrapping paper to reveal a Nintendo Entertainment System—the one thing he had wanted. Unbeknownst to him, another package would await under the tree the next morning: *The Legend of Zelda*, complete with all its gold-colored glory, *Contra*, and *Punch-Out*, for the enjoyment of their family and friends.

Unaware Layla had followed him outside, Calvin found her playing in the slowly falling snow. She threw snow into the air, forming snowballs before brushing snow off the swing attached to their massive backyard tree. Sitting down, she began swinging gently, causing snow on the branch above her to fall on her head. "That's cold!" she playfully scolded the tree.

As Layla swung, humming a tune, she gazed into the woods ahead. Sparse bushes rustled, catching her attention. After the past few months, she had learned to associate the woods with trouble—until now. Layla heard a faint mew in the distance. "Could it be?" she whispered in her mother's accent.

A cat emerged from the woods and meowed at Layla. "Hi, kitty!" she exclaimed, hopping off the swing to pick up the white cat. Layla noticed its black feet—a distinctive feature. She turned the cat around and found a tag: "My name is Boots. If found, please return me to the nearest animal shelter."

"But you don't have a home anymore. So, you can stay with me! I'll take care of you!" Layla beamed, overjoyed to have found the cat she had been looking for over the past two months. "Hi, Boots-Boots! I'm Layla, but you can call me Layloo."

Layla examined the tag again, removed the collar, and assured Boots, "Mom and Anna will be so relieved you're safe. You can stay with me if you want. I'll ask Dad, but I'm sure he'll say yes. We're a good family. You'll like it here!"

Yes, we are. We are a great family.

THE END

SPECIAL THANKS

I need to thank the 80s and my hometown for shaping me to be who I am today before technology took over.

Blockbuster Video-for giving me hours of memories being in your stores and eventually managing a few of them when I was nineteen years old. Most of the time, I had no idea what I rented, but that was a good thing.

Stephen Graham Jones and Stephen Markley-for helping get out of my writing funk with the books, *The Only Good Indians* and *Ohio*. And Clive Barker for writing, *The Thief of Always*.

The Booktokers- DarkAngelMisty, Yayasworld04, Calista, TessaMcBessa, Bookish Wh0r3 Kiki, Timothy King, Horror Movies & Shit, Veronica, and Kirsty_justsaying, for checking this and my other 2024 stuff out even if it may have not been your thing.

And, of course, my wife and daughter who humors me and listens to my weird ideas and occasionally placate my ego.

ABOUT THE AUTHOR

Bryan Wayne Dull writes books, which makes perfect sense if you really knew him, and it's all he has done since sixth grade, spinning a yarn at a moment's notice. He is best known for writing horror and suspense stories. Solstice was his first novel and foray into publishing (it was a bet to do it), then its sequels. He lives in Spartanburg, SC, with his wife and
daughter and plans to write more stories with something to say in this strange world we live in.

OTHER WORKS BY BRYAN WAYNE DULL

Solstice
Equinox
Ecliptic
Celestial

Pill Hill
The Pressure
Small Hearts

Milton Keynes UK
Ingram Content Group UK Ltd.
UKHW041352041024
2011UKWH00031B/72/J